THE

ALTERNATIVE

A Novel

WILLIE O'REGAN

This is a work of fiction. Names, characters, incidents and dialogues
are products of the author's imagination or are used fictitiously. Any
resemblance to actual people, living or dead, events or locales is entirely
coincidental.

For all those that helped along the way

ACKNOWLEDGMENTS

First and foremost to the town of Castlemaine, Australia, for providing me with the inspiration to begin penning a book. A day off from picking apples, an empty bank account and forty degree heat gave me the idea to spend my day writing a book. It took many more days and nights but it all started in Castlemaine.

To Adrian, Curley, Michelle, Laurence and Ben for both the support and the slagging when I chose to write by the River Yarra instead of find a job. To my family, Jim, Marjorie and Michael, for supporting me when I came home to the farm from travelling and wrote some more instead of milking the cows. And finally, to Wendy for supporting me to use my time to finish the book.

Thanks to those that helped proofread the book, Ciara, Aidan and especially Wendy who put in some serious hard yards. Huge thanks to Peter Howell who designed the cover.

Prologue

Summer 2008

The carriage doors open. The screams are deafening. Panic is in the air. Andy does a double take. To his left a man lies on the platform covered in a pool of fresh dark blood.

He pulls out his phone and rereads the text message he has just received.

You will see – look left at the platform. Red is the colour.

Part 1
Before

Two Days Earlier

1

'Wear Sunscreen' Andy remembered the words from the popular nineties chart hit as he left Baker Street tube station. It was a sweltering thirty degrees Celsius day, an unusually welcome occurrence for the English capital. Andy had forgotten his sunscreen and just knew his unweathered nose would be transformed into Rudolph the reindeer by sundown. Andy had always liked the Baz Luhrmann song, even if he always didn't follow its advice. The lyrics questioned life, its twisty turning road and our role in it. It then dispensed advice on how to steer through it, hitting the kerb a few times to remind you that you're alive, but at the same time never crashing and making that finish line with a hint of a smile. Lately Andy had begun questioning his own life and was searching more and more for that hint of a smile.

Directacom was on floor number 7; Andy had worked here for seven years and had worked his way up to Area Manager. He had his own office with 'Andy Pickering - Division Manager' on the door. The maintenance department hadn't quite got around to changing the sign yet. Andy was promoted six weeks earlier and that was the pace things were done around here. Each action needed a mandate, the mandate needed to be signed by all affected managers and once the relevant signatures were in place, the document would go to the boss, who's final signature would finally enable work to be done.

'Directacom is a telecommunications company specialising in mainstream mobile communications'

Andy never really knew what Directacom did but the above was imprinted on the heading of all official paper and whenever anybody asked what the company did, Andy had his prepared response. Besides, the quote was impregnated in his mind at this stage as all Andy's job seems to entail these days was signing some correspondence or another.

As he entered the office he could see another pile of papers to be signed on his desk, luckily Andy had ordered replacement ink cartridges for his lucky fountain pen last week and these lay next to the papers. Stationary was the one item that did not need to be signed off by everybody as it was seen as critical to the internal cog of the Directacom machine. The office was a master bedroom size box, complete with a window and view of another office block, tile carpet floor, stuffy air, a filing cabinet and desk, and two near dying plants by the door. It was what he had worked towards, for seven long years.

Sarah Cripwell knocked on the door. She just joined the company and felt she should introduce herself to her new area manager. The man she saw when she opened the door was in his mid-thirties, approximately six-foot tall, slim build, hair beginning to recede and nose a little red. He wore a black pinstripe suit, the type that was not too flashy, and accompanied it with a white shirt and red tie. Looking at his eyes she could see they were kind but distant. Sarah made her introductions and left, a welcome break from signing his name for Andy.

2

Andy left work at 4.30, this was a little earlier than usual but this was no usual day, it was payday. On the last Wednesday of every month for as long as he could remember, Andy had his payday ritual. First he would walk around the corner to his branch of Nationwide Bank and put some of his money in government Premium Bonds. Unsure of the markets and having been stung previously with dropping house prices, Andy preferred to give his financial future the security it needed, namely guaranteed government backing. As a child Andy had won £200 on the bonds his grandmother had given him for his twelfth birthday. He could still remember the day he received the letter with the good news. Her Majesty's Government Coat of Arms was watermarked on the page to show its authenticity, the letter was signed on behalf of the Chancellor of the Exchequer, Government Buildings, Westminster, London, by a William somebody, he could never quite figure out the scrawl that was William's second name.

Next only one street down it was to the quaint, but tremendously successful, *Vanessa's Flowers*. Andy always got his wife Victoria a bouquet on payday. It was while on holiday in the south of France that the couple had met. Victoria was working in a coffee shop in Nice during her summer holidays from university. She had always enjoyed different languages and cultures so each summer she decided to discover one; previously she had worked in Barcelona, Stockholm and in Edison a satellite town of New York City. The relationship was quite a passionate affair. Within three hours of their meeting in a cafe in the town square, they were skinny dipping together in the Mediterranean Sea under a full moon. Passion is what drew the couple together and it's what had kept them together for so many years because Andy and Victoria did not have much else in common. Andy enjoyed a BBQ, a beer and watching his beloved Arsenal play. Victoria had seven cookery books, didn't drink too much apart from a nice glass of wine to accompany a meal and enjoyed going to a West End show once a week with her best friend Jennifer. Their friends could never understand how they ended up together, only Victoria and Andy's hearts could see how.

Andy decided on a bouquet of tulips. He could not help but look at the other men dressed in their suits buying flowers for their loved ones. He wondered if their marriages could be gone as flat as his own. He wondered if marriages were supposed to be this way, if time was to change all marriages from thrilling to turbulent to tolerable. Andy was certainly at stage three with Victoria. It had been twenty-two days since they last had sex. Twenty-two days and seven hours as Andy recalled. Sex was now on the cards but once a month, twice maybe if luckily a birthday fell in that month. *Sexnight* as Andy called it in his own private thoughts was when Andy himself took his wife to a West End show and Jennifer was left at home. It now it felt more like a thank you gift rather than lust or love. Before they had their first child, not a day would go by without a mattress, kitchen table or partition wall having its structural strength rigorously tested. Something had now died in the marriage and they both knew it deep down even if it was not talked about.

Jack was their first child. He was now five, had fair hair, blue eyes and many plasters over his constantly cut knees. He had begun school and loved *Sponge Bob Square Pants* cartoon and Arsenal football club in equal measure. Anne-Marie was their second child. She turned three last month and had an outstanding vocabulary for her age. She had strawberry blond hair and blue eyes but she seemed to avoid cutting her knees much better than her older brother. Andy was so proud of his children, he felt them his ultimate achievement in life and one of the best reasons to roll out of bed each morning. When Victoria first got pregnant Andy had mixed emotions. While delighted as they had been trying for six months, he was also very apprehensive. He was concerned that he would not make the cut as a father. Andy didn't have any great love for children up to that point in his life and prayed that he would love, cherish and raise his new child to the best of his ability. That he had done for the past five years and it cheered him up anytime he felt down. Just to see Jack and Anne-Marie's faces smile brought joy to Andy. This is why Andy's next stop was the corner shop outside Baker Street underground station. He picked up a few chocolate mini eggs and some sherbet, paid for them and made his way to the tube.

3

'How are you Peter, hope you take it easy on my shins tomorrow night'.

'They invented shin guards for a reason Andy, and you know I'm that reason.'

They both shared a laugh. Peter was a work colleague of Andy and lived in the same suburb as him. More often than not they would end up meeting on the tube, if not going home, then probably on the way to work. Today was no different. Peter organised the Directacom 5-a-side on Thursday evenings, and he certainly knew how to tackle. 'Fracture' was his nickname on the astro-turf as he had broken Jeff, another workmate's, leg in three places. He was a tough man, he stood at a mere 5' 5" in height but nobody messed with him. Andy had always liked him though, he was a genuine guy, and a good laugh too. In an office of pen pushers, suits and ties Peter told it as it was and was a breath of fresh air to Andy.

As Andy and Peter jibbed over who was going to win the big match between Arsenal and Tottenham, Andy couldn't help notice the bruises on Peter's face. Peter had a bluely purple blotch on his chin and his left eye was visibly black. Andy wanted to ask him how he got these marks but Peter was only a colleague, not a close friend. Andy decided not to bring it up; perhaps discretion was the better part of valour.

'Say hello to that lovely wife of yours for me' said Peter as he got out of the carriage. Lately Peter kept getting out at Finchley Road, a stop before West Hampstead where they both lived. Again Andy had not asked him about this, Andy thought maybe Peter was back on the drink and drinking in nearby Frognal so that nobody would find out. He was known to have a drink problem in the past and this might explain the bruises too, for he was not a man shy of throwing his weight around on the football pitch. Andy could only imagine him being confronted after a few drinks.

'West Hampstead station, please mind the gap' Andy got out and walked the five minutes home.

4

No. 41 Thompson Avenue was a fully detached house with a front and back garden and a black picket fence separating it from the footpath. Thompson Avenue was a street of redbrick houses and the Pickering's home was no different. After the prize bonds, flowers, and chocolate, most of Andy's pay packet went on his £600,000 mortgage. West Hampstead was a quiet and nice area and Andy was only too happy to spend the money, such that his two treasures could grow up, playing hop-scotch on the road, or kicking a ball down at the park, without Andy and Victoria having to worry about them.

'Thank you so much for the flowers, they're lovely' Victoria said as she took a vase from the cabinet underneath the kitchen sink. Victoria was a few years younger than Andy and was in excellent shape. She had lost none of the looks that attracted Andy to the Mediterranean Sea twelve years ago. She wore tight leggings with a hoodie jumper and her long dark blonde hair was dripping wet. She had just climbed out of the shower.

'How was your run Vic?'

'Very good, I just got back, 44 minutes for the 10k'

'If you keep on at this rate you'll be heading down the road for the 2012 Olympics'

'Did I not tell you that's the plan?' Victoria joked

Over the last few weeks Andy felt their relationship had been improving. Victoria was in good form more often; she had started exercising more regularly, had joined *Curves*, a new gym programme, and was dressing sexier than usual. Andy hoped if he could play his cards right that the bunch of tulips, together with a bit of old fashioned TLC could make tonight that rare commodity *Sexnight*.

'Do you have anything planned for tonight' Victoria said in

her sweet but slightly raspy voice. Andy's hopes started to grow as he told her that he didn't and was available to do whatever she wanted this evening.

'Excellent, you can look after the kids, me and Jenny are going to see Billy Elliot this evening'

Andy's heart sank a little, but he knew deep down he shouldn't have let himself believe in the first instance.

Andy spent that night watching *Sponge Bob*, helping Jack with his homework and stopping the two from fighting as they liked to do on occasion. After eventually getting them to sleep Andy poured himself a small glass of brandy, sat by the fire and pondered whether this was as good as it gets. At thirty seven, he had a wonderful home, a well-paid job with a secure company and arguably the most beautiful wife in the neighbourhood. Nobody he knew would guess how unhappy he really was with the falseness of his entire life. The reality was, his wife no longer loved him and they had nothing in common, he was beginning to go bald, five-a-side was getting more and more strenuous and to top it off, a monkey with a good right arm and a fountain pen could do his job.

This just can't be as good as it gets he thought to himself, feeling guilty for thinking these thoughts and not being more grateful for all he had.

Chris O'Neill was the only person in the whole world who knew Andy was not the happy man he outwardly displayed. Chris was Andy's best mate since university. Andy, Chris and another two friends were actually on holiday together in Nice when he found love. He had always been there for him and vice versa. Andy gave Chris a call and arranged to meet him tomorrow night for a few drinks after the 5-a-side. He had to get all this bottled up frustration off his chest, get a few wise words on it all and have a good night out while doing so. It was now midnight, Victoria had not yet returned as Andy went to bed.

5

The world's most annoying sound woke Andy. It was his little black alarm clock. Every morning he promised himself he would buy a better one but he still had the same alarm clock for the past five years. 7.00am was the time, time to roll out, shit, shower, shave, on with the suit and out the door. Another day with nothing changing each morning only the weather on the five-minute walk to the station. Andy left Victoria a note of his plans for tonight on the bedside table. Then as he went to kiss Victoria on the head before he left, he noticed she was still wearing her evening dress from the night before. She also smelt of alcohol, which was quite unusual. Jennifer must have got her to loosen up last night; I must get a few tips off her he thought to himself. He landed a soft kiss on her forehead, walked down the corridor and out the door.

Once the teams were picked, Andy breathed a sigh of relief; 'Fracture' was on his team. Andy and Peter contributed two goals each in a 5-3 win. Peter suggested a drink to celebrate the victory. It looked like he was definitely back on the booze. Andy thought what could he do to stop him drinking, besides he enjoyed his company, so he asked Peter to join him at his mate Chris' place and they would all have a drink together.

Chris had the kind of flat everybody wanted to hang out in but nobody would want to live there. It was a new spacious apartment but in the sitting room Domino's pizza boxes lined the floor and the couch seemed to be growing things. Their television was a 50" flat panel but it had a crack in the screen from a stray beer can that had been flung from the fridge but didn't make its intended recipients hand. The fridge itself had not seen something green in it since Terrence the young go-getter hairdresser moved in. Needless to say he didn't last there very long. The kitchen on the other hand was just a no go area, even for men with the toughest constitutions. Chris even recognized it was a bit disgusting so he moved the fridge to the sitting room so he wouldn't have to look at it when getting himself a beer!

Chris and Andy both studied marketing in the University of London. They knew how to party, how to do nothing and how to eat 300% of your RDA of fat everyday and still get onto the university football team. Andy had moved on from this for the past fifteen years, Chris had not. Somehow he got trapped into the way of life and couldn't seem to come out, nothing had changed for Chris except now he couldn't even make it onto his pub football team. The apartment aside, Chris was an extremely likeable guy and had an infinite number of friends. He worked in advertising where he had become quite a success. He now had full directive control over all *Coca-Cola* television, newspaper, billboard and radio advertisements in the UK. When it came to going out, Chris knew so many people that he'd never queued for a nightclub in his life. In his youth Chris seemed to find women who wanted to sleep with him easier than finding the free transformer robot in a pack of cornflakes. These days he still had the quick wit for the ladies but his gut had started to hinder his love life.

Andy introduced Peter to Chris and out they went to Kitty O'Shea's, an Irish bar and Chris' local. While Chris was born in England both of his parents were Irish and the Irish fondness for the odd beverage had certainly not been lost on Chris. Kitty O'Shea's had an authentic Irish pub feel to it, unlike many of its competitors across London. This was helped by the fact that it had Irish owners; Chris' parents. Mr. and Mrs. O'Neill had purchased the then rundown bar before Chris was born and had refurbished and ran the establishment for the past forty years. Peter got the first round in. To Andy's surprise he ordered a squeezed orange juice for himself. Andy plucked up the courage to ask him if he drank alcohol anymore. Peter responded that he hadn't taken a drink in two years. Andy, although thrown by the answer, congratulated Peter and jokingly told him that must be the reason why he is so competitive at the 5-a-side.

Two hours later and the few drinks had loosened up both Andy and Chris. The conversation had gone from football, to the economy, to which member of the royalty has the nicest bottom and back to football again. With his vocal cords oiled from the ever-sweeter tasting beer, Andy explained the thoughts he had as he sat by the fire, brandy in hand, the previous night. He didn't care that Peter, a man he barely knew, would find out about all his life, in fact he was happy he was there. Peter was as straight as shooter as it got so Andy knew he would get Peter's real views, whether he would like them or not. Chris was the first to speak after Andy had explained himself thoroughly.

'Well first of all Andy, you know how I feel about you and Victoria, but let's not go there again.'

Chris then told Andy that he wanted to be either a private eye or a professional footballer but things don't always work out as you have planned. He explained in his unique Irish/English accent that

'We all might want to go down different roads to find the perfect job but we never know if that new road will get us to our desired destination or not. I think sometimes its wiser to stick to the road you're on, you know the road so it's easier, you probably won't crash and despite what you think Andy, everything could change for the better around the next corner.'

'Very philosophical indeed' Andy retorted 'Thank you Dr O'Neill, how much do I owe you? Another pint I suppose!'

As they joked Andy took the advice on board, Chris was making sense, and maybe he was right after all.

From the corner of his eye Andy spotted Peter's glass

falling from the counter, swiftly he stuck out his hand and caught it.

'Here you go Fracture, do you just break everything, bones, glasses, whatever's nearby!'

Peter accidentally knocked his glass off the bar, luckily Andy caught it, and he caught the opportunity to give him a dig as well.

'Careful Andy, you're nearby!'

Everybody shared a laugh.

Soon it was time to go.

'Thanks Chris, now go get the hoover out and tidy that sitting room' Andy roared across the street as he said goodnight to his best friend and newfound psychologist. The two men went back down underground and onto the tube again. Andy wondered how many hours of his life he had spent on this damn transport network. Then his thoughts turned to his newfound buddy Peter. Where would 'Fracture' get off this time, West Hampstead or Finchley Road? Then suddenly he just blurted it out

'Why do you always get out at Finchley Road on the way home from work Peter?'

Peter had been studying the tube poster that was on the wall of the carriage near the door, he had been in a world of his own, but he was instantly snapped out of it by this question. With the alcohol coursing through Andy's veins like a greyhound round a dog track he whispered to Peter

'And what's with all the bruises on your face?'

Peter initially fazed, responded by laughing and saying it was top-secret information. Peter went to briskly change the topic of conversation but when he turned to Andy he could see there was now no need. Andy's head was turned up to the ceiling, his eyes firmly shut and a slight purring noise could be heard from his mouth. The night was well and truly over for

Andy as he sat sleeping upright on the Jubilee line.

Smack. Peter had just hit Andy in the face.

'We're outside your front door, goodnight Andy' Peter said firmly as he turned to walk in the direction of his house. Then he whispered in Andy's ear 'check your left hand coat pocket in the morning, it will explain everything'. And with that Peter was gone.

6

'Twenty-three, twenty-four, twenty-five.' A broad chested man, wearing only a pair of skimpy running shorts, laid breathing rapidly on a bench press. Fifteen seconds passed in silence, then the sizeable figure of the bare-chested man got up and added another ten pounds to each side of the weights bar. A minute later twenty-five more chest presses were complete. The room was large and dark, and between the lack of light and lack of sound, there was an air of tranquillity about the basement. Paint peeled from the walls and damp grey blotches were noticeable on the ceiling. The carpet on the floor in contrast was in relatively good condition and was obviously laid much more recently than the walls were painted. Upon the dark blue coloured carpet lay a multitude of body building equipment. The machines were positioned in a circle next to the walls and in the centre of the room the bench press, which had just been used, was given pride of place.

After a well-earned shower he, now clothed, walked over to a small office area in the corner of the basement furthest from the stairs. He switched on his laptop and opened his diary. He could see development drawings of an apartment were due for collection today from a William H. Murray. Upon opening his inbox he saw a new message from Murray & Associates Developments. He was to meet a man with a black pinstripe suit, white shirt and blue tie in Cafe Rosa near Canary Wharf. Just as he was penning the details into his trusty diary his mobile vibrated on the desk. The new message received simply read

Yes, but I want the cash this morning.

Just another errand to run thought the man.

20-01-1975 was the man's birth date, and it was also the code to his safe located under his desk. He opened it, took out

£500 and shut the door again. All the money in the safe belonged to his clients. He never really knew quite what his job was, there was certainly no title for it in any job recruitment office, but he knew it was well paid and that's all that mattered.

Up the basement steps, through the corridor and out the front door. As he walked over to his navy BMW *5 series*, he could hear his elderly neighbour walking along the pavement in front of him.

'Good morning Terry, what a wonderful spell of weather we are having' the neighbour said over the fence as he looked towards the heavens.

'Long may it continue' added Terry as he closed the door of his car. Nobody on his street really knew what Terry White did for a living. However, he had never been any trouble and always paid the residents collection to cut the streets common green area, so he simply managed to go about his days usually without being noticed much by anybody. He flicked down the sun visor, put on his secret service style shades and sped off into the direction of Canary Wharf.

7

Andy was rudely awakened from his slumber by the world's most annoying sound. Again he promised himself that today he would definitely purchase a better alarm clock. Andy was a bit more sluggish this morning; the shave had to be cut out of the traditional shit, shower, shave routine such that he could make work on time. He gave Victoria the usual kiss on the forehead and headed out the door. The fresh air from the five-minute walk to the tube definitely helped soothe the pounding that was taking place in his head.

At least today is a Friday he thought to himself.

The sardines went into their can one last time. All on the carriage must have been thinking the same thing as Andy. As he squeezed between an overweight man's buttocks on the left and a young elegant businesswoman's bust on the right, inevitably, almost involuntary, leaning slightly more to the right, Andy began to recall the antics of the previous night.

Suddenly he put his hand into his left pocket, the accidental contact with the large man's bottom making Andy shudder. He didn't care though, he was too excited, it would explain everything, that's what Peter had said if his memory, his drunken memory, was correct. He reached and fumbled and went right around the pocket lining but there was nothing in there but his mobile phone. He hoped against hope that he had not lost it, whatever *it* was, when he took off his trousers last night. As he cursed his luck he pulled the phone out of his pocket, maybe the phone itself might be a clue. How he wished Peter had put the item in his other pocket, the man's enormous sweaty behind almost wedged against his trouser pocket. Eventually Andy yanked out the phone, promising himself that he would wash his hands the moment he arrived at work.

'1 message received' it stated on the screen of the phone; it was from an unknown number

Hurriedly he opened it;

You will see - Look left at the platform. Red is the colour.

That's all it said, a disappointed Andy put the phone back in his pocket. Explain everything my arse he thought to himself, and besides, he was in no mood to turn left at the moment, with the low lying trousers of 'Mr Big' not covering the top of his huge white rear. The crack of the man's ass was evident for all to see but Andy was the only one on board to get the 'privilege' of having it occasionally press up against him with each bend in the train tracks. His head was also beginning to pound again, the sweat of the people and the stuffiness of the air combined with last night's alcohol had Andy severely dehydrated. Now he just wanted to get off the tube, and when 'next stop Bakers Street' was announced he began to breathe a sigh of relief.

The doors opened; Andy heard the screaming. People were running across the platform, pushing those in their way. Others lay on the ground with their hands over their head. One girl caught Andy's eye. She must have been about the same age as Anne-Marie, wearing a red summer dress and holding a brown teddy bear, with tears rolling down her face. His brain was in a whirlwind but within an instant he was snapped out of his state by the mass heaving of the crowd behind him. It seemed everybody wanted to get out of the carriage fearing they were the target of a terrorist attack. He too wanted to get out but was stuck behind 'Mr Big' as he had christened him. He forced his way to the fresh air he had earlier craved. Less than ten yards away from the door to his left-hand-side laid a man covered in a pool of fresh dark blood. A section of platform had been coloured red by the bodily fluids that oozed from his wounds. Policemen stood around the body as they watched a passing doctor attempt CPR on the victim. Even the police looked shaken by the events. Andy tried to get a good look at the soon to be dead man's face. Before he could venture any closer a police officer, armed with a very real looking machine gun, grabbed him and told him to move to the nearest exit. The station was being evacuated. As Andy peered over the officer's shoulder to the body, the policeman shouted angrily at him 'Now Sir'.

Andy was again back with the sardines as they left the station. Now everyone was huddled together like a scared flock of sheep after they saw a fox in their field. For a change he didn't care about the sweaty shirts touching him. His heart was racing again; blood was being pumped around to his vital organs at a rate that had not occurred in years. While all around him were petrified, Andy was getting excited, he was buzzing. With his senses heightened from the adrenaline rushing through his system he pulled out his phone again.

You will see – Look left at the platform. Red is the colour.

Question after question started to come to his mind. Who was the man gunned down on the platform? Was it really terrorists that shot him? Is Peter linked to terrorists? How could he possibly know the exact time of the shooting? The timing of the event was so precise to my movements, was the situation staged just for me?

Now out on the street, he turned slowly trying to spot anybody looking at him, or even looking suspicious. He gradually made his way round a full 360 degree turn, but spotting anything was next to impossible in this melee of ambulances, fire engines, police, bomb disposal men and hundreds of panicked people. The beeping of horns and the symphony of sirens was now just disorientating. He knew what he had to do, turning on his heels he began to sprint, there's life in the old legs yet he mused.

'Get me the records of all Baker Street Directacom staff

mobile numbers' he directed the new girl Sarah Cripwell, still panting from the unusual burst of exercise, Sarah duly passed him an A4 page with all the information required. Andy quickly scrolled down through the sheet.

Jaroick, Jeffers, Johnson. Peter Johnson, he checked the number on the page to the number on his message received. Bingo, it definitely was Peter who sent the message. Hurriedly he walked into his office, logged onto his computer and checked the office personnel tracker.

Peter never signed into work today. Could it have been Peter who shot the man?

As if to snap him away from his thoughts his phone beeped in his pocket, causing a startled Andy to jump in his chair. Without hesitating he pulled the phone out, the message was again from Peter. It read *10.00am, West India Dock Guard House, no police.*

8

Victoria awoke from her sleep to the stench of her husband's liquor. This was an unusual occurrence for Andy, and Victoria recognized that; he was a good father to her children, if not a good husband to her. Victoria got up and went straight for the shower. These days she had a spring in her step and an excitement in her voice, and it was certainly noticeable as she sang loudly and with passion in the shower. Jack greeted her when she opened the bathroom door. He said he was sick and needed the day off school. Victoria recognised that although he had the face of an angel, he didn't have the mind of one. She placed her hand on his forehead and told him he was perfectly fine and to stop being such a rouge.

While waiting for the kettle to boil, Victoria listened to the morning radio. *Classical Radio 105* was her favoured station especially the 7 to 9am Breakfast Show that played hit scores from popular musicals and films. The title track to the film The Mission was now playing and it seemed to din the sound of Jack and Anne-Marie as they squabbled over the last fun size chocolate bar for their lunch box. Unfortunately it had to be 8.30am and the news interrupted, it always seemed to interrupt as it was regularly about this time that the radio was turned on.

'In breaking news there has been an unconfirmed terrorist attack at Baker Street Station this morning. A man in his thirties was fatally wounded in a shooting at 8.15am, while he stood waiting for an underground train on platform 2 of the station. The man's identity has not yet been released until all family members are informed. Baker Street Station remains closed and The Jubilee Line service has been suspended until further notice.'

The news hit Victoria like a tube train itself.

'Mummy, Mummy, Mummy' Jack petulantly screamed, 'Is that not where Daddy works, is Daddy okay?' Jack's words were the reality that was worrying his mother.

'I'm sure he's fine, Daddy goes to work earlier than that, so he is fine.'

But Victoria's expression didn't add up with her response. She was worried, she was really worried and Jack knew it too. Victoria went to the sitting room, lifted the receiver of the phone and punched in the numbers. The phone was ringing; as she waited the time seemed to stand still. Finally a man's voice answered the phone. With anguish, and a quiver in her voice, Victoria asked

'How could you do this? How could you do this? We hadn't talked about this.'

9

'I'm afraid I'm feeling ill today, I'm going to have to take the rest of the day off and go home to bed. Sarah is re-arranging my appointments as we speak.' George Brownlow, Andy's boss, hardly looked at him as Andy explained his situation.

'No problem, we'll see you when you are better' George responded. Andy couldn't believe how easy that was; he was expecting a response similar to how his wife reacts to his son's sick day requests. It was Andy's first false sick day with Directacom but he had a funny feeling it would not be his last.

It was 10.05am when Andy arrived at the guardhouse. With the tube line shut, Andy had to take a taxi, but now traffic was also heavily impeded by the extra security on the streets. One stop at a police checkpoint cost Andy twenty minutes and fifteen pounds. At this moment Andy was more concerned about the time than the money. Andy wondered had he missed something he was supposed to see; he hoped against hope that whatever it was it would not be another dead body. It was now 10.10am and Andy could see nothing, the little guardhouse had been turned into a quaint newsagent. There was no customer inside the shop and nobody behind the till. This began to worry Andy as he stood at the door looking in.

Is it me who is the target this time? he thought to himself.

Just then the fallen leaves next to Andy were whipped up into the air, and performed a little dance on their way back down. Quickly Andy turned but all he could see was the back of a car that was speeding down the street, Andy recognised the make of the navy car, it was a BMW *5 series*.

Terry White pulled up outside Cafe Rosa, he took of his shades placed them on the dash and locked his BMW. Terry had already handed over the envelope containing the £500 earlier this morning and was now on his second errand for the day. The man he would be looking for would be wearing a black pinstripe suit, white shirt and blue tie. Terry opened the door and stepped inside. With razor sharp eyes he scanned the room before him, but after a few moments he came up blank. Biding his time he sat next to the window and ordered a flat white coffee, with no sugar. It was highly unusual for any of his meetings to run late.

Andy's own eyes were scanning for activity. He meticulously checked the guardhouse itself for any writing or any clues but all it contained was a small plaque containing the words John Thorne - In love and war he conquered 1874 - 1918. Could this be the clue he was looking for, and if so what did it mean. Andy was now getting frustrated, what was Peter doing? He felt that if he could not understand what was going on then maybe he should bring in the police, after all a man had already been murdered this morning. As his mind raced he began to take more notice of the BMW man sitting by the window in the cafe across the street. Andy felt he just looked out of place, in a part of the city of flash suits and false demeanours, his suit was rigid and his demeanour unwavering. At that moment a brand new black Mercedes pulled up outside the tiny cafe. Either this place has the finest coffee beans in the world, or something serious is going down there. He wondered what it could be.

As Andy pondered what could be taking place in Cafe Rosa a man hovered up behind him and pulled a small black sack over his head. A black van reversed up to the guardhouse, Andy took a heavy punch to the rib cage and was then bundled into the van. Andy lay aching on the floor of the transporter, all he could see was the black bag over his head and all he could hear was the sound of an ear aching Garth Brooks song pounding out over the speakers. Eventually the song 'Friends in low Places' was dulled by the sound of sirens. He wondered was he being brought back to Bakers Street, but how could these people get away with it and why would they want to bring him back?

'Why me?' He said to his attackers with an air of panic,
'Why me?'

10

Victoria was now in tears on the phone. She thought she could trust this man, out of anybody she thought he was the man she could place her faith in.

'Calm down Victoria, calm down, I only did exactly as we agreed. Exactly, no more, no less' the man told her.

'But the radio, 8.15am, Bakers Street, thirty something year old man - dead' she said with a quiver in her voice.

Jack had now entered the room, the moment he saw his mother crying he ran over and wrapped his little arms in a bear hug around Victoria's legs.

'Are you talking to Daddy? Is he okay, can I talk to Daddy?' Jack asked.

'No honey, this isn't your father, I'm just taking with Jennifer, Daddy is fine, absolutely fine, now go back to the kitchen and pack your lunch-box.'

'Can we ring Daddy, please?'

'Okay, we'll ring straight after I'm finished talking with Jenny.' With that, Jack went back to the kitchen and Victoria took her hand off the receiver.

'He better be alright, he is a very good father'. Victoria then slammed the phone down.

Victoria felt as though she might faint, she braced herself against the fireplace mantelpiece as she took shortened breath after shortened breath. Victoria had been in this situation before. Suffering from asthma when she was young she occasionally hyperventilated. It was an occurrence of only once every five years or so but instinctively she grabbed a paper bag from under the coffee table and placed it around her mouth. As she breathed into it she noticed the decrease of oxygen going to her head and soon Victoria was taking regular breaths again. If only she knew that in an hour's time her husband would also be breathing through a bag, but this time not by choice.

Gathering her thoughts, and taking one final deep breath Victoria rang her husband's mobile, but it went straight to voicemail. This was not unusual as Andy always turned off his mobile during business meetings. Unfazed, Victoria dialled his direct line at work. Once again Victoria got a pre-recorded message, but upon hearing this recording Victoria's jaw dropped. It would have been common to hear a message that Andy was in a meeting and would ring back at his earliest possible convenience, but this message was extremely unusual. It was Andy's sick day message.

'You have reached the Voicemail of Andy Pickering. Andy is currently out of the office today for personal reasons, please contact George Brownlow for any urgent queries, Thank you.'

Clearly Andy was not at work and somebody had set up his voicemail to suit.

'He's dead, he's dead, I did this, God damn it I did this.' Victoria whispered under her breath as best she could, the rapid breathing now starting to take her over. Jack, getting impatient, came back into the sitting room to talk to his father. Upon entering he saw his mother lying out cold on the floor, one arm was resting upon her face, its hand holding the receiver to the phone.

11

Slowly, very slowly, Andy began to open his eyes. He was groggy and everything around him looked unfamiliar, strange, confusing even. His ribs hurt, he tried putting his hand on them to check if they might be broken, but found his hands were bound together tightly. Andy tussled with the ropes for a short moment but deep down he knew it futile. He was stuck here and he was at his kidnapper's behest. He was now regaining his normal conscious, but he might as well have remained unconscious for all the good having his faculties back would do him. Andy was sitting in a chair. His legs were also bound and his chest was wrapped to the chair with sailor's rope. Andy now understood why his ribs were so sore, the rough rope digging into his side where he had earlier received a heavy blow. The chair was the only chair in the room, in fact it was pretty much all that was in the room, except for a projector screen that was currently wrapped up. The room had white walls, a white ceiling, and most disorientating white carpet. Andy, seated exactly in the middle of the room could not take his eyes off the carpet. He was transfixed on the floor. The carpet was white but it contained some red patches as well and the patterns lack of symmetry were making Andy sweat. The red patches were most definitely blood, spatters lay everywhere; the walls were obviously easier to clean than the once fluffy carpet.

His thoughts now turned to Jack and Anne-Marie. Even though he was bound, disoriented and in obvious pain with his ribs, he could still afford a smile with his treasures in his thoughts. Surprisingly Victoria was next in Andy's thoughts. Chris had told him many times to accept it was over, that it had been for many years now. Chris had told him to move on while he still had hair on his head. 'Women and scalps just don't mix',

Andy had heard this phrase from his best friend on many occasions. Chris definitely always talked sense but he had a heart that wouldn't need to acclimatise in the North Pole. Sometimes it takes an accident or illness to realise who the ones you really love are. This was that moment for Andy, he knew he still loved Victoria, just the same as the night they first met. If only she could somehow see back to that night and find that love for him again that had now been lost.

'When you wake, please press the button on the control between your knees, this is a recorded message and will be repeated every five minutes'. The message from the speakers startled Andy. With all the events unfolding, both in front of him and in his mind, he had not noticed the simple remote placed between his thighs. It had one red button on it and a sticker which read *Press here for Assistance*. Andy's first instinct was that the button would detonate a bomb; it just seemed like something out of the movies. Maybe it would be a bomb in an underground station to continue the chaos caused earlier that morning. It all made sense to him now. He had pestered Peter about what he was doing getting off at the wrong tube stop and why he has all the bruises. Peter left the note saying he would explain everything. Now he had shown him he was a terrorist, and to put the cherry on the cake, Peter was going to make him detonate the bomb to bring death, to bring motherless children, to bring sonless mothers, to central London.

Of course Andy knew if he didn't press the button, there would be consequences to him. Soon his own blood would surely be staining the white carpet floor. He thought that maybe he should just press the button. Peter and his group would detonate the bomb anyway and there wasn't much point in him getting tortured to attempt to stop the inevitable.

If only I could warn somebody, if I could just stall them long enough to evacuate the underground.

Andy manoeuvred to attempt to retrieve his mobile phone from his trouser pocket. His hands were so tightly bound that it proved difficult, but he could feel the phone, he knew it was still there. Who to ring he deliberated, and who would believe him. Only the Prime Minister might have the power to evacuate the whole underground system and unfortunately Andy did not happen to know the Prime Minister on first name terms. If he rang 999 nothing would happen, they would take his name, number and details and say they would investigate the claim straight away. This is what the police telecommunications personnel are trained to do. The whole country would be shut down every day if all hunch and prank callers were believed to have one hundred percent accurate information every time.

Andy rattled his brain; he clenched his fist and concentrated hard.

Who do I know with power, who do I know who knows someone in power.

Andy knew Sergeant Green pretty well, he was the local sergeant in West Hampstead. As a good football player Andy even invited him to the Directacom 5-a-side on two occasions when they had been short, but he was unavailable both times. Still, he just would not have the power. Then it clicked. Victoria's best friend was Jennifer, Jennifer had another friend that Victoria didn't know personally, but that friend's brother was a government minister. Andy couldn't remember what minister he was but he knew who he had to ring. He had one call to make and he had to make it fast, he was sure he was being watched. Andy thought if a government minister cannot be taken seriously then who can, and he attempted to yank the phone from his pocket, with his bound hands, to ring Jennifer. Then suddenly it happened. Andy heard the noise and spun his head around to find the remote had fallen to the floor. Worse again the controls landed face up again, but the red button was now firmly depressed. He waited for the deafening bang followed by the screams of panic and pain.

12

Once again Terry White took off his dark shades and placed them on the dash of his car. His BMW fit in quite nicely in this neighbourhood. Terry reached out of the window and pressed on the intercom that lay before him.

'Mr White, password Thomas the Tank Engine'. Terry's client was a man of much wealth and his security was no laughing matter but each week he would change his password to a new children's cartoon character. It was an eccentricity a man of such wealth could afford himself. The tall black cast iron gates duly opened and before Terry lay a tarmac drive that twisted up to his client's residence. The house was Victorian and in excellent condition as it had been recently refurbished. In recent years money was becoming much easier to come by for his client but then again it was no coincidence that in recent years Terry had worked for him. Terry knew his client as Mr B and had never referred to him by any other name. This was simply for security reasons and Mr B never skimped on security. Mr B was in the line of business where phone tapping had occurred in the past, many were also getting suspicious of his new found extra wealth. The combination of these factors meant Terry could never, and did never, refer to him by his real name.

The grand two story house was set on two acres of land and Mr B had two foreign men employed full time as gardeners and lawn manicurists. It was Pavel that Terry first met after getting out of his car.

'Where is Mr B?' Terry asked Pavel, his voice deep, his tone firm and factual.

'You will find him in the conservatory Mr White' Pavel told him, with hedge clippers in one hand and a bottle of water in the other. Today was another roasting day as the heat wave continued, and Pavel was certainly feeling it.

'Thank you Pavel, now go put on a hat' Terry told him as he began making his way towards the conservatory. The conservatory was Mr B's latest and most extravagant addition to the house. Unusually it was two stories in height. It could be accessed from both his bedroom on the first floor and the sitting room on the ground floor. The first floor was made from glass so the sun could beam through to the couches below. It was double glazed with a blind in the centre to give privacy to the 'Bedroom under the Stars'. As Terry approached the conservatory he looked up and could see the blind on the first floor was closed; it was a warm day and if it was still open Mr B would surely have been waiting for him in a human oven.

When Terry entered, Mr B was indeed awaiting his company.

'You're late' Mr B snapped.

'Yes Sir, traffic was gridlocked due to the police checkpoints today, my apologies again Sir.'

Mr B knew that Terry was telling the truth, but he remained austere at all times. He was a man of forty five or so years and good looking in a powerful sort of way. He had no stand out features but his manner, dress sense, quick wit and knowing smile made him a hit with many a beautiful woman. He was also a caring father in his time off, his wife having died in a tragic car accident nine years ago. His two boys were now fifteen and sixteen and were developing the same alluring smiles as their father was noted for. Not that he saw them that often now at any rate; both boys were away in public boarding school. This meant that unfortunately Mr B only got to see his boys at the weekends, but fortunately for him this meant a free house for five productive days a week.

'Did you get the package I require' Mr B asked.

'Yes indeed sir' replied Terry as he placed the briefcase he had been holding on the coffee table in front of him. With a snap of his fingers the case was open and Terry produced two A4 size envelopes.

'Two copies as requested Sir, only the original remains, the master copy, and that is securely in Mr Murray's safe.' Terry stated.

'Thank you Terry, that's good work. Did you deliver the envelope to the other gentleman this morning?'

'I did indeed Sir, he assured me everything was in order.'

'I have become concerned about this individual Terry, I am not sure he can be trusted, do you believe I should trust him?'

'Sir with all due respect, I am not here to judge people's characters, nor am I concerned be they of good or bad nature, it would be a conflict of interest to my job if I did. But I do believe him to be efficient Sir. Will that be all Sir?'

Mr B knew he should not have asked the question in the first place, but Terry White's answer was wise and insightful as always. Mr B was glad to have Terry working for him. His record was flawless, his work was generally simple, usually collecting and distributing, but he did it with such efficiency, accuracy and reliability that Mr B had come to rely on Terry. In truth, Mr B wanted to know more about Terry, what his background was, had he been in prison, what was the worst thing a client asked him to do? But he knew this would jeopardize everything. Why try and fix what isn't broken Mr B always said and in his relationship with Terry this was no different.

It was a fellow colleague who recommended Terry. He had held Mr B's job previously until a sex scandal involving two Thai girls, some leather, a dog lead and a video camera, had brought a crushing and decisive end to his job and his marriage. Terry had served his predecessor well and his performance for his new client had been no different. Terry did not like Mr B's last question, Terry was no friend of Mr B's, in fact he secretly thought what he was doing was a disgrace, but his job was not to judge, and Terry took his job seriously.

'That will be all for today Terry, I will be in contact with you via e-mail.'

Terry picked up his suitcase, turned, left the conservatory, and walked back to his car. Once sitting back into the driver's seat he opened the glove compartment and took out his trusty diary.

'What does The General want this time?' he said to himself, as he put the diary back into the glove box. Quickly he put on his shades and started the engine. The wheels spun and smoke rose from the tarmac as he left Mr B's drive. He was heading back towards central London, some twenty-five miles away.

13

The stainless steel handle on the large white door began to turn. It was a little less than one minute since Andy had inadvertently pressed the red button on the remote control. No bang was heard, no screams piercing Andy's ears, nothing but one never-ending minute of silence. The door opened and Andy held his breath. Two contrasting people walked in the door. The man was dressed head to toe in military camouflage uniform. His steel toe cap boots were freshly polished, his trousers and jacket were a combination of the thirty shades of green, and he wore a matching camouflage peaked hat on his head. His face was clean shaven, showing the sharp bone structure to his jaw. The man of strong build and average height looked at Andy as he began to walk towards him. Andy tried to read into the soldier's eyes, but they were cold and distant and gave nothing away. Andy's eye was then drawn to the second individual.

She was dressed in a short blue skirt and a white blouse with a lab jacket partially covering both of these. She wore shoes with a slight heel, which gave lift to her calves which looked toned and shapely, as they kept drawing Andy's eyes up to the point where the woman's legs met her dress. Her face was more kind than the man's, but none the less it remained serious. She too walked toward Andy holding a briefcase in her left hand. Her hair was tied in a bun which allowed the beauty of her face to be shown. The only kind of physical flaw Andy could see on the beautiful woman was a large dark birthmark under her left ear. Snap out of it Andy told himself as he realised that he was ever so slightly leering at the woman.

The two were now side by side and standing directly over Andy. The man spoke first.

'My name is Corporal Derek Cleaver. On behalf of the

team I hope your visit to our headquarters has not been too much of an ordeal for you. Privacy is imperative to us, hence the bagging on your way to our facility. You have already been injected with some drugs which will affect your brain in different ways. You will require another shot to complete the course.' Corporal Cleaver then motioned with his arm. 'This is Corporal Amy Fisher, she is handling the medication.'

'Good afternoon Mr Pickering' the woman said with a voice much more coarse than Andy had expected. She placed the briefcase in Corporal Cleavers hands and flipped the lid open. Andy could now see what was inside. The case was filled with a black infill, in which one large vile, and one equally large syringe were held. Andy began to sweat again, in fact since he regained consciousness it had never stopped. The droplets trickled down his neck getting absorbed into his dripping shirt when they hit the collar. Andy had not said anything to the two captors so far, he had waited for Corporal Cleaver to tell him about the bomb, but no information was forthcoming. Instead all he had told him about was some medication, maybe they were trying to ease the pain in Andy's ribs, but Andy didn't care about them. He needed to know; after all he had been the one to press the red button.

'Where is the bomb? How many did it kill? How many did I kill?' Andy exploded

'Excuse me Mr Pickering?' responded Corporal Cleaver.

'You heard me, the God damn bomb, where did you plant it? What is your cause? Why are you doing this? What is your cause?

Corporal Cleaver gestured toward Corporal Fisher and she duly nodded back.

'I'm afraid the medication has played tricks on your mind Mr Pickering, it is a common side effect of the drugs we use. Please put your mind at ease sir, there is no bomb we know of.

Now a moment ago you said how many did I kill.'

Corporal Cleavers voice straightened and became extremely authoritative. He stared Andy right in the eyes and asked him

'Who do you think you killed? Who do you want to kill?'.

'What?' Andy answered in disbelief. 'Are you seriously trying to suggest I would want to kill somebody, anybody?'

'Well why would you say it otherwise?' the Corporal retorted, now bent over staring Andy in the eyes. His nose could be no further than an inch away from Andy's at this stage. Somehow the situation had turned 180 degrees, Andy was now being accused of wanting to kill people.

Although he felt the Corporal knew well what he was about to say, Andy felt he had to say it anyway.

'I got a message on my phone, I was given front seat viewing for a terrorist attack in Bakers Street station, I got another message, it told me to go to a guardhouse. There I was abducted by the terrorists, I wake up here, bound, surrounded by blood on the carpet and am given a detonator to press. I swear I didn't press it, I just accidentally dropped it' Andy's voice was becoming more defensive.

'So I detonated the bomb by accident, but it wasn't me who planted it and it wasn't me that killed those people, okay. It was your group, it was your group, not me.'

On hearing the story Corporal Cleaver backed off. The chain of events made sense to Corporal Cleaver; Andy had just put two and two together and got five.

'Once again Mr Pickering, calm down, I assure you, you did not detonate any bomb today. Let me try and explain things to reassure you that everything is fine and we are not terrorists.'

Andy was predicting what he was about to hear, some pathetic story that justified shooting people, or possibly even bombing people, but what he would hear was very different indeed.

14

Corporal Cleaver began 'You are here because you wanted to be here. What we need to know is if you want to stay here for longer. The group we belong to is called Unit Firestorm and your work colleague Peter Johnson is a member of our unit. Peter informed us that you passed his reflex tests in the public house. You caught the falling glass that Peter knocked off the table when you were intoxicated. He also informed us of your melancholy with the world, how you had begun to question your life and how you felt nothing that you did really mattered. This is the reason most people end up in this room, because they feel exactly like you. You would be surprised by how many people out there experience the same emotional discomfort about their life as you. These emotional discomforts are exactly what our group thrive on, we would not exist without them. We are always looking for people who need a change in life before they end their own. Basically, we look for people who need to be brought back to life, but in doing so we will bring them much closer to death. We are looking for someone who does not question authority, who always puts Firestorm number one, who isn't afraid to lose friends but will definitely make some real friends. Friends you are willing to die for, not so called friends that you debate if you will give them the £50 loan they are looking for on a Saturday night. Our work is to kill or be killed, and we like to kill. We are looking for a person who wants all these qualities and who deep inside has all these qualities. Mr Pickering, we are looking for *you*.'

Corporal Cleavers speech struck a chord with Andy, his life was indeed as he described and he wished for something more real in his life for as long as he could remember. Andy did want a change. He did want people he would die for or that would die for him, but he had no interest in achieving this by volunteering for a bunch of ruthless terrorists.

'You say you need to know if I want to stay for longer, then if it is by my choice that I am here why bind my legs and wrists, and tie my chest to this chair? Why is the room all white? Why is there blood spattered all over the carpet and why on earth is there nothing in the room bar a projector and screen?'

'You have many questions and this is understandable' replied Corporal Cleaver.

'I am but a Corporal, you will have to ask the Marshal to find the answer to some of those questions but I will tell you what I know. You are bound simply because it keeps you limited as to what you can physically do, hence you are much easier to transport and detain. Your chest is tied to the chair because it ensured you would be sitting upright at all times and thus not harm yourself by falling as the drugs we have administered to you kick in and out. This room is all white as it is used to disorientate people, it is a torture room and that is why the blood is on the floor. We also use it to educate new candidates to Firestorm; you are about to watch a short film hence the projector. I hope I have answered all you questions, now if we could get back to the programme Mr Pickering.'

'Yes Mr Pickering, as per programme you are due your booster shot of medication' said the patiently waiting Corporal Fisher. She moved in closer to Andy. 'I am just rolling up your shirt sleeve to administer the shot' the Corporal told him. When she had lifted his sleeve he noticed an area of bruising at the point of soft tissue flesh in the crook of his elbow. At the centre of the bruise was a pin prick. He had definitely been injected already. This startled Andy. Although they told him that he had already received some of this 'secret medication', he just assumed that these people lied about a lot of things, this medication would just be one more to add to the list. The shock broke Andy's short silence.

'What the hell have you put into me?' He roared at Corporal Fisher. He was now fruitlessly wrestling with the ropes that bound him.

'The drugs are perfectly safe Mr Pickering' Corporal Fisher responded 'but I must carry out some precautionary checks before the final dose is given.'

'What if I don't want the damn injection?' he asked wishfully, knowing only too well what the answer would be.

'I'm afraid it's too late for that now Mr Pickering.'

Corporal Fisher then removed a clipboard from the brief case.

'What is your name?'

'Andy Pickering.'

'What is your age?'

'Thirty seven.'

'What is your wife's name?'

'What the hell does that matter' Andy said as he began to raise his voice. 'What if I just refuse to answer the questions Corporal?'

'I will just give you the shot anyway without knowing if it is safe or not, remember Mr Pickering, you are bound and tied to a chair.'

'Victoria' Andy mumbled.

With that Andy felt a piercing of his skin; it was the unmistakable pinch of a syringe needle. Andy watched as the liquid level in the syringe reduced further and further, soon it was empty and he could feel his whole body relaxing. He fought to stay awake, to stay alive but the drugs were strong. As he slipped in and out of consciousness he could see the corporals walk to the door, a moment later it was shut behind them. Andy was left on his own, bound, tied to a chair and fighting his body for consciousness.

15

'You have a visitor Mrs. Pickering' the nurse said as she quickly snuck her head in the ward. Victoria was now in Hospital; it was only precautionary but she would have to stay overnight for observations. When Jack found his mother sprawled across the sitting room floor he reacted in a way that would surely have made his parents truly proud. Instead of crying, instead of screaming, instead of running into his neighbour's house, Jack dialled 999 for the emergency services and gave them the exact address of their house. The ambulance driver said it was truly amazing and told Jack he was a hero. The Sullivans, the Pickering's elderly neighbours, were now looking after both Jack and Anne-Marie. As his mother lay in hospital Jack epitomised the innocence of youth as he grinned from ear to ear. Jack had managed to get the day off school and was being spoiled with chocolate by the Sullivans, his new biggest fans.

Victoria had had a panic attack, she had been seven years old the last time she found herself in hospital after a panic attack. That time she found her pet cat 'Misty' run over by a big truck, this time she feared her husband was dead, and all because of her actions.

Jennifer followed the nurse into the ward, she looked truly worried.

'My God are you okay Vic? what happened to you pet?'

Jennifer had been Victoria's best friend since they met by accident in Edison, a satellite town of New York City. Victoria loved to travel and did so every summer break from university. That year it was the turn of New York City or more specifically Edison where some relations lived. Victoria was waiting in the kitchen of a *Starbucks* coffee shop for an interview. Jennifer happened to be in the same kitchen at the same time, looking for the same job as Victoria. Neither of them got a job that day but they did get a friend. A week later they had rented out an apartment together, three months later they came back on the same flight to London. Jennifer was bridesmaid at Victoria's wedding and celebrated in the good times with her best friend.

Over the past couple of years she had been a shoulder to cry on when Victoria's perfect marriage started showing signs of cracks, but for the last few weeks Jennifer's shoulder was not necessary. In fact they had only met up twice in the past six weeks. Usually not a week would go by without Vic and Jenny meeting up at least on one occasion. However, Victoria wasn't able to make the time lately. Jennifer understood that she had joined Curves and was as a result busier than usual. Still, Jennifer, for the first time in her life was not sure if she really knew Victoria. Victoria had always told her everything. Jennifer knew of her fear of lifts, she knew of Andy's refusal to ever sleep in the top of a bunk bed for fear of falling out, she even knew when and where the Pickerings had sex. Now she looked at Victoria lying in the bed beside her and she just knew she was hiding something from her, something big. Jennifer had tried bringing this very topic up with her on the phone only last week but immediately Victoria became defensive.

'There's nothing going on Jennifer, I'm just trying to improve my life by getting into shape and its taking up a bit more of my time, I'm sorry if that's a crime.'

Victoria certainly put that discussion to bed and Jennifer had not dared to bring it up again.

Victoria explained what had happened to her. She was listening to the news on the radio when she heard of the terrorist shootings in Baker's Street station. It was at the time Andy would have been there so she had rang his mobile and his office phone but got no answer. She feared the worst and had a panic attack. Jennifer attentively listened to the story. It was a touching tale but it just didn't add up. What would the chances be of Andy being the one person to get shot in London this morning and why get a panic attack over him doing a common thing like not answering his phone? Jennifer really wanted to question her friend but she knew she couldn't. Somehow, and a lot more subtly she would have to find out the truth.

'So how is your love life? Did you meet up with that engineer Dave in the end?' Victoria asked her visitor.

'No joy I'm afraid, he was a nice guy but just a bit too nice if you know what I mean.'

Jennifer's love life was like a Boeing 737 with no fuel, it just wasn't taking off. Jennifer was about 5'7", had a pudgy build, long brown hair and a gorgeous smile. Many a man had got lost in Jennifer's smile and it was easy to see why. Jennifer had been slow to open her heart up to a man for the past two years. It was that long ago that she and her boyfriend had split up. It was a bad break up with Jennifer having never spoken to her ex since the day of the break up. Despite what she said, it still affected her and the scars left over were slow to heal.

'Special Delivery for Victoria' one of the nurses shouted as she came from down the hall and into Victoria's ward. In her hand she held the most beautiful, fresh and colourful bouquet of flowers.

'Mr Pickering has splashed out for his lovely wife, they are just gorgeous' she said as she lay them on the bed beside Victoria.

'Well my husband is alive and well' Victoria said.

It was a forced comment and lacked sincerity and Jennifer picked up on it straight away.

With the impatience of a child getting up on Christmas morning Jennifer blurted out

'Read the card, read the card.'

Victoria cautiously looked at the card.

'Awh, from you know who it says, isn't Andy great'

But who really was the 'you know who' Jennifer silently wondered.

16

Déjà Vu. Andy's eyelids began to flicker. Soon they were again wide open surveying what lay in front of him. Andy was still bound and tied to the chair in the white room. Nothing seemed to have changed since he was talking with the two Corporals, except that his ribs had gotten more sore. Andy couldn't help but think about what kind of poison had been pumped into his body and the reason why it was administered to him.

Andy snapped out of his thought process when he looked down at his hands. He was holding the red button control. He re-read the sign on the control ' Press here for assistance'. Assistance had arrived in the shape of the two corporals when the button had been accidentally pushed in. Also, he had heard no explosions, no piercing screams. The corporals had told him he was here because he choose to be here and were suggesting a future that promised so much. To hell with it.

The red button was once again pushed. To Andy's relief there was no bang. The latch again began to turn on the large white door.

'Good evening Mr Pickering, you have been asleep for the past four hours, you are now ready to watch the presentation' Corporal Cleaver told Andy as he pulled down the projector screen over the wall. The white projector screen over the white wall seemed a bit pointless to Andy but he was in no position to argue.

'Hello Andy, I hope the white room hasn't thrown you too much. When I was first bound in the chair I thought the red button was going to electrify the chair. The room can really play tricks with your mind. Anyway I promised I would tell you everything and I will stay true to my word.'

Andy recognised the man on the projector screen, but he was dressed in a much different manner than he had ever seen him before. Only the upper part of the man could be seen as he sat behind his desk. It reminded him of how a news anchorman looked on television. He wore the same uniform as Corporal Cleaver, a green camouflage jacket with a matching peaked hat. The man had a black eye and an area of bruising around his chin; it was unmistakably Peter 'Fracture' Johnson. Andy sat engrossed as Peter began to shed some light on the past 12 hours.

'First of all, let me explain the medication. It's called Alphatex and is a substance which government scientists invented around five years ago. Its use is very simple, it alters the brain's memory patterns. The effects last ten hours from the first injection so I would guess that from now you have about four hours of altered memory collection left. In short, we've funnelled all your memories into one tiny section of the brain. Normally, memories are channelled to different parts of the brain, usually being classified by association. The difference of knowing exactly where your memories are is that now we can kill them, we can erase your memory. When this film ends you will be given two separate contracts. You will have to sign one of them. If you sign the 'opt out' document then you will be free to go return to your normal life. Nineteen out of twenty people choose to sign this. We will then inject you one last time, this injection is indeed poison, but it is focused poison. It will kill a tiny section of your brain, the section that contains all your channelled memory since your initial injection of Alphatex. You will then be relocated to wherever we picked you up, in this case the guardhouse by Canary Wharf. You will wake up, be disappointed that all the wild goose chase did was get you mugged by a group of men who put a black bag over your head. Most likely you will then ring to cancel your credit cards. You will probably find out the time at that stage and be amazed that the knock you got had you out cold for the past ten hours, and that nobody had come to help you. You would still be suspicious of me, but there will be a text on your phone sent at 10.20am this morning from me stating that I had waited from 9.50am to 10.05am at the guardhouse for you but you never showed, so I left. Because of the shooting at the station you will probably get up the courage to ring me, I will simply tell you what you were most likely thinking already. On the left as you got out of the tube there was a large red billboard for the A.A., the alcoholics anonymous. I would tell you that I had been attending meetings but was finding it difficult. I now often drank in Frognal as none of my friends and family would be there. I had also gotten the bruises from some fights I had got myself into. You would be so disappointed by the news, but it would appear real to you straight away, much more plausible than the crazy 'Peter is a terrorist' idea you held earlier in the day. You will promise to help me, whether you will actually try or not, only time will tell. But you will go back to your unloving wife Victoria, your 'monkey can do' job, our Directacom 5-a-side and you will grow old thinking this is all there is to life.

There is an alternative. If you sign the other contract your life will change forever. We hope that you will be one of the one in twenty who chooses this exciting and rewarding road. If you do sign this document, you promise never to speak of Unit Firestorm to anybody who is not in it, the punishment for doing this is death, along with whoever you told. There are many other clauses and fine print in there, but take it from me, that is the most serious clause both for you and for the rest of the Firestorm team. Signing this document makes you a member of the Firestorm training division and you will be unbound, untied from the chair and walk freely out the door with Corporal Cleaver and Corporal Fisher, two people you will soon be willing to die for.

Now to answer your earlier questions, the bruises I have are from the aggressive training regimes we undergo here, the reason I get out at Finchley Road on the way home is because I need to change lines. I end up here, where we train, where we get briefed, where you are right now. Now you will need to know who you will be working for.'

Although bound and strapped to the chair Andy had shuffled as much as he could and was now on the edge of his seat. He was about to find out who wanted the man at the station killed.

17

The blue BMW was now very close to the location for Terry White's next meeting. If Terry didn't like what Mr B's money making activities were, they were but a drop in the ocean compared to 'The General'. The man he was about to meet was ruthless. Terry had never questioned what was in the packages he delivered, but it wasn't hard to tell. Each time he distributed the packages to the different recipients he held his breath, secretly of course, as Terry always kept his unmistakably stern demeanour. These were dangerous drop offs but each was well rewarded for Terry. One of The General's drop offs involved Terry parking in an underground car-park in space no. 627. He never forgot that number. He was to wait for two men, one would knock on the boot and remove the goods, the other would give Terry a brief case through the driver's window. Terry had parked in the assigned car park space, but he was unaware the plan had been infiltrated by rivals earlier that evening. The General told him he would rendezvous with two men both wearing Chelsea football jerseys. Two men approached Terry's car, but there was no sign of the blue colours of Chelsea. During The General's drop offs Terry was always on edge, and as soon as he saw the two men approach he turned on the ignition. Terry was going to listen to no excuses; a change in plan meant an aborted plan. He pushed the gear stick into reverse, hit the accelerator pedal and spun the leather covered steering wheel. Now back on the car park road Terry quickly grasped the gear stick and shoved the lever into first, then second, then third. Behind him he could hear gunfire. Terry loved that Porsche *911*, it served him well for many years but he knew now it would be time to move on. It wasn't that the car was not fast enough for Terry, it was that it now contained seven bullet holes. It could probably have been repaired but Terry wasn't going to risk everything by giving a car with seven bullet holes over to a garage. Too many questions, too many suspicious eyes, too much potential trouble. The Porsche can now be found somewhere at the bottom of the River Thames. That was over six months ago and Terry was now used to the BMW and was quite happy with it too.

'Welcome to Hell' the faded sign read as Terry's car went whizzing by. The last word on the sign looked somewhat different to the rest. Obviously the local youths decided that an aerosol can of paint, could better describe their locality than its real name ever could.

Terry passed the grain store. He had no idea what happened behind the perimeter fence and did not dare to ask. The General did not even have the power to let Terry in beyond the boundary. The area covered as a grain feed warehouse facility, indeed at one time it had been, but with a ten foot electric perimeter fence, Terry did not believe the cover for a moment. The agreed meeting point was a mile away at the local Tesco supermarket car park. The General seemed to like car parks. He felt with so many people around nobody is looking at you. Terry always thought it was too many sets of eyes around, it only taking one set to blow everything apart, to end his career and to send Terry to jail for a long time. Terry didn't argue with The General though, he was pretty sure nobody argued with The General.

The passenger door of his car began to open and a short, heavily overweight man sat into the seat next to Terry. He wore black trousers and a black short sleeved shirt. The shirt was not tucked into his trousers, his large belly not making this a possibility. His shoes were black leather and recently polished. It was an obscurity Terry had often noticed, The General's shoes were always freshly polished, without fail. He was bald as an eagle on the top of his crown, with black hair on the back and sides. He made up for the lack of hair on his head with a big black bushy moustache.

'Good evening Terry, inside this envelope is all you need to know. It's a big shipment this time, the biggest yet and I intend to take my slice. There is simply too much for me to smuggle out and hide, this means I need you to enter the facility. I think I can get you about five minutes. This is serious shit Terry. For fuck, sake don't fuck it up. Give me a call on Monday and we'll fix the time and date for the operation. I expect you'll have no questions, but if you do, then is the time to ask me. Now enjoy your shopping at Tesco. I heard they have some great deals at the meat counter, let's just make sure we don't end up as dead meat ourselves.'

With that, The General left the car. Terry didn't even get to say one word, not even a 'hello', not even a 'goodbye'. He was used to this treatment now, this treatment had afforded him his new BMW *5 series*. Terry pulled a flick knife from his pocket and used it to open the top of the envelope. It contained maps, letters, positions of security cameras, a hand written note from The General, and £25,000 cash. Terry usually got paid £10,000 for each job he did for The General. This must be a dangerous operation Terry thought to himself. Terry remained unfazed, confidence is something he certainly did not lack. Terry laid the information out on the passenger's seat and got to work, confident nobody could see him through his black tinted windows.

18

Andy, on the edge of his seat as much as was physically possible sat glued to the projector screen. He would be amazed to hear what Peter was about to tell him. Peter explained

'I work for the British Government, both Corporal Cleaver and Corporal Fisher work for the Government and we want you to work for the Government too. The name of the man you saw in a pool of blood at the station today was Regulo Velasquez. Corporal Cleaver shot that man.'

On hearing this Andy started to become very uneasy, Corporal Cleaver was standing only a couple of feet away to his left, but he had no time for questions, the pre-recorded video rolled on.

'The British Government shot that man, they shot him for the good of Britain but nobody knows about it except Unit Firestorm and three other men. Velasquez had just brought in a large shipment of cocaine into England. Unfortunately the police, the British Army, even MI5 would not have been able to catch him, or the drugs. Unit Firestorm is permitted to use alternative methods to extract information from detainees. The room you are in now is where much of our information comes from, the torture room, the white room. We also have the ability to take down major dealers and drug lords by shooting them dead, no questions asked. This takes the drugs, the terrorists, and the corrupt, off the street immediately. If regular channels were gone through it could be a year before a dealer or terrorist are put behind bars. In the mean time they would have passed on their trade, their information to the next in line and nothing would change. Our methods stop the activities at the source and these peoples secrets die with them. How are we legal? How are we regulated? I assume you must we wondering.'

Peter hit the nail on the head, this is exactly what Andy was thinking; it's all very well to have Batman and Robin, but people can't just take the law into their own hands in real life, how can Firestorm get away with it.

Peter continued 'All intelligence for each operation is compiled and encoded. This is carried out by our sister unit *Recon*. The decision on which operations to carry out rests with three powerful individuals. The information compiled by Recon is electronically mailed via a secure network line to these three people. They have the codes to unscramble the encryption and extract the intelligence. If they are satisfied that the mission should go ahead then they return their mail electronically with the code for 'go ahead'. Else they return a code for a 'no-go'. It takes a 'go-ahead' from all three to form a mission. They are the only people with access to these codes and are the only people outside of Firestorm to know of the unit. They have also signed the document that lies in front of you. If they ever speak now, or in the future when they retire from their posts, they along with those they told will be assassinated.

These people are: The Chief of the British Army, he looks at the strategy of the mission and assesses its impact. If he believes the mission should be carried out in an alternative manner he can veto the operation and suggest his recommendations. The second person is the Prime Minister; their role is to look at the mission from a moral stand point. As leader of the country, their position is to do what is for the greater good. It is one of the most important roles the Prime Minister will take on when he enters office, but nobody knows about it, not even himself or herself, until we make our first contact with them. Finally the third person is the Chancellor of the Exchequer. He checks the mission from a financial point of view. As minister he has the arduous task of hiding the money allocated to Firestorm on the government books. Any government 'hot' money, money that they do not want showing up anywhere is used to fund the unit.

I appreciate that this is a lot of information to take in so let me summarise. Our sister unit Recon gather information, the three wise men decide our orders, we carry out those orders. None of these cogs make contact with the other cogs that make up the Firestorm machine.'

Andy's mouth had gone dry; it had now been gaping open for quite some time. Andy was definitely unsure about joining the organisation but he was gutted to think that if he signed the 'opt out' document that he wouldn't remember any of today's events. Despite the high blood pressure, paranoia, near death experiences, sore ribs and amazing revelations, this had been a damn exciting day and Andy knew it. In truth he had been crying out for a day like today his whole life. He almost felt his receding hair line growing back, he was feeling young again, rejuvenated. Then Andy's sensible self kicked in, he reminded himself of his two fantastic children, his wife, his job, his life. This sensibility started to take him over as he listened to Peter's next words.

'Make no mistake, if you join Unit Firestorm, you join for life. We will provide you with the best training and latest technology available but you must be mentally ready for the challenge. Basically, you have two questions to ask yourself. One; Do I want to radically change my way of life? And Two; Am I willing to kill or be killed? I let it in your hands, if I don't see you outside the door of the white room, I will see you at work Monday morning.'

The presentation was over. Corporal Cleaver left Andy's side and walked up to the screen. He pulled the chord and it rolled back up. He then went to the door and wheeled in a small table from outside the room. The table was placed in front of Andy. Corporal Fisher produced two documents from her briefcase and laid them on the table. Corporal Cleaver once again left the room, this time he returned with a silver pistol in his hand.

'We will unbind your hands so that you can read the documents, but take a good look at my magnum before you contemplate anything stupid.'

Andy heard the Corporal loud and clear. He was then given a pen and told one of the contracts needed to be signed in the next thirty minutes. The pen then dropped to the floor. Andy was so nervous and yet excited that his every sweat duct was now emitting liquid and the pen slipped through his fingers. Corporal Cleaver picked it up.

'No funny business Pickering' he warned Andy.

But Andy was in no mood for funny business, these were the most serious thirty minutes of his life coming up, it could change everything, it would change everything. Andy picked up the 'conditions for membership of Unit Firestorm' and began reading. After completing both documents, Andy put the contract back down and wiped his right hand on his trousers before he picked up the pen again. Andy's signature had never looked so shaky but it was done, he had signed his name to one of the documents.

Corporal Cleaver then marched towards Andy. Andy clenched, unsure what would happen next. Cleaver stopped behind him and bent down on one knee. Andy remained frozen, he could no longer see what Cleaver was doing. As Andy sat motionless the ropes dropped from his waist. Cleaver unbound his legs and untied him from the chair. Cleaver got up and now stood in front of Andy.

'Welcome to Unit Firestorm Pickering' he announced.

Cleaver motioned for him to stand up and the three of them walked to the large white door in the room.

Just at that moment Andy's mobile rang. He looked up at

Corporal Cleaver. He gestured to answer it. The number was Victoria's.

'Hello honey' Andy said in a tone as relaxed as he could achieve.

Victoria was relieved to hear Andy's voice. She had heard the man in Baker's Street station was identified as a Columbian national, but yet she had been unable to get through to her husband all day. Victoria wasn't supposed to be using her mobile phone in the hospital but she had just thought of a great plan to boost her spirits.

'I'm still at work' Andy told Victoria 'but I should be finished up in the next hour.'

Andy looked at Corporal Fisher who was nodding in agreement. Victoria informed Andy about her earlier panic attack and that she was in hospital for observations. She said she was absolutely fine, but no visitors were allowed in the ward after 8pm. She told him that the kids were at the Sullivans and to collect them on the way home. She assured him she was fine and there was no point in trying to come to see her.

'I'll see you tomorrow, I should be home about noon, tell Jack and Anne-Marie their Mummy loves them very much and will see them tomorrow.'

The couple said their goodbyes and he put the phone back in his pocket. It had been one hell of a day already and he could only imagine what lay outside the large white door. 'Go ahead' Corporal Cleaver told him. He placed his fingers around the stainless steel handle and pushed down.

19

Victoria was now fully dressed and waiting patiently at reception. The receptionist had gone to get the ward matron. Victoria had requested to sign the 'self discharge' sheet but only the matron had the authority to oversee a signature. After phoning Andy, she had made one more quick call. He was delighted to hear her voice and to hear of her new found availability. He had told her that he would immediately cancel his plans for the evening, nothing could be more important than a visit from Victoria.

'I believe you wish to discharge yourself Ms' the matron had arrived and had brought her unhelpful attitude with her.

'You do realise our staff have thoroughly assessed your situation and we highly recommend you stay the night so that we can observe you. You have had a serious panic attack Mrs. Pickering; these can have consequences which may only become apparent sometime in the following 24 hours.'

Victoria knew all of this, but this unfortunate panic attack had presented Victoria with a rare opportunity and she wasn't going to turn it down over some precautions.

'I fully understand what you have told me matron, but nevertheless I wish to sign the form' Victoria argued.

'Very well' said the matron with a resigned tone.

Victoria signed her name, walked out the exit and headed for the close by taxi rank. Where she was going was not on any underground line, it was much further away and would require a train. After the shooting earlier in the day, and considering she had just left hospital, she thought it best just to splash out on the taxi.

Victoria couldn't help but feel a little guilty about what she was about to do, but the past six weeks had been magical and she just couldn't resist. As she thought more about her deceit, she fully understood that her pathetic marriage to Andy was truly over for her. Although he was a great father, her love for him was no more. As Victoria got into the back seat of the taxi she realised that she felt more guilt for lying to Jennifer than to her husband. It killed her that she was jeopardising her friendship with her best friend. She could tell Jennifer wasn't buying all her recent excuses for not meeting up. Worst of all, it appeared Jennifer suggested that the flowers that she had received might not be from Andy. And she was right; they were from a man who would be getting a welcome visitor in about half an hour.

The taxi rolled up outside the front door, Victoria paid the driver and climbed up the steps to the large red door. Victoria lifted the big brass knocker and gave four knocks. As she waited she brushed her long blonde hair with her hand trying to ensure she was looking perfect for her host. The door opened and immediately the two embraced and shared a passionate but short kiss on the doorstep.

'I'm so glad you're okay, I hope you liked the flowers' the man said.

'Oh John they were perfect, just absolutely perfect.'

John and Victoria had first met six weeks ago and it had been a steamy affair since that fated night. Victoria met Jennifer outside the theatre as she often had done before. Jennifer had told Victoria that she would have some friends of hers joining tonight. Victoria was introduced.

'Meet my good friend Emma and her brother John.'

Although it was raining, and all four were stuck in the queue to get into the theatre, Victoria didn't care. She was simply drawn by John. She loved how John oozed sophistication. He was dressed in an Armani suit on the night and it looked as though it had been made just for him. He wore a designer felt fedora hat that accentuated his strong facial features. It was a bold hat, but he was a bold man and could pull the look off with ease. In the theatre Jennifer sat on one side of Victoria, John on the other. Victoria laughed at every quick witted comment that came from John's lips. Then the lights came down and the performance began. John had his own performance in mind. He began by rubbing the back of his index finger against the outside of Victoria's dress and along her bare leg. With no signs of discomfort shown from his recipient, the outside of his finger changed to the inside of his hand. The discreet fondling continued until the show reached its climax; Victoria almost reached it as well with John's hand now drifting inside her knickers.

John and his sister had to leave straight after the show to a prior engagement but he left Victoria with his business card and whispered in her ear to give him a call. John always maintained the exterior of the utter gentleman and Jennifer knew no different. Never for a moment did she suspect the activities that had taken place in the seat next to her earlier that evening.

The next day Victoria removed the card from her wallet. Jonathan Black MP was the title. John Black did not just look and act like a man of power, he genuinely was a man of power. The power drew in Victoria like an expensive French perfume. For two days she looked at the card, for two days Victoria considered saving her marriage. Then she picked up the phone early on a Friday afternoon. Within an hour she lay naked on the bed in the penthouse suite of the Ritz Hotel. It was a whirlwind romance and six weeks later nothing had changed. Joining the weight loss program Curves was just a cover to meet up. Westend night was now abandoned in favour of John. Victoria was a little concerned that Andy would be suspicious after she had woken up the other morning still in her evening dress. She had told Andy that she was going to see Billy Elliott with

Jennifer, but in truth she had a champagne meal on a private boat on the River Thames. She had drank a little too much which definitely was a rarity for Victoria, and she just fell into bed with her dress still on. She knew it was only a matter of time before she would get caught by Andy.

Victoria had also come to realise that her husband had become apathetic towards life. Maybe this was the reason she no longer loved him, maybe it was just one of them, maybe there was just no logical reason. Love isn't logical very often. Although Andy never discussed his feelings with her, Victoria knew her husband, the man she had shared a bed with for the past ten years. As if proving love's lack of logic, Victoria told of her husband's troubles to her new love. She may have only known him a mere six weeks but Victoria had fallen for John in a big way and felt she could divulge anything to him.

To her surprise, John responded with a plan. A plan to solve all her troubles, all her worries, he told her he could kill two birds with the one stone. It seemed too good to be true, it seemed science fiction. Then John told her that he could prove it all to her, he really had the power to make all their dreams a reality. John duly did as he had said. John predicted that a man would be killed in a tragic road accident in Paisley, a small town, twenty miles west of Glasgow. He told Victoria the name of the man who would be killed and exactly how the terrible crash would occur, he said to listen to BBC Radio Scotland in the morning for all the details. The next day, Victoria tuned into morning show on the radio station. The 8.30 news interrupted the programme.

'In other news, a man was killed this morning in a single car accident in Paisley, close to Glasgow. The victim's details have not been released but he is believed to be from the locality.'

Victoria didn't need to know the dead man's name. This was enough coincidence for her. Victoria was in shock; John

Black knew more information than she could ever want to know. This meant that he was correct, he could provide the solution to all their problems. And he would provide the solution.

20

Peter greeted Andy outside the door of the white room. He had been viewing events closely from the surveillance room and was delighted when Andy signed the contract to join Firestorm. Peter felt like Andy only two years ago. At the time he also had a drink problem. It was another Corporal that invited him to join. He was a counsellor at the A.A. and felt, bar the drink problem, that Peter was an ideal candidate. Peter still held a special relationship with that Corporal and had stayed off the drink as much in respect for him as for himself. Two years on, his life was one of joy, one of meaning.

It was only on Wednesday night that Peter got a phone call from a man he did not know. The caller divulged

'I am from within your organisation and I know of an ideal candidate. I am unable to bring in this man for reasons I cannot explain right now. Can you please offer this man the same chance you had. Please confirm via text to this number. For your co-operation I will send a gift of £500.'

Peter was a man of substance and a bribe of a paltry £500 would not sway him. Peter had to find out for himself if Andy was in fact an ideal candidate. Directacom 5-a-side was the perfect occasion to try and go for a drink together, to check Andy's character, his dulled lust for life and lust for change. A couple of drinks later and Peter easily extracted all the information he needed. The die was cast and Andy would be receiving a text message that would have far reaching consequences on Andy, and on almost everyone he knew. Peter met an unknown man in a BMW *5 series* car, accepted the gift and the wheels were set in motion.

'Welcome to Firestorm, welcome to the family Andrew Pickering' Peter said as he grabbed Andy's hand and firmly shook it. Peter was dressed, as he was on the video presentation, top to toe in camouflage gear.

'Thanks Peter, my head is a bit fucked right now, but it's good to see your face. I wouldn't have signed to join only for you, I'm trusting you Peter, I hope I am right' Andy told Peter as he held his head in his hands. Andy's head was sore, but it was a very different type of headache to the drink fuelled one he felt earlier that day, this time his mind was struggling to process all that had happened. It was also churning out the possibilities of what could happen next.

'Deep breaths Andy, deep breaths, let's take this thing one step at a time. Your head is supposed to feel like this, it means you're human.' Peter reassured Andy. 'The last ten hours ensured your head would feel like this. The texting, shooting, bagging, white room, medication, even the button ensured you would feel as you do now. We needed to know that even after all you had been through, with all the paranoia making hysterical waves in your brain, with the physical pain that you felt, that you still felt that this crazy, dangerous, disorientating life was better than the one you currently live. Usually the day proves too much for people, we root out the weeds and keep the budding plants. With training you will become an oak tree, strong, old but wise and with many branches to your life, but your roots will now be in Firestorm. Firestorm will keep your life crazy but your mind sane. Now welcome again to Firestorm'

Andy had just heard the news of his wife's panic attack and didn't want his kids left with no parent to take care of them because they were both in hospital. He took Peter's advice on board and began to relax his muscles and his brain with long deep soothing breaths.

'Okay, so what's the story with work? How can you be a member of this unit and still turn up on the seventh floor every day?' This was the first of many questions on Andy's mind.

'Oh but do I' Peter replied. 'As part of the contract you signed you must do everything in your power to maintain as normal a life as possible to those that you know, remember if anyone you know finds out about Firestorm they will be assassinated.' Peter then paused for a moment and began speaking slowly ' It has happened before, and believe me mate it's a harrowing experience to see a loved one killed because of you.' Peter resumed in his usual tough talking tone 'Check how many days I've actually turned up to work in the past year, I bet you'll be surprised. You don't miss me not being there, why would anybody else.'

'So I have to keep my job?'

'Absolutely, get inventive, you'll be surprised how little work actually needs to be done. I know I used to always make work for myself.' Peter then smiled and said 'Stop making the work and you don't need to do it any longer.'

Andy could have stayed for the day asking questions but it was now only Peter and Andy who remained standing outside the door of the white room. As Andy looked around the corridor, it reminded him of a hospital corridor. The floor was a dull grey vinyl, the walls were painted magnolia and the grid ceiling had cream ceiling tiles. It was boring, but effective and it all looked brand new.

Suddenly the lights shut off and only faint emergency lighting remained. It was getting late and everybody had gone home for the night. Andy still had so many unanswered questions but Peter told him they would have to wait.

'Your brain is in no fit state for the answers right now, you need to rest. And besides I've got to get home to Max and my dinner.'

Max was his dog, Peter knew Andy didn't know this but he thought he might as well leave one more question hanging in Andy's mind that night. It had been a serious day and they would both enjoy a laugh when he told Andy about his Alsatian.

'Go to work tomorrow and put everything in place, we'll see you here at 6.30 Monday morning.'

Peter walked Andy to the side exit of the building and took him to security.

'The tube is about seven hundred metres down there' he said as he pointed down the road. 'Now get some rest.'

As Andy walked toward the station he couldn't help notice a car parked all on its own outside the facility. It was half up on the grass margin, half on the road. It certainly wasn't a natural place for a car but nowhere on the road outside the facility perimeter catered for parking. The type of car made Andy suspicious as much as it's bad parking. It was a BMW *5 series*, and it was coloured navy. Surely it was not the same as that parked earlier today outside Cafe Rosa. It had been a long, long day and it was definitely time for Andy's weary head to hit the pillow. As a result he put it down to coincidence

Get a grip Andy, get a grip, the world doesn't revolve around you.

But it certainly seemed like it was starting to.

21

It had been a beautiful night. With the spell of good weather there was not a single cloud in the sky, a sky illuminated by a near full moon. The stars had come out to play too, even a lone shooting star was spotted. The city's lights had dimmed this image for too long. It was the perfect setting, and this was not lost on each other. The passion steamed the glass, the condensation dripping down every corner. Screams of ecstasy could be heard in the surrounding gardens. Then there was silence once again, only now no star could be seen, only the faint outline of the once bright moon could be made out through the fogged up glass. The 'bedroom under the stars' had once again proven a success.

When Victoria had arrived earlier that night the taxi stopped outside large cast iron gates.

'Can I have your name and password please' the intercom sounded. Victoria rolled down the window and stuck her head out

'Victoria Pickering, Thomas the Tank Engine'.

Now Victoria lay in the top floor of John Black's extravagant conservatory, it was an amazing way to spend the night making love under the stars. Victoria was truly taken in by the magic of it all. She was truly taken in by John Black, by the irrepressible Mr B.

It was three days ago that Victoria stood dumb founded as she listened to the nine o'clock news. The man from Glasgow died exactly as John predicted, in the exact location he said. John had told her he could solve all Victoria's problems, that he could give them more time together by keeping Andy more occupied, and he could bring Andy back to life as well. He explained that, as an MP, he had certain privileges of confidential information.

He told Victoria there was a secret group which Andy could join, which sets about revitalising the depressed with life by getting them to serve their country on dangerous missions. As the missions were undercover their outcomes often had to appear as accidents. John Black was not just an MP but the Chancellor of the Exchequer, he was actually inside Firestorm. He knew if he could get Andy to join it would considerably tie up his time. John called Terry, his right hand man, and got the ball rolling. However, John was also afraid of the plan; he wondered should he have just taken on the task himself, if he should never have said anything to Victoria. Although she didn't even know the name Firestorm, not to mind the dynamics of the unit, John had certainly, if inadvertently, put her life under threat, along with his own.

22

A sky scraping pile of documents lay on Andy's desk. Andy had got up early this morning, left Jack and Anne-Marie back with their new fans, the Sullivans, and come to work to put 'everything in order' whatever that meant. As it was a Saturday, bar two cleaning ladies, he was the only person in the Directacom offices. What to do with the pile of documents he wondered. Each contained the main content, a front page which summarised the proposal and a budget cost, and a back page where all managers' signatures were required to see a proposal through. If a manager was against a proposal they would simply staple on a page over the front of the document, explaining why it was rejected and signing their name. Ahead of Andy lay a day's work. He needed to devise a plan to get it done in thirty minutes, and he did just that. If any proposals cost exceed £50,000 then it would be shot down, this was only one in a hundred proposals. Also if David Sharpe had disagreed with any proposal then Andy would also do so. Sharpe by name, David was also sharp by nature and he was always clued in to the company's best interests. Last but not least Andy changed his signature to his initials, another time saving measure. 'Genius' he thought as he gave himself a virtual pat on the back. It was a delicate balance but Andy felt he had got it just right. If he signed off every document, his boss, George Brownlow would be on his back, if he didn't sign off on a lot of proposals then everybody would be coming knocking on his door looking for answers. Next he had to ensure he wouldn't be available if anyone did come knocking.

Andy sat at his desk and turned on his laptop. As he waited for it to boot up he sat in silence with a wry smile on his face. It had been an unbelievably productive morning so far. Andy logged on and checked the company personnel tracker. He had wondered if Peter really wasn't coming in to work. He had never noticed him missing, then again there were so many people employed here, it was hard to keep track of them all. He tried to access Peter's attendance record.

Please enter administrator code requested a dialogue box. Andy had forgotten that one can only access that day's records for all personnel. He could only access his own records on the tracker, unperturbed he tried 'password', '0000', then '1234', then he left the dialogue box empty and just pushed Enter. Andy was on a roll now and felt as though his luck would carry him over this minor hurdle. He saw 'incorrect password' on his computer screen, all four times, he attempted another few efforts but to no avail. Andy was coming back down to earth, he was human after all.

George Brownlow had the password, he had all IT passwords for the company, unfortunately for Andy, his office, like all the offices, was locked tight. What now he pondered to himself as he sat twirling his chair and tipping his fountain pen back and forth against his bottom lip. Outside his office the cleaners were just about finished. Then Andy's door opened.

'Sorry Sir' the lady said in a cockney tone. 'Would you like us to clean your office?'

'No thank you Sally' Andy responded. He saw a Sally, age 25, and a Theresa, age 43, were on duty today, the personnel tracker had come in handy for something. He always appreciated how important it was to greet people by their names. It made you feel better for knowing it, it made them feel better for knowing that you knew it, and it made good business a whole lot easier.

Then it came to Andy

'Sorry Sally, could you do me a small favour. I've left the Dobson Report in George's office. He needs it up to date first thing Monday morning. Would you be able to open his office a moment so I can get the report?'

'No problem, glad to help.'

'You're a lifesaver Sally' he added as he got up from his chair. Sally was now quickly fumbling through her keys. She felt she was just about to complete her most important task of the day, and it was all for the boss of the company.

Andy was in; now to find the administrator password. He closed the door behind him. Outside Sally and Theresa began to chatter. He knew he had about one minute before the girls would get suspicious. He hoped whatever they were discussing would keep them distracted. Andy loosened his tie, quickly surveyed the room and got to work. First he read the stickers stuck to the monitor of the P.C. '2 pints of milk, peppers, and curry powder'. Although he had no time for it, he laughed to himself, his laptop still contained a shopping list Victoria had given him last week. 'Move, move, move' he muttered snapping himself out of it. Next were the drawers on the desk. Drawer one, stationary, drawer two, newspapers, drawer three the final drawer contained among other things George Brownlow's diary. Quickly Andy flicked through it.

'Are you okay in there' Sally said, in a more concerned than suspicious tone.

'I'm fine thanks Sally, one moment and I will be out to you'

The heading on the back page of the diary was 'CODES' his index finger trawled through the page until he got to Administrator Password. 'Bingo' Andy said as he wrote the code on a yellow sticky pad. He closed the diary, put it back as he had found it and pushed the bottom drawer back in. He then regained his composure, straightened his tie, and left the office.

'No luck finding it then' Sally asked Andy as he emerged from the office. He was empty handed. It was a faux pax and he knew it, he had meant to pick up an empty file on the way out but had forgotten in the excitement. Thinking on his feet Andy responded

'I'm afraid not, I guess I'll just have to deal with George Brownlow's wrath on Monday morning.'

'I'm so sorry to hear that' Sally responded as she once again locked the boss's door. 'Try and have a nice weekend anyway.'

'Thanks again for your help, don't mention this to Mr Brownlow, he would kill me if he knew I'd misplaced the report even for a moment.'

'Mum's the word' she said as she and Theresa left him for the exit.

Andy quickly typed in the password into the computer. Unlimited access to all tracker records, it was hard to control himself, he could look up anybody. There were profiles on all people, there were CV's attached to each profile. There was definitely some juicy stuff in here, who to look up Sarah, the new girl, Brownlow, or even Brownlow's attractive P.A. It would certainly be interesting to see if her C.V, matched her position. However, Andy always had reasonably good morals, and he wasn't going to let one crazy day change all that. His fingers hit the keyboard typing *Peter Johnson* and pressing enter. Peter was down as a full time employee and was tracked in practically every day. It didn't make sense.

How could Peter be in two places at once, does he have a private jet pack to shoot him around the city?

Andy afforded himself a smile, but it all seemed a bit impossible. Peter had a few more sick days than him, but then again, everyone had a few more sick days than him. Since yesterday morning he vowed that that would change, his brief chat with George Brownlow showing that taking a few of these days was all too easy. What wasn't easy was figuring out Peter's double life. He clicked on the 'sign in time' for a random day, more out of frustration than any productive reason. Then the answer stared Andy in the face. It was so obvious. He had heard of a few employees using this facility but he never thought it would suit himself. It all seemed a bit anti-social, but it was also perfect for Peter's needs. Peter was making use of the company 'work from home policy'. It was originally developed such that maternal mothers could work a little longer before they took their leave. Legislation later dictated that men should be entitled to the same rights as their female colleagues. Andy always thought only loners had used this possibility, obviously not. When he clicked onto the 'sign in time' it brought up the location of sign in, Peter more often than not had *remote location* instead of the standard *Directacom 1, 2 or 3* swipe points. He had a feeling he would be working from home a lot more from now on.

Andy opened his diary. Appointments were spread sporadically across the five days of the week. As he analysed the appointments he saw that all but one could be moved to a different date if required. There was only one meeting that was steadfast. This was the Managers Progress Meeting, held with all area managers and George Browlow himself. This was the focus of the week and was held on a Thursday afternoon just after lunch. This explained exactly what each manager achieved last week and what would be their goals for the coming seven days. Once this meeting was over, a sigh of relief was let out by all concerned. Ahead of Andy that night was the 5-a-side, a shorter day on Friday and a weekend round the corner. In truth, he felt once this meeting was over the weekend had begun. Andy now knew what his first job was on his first day back at work. All appointments for the week would try and be changed to Thursday; this would mean a necessity only to turn up to work one day a week, maybe two to reduce suspicion. The plan was set. The sickness that began yesterday would continue next week. A guilty Andy would ring Mr

Brownlow someday next week and confess that he was feeling guilty about the work he was missing out on while being sick.

What a hero Andy mused.

Out of nowhere he would come up with a genius plan, he would remotely connect to the network and do some work from home. It will revitalise him and he would decide to tell his boss that he will work at home more often now, even when he wasn't sick.

Andy logged off, closed his laptop, filled his brief case with any necessary files to work from home and left his office, locking it on his way out. He left the office with a hearty smile on his face and a spring in his step. If he hurried he would have collected the kids and be home before noon to welcome his wife home from hospital. He decided it only right to call by Vanessa's Flowers before he got on the tube.

She may not love me right now but I'm about to be a different man, a man of excitement and spontaneity, and here's the first step.

Andy purchased a dozen red roses and headed down the escalator around the corner. For most of yesterday he wondered would he ever be able to face Baker Street station again after what he had witnessed, but there was a new steel to Andy, a hardness manufactured through terror.

23

It was his day off and it felt good. Terry was a man of precision but this morning, unusually, no alarm clock had been set, the shutters in the room were closed tight and only a single ray of light peered though the centre where they met. The one tiny slit illuminated thousands of dancing particles of dust. They seemed to avoid the laws of gravity as they bobbed up and down in the air. The room was a large airy bedroom with a huge master bed. Terry's muscular long arm lay stretched across his bed. It reached as if looking for someone at the end of it. It had been a long time since there was someone next to him to hold. Terry longed for someone to hold, someone to be there on his occasional mornings off, someone to welcome him home if he was after a challenging day at what he called work. Terry knew it wasn't easy. In his line of work meeting people was difficult. Unless of course he was looking to fall for some kind of tough man wielding a revolver, which he certainly was not.

Terry tossed and turned a little longer but his natural body clock told him it was time to get up. The time was 8.30am. Terry usually started the morning with a protein shake at 6.00am. This was a long lie in for Terry. Terry opened the shutters and welcomed the new day. Although he planned on taking the day off, Terry had nobody to share it with, at least nobody worth sharing it with. Terry's family was from a large industrial town in the north of England. His days in school there were marred by expulsions and he went from school to school quickly making new friends, and quickly loosing them again. At the time, Terry had an appetite for driving, the only trouble was, he didn't own a car. Some kids play rugby, some play football, joyriding was Terry's sport of choice. Terry's reputation began to precede him, and finding an employer willing to take him on proved difficult.

Others in the community could see the potential in him. Unfortunately for Terry, these were the unsavory drug dealing gangs in the town. Terry was recruited by one of these gangs and quickly developed a reputation as reliable, efficient, an excellent driver if police were in pursuit, and a menacing force when necessary. Terry had certainly gone down the wrong path as a youth.

One morning as Terry lay in bed in his mother's house, a broken piece of concrete block was thrown through the window. Tied to the block was a note. 'Get out of town or go six feet down'. It was a short message but a very straight forward one. Terry was working for tiny money and his life was in danger. He knew that this was not the life for him. Having no friends of note, his mother was the only person he would miss if he left. He did leave and he still missed her. He moved to London, the obvious choice eight years ago. Again 'straight' work was very difficult to come by. Terry had no qualification, he had not even finished school and he had a petty crime record to rival with any delinquent.

It was just another Monday morning, and Terry had purchased the local newspaper. He stood in a payphone box, one hand holding a highlighter pen, one holding the paper and his shoulder and neck combining to balance the receiver of the phone. Four refusals without even an interview, Terry had one twenty pence piece remaining. The last job he tried for was as a driver. The ad looked for someone trustworthy and reliable. The only qualification required was to hold a drivers license. The three month ban on Terry's license had just finished. The call turned out to be the best twenty pence Terry ever spent.

The man on the other end of the phone actually appreciated that Terry had a criminal record; the fact that his driving license had been revoked for a while was also a plus. The final factor that Terry was from the north of England and knew nobody ensured he was the man for the job. His employer was the then Chancellor of the Exchequer. He had packages to deliver to different people and even bought Terry a car to get him off the ground. He warned Terry never to look at the packages contents, never get caught with them and to never ever speak of them to anybody. Terry was taken under his wing, and his name started to be spoken of in underground circles. Soon the Minister was but one of his bosses. His new clients offered substantially larger rewards, but with that came many extra dangers.

As Terry's reputation grew, so did the pressure to live up to it. It was said that it would take five strong men to wrestle him to the ground, that the man did not know what sweat was, and that a world rally team had approached him to test drive their car. With his new found cash flow Terry invested in a nice property in a pleasant neighbourhood. The beauty of the property was its huge cellar. Terry got to work. Soon he had built his new office, an office that was hidden away from prying eyes. Terry built up his collection of gym machines; with each new job he rewarded himself with some new equipment. He stepped up his training. Terry began to believe in the stories himself. The other section of 'the office' was originally a couple of bookshelves, a desk and chair. He could read and write but at a basic level. He began to buy books to fill the shelves. He read them as part of his daily routine and he began to enjoy them. Soon he moved from fiction to fact. He read up on weaponry, martial arts and even the arts themselves. He became a rounded individual and a very knowledgeable one at that. The shelves looked less empty each week, now they were full and Terry had his own personal library.

He then attended a computer course for the first time. He knew that he needed to use email to communicate with higher profile clients. It would open new and more financially rewarding doors for him. Terry was not an easily distracted man, but every Tuesday night the woman who sat next to him on the course melted his cold exterior. She was bright and bubbly and fascinated Terry. It was to be his first love. Terry adored the woman and the more she got to know him the more she loved him back with equal measure. His intellect was astounding, his manner always exemplary, his wealth was alluring, and his stamina under the sheets was mind blowing. Unfortunately for Terry, he had to hold back his true identity, so he told her that he worked in insurance. Terry was both happy and successful; life had changed substantially from his troubled days in the north. Life was now perfect. One moment changed all that, one unfortunate moment insured the woman he loved would not be next to him this morning as he lay in bed. How he longed to feel her warm touch again. Terry knew it was probably too much to hope for that the relationship could work, in reality he would have to choose, work or love. As he dressed himself for the long day ahead he wondered how different it all could have been if his lover had not been with him that fateful summers morning. Terry shook his head, poured water over his face, and walked down to the kitchen where he started to prepare his morning protein shake.

24

There was a knock on the door, 'I'm home, mummy's home'. Jack and Anne-Marie ran to their mother and embraced her. While the Sullivans had packed them full of sweets, it was still no replacement for mummy. Andy had arrived in the door only five minutes earlier, still in fantastic form after his ultra productive morning. He had never seen his family look so happy. The night in hospital seemed to have done wonders for Victoria. She stood in the corridor with a beaming smile across her face. His two children were ecstatic to see their mother, although their hyper happiness was no doubt helped by the sugar rush. Andy himself could feel mussels being used on his face that had been redundant for some time, caused by a long lost smile. Andy blinked and took a mental picture to ensure he kept this memory. Why can't it always be like this? he said to himself.

'It's great to see you Vic, I got you a few roses to welcome you home' Andy said as he produced the bouquet from behind his back.

'We all missed you.'

'I missed you guys too' Victoria said.

She placed Andy's cheek in the palm of her right hand and gave him a gentle kiss on the lips. Andy felt his heart flutter just a little.

"You look great, tired after the ordeal for sure, but there is a beautiful glow from you. They must have been spoiling you in hospital?' Andy joked.

'They were great, couldn't have asked for better, but I'm afraid the attack really did take it out of me, I'm still feeling exhausted. I'm going to pop into bed for a few hours. I'll see you later on. Thanks again for the flowers honey.'

'You're welcome, sleep all you need, I'll take the kids down to the community day in the park and we'll see you for dinner. I feel like cooking for a change.'

'Excellent' Victoria said 'looking forward to it'.

Victoria slipped under the covers. It had been a long twenty-four hours that included a panic attack and a night of passion under the stars. John had only afforded her two hours sleep last night so she was physically and mentally shattered. She spent the brief few moments before she fell asleep thinking about Andy. Whatever John had got him into was certainly working a treat. Her new lover had somehow managed to get her husband to buy her a dozen red roses. It was all very complicated but it was fabulous nonetheless. Everything seemed to be working out for Victoria. How it all would change.

Andy spent two hours preparing dinner that night. It was rare he cooked, but when he did he liked to get it right. Tonight was no exception, in fact tonight he wanted to make it perfect, the perfect meal for Victoria to awake to. Andy called his wife when it was ready and she said she would be down in a couple of minutes. He waited fifteen. Again he went up to Victoria, this time she told him that the attack had taken it out of her more than she had first thought, unfortunately she would have to stay in bed for the rest of the night. He told her it was okay, but deep down he was gutted. Three Pickering's sat down to dinner that evening, the other lay in bed too tired to even feel guilty.

25

For a change, Andy was not woke by the most annoying sound in the world. It was a pleasant change and a pleasant surprise, especially considering he had not purchased a new alarm clock. It was pitch dark as he rolled out of bed. The excitement of the day ahead had awoken him naturally. He couldn't recall if his body clock had ever woken him on a Monday morning before, he was pretty sure it hadn't. There was no need for him to miss out on the shower this morning; he had plenty of time for his routine. Andy kissed Victoria on the forehead and left for the tube station. He could see a familiar face waiting on the platform as he came down the station steps.

'Good to see you soldier' he joked.

'Good to see you too Peter, I really didn't even know the underground ran at quarter to six in the morning.'

'There is a whole other world that operates at this hour of the morning from nurses and doctors to bin men, and you'll get used to seeing them from now on. So how was your weekend, get everything sorted at work?'

The tube arrived as Andy proudly explained his productive Saturday.

Andy waited in the office. It was now bright and the sun made its way in, despite the closed set of blinds that hung over the only window in the room. It was the most ordered office Andy ever saw in his life. David Sharpe, a colleague from work had a tidy office, but it paled in comparison to this one. Large maps and aerial photographs were tacked to the back wall, each laid out with an inch, no more, no less, between them. The bookshelf, which stood against the side wall without the window, was unexceptional in itself until he took a closer look. It was then he noticed that every book was placed perfectly in alphabetical order. The desk was not cleared but all that was on it was in neat bundles, the edge of each bundle either parallel or perpendicular to the edge of the desk. The only thing at a slight tilt was the name plate that lay at the front of the desk. The name on the plate was Marshal Anthony Pearson, Peter directed him to his office as soon as Andy had entered the facility. Andy stood waiting patiently, then heard a beeping noise and turned around to see the digital clock on Marshal Pearson's wall had just turned to 6.30am. Instantaneously the door to the office opened. The Marshal was a meticulous man and his time keeping was no different. He was a tall, thin man, dressed in a navy coloured suit. Andy saw no medals attached to his jacket, neither did he see any stripes on his shoulders, but five minutes into his first day, he was not going to question why.

Firestorm's leader reached out his hand, Andy grasped it and the two shared a firm handshake. There was something funny about the handshake, but before he could think what, the Marshal began to speak.

'Welcome to our family Andy. I have heard much about you, and we expect much from you too. I don't have long but let me first introduce myself; I am the head of Firestorm, Marshal Anthony Pearson. If you do not see much of me it means that you are doing very well, but if you do need to talk to me, please feel free to arrange an appointment with my secretary. First let me explain the basics, then our team will take you on and toughen you up. The basics are that this is a secret organisation, and must remain so. If you ever put that in jeopardy, you will experience the consequences, unfortunately due to the critical nature of remaining undercover, we will act first and ask questions later. Do you understand Private?'

'Yes Sir' he replied. He didn't understand much but he certainly understood this. It had been drilled into him Friday and he wasn't about to forget any time soon.

'The basics are the one, two and three. One; we never say the name Firestorm unless absolutely necessary. There is a code that changes each week. This will be texted to you each Monday morning. You will need this code to get through security. This week the code is BigFish.

This week our unit is Unit BigFish, do you understand Private.'

'Yes Sir' Andy quickly responded, he didn't know the Marshal long but he definitely got the feeling he was a man not to be messed with.

'What is the name of our unit?'

'Unit BigFish Sir'

'Good, now number two; we do not greet each other by salute as traditional in the army as we're a secret organisation. When in disguise or meeting people from our other branches it may be hard to recognise each other, that is why we have a number of options. If you are giving a handshake then bend your thumb and place its tip on the top of your acquaintances index finger knuckle. It is subtle enough for the average person to not recognise that anything different occurred, but Unit BigFish members will have revealed themselves to each other.'

It clicked with Andy, there was definitely something strange about the handshake that he just shared with the Marshal, but like any member of the public, he didn't realise its significance. The Marshal continued,

'This is an old Masonic handshake, used in past times by the secret organisation. They called it 'Boaz', we simply call it *The Greet*. This is the main way of revealing yourself to fellow members, we have others, these will be taught to you in due course. Please remember that people are only referred to by their rank inside these walls, and when in uniform on missions. At all other times, never refer to people by their rank, even me. Three;

Tactical Tuesdays. This is the most important day of the week and cannot be missed. Tactics and missions are discussed with all on Tuesdays. It is the only day of the week that we require everybody to be in attendance, and seeing as it is the only day, we expect to see you there, without fail, am I understood?'

'Yes Sir' Andy said sharply, he was starting to feel like he was in the army now. He was glad the Marshal only had three rules, he was beginning to feel uncomfortable in his presence and just wanted to leave the office at this stage. Again the Marshal briskly continued his instruction.

'We do understand that all in the unit must continue their outside lives as normal, and this is extremely important too. We monitor your progress inside these walls but we expect you to monitor your own progress in work and life. Any slackening off in performance in these areas only draws attention to you which draws attention to us. The best piece of advice I can offer to you is that we always make work for ourselves, stop making the work and you don't need to do it any longer.'

This was the second time Andy heard this phrase, Peter had obviously picked it up from his induction talk with the Marshal. How true it had proven to be.

'I assume you understand the basics of the one, two, three Private' Marshal Pearson said as he stretched out his hand.

'Loud and clear Sir' Andy replied as he shook the man's hand.

It was a firm handshake, then it seemed as if the Marshal was squeezing Andy's hand. After a moment it clicked with him and he quickly put his thumb onto the Marshal's knuckle. Instantly the squeezing released and he knew that he had made his first mistake as a member of Unit BigFish. Wake up he told himself. Maybe he could forgive himself, as he left Marshal Pearson's office he noticed the clock on the wall said 6.37am. Andy would normally be sound asleep at this time. Peter was waiting for Andy outside the door. Andy was a bit pale after his first meeting with the Marshal and Peter could see it.

'Come on mate, you've got a long day ahead, if you're pale after Marshal Huggy Bear Pearson I think I might get to practice my CPR after what you're going to see today!'

They walked down to the bottom of the corridor where Andy was due for his next appointment. It was going to be a long day.

26

The sweat was evident for all to see. Although she had taken off her check jumper and had unbuttoned as much of her light white blouse as decently possible, she still couldn't hide the perspiration covering her face and chest. She sat in discomfort behind the main information desk. Everybody else in the room felt it too, and hence the room was nearly empty. Normally the library was full on a Monday morning, the advent of computer access swelling the number greatly. One hundred computers were installed last year. It was envisaged they would increase peoples search capabilities for books, and aid research. They proved an instant hit with queues developing to use the machines. One of Jennifer's jobs was to ensure that people only used the machines for educational purposes. It was an impossible job and she had given up on it a long time ago. Trying to get teenagers to stay off *Facebook* or *Gmail* and stick to the library database or *Amazon.com* was like trying to tell a mouse not to take the cheese from the mousetrap, it was just too tempting. Every computer desk still had a large sign explaining the rules of use but everybody, including Jennifer, knew the reality, it was free internet access, simple as that. For a change there was no queue for the machines, neither was there a queue for information, there was probably only ten people in the enormous room.

Now her bottom began to stick to the chair. It was unbearable. Jennifer marched up to the library director's office, knocked on the door and walked straight in. She was not in a mood for messing about.

'I know, I know. We're trying to sort it out as quickly as we can. It's hell for all of us' the director said.

But she had had enough,

'I'm out of here. There are only ten people out there, they are crazy for being here anyway. I'll tell them we are closing the library for the day. Trust me they will understand.'

'Very well, they're due here any moment, I guarantee you that the air con will be sorted tomorrow.'

'See you tomorrow' she said and like a shepherd started to gather the flock that was spread out all over the library. One by one they made their way out. Jennifer couldn't understand what they were doing there anyway. At least she was being paid to put up with the 30 degree heat and crazy humidity. Soon the place was cleared and she locked the doors to the main hall, that was her area and it was now closed for business. She handed the keys to the security man stationed at the front door and rushed outside. It wasn't exactly the cold shower she was looking for, but although very warm, she certainly appreciated the fresh breeze that was starting to cool her down.

With nothing else pressing, Jennifer thought it an excellent idea to visit her best friend. Maybe a nice afternoon coffee might reveal if Victoria was hiding something from her, or if she was just being paranoid.

She arrived at the Pickering's door and knocked on the big brass handle with her right hand, her left hand was holding some recently acquired shopping bags. On her way to the tube she couldn't stand the sticky sensation that she felt from top to toe. She kept pinching her clothes and pulling them away from her body, but they kept pulling back toward her skin as if she was being vacuum packed by her blouse and skirt. Jennifer decided to make a few purchases. Now she stood at the door as much hoping to see Victoria's shower as Victoria herself. Then the door opened, the person behind the door was definitely not who she expected to see.

'Hello and who might you be?' asked the man at the door.

'I could ask you the same question' said Jennifer

'I assume you're looking for Victoria, I'm afraid she's gone out for the afternoon.'

She was now a little confused, all she wanted was a nice shower and to meet her best friend. Instead she was now about to be turned away by an elderly man. She queried the man

'I'm sorry, but who are you again?'

'I'm Martin Sullivan; I am the next door neighbour. That's my house over there.'

She turned around and looked in the direction that Mr Sullivan was pointing.

'Victoria asked me to look after Anne-Marie for a while as she needed to go to town to run an errand.'

Jennifer explained that she was Victoria's best friend and she had come to see her. She then explained her day to the man and was hoping there was a possibility that she could have a shower. Right now, in her sweaty state, she was still more concerned about the shower than Victoria. Mr Sullivan apologised, he couldn't let someone into the house he didn't know. He said he would leave a message that she had called by, but that's all he could do. Just as the door was about to close Jennifer heard her name being called out. It was by a much different voice than Mr Sullivan's, it was female, and it was young, very young. She turned around to see Anne-Marie at the door with her arms wide open for a hug. Jennifer picked her up and twirled around with the girl in her arms. Anne-Marie just loved getting spun around, it made her feel dizzy, but strangely happy. The next voice she heard was Mr Sullivan's

'Come in Jennifer and enjoy your shower, if little Anne-Marie knows you that well then you're definitely a friend of the family.'

It was the most enjoyable shower she had had in years. Refreshed, revitalised and wearing her new outfit, she came down to the kitchen to thank Mr Sullivan. On the table lay a spread of sweet cake, biscuits, homemade apple tart and of a pot of tea.

'You'll join me for a cup and a chat?' said the old man.

It would prove to be an enlightening conversation. Jennifer found out that it was only once in a blue moon that Mr. or Mrs. Sullivan were asked to mind the Pickering's kids. Lately though the trend had changed. Now at least two days a week Victoria would ask could they take care of Anne-Marie. Mr Sullivan said it was no trouble but he just thought it all a little strange. He asked Jennifer if she knew what errands Victoria had to run in the city. She didn't have a clue, but she was certainly determined that she would find out. Jennifer was happy with her trip to the Pickering's home that day. She had gone there for a shower and to find out some information about Victoria, and although she never got to meet her, she'd done what she had set out to do. Mr Sullivan had confirmed her suspicions, now she would find out the truth.

27

Plans lay strewn all over the table. They looked like plans to a prison; the building was such a maze. The General had been studying the plans for some time now. It was going to be a difficult job, but the rewards would be great. He was lucky to have a guy like Terry. Although The General ruled with an iron fist, Terry was a man he would listen to. Terry made his wealthy life possible. The General was due a phone call from him this morning. He hoped Terry was up to the task he had given him.

The General had three jobs. It confused even him at times, but he felt he had to satisfy his greedy nature. His primary job was as a horse dealer. He had an eye for talent. He was a professional jockey in his youth. He rode all over England and made many contacts through his trade. He was never the best jockey on the circuit, but he was still a jockey in demand. If ever a race needed to be fixed, then a trainer wanted him in the race. An unlucky fall here, accidentally taking down another horse there or whipping a horse but actually hold her, he had every trick in the book, and more. If there were to be a book written on throwing races from the saddle, The General would be its author. It helped that one bent trainer in particular liked what he could do. The trainer also had a big yard, this gave him full time work and less people were likely to find out about his underhanded trade. He was so good he was never caught. The only reason he had to pack it in was that he started to struggle to keep off the pounds. He was spending most of his day in steam rooms and this was not the life for him. Now days, he never went to steam rooms and it showed. The horse dealing was a success, but it couldn't generate anywhere near the money that his unscrupulous horse riding could.

Then a new opportunity came his way, job no. 2, Unit Firestorm. He would have to tidy up his plans in a moment, he was currently at this second job and was expecting company in about ten minutes. However, for now he was concentrating on job no. 3.

It was definitely his most fruitful work. The plans had been over marked with a series of lines, all started from the same point and ended at the same point but the route chosen to get there was different. The General was now trying to measure all these lines with a ruler and calculator. From the corner of his eye he could see the phone on his desk. He was trying to concentrate on the plans that lay before him but now he found himself starring at the phone. Then it rang. Terry was always on time. The two discussed the operation for a few minutes. The General got the answer he wanted to hear.

'I'll do it, I'll be outside sector 4 at 9.50pm, make sure what we have agreed is there. Any changes in circumstances, if I see anything is not right then the deal is off, okay General.'

'Perfect, I will get everything in order. Thank you and goodbye'

The General hung up the phone, a wry smile took over his face. Tomorrow night would be the pinnacle of his corrupt life.

His short moment of happiness was broken by a bang on the door

'Your eleven o'clock is here sir. Shall I send him in?'

He folded his maps as calmly as he could and told him to let in his appointment.

The door opened and in walked a man. Although they had never met before, each man would end up altering the other man's life more than they could ever have realised. Eventually each would want the other man dead.

28

Andy sat on an uncomfortable seat in the corridor. Peter told him to wait here while he checked if the next ordeal he was to go through was ready for him. Peter had warned him that this would be the worst five minutes he'd experience, worse than any physical training, even worse than the white room itself.

Andy's morning had been pretty productive. First he got his picture taken for his security badge. It was no average badge though. Andy was still in pain from the needle but he tried not to show it. This was no place for wimps, and Andy was not going to show himself up on his first day. All Andy's information was now on the Unit BigFish database. It contained his picture, height, weight, age, medical history, career, even his fingerprints. Every morning he would go to the interlock room. This was the only way in and out of the facility. The interlock room was a solid steel box with a door at either end. Mounted on the wall was a keyboard, computer screen, bar code scanner and surveillance camera. Whoever wanted to enter the facility had to type in that week's unit name, the scanner was then activated. This is the part Andy was still in pain from. Andy had never got a tattoo before, he had often debated about getting one when he was young, but he had chosen the sensible route as he often did. It was about the size of a baby toe nail, but under the microscope it was a perfect bar code. It was possible to make it so minute because a machine did the work as opposed to the flawed hand of a human. The mark was just below Andy's wrist on the inside of his right arm. Andy would place his wrist up to the scanner, the security man's screen then showed Andy's database. Once the database was up, the security man had fifteen seconds to decide if the man he was viewing on the interlock surveillance camera was the same as that shown on the screen. If satisfied he pressed the flashing acceptance button and Andy would be in. The acceptance button only worked during this fifteen second window. It would be tomorrow morning before Andy could get to experience Unit BigFish security at its best, the tattoo was still too inflamed for the scanner to read it perfectly.

Next it was breakfast time. This was Andy's first look at the canteen and his first introduction to his new team mates. The canteen was as bland as the never ending corridors of the facility. Choices for breakfast were limited. The canteen only contained a water boiler, a toaster and a dishwasher. Tea and toast it would be. There were about thirty people in the canteen, some were dressed in camouflage gear, some in lab jackets and some in civilian clothing. As Andy was surveying his new surroundings Peter caught the door to the room and banged it shut. Everyone turned around.

'Morning folks, this is Private Andy Pickering, he is our latest recruit so please try and be nice to him.'

One or two of the people greeted Andy with a quick 'Welcome' or 'Morning' but most just turned back to their food and conversation without batting an eyelid.

'Don't worry' Peter said to Andy 'Trust me, these are about to be your new best friends.'

Andy sat down with Peter and spread some marmalade on his toast. While he covered his toast with his coarse cut fruit preserve, he could hear people talking about stock markets, about insurance and about meetings. The whole canteen seemed to be using the few minutes break they had to carry out any outside world work that needed to be done. Andy too pulled out his phone. Mr Brownlow actually sounded concerned for him when he informed him that he would not be able to come in due to the sickness again today. Again, he heard 'Take as much time as you need'. This shit's just too easy he thought to himself. He could now see how he was going to trick Brownlow into being able to work from home. Confidence was up and Andy was starting to talk the talk.

It was now three hours later and he was not so sure that he could talk the talk any longer. After breakfast he had gone for a quick health and safety induction for the facility, then he got his camouflage gear. Now he sat waiting. His boots were shiny, his clothing wrinkled and bright and the peak on his hat was straight even though he was trying frantically to make it curve a little. Andy definitely looked the new guy, and he was about to be thrown into the lion's den.

Peter came around the corner,

'He's ready for you.'

It was now 11.00am as Andy walked in the door to the Bulldog's office. Peter had told him that everyone around here called the Marshal Huggy Bear. The man Andy was now introducing himself to was often called the Bulldog, but in his office, he would strictly be called General.

'Welcome Mr Pickering' The General said. He was still putting away all the plans he had just folded into his desk drawer.

'Take a seat.'

'Yes Sir' he replied as he made his way sharply into the seat in front of The General's desk. The office was very different to the Marshal's, in fact they were poles apart. Maps and aerial photographs were also on The General's walls but they were simply stapled on, some over lapping, some at slight angles and many defaced with writing and lines in marker. The General had no library of books, but his desk was strewn with them all over the place. Everybody that ever entered the office must have wanted to suggest that The General get a bookcase. Andy doubted if anybody had the balls to say it. As soon as Andy sat down The General got up and began to walk around slowly behind his desk.

'Why are you hear Private?'

The question slightly threw Andy but he did the best he could.

'I am here to serve Britain as best I can and improve my life in the process.'

'Very good Private, did you get that from one of the flyers we hand out on the street? Let me rephrase , do you know why you are here?'

'Please tell me Sir' Andy wasn't going to get caught playing word games with The General, he just wanted to get in and get out and have the experience over with.

'You are here because I asked for you to be here at 11.00am. If I ask to see you in my office tomorrow at 11.00am you will also be here. If I ask you to clean my toilet, you will clean it, if I ask you to clean my boots you will clean them and you will be able to see your reflection in them. Is that clear Private?'

'Absolutely Sir.'

The General quickly moved up to the desk, he leaned forward and placed his two hands on it.

'Pickering. Never call me Sir, do you hear me? You will address me as General at all times, do you hear me Pickering?' Andy was starting to feel spittle on his face from The General's rant, he was also starting to feel very uncomfortable.

'Yes General, absolutely General' he replied.

'As you may have noticed I do not have a family name on the name plate on my desk. People used to always call me The General anyway so I decided that is all people would call me. Make sure that is what you call me Private.'

'Yes General' Andy had a feeling he would be saying this phrase a lot over the next few minutes.

'Take a good look around Private, this is my office. I doubt you will ever be in it again. Nobody enters my office without my permission, absolutely nobody. I don't care if there is a fire and the only way out is through my office, you do not go through my office. Trust me a few hot flames is a lot easier way to go than what I can have done to you. Do you understand Private?'

'Yes General, most definitely.'

'I assume the Marshal has told you about Tactical Tuesdays, this is the day you will see me each week. I am in charge of tactics for all missions, that is my role. You will never question a tactical decision of mine; you are here to perform the function of a soldier. Leave the strategies up to me. Understood Private?'

'Yes General.'

'Good, then I will see you tomorrow.'

It was like a seesaw, as soon as Andy went to stand up, The General sat back down on his chair.

Peter was waiting for Andy outside the door. As soon as he saw Andy he broke down laughing. He was pale as a ghost, for the first time that morning Andy had not thought about the pain from his new tattoo.

'Come on mate, toughen up or you won't even survive day one' Peter told Andy.

They walked together to the next room on the itinerary. The talking was over and the action was about to begin, but Andy still didn't look well after his last encounter. Then without warning, Peter punched him in the stomach.

'Snap out of it, if you go in there like this you'll get killed' Peter said as Andy tried to catch his breath.

At this instant he wasn't overjoyed by Peter's actions but as he recovered his breath he recovered his colour too. It would not be long before he would lose them again.

29

Andy rolled out of bed. Again he had defeated the dreaded alarm clock and again it was dark outside. Yesterday morning he had a spring in his step, this morning he had a limp in his step. Yesterday afternoon contained martial arts exercises, obstacle course training, a five mile run and some good old fashioned hand to hand combat. It was when Andy was in the shower that he noticed all the bruises that had come up on his body from the previous day. Luckily there were none on his face, Andy wouldn't have to start explaining his severe bruising just yet. Andy was excited about the day to come. A lot was going to happen. He was due to handle and fire weaponry for the first time, be at a Tactical Tuesday meeting and at the end of the day receive his BigFish training programme. All the exercises he would perform would be analyzed and timed. A specific diet and exercise programme would be required for six months to reach a target level of strength and fitness. It would be at this point only that he could graduate to become a Corporal and be allowed go on his first official mission. He kissed Victoria on the forehead and headed to his new 'work' place.

Andy stood and waited. He was unsure if it was going to work already. Andy looked into the surveillance camera, then the door opened, he was in.

That's so fucking cool he said to himself as he looked closely at the mark on his wrist, almost in disbelief.

The sun was now just peering its head over the horizon. It was a wonderful time of the day that Andy had overlooked for so long. The air seemed fresher and cleaner than he was used to. After a week of a heat wave he thought that this was the time of the day that everyone should be working. Andy was heading to one room and one room only this morning, he had been looking forward to it all the way in on the tube.

Weapons Room. He tried to open the door but it seemed to be jammed. There was no lock on the door so Andy put his shoulder against the cold steel door and gave it a shove. Again there was no movement, then he noticed a scanner embedded in the wall to the side of the door. Andy remembered the swipe card he had been issued with yesterday for the internal doors. Andy flicked the card towards the reader and the lock disengaged.

Ahead of him was a sea of killing machines. There were handguns, snipers, machine guns, grenades, RPG's, even some two foot long missiles. There were even things that looked dangerous but he had no idea what they were. Andy was a bit disturbed by what he was feeling. He was almost turned on by what he saw. He just wanted to touch one, to feel its smooth curves, then to pull the trigger and experience its power.

'I see you're drooling Private.'

Peter was at the door behind Andy and could see the shell shocked look in his face. Andy quickly snapped out of it and knocked the glazed look from his eyes.

'Don't worry about it Private, everybody reacts the same way at first. Soon enough you will grow to understand what all this plastic and metal can do, you will never love these machines, but you will respect them more and more every day.'

Peter walked down to the racks holding the hand pistols. He picked one up. With hands faster than a magician he disassembled it into its six constituent parts. Then as if showing it to the audience, which was Andy, he flicked his wrists and abracadabra. It was once more whole. Peter's stance had now changed and he was holding the gun as if he was about to shoot some invisible man.

'You need to be able to do this as quick as me, and you need to be able to do it out in the field with gunfire around you when your semi-automatic has jammed, which it often can.'

Peter grabbed a book which was on one of the racks. Then he threw it over to Andy.

'Here, this is your homework for the next week. You'll know the make, model and number of each weapon in this room. You will even know the year each was made. You will learn how to assemble and disassemble each and every one. Most importantly you will know the advantages and disadvantages of each. For each mission you must select the right weaponry. Weaponry selection on a mission is your responsibility, you better make the right choice.'

The organisation didn't mess around and Andy was starting to question if he was able for the training. He looked at the thick volume book in his arms, he felt like he was back in university, but without all the drink.

'Okay, let's use up some ammo, you're going shooting.'

The words hit Andy like a defibrillator on his chest, his heart was now pumping and he could feel it, he could even hear it.

Andy never liked guns and never really had an interest in them. He couldn't understand how you could own your own riffle in the United States at eighteen, but couldn't drink there till you were twenty-one. Andy liked a drink, so for anybody to have to wait until twenty-one to feel the soft sensuous taste of malt barley and hops against their lips seemed an absurdity. Andy was always glad that Britain had logical gun licensing laws.

If the criminal finds it harder to get a gun then I don't need one was how he always thought. However, as Andy felt the smooth curves of the Magnum Desert Eagle in his hands, he was surprised by how he was drawn to the weapon. It just felt 'right' in his hands. Andy was now standing in the indoor firing range arena. Ahead of him was a jet black man he had to shoot. It was a cardboard cut-out and he would receive the results of

Andy's first pull of the trigger. He turned to his side to see Peter's lips moving, but he couldn't hear anything. Andy took off his ear-muffs.

'You've seen me do it, repeat the stance and fire, your magazine holds eight rounds. Use all eight, leaving one second between each shot. Best of luck.'

Andy took Peter's advice on board as he put back on his ear muffs. The magazine slipped into the gun with ease. Andy stood and pointed the gun using both hands. Andy's finger hit the trigger.

Eight seconds later the magazine was empty, in contrast Andy was full, full of endorphins. Peter hit the button in front of Andy and the black cardboard man made his way up to meet his assassin. All eight shots hit the target, only one was in the zone Peter told Andy to aim for, but this was a good start.

'We've a natural. Catch' Peter threw Andy another mag.

'You'll be sick of this in a half an hour, trust me.'

Thirty minutes passed by and Andy was still asking Peter for more ammunition. His hands hurt like hell, his elbows ached but he wanted to get the perfect eight.

'That's it for today Private, no one dares to be late for the tactical training meeting.'

They walked down the never ending corridors once more. He had seen much of the facility, fought hand to hand combat, been through the mill in the white room and even fired fifteen live rounds of ammo. He was starting to believe he was one of the unit, that he was a soldier.

'Tactical Tuesday Meeting' was big, very big. The conference room was state of the art. The seating was sloped like a stand at a football match. Each seat had a desk in front of it, each desk had an in built computer screen. The screen was a touch screen as Andy found out when he accidentally leaned on it. It seemed to Andy as if there were around thirty people in the room.

'This is everybody' Peter, who was sat next to Andy, whispered to him. 'Basically, you're on your death bed, or you are at this meeting.'

It was the Marshal that opened the meeting.

'Good Morning unit, first of all has everyone signed in.'

Attendance was noted at the meeting. Peter had only missed one meeting every year for his summer vacation since he joined.

Again, Andy noticed a little scanner embedded into the side of his desk. He flicked his wrist over it, immediately the screen in front of him said Welcome Private Pickering, You are signed in at 10.01am. Andy hoped the fact he was signed in a minute late would not bring the wrath of The General on him, but The General had a lot more on his mind than Andy's time keeping.

The first hour of the meeting reviewed last week's operations. The only one that Andy was aware of was the Baker Street station killing, but it turned out there were another two operations that week also. One was in Paisley near Glasgow, the other was also in London. Andy listened attentively as they discussed how the operations were carried out, if they were carried out correctly, the level of public suspicion, and improvements that could be made for future operations. The floor was open and almost everybody contributed. Tactical positioning could be communicated to all by hitting the 'Projector' button on the screen on each desk. This enabled one to draw on plans on one's own screen and show it to everybody on the main projector. I doubt I'll ever have the balls to hit the 'Projector' button Andy thought, but he would end up surprising himself. Once last week's missions were complete, the Marshal sat down and The General got up, it was just like the seesaw effect Andy had seen before in his office. The General started into the coming missions, concentrating in particular on the missions due to take place next week.

Forty minutes into the meeting The General's phone rang, he looked at the caller ID and told his audience he would be a moment. The General moved into the corridor.

'I received your message, I don't like, I don't like the change of plan' said the man on the other end of the line.

'It's fine, I guarantee it' The General promised.

'I have too much to risk by meeting you myself. If they find out the cocaine is gone all the evidence would point to me.'

'But this guy isn't stupid, he will suspect something, he will get us all caught' said an unassured Terry.

'No he most certainly won't, he's brand new to the facility. He barely knows how things are run around here, and I'm pretty sure he is very much afraid of upsetting me. He will be a piece of cake trust me.'

'£50,000 or its all off.' Terry felt he deserved a little extra reward for the all the extra risks involved.

'Fine, no more questions, just get the job done.' The General felt it was worth a few extra pounds to ensure there was no connection to him if Terry was caught.

The General put his phone back in his pocket and re-entered the auditorium. As Andy enjoyed his brief reprieve from the intensity of all the new information being thrown at him, little did he know that later that evening The General was about to put his reputation, and his life in jeopardy.

30

Jennifer was on the tube to West Hampstead, she was on a mission. Earlier that morning the library director rang her to say that the air-conditioning wasn't fixed yet. In light of the mess that was the previous day he had decided not to open the library today. He told Jennifer to enjoy the day and that she would definitely be at work the following morning. Since the revelations the previous day at the Pickering's house, Jennifer was determined she was going to find out what her friend was up to. The day off could not have come at a better time, she was grabbing the bull by the horns; she was going to get answers. Jennifer was wearing her long chestnut brown hair in a bun, over that she wore a New York Yankees baseball cap. Jennifer also wore oversized sunglasses. The days of asking questions were over, today Victoria was going to be followed and Jennifer was determined not to get caught.

Jennifer purchased a newspaper at the station and walked to the Pickering's house. Across the road from their red brick house was the entrance to the local park. She entered the park and waited. It could be a long day. Mr Sullivan had said Anne-Marie was dropped off at their place only a couple of days a week. Jennifer was banking on today being one of those days. She opened the newspaper and began to read.

It was over two hours since she first sat down on the park bench. She read articles in the newspaper she wouldn't dream of reading before. She even had a flick through the sports pages, a definite first for her. Jennifer actually got caught up in one article in particular. It was about new techniques in preserving old books. The technique was originally developed to preserve fruit but it didn't pass clinical trials. The process was then tweaked and applied to books where it was proving a big success. Ink did not fade under light after the pages were treated with the radiation treatment. It was interesting reading, it was too interesting. When Jennifer lifted her head above the paper she saw Victoria leaving the Sullivan's house. She had a bag in her hand and a bounce in her step and was now headed in the direction of the tube station. Jennifer folded the paper and placed it under her arm, she was now in pursuit.

Both of them sat in the one carriage, six seats separated them. The tube was comfortable for a change, it was a new carriage and rush hour was well and truly over. Jennifer looked across at Victoria, she began to feel that they were not just physically separated right now, they were beginning to get separated emotionally as well. She was about to find out what was jeopardising years of friendship.

Out of the tube, up the stairs, through a couple of streets and into a cafe. Victoria could really move when she wanted to and Jennifer was at full tilt to keep up with her. She clung on to Victoria's imaginary coat tails until she stopped outside the cafe. Jennifer was glad that Victoria was at her destination, she might have lost her if the pursuit continued much longer. Slowly Jennifer walked up to the small coffee shop. Still wearing her baseball cap and sunglasses Jennifer put her head up against the front window. She didn't want to be so obvious but the reflection of the midday sun meant that she could only see herself until her nose just about hit the glazing. What she saw confused her. The cafe was reasonably small, having no more than ten or fifteen tables. It was busy though and there was a good atmosphere inside. What confused Jennifer is that she surveyed the thirty or so people dining inside and Victoria was not one of them. She was disappointed. Whatever Victoria was up to she would not be able to find out. She assumed Victoria must have gone into the kitchen. Maybe she was learning to be a chef. Whether it was the hot food or indeed the hot chef that attracted Victoria, she could not go back there to see without getting caught. She decided to stay across the road and wait for Victoria to come out. It could be another long wait. There were no benches on the street so she decided to sit on the pavement. She prayed that nobody she knew, not just Victoria, would recognise her. All she needed was a cup and a poorly cut cardboard begging sign and she would fit right in.

The cafe door opened for the first time since she had sat down. It had been a long five minutes for Jennifer and her dignity. Again she was surprised by what she saw exiting the cafe. It was a new and improved Victoria. Jennifer now understood why she had not seen Victoria through the window. Victoria had gone to the toilet to powder her nose. She left the cafe in a pair of high heels, a stunning summer dress and her hair was freshly brushed. Victoria's trainers, jeans and top were now in the bag she carried with her. Jennifer's short stint at being homeless was over, she was now twenty yards behind Victoria and closing fast. Victoria's pace had slowed considerably since she put on the stilettos. Jennifer thought Victoria must have been close to her destination, and she was right. Victoria turned the corner and greeted a tall man wearing a top hat. He was dressed in black trousers and a maroon coloured jacket. They were in Piccadilly and he was the usher at the main entrance to the Ritz Hotel. Once again, Jennifer viewed proceedings inside through the impressive atrium glazing. Luckily a shadow was cast over this side of the building and she didn't have any of her earlier troubles with unwanted reflections. As she stood from a far on the pavement, Jennifer could see her friend talk to the receptionist, receive a key, walk across the marble floor and enter the lift. As soon as the escalator doors closed Jennifer removed her hat, let down her hair and put her shades resting on top of her head. If she was to enter the Ritz of all places she would be doing it without wearing a Yankees cap.

'Good Afternoon Madame, how may I help you?'

It was a mature man who offered his assistance to Jennifer. He was in uniform and stood behind the hugely impressive reception desk. He looked as if he was born to stand behind the desk at the Ritz. Jennifer never met the man before, but she could tell he took much pride in his job, much pride in himself, even much pride in the reception desk he controlled. And he did, the handsome crescent of mahogany was restored a number of years back and it was his responsibility to ensure the desk remained in pristine condition to continue the service of his predecessors and keep the name and standard of the Ritz alive.

'Sorry Madame, can I assist you in any way?'

'Yes, the lady that was just talking with you a moment ago, her name is Victoria Pickering, can you tell me who else is sharing her room?'

'I'm sorry Madame, I don't know of any Ms. Pickering, unfortunately I am unable to help you' said the man in a polite but stern manner.

'But she was just talking to you a moment ago' Jennifer protested.

'I'm afraid you must be mistaken Madame.'

She knew it was a lost cause, the old man was going to die with all the sordid secrets he knew over the years, and no money or no words were going to change that. She left disgruntled but not despondent. This time there was a bench on the pavement. It was time to play the waiting game again.

Jennifer was exhausted. She knew after today that she would never become a private investigator or police detective. Being on a stakeout was hard, very hard. Her eyelids were like melting snow on Alpine peaks. If they fell it could have disastrous consequences. It was only two o'clock but it had been a long day. Jennifer was starting to hallucinate now; two hours of looking at the same front door, the same purple usher, the same street litter bin only a few metres away. The bin began to dance and Jennifer's head began to bop to its movements. Somebody spitting chewing gum into the bin awoke her from her merry way. She could almost understand how somebody stuck in a prison cell looking at the same four walls every day could go insane. Jennifer had read of the phenomenon and dismissed it, but today's experience had shown in a small way what the harsh realities could be like.

The usher reached and pulled the door open. A summer dress flowed out, this time the owners hair was ragged and tossed about but the glow on her face made up for the erratic nature of her hair. A man walked out in her arm gave her a quick kiss on the cheek and hopped into a waiting taxi. In an instant he was out of sight. Jennifer rushed over to Victoria. There was about to be a confrontation Victoria certainly did not expect.

31

It was immense, it was incredible, it was almost sore on the eyes. The room was bright white, wall to wall, floor to ceiling. Andy was looking at forty million pounds, and it was all going to be destroyed tomorrow. It seemed almost a waste. Andy had never taken cocaine before but knew many friends who did, how their noses would sniffle if they were standing next to Andy right now. Tattoos, guns, cocaine, Andy was living his youth again, but he was getting paid by the government for it this time. He was standing in the contraband room. Peter had to show this to Andy, it was just too amazing to miss. There were 1.4 tonnes of cocaine in the room. The haul was the largest the unit had taken in for some time. Colombian, Regulo Velasquez had made the call to meet his accomplices last Thursday. Unit Firestorm knew of Velasquez activities and had his phone tapped many weeks ago. When they intercepted the call the foundations were laid in place for the following day. Velasquez had told the man he would meet him at Neasden station at 8.30am. Velasquez was living next to Baker Street, the unit deduced that he would take the tube, leaving around 8.10am. Peter explained all this to Andy as Andy got distracted for a moment from his white powder trance.

'So the shooting had nothing to do with me at all, it was all just a convenient coincidence?' Andy queried Peter

'You're starting to catch on Private, I was aware of the mission, and it gave me the perfect opportunity to test your mental strength and see if you were a man we wanted on our team. It's amazing how one short text can change a man's life.'

'So how did you find the coke?' questioned Andy

'We sent a man in to replace Velasquez. Sometimes we wear camouflage, sometimes not, in this instance The General got camouflage of a different kind, he got a new face. After the phone call was intercepted Thursday evening, two of our men went around to Velasquez's place. They gained entry and spiked his bottle of bourbon. He had been under surveillance for some time. Velasquez was an eccentric man, a mean man, a man that was hard to predict, but for as long as we were watching him, every single night, the man drank a half glass of bourbon. Velasquez kept to the plan and soon he fell asleep on the couch. We had spiked his drink with Alphatex. When Velasquez woke up we were still cleaning the plaster from his face. He had been taken here, he sat in the same seat as you in the white room. As you can imagine he was terrified when he woke up. His hands and legs were bound and his chest was tied to the chair. He saw the blood all over the floor and he presumed his blood would join it. I was in the room along with Corporal Cleaver and Corporal Fisher. Corporal Cleaver was the first to speak. "Whatever you thought we were going to do to you, it is going to be worse." With that Corporal Cleaver beckoned to the rest of us to leave the room and we walked out of the room with the Corporal. Ten minutes later we re-entered, Velasquez was covered in sweat. I love to see a bastard like that sweat. Then we told him exactly how the next twelve hours would play out. How there would be no thirteenth hour for him, that hour would be spent in the morgue. Velasquez now knew his own fate, he knew that he was going to walk into a trap but yet he would walk into it anyway. I've seen a lot but I've never seen a man spasm so bad that he knocked himself unconscious. Velasquez was out cold when we gave him the final injection such that he would lose the memory of the past ten hours. He woke up on his couch slightly dazed and confused.'

Today had been a roller coaster ride for Andy, and Peter's stories had him back up at the top of the lift hill, it was amazing, and Andy now felt he was lucky with the treatment he received in the white room. Peter continued.

'Velasquez must have been disappointed with himself that he slept on the couch before the most important day of his life. He made his way, still slightly groggy, to Baker's Street station. When he arrived at the platform, The General was already on the previous underground to Neasden. He was wearing a mask of Velasquez face, fabricated the previous night. The latex took four hours to set perfectly over the plaster of Paris, but it was worth the wait. Not only was The Generals face similar to that of Velasquez, but his build was the same, and his harsh demeanour, the demeanour you got the pleasure to experience, was almost identical. The General was also more focused than I had seen him before. He really wanted this mission to go perfectly, he wanted to nail these bastards. And he did.

The General met a man at the station, they exchanged brief pleasantries and got into his car. He took them to the local park which contained an old World War II underground bunker. It was not used in years and the entrance was completely covered over with gorse. It was perfect. They both walked down the steps to the bunker. The man turned on his flashlight, ahead lay a powder heaven. The General pulled a pocket gun from his sock. These guns are so small that they are absolutely useless unless you are only a few feet from your target. He stepped in to shake the man's hand, the haul was exactly as he had described. Instead of four fingers getting wrapped around his hand, four bullets were now wrapped around his heart.

We left the cocaine there under armed guard for the past four days until we had all provisions in place to move it safely here. Take a good last look Corporal because it will be destroyed in our incinerator tomorrow morning.'

These guys are good, these guys are real good Andy thought to himself, and now I am one of them. It had indeed been a roller coaster week, he may have been at the top of the lift hill now, but after the hill always comes the fall. The General was about to insure that.

The plan was in place. It was going to be gruelling but, then again, that was the whole idea. Peter said he would be behind Andy all the way, he would help him emotionally or physically any way he could. Andy looked at the print out, his program had been set out for him, every stomach crunch, every mile of running, every hit of the punch bag and every shot to be fired.

'This is going to be hell isn't it' Andy said to Peter.

'I'm afraid so, but if you don't make the mark you can't go on the missions and you don't want to be a failure now do you!'

'Thanks for that wonderful support of yours' he joked. It was the end of another long day and Andy was ready for bed. They made their way down the corridor in the direction of the exit.

'Corporal Pickering, can I see you in my office.'

Upon hearing this Andy turned around. It was The General, just who Andy didn't want to see. He was only one minute late signing in for Tactical Tuesday's meeting but he was still terribly uneasy about entering The General's office.

'You're fucked now!' said Peter to Andy in a playful manner.

'I thought you said you were going to be there for me emotionally Peter, that shit's just not helping at all.'

Andy rarely used coarse language. The only time he might let his tongue slip was when his blood pressure was really up. Andy surprised himself by how much coarse language he had used over the past few days.

'See you tomorrow' Peter shouted down the hall as Andy entered The General's office.

32

'Have a seat Private Pickering' The General said. Andy sat down, at that instant The General got up from his seat. It was like clockwork.

'Yes General' Andy said.

'I have an important job for you. It is top secret and nobody in this base is aware of it. Please understand it must remain that way. The Manchester unit is performing a mission in Bolton. One of the informants is currently in London and a Corporal Jack Ryan, a member of the Manchester unit, is tracking him down here. The Marshal of that unit just telephoned me a moment ago to ask if we could give Corporal Ryan access to our weapons as he cannot afford to go back to Manchester and risk losing the suspect. I have a family function tonight, thus I have selected you to leave Corporal Ryan into the facility. He is aware of the processes involved and the layout of the facility. Your only function is to allow him access to the weapons room. You may then leave, Ryan has our full permission to do what he wants with the weaponry, he will use our sign out sheet to declare what he took. As you know, he will have no access to any other part of the facility without a scan so he can be left to do what he wishes. I haven't informed our security as this is technically a breach, but we need to take this gun-running bastard down and Ryan is the man to do it, the Marshal assured me of that. Do you have any questions Private Pickering?'

Andy had so many questions he did not know where to start, but he was frozen by the cold stare of The General

'What time do I meet him and where?' Is all Andy could muster to ask.

'8.00pm, across from the large oak tree, 150m from the

entrance on the way down to the tube station. He will be parked half on the road and half on the grass so you will be able to recognise his car, knock once on the driver's window.'

Andy's left eyebrow was slightly raised, he didn't mean it, nor did he know it, but The General saw it straight away.

'Have you got a problem with this Private?'

'No General, that's no problem General, loud and clear.'

But Andy did have a problem with it. The meeting point described by The General was the exact same location Andy had noticed the suspicious Navy BMW parked on Friday. If Jack Ryan drives a navy BMW then something well dodgy is going on here he thought to himself, lowering the eyebrow he now had noticed was raised.

'Good. No questions, no answers, this meeting never took place and you never met Corporal Jack Ryan. Understood?'

'Yes General, one hundred percent.'

'Your first mission has come up early, don't fuck it up Private.'

'I won't, I promise.'

The General grabbed his backpack from under the desk

'Come on Private, move your ass, I gotta go.'

Andy got up from the chair and left The General's office. When he turned around he almost expected The General to have sat back down just to continue the seesaw trend, but it was not to be, The General was locking the door. Andy had to pass away the next hour on his own until his first mission.

It was a long lonely hour. The facility felt creepy when the main lights were turned off. It was a power saving exercise that could be overruled if required. Unfortunately, Andy didn't know how to get the main power back on again. The emergency lights were forming long vague shadows in the corridor. Andy had to blink a few times and focus hard. As a child Andy never liked the dark, he liked to see his surroundings, to see light. Darkness was just plain evil. If he tried to sleep in pure darkness the nightmares would follow. And they were bad nightmares, his mind could dream up ideas that horror movie directors would kill for. Andy used to describe what he saw to his parents; soon they started to think that he might be a deranged child. They even sent him for physiological tests. The shrink told Andy's parents to let his bedroom door slightly ajar to allow some light from the hall into his room as he slept. It was a miracle to Andy, he could sleep, he could wake in the morning and he could be happy. Unfortunately, all this had a result on Andy, he now had a complex. Total darkness just freaked him out. It was a secret he kept to himself but it was as real today as it was when he was a child.

Andy was now in the canteen studying the weaponry catalogue book. His field torch had finally come in handy for something.

Make damn sure you always have your torch Andy.

The last thing he wanted was to freak out in the middle of a real mission and get everybody killed in the process. He doubted if the unit would even have taken him on if they knew of his phobia. The book was proving interesting, especially the hand gun section. Revolver vs. Semi-automatic. Andy didn't even know the physical difference before he started reading. He could now choose his weapon based on reliability (likelihood of jams; how to recover from jams; how to recover from misfires), degree of user training needed, degree and frequency of gun cleaning needed, ammo capacity, weight, speed and ease of reloading and of course bulkiness with regard to concealment. It was fascinating. Today Andy had pulled the trigger on a semi-automatic, tomorrow would be a revolver. He was licking his lips at the thought. There was something attractive about the old fashioned revolver. Andy wasn't sure, was it the way the bullets were loaded by flipping out the barrel or the many films portraying the game Russian Roulette, but he knew the next time he squared up to the black cardboard man, he would tell him 'Make my day punk' before pulling the trigger. The book had certainly helped take Andy's mind of the eeriness of his surroundings. It took the alarm he set on his phone to pull him out of chapter five. 7.55pm it was time to meet Corporal Jack Ryan.

It was a banger in every sense of the word. Terry had handed over the money. £5,000. It certainly still had a good engine and that was all that concerned Terry. The sales man had never had a test drive like it, he didn't even know that speedometers could reach the end of the dial, but Terry showed that anything was possible. The salesman was left out of breath, but happy with the ball of cash that was in his hand. Terry also left happy, he was content that if anything were to go askew on this task, dumping a seven year old Alfa Romeo *147 T.Spark* was a lot easier than dumping his pride and joy. Terry now studied the plans one last time as he sat in the car. The car itself was parked in one of the two locations where CCTV cameras did not cover the facilities exterior. That was the reason he had to park half on the road, half on the grass. The General had done his research and Terry had studied it hard. Everything was in place, as each minute ticked by Terry's heart rate increased. It was 7.59pm. If The General's confidence was not misplaced, then a man would knock on his window in less than a minute.

Andy increased his walking pace, one thing he did not want to do was upset The General by being late. He was adding two plus two together since his captivating meeting with The General. The answer he came up with was a navy BMW. Andy exited the compound. To his surprise a red car was parked exactly where he expected a navy one. It slightly threw Andy, but it also relieved him. He had seen the navy car at West India Docks on the day all this craziness began, he saw it again that evening. It seemed to Andy like the navy car had something to do with him, something he didn't understand, but something that wasn't in his best interest. He relaxed a little as he walked up to the car, he knocked on the window, just once as instructed. The electric window lowered.

Terry saw the man approach the car. There seemed to be something familiar about his outline as it was sporadically illuminated by the orange street lights. Terry lowered the window. To his shock and horror he recognised the face that was staring back at him. Terry had worked for many years, on many assignments, in many places, but never had he come across someone he knew on a job, worse again it was someone who knew him. He wished he had done more with his disguise, but he could never have seen this coming. It was too late to turn back now. Pickering could be dealt with, but Terry wasn't going to mess with The General.

The door opened. A tall, well built man now stood before Andy. He had a moustache, glasses and a large birthmark on his left cheek. He also wore a baseball cap and was chewing gum. He was an intimidating size and Andy knew that just like The General, there would be no arguments with this man.

'Pleased to meet you' Andy said to the man.

'Likewise Private' the man responded as they shook hands.

Unwittingly Andy had given Terry a little test. The General had prepared Terry well and Andy received *The Greet*.

'My name is Corporal Jack Ryan. Can we keep this moving, my target is due in Leicester Square in an hour' Terry barked.

'No problem Corporal' Andy replied as he turned on his heels and began to walk in the direction of the facility entrance. Andy had no idea, but right at this moment Terry, aka Jack Ryan, was perspiring more than Andy. It was dark out on the street, but Terry was concerned that once they hit the lights of the facility he would be recognised. After all, a moustache, glasses and fake birthmark may make you unrecognisable to the public, but to someone you know, it was a different story.

'This is the interlock, you stand behind me in the corner, the surveillance camera can't see you or it's all over.'

Andy and Terry stood inside the interlock. Andy dispensed his words of wisdom, typed in the password and got his wrist scanned. It was now down to the security man. Andy looked up at the surveillance camera. There was silence as the two men waited for their fate. Either the door would open and allow them into the facility, or they would be locked in, Andy didn't want to contemplate what would happen if they were caught, maybe the white room, maybe worse. Terry was welded to the back wall, he attempted to minimise his large frame as much as possible. Time stood still. The silence started to make Andy's ears hurt.

Click

Both men heard the obscurely beautiful sound. It had broken the silence, and it had also broken Terry in.

'Let's go Private' Terry motioned to Andy.

Terry now stood outside the door. It read Weapons Room. Andy swiped his card in front of the reader, there was another click, Terry was in.

'Goodnight Private, Thanks for your co-operation, I'll make sure to get that gun smuggling bastard tonight.'

'Goodnight Corporal, best of luck.'

Andy wanted to stay and spy on Jack Ryan. It was all just so suspicious. However, it was The General he was dealing with. This was only his second day and he would quite like to see day number three. He decided to call it a night. It had been another very long day. His head was dizzy from the information overload and a good night's sleep was rarely more needed.

Andy made his way past the red Alfa Romeo. Like The General said, just forget it. 'No questions, no answers, this meeting never took place and you never met Corporal Jack Ryan' Andy quoted The Generals words back to himself. Of all that was going through his mind these words actually made the most sense. Andy would never speak of tonight again.

Terry let off a sigh of relief. He was extremely pleased to see there was only the pale emergency lighting on in the facility. His weak disguise might just work after all, and it had. The General was correct as always 'Don't worry about him he will be a piece of cake', Andy was just that, a piece of cake. Somehow The General always got his judgment right. Terry headed to the rack with the machine guns. Even from here he could smell the white powder. The plans in his hands showed him how to get the cocaine out. He was about to make The General a very rich man.

Part 2
After

About Seven Months Later

33

'Get down, get down, three men approaching from the left' crackled the earpiece.

Andy dived behind the large stone flowerpot next to him. He peered between the leaves of the palm tree growing from the pot. The leaves were wet, so was Andy. The rain hadn't stopped all night. It had been nearly seven months since he first joined the unit. A lot had happened since that incredible day at Bakers Street Station, but he knew that this situation was the most dangerous one he had encountered yet. Andy was now a Corporal and this was his fourth mission. The previous three had been roaring successes. Although he hadn't assassinated a human being as of yet, Firestorm were very pleased with him. The Marshal even picked Andy out for special mention during one Tactical Tuesday meeting after he had spotted a television crew making a documentary. Unintentionally, Firestorms activities, which involved murdering two people, were caught on the tape. Andy 'accidentally' bumped into the camerawoman going down the street and knocked the camera to the ground, thrashing the tape and ensuring Firestorm's cloak of silence remained. Andy felt the gruelling six months of training had definitely been worth it. He was in superb physical shape, better educated, and his self-esteem was through the roof. Surprisingly his work at Directacom was going well too, Brownlow, his boss, was now encouraging other people to follow Peter and Andy's example and work from home a few days a week. Brownlow felt Andy was more tuned in when he was at work, that his eye was sharp and his mind quick. Brownlow was right. Andy was actually enjoying work. A week's work was packed into a Thursday. This day was intense, but he was dynamic and everybody listened when he barked.

Barking is one thing Andy had no intention of doing right now. He held his breath as the men passed him.

'Allez, allez' said one of the men as they made their way back out toward the main gardens.

Each had a pistol in their hand. They were sure to have received orders of shoot to kill. The stone flowerpot Andy clung behind was one of many at the foot of the stepped entrance. At the top of the entrance was a mansion, a chateau. It was a simple mission but one mistake had cost them dearly. Inside the chateau, located a few kilometres from Bordeaux, an Englishman was to be asleep in bed. This was one of his many foreign homes. Interpol had tried to catch the man for years but through a series of different identities he had eluded their grasp at every turn. Four teenagers died from his 'ecstasy' the previous week in London. He was a ruthless man. The youths may have thought they were taking ecstasy, but they were just branded pills. Under pressure to meet demand, the drug lord, Archie Carlisle, flooded the market with an entirely different substance called PMA. PMA can seem like 'weak' ecstasy at low doses; it takes about half an hour longer to come on, then produces mild euphoria, minor hallucinations and a stimulant effect. However, at higher doses it causes dramatic increases in temperature, blood pressure and heart rate, potentially leading to convulsions, coma and death. In last week's case it led to death. The youths just felt that they had got cut ecstasy because the effects took so long to come on. They popped more and more pills waiting for the kick. When the kick eventually came their hearts had no chance. The Prime Minister had no problem signing for this mission, and Andy had no problem doing it. It was his first assassination assignment. He was chosen as the one to pull the trigger. The Marshal felt he was ready, even The General felt he was ready. Most importantly Andy felt he himself was ready.

Except now everything had gone pear shaped.

'I'll take the heat outside here. Just go in and get the job done. He's not going to be asleep in bed now so be prepared.'

Andy's earpiece crackled again. The man at the other end of the line was Corporal Cleaver. Peter was right all that time ago - one day you will be willing to die for Corporal Cleaver and he will be willing to die for you. Andy hoped that it would not come to this, but it certainly was getting messy. There had been a detection laser located inside the main gates that Recon had not informed the team about. Once the team, simply being Andy and Cleaver, had got over the external wall they made their way to the front entrance dodging the many security cameras about the gardens. The laser was activated without them even knowing. Something had gone tits up and now all plans were out the window. At that instant the men did what they were trained intensively to do, they split up and ran like hell. Corporal Cleaver now found himself lying inside a fountain in the middle of the majestic gardens. He was already soaked from the torrential rain so a swim in the centrepiece didn't make much of a difference. Andy had dived for cover behind one of the many large flowerpots at the end of the garden. This was it, training had prepared him, now was his time to shine.

As he readied himself to come out from behind the cover, an image of Corporal Amy Fisher flashed before his eyes. The two had certainly grown a lot closer over the past few months. Corporal Fisher always got on well with Andy. She knew how to share a joke, drink a beer and she even had a passing interest in football. The fact that Andy thought she was almost physical perfection itself certainly helped draw him in too. It had always been a platonic relationship. Andy was married, and Corporal Fisher was gorgeous. These two large stumbling blocks ensured the relationship would never be taken any further. However, she was showing a lot more interest in him lately. Maybe it was the fact that she had just broken up with her latest boyfriend, or maybe it was the fact that Andy was now a prime bit of meat himself after his six month work out. Regardless there was definitely a new twinkle in Corporal Fisher's eye when they met up. It was a twinkle that worried Andy. It was always fine to be around Fisher, to enjoy her company, even to enjoy her beauty. Now things had changed and it was a major concern to Andy. If the woman he had sometimes fantasised about was interested in being with him, it was going to take a heroic amount of self-restraint to resist her charms. Nevertheless, Andy had managed to do it thus far. He was still a married man, he had to think of his fantastic kids as well. His thoughts were quickly interrupted.

'Are you in?' It was Corporal Cleaver and the sound in Andy's ear was more crackly than ever. Water had got into the Corporal's mouthpiece.

'Negative, I'll report status in a minute.'

He took a deep breath for it could be his last. Then he sprinted up the steps of the mansion and shot a round of bullets into the many locks on the door. Although he was using a silencer he still wasn't sure if anybody had heard him. He threw his shoulder against the oak door. It swung in and Andy followed it landing on the doormat inside the house.

'I'm in, what's your status?'

'Still in the fountain, the dim wits haven't looked in here yet but I don't know how long I have, get a move on.'

'I'm on it' Andy replied.

That was the first time he had fired a gun in anger on a mission. Fifty-year-old oak had felt his wrath, it had been easy. Andy hoped he would be able to pierce some fifty-year-old flesh with the same ease.

Andy couldn't believe what he was about to do. It was one of the scariest things that could happen to him and he was about to do it to himself. He reached up, and pulled out the wires leading to the trip switch. Power to the chateau was gone and with it came the darkness, the darkness that he despised. He was prepared though, he switched on his night vision goggles, and the green tinted vision regained his composure. Andy headed straight for the drug lord's room. He was supposed to be asleep, that's what they had trained for. He knew that there was going to be no easy shot tonight. If he were to kill his first man he would have to work for it.

34

Creak, creak, creak. The timber steps of the flight of stairs moaned with every step Andy took. The grand old staircase must have been over a hundred years old. Andy knew that the steps would squeak but with the silence, combined with his raised sense of alertness, each step seemed to send echo's throughout the old chateau. He paused for a moment to reassert himself, then Andy began to move faster and faster up the staircase. Carlisle's room was the first on the left at the top of the stairs. Andy now stood outside the door. Three deep breaths were followed by Andy swiftly opening the door. Andy's two arms were now out stretched, his fingers wrapped tightly around his semi-automatic. Left, right, up, down. Andy moved his arms rapidly and with precision, but everywhere he looked there was nobody to be found. After checking underneath the bed, in the en-suite and in the wardrobes it was clear that the enormous master bedroom was empty. The white bed sheets and two bulky pillows were strewn on the floor. His target had certainly left in a hurry. Andy sighed, he would have to search every room in the large chateau to find the baron, and the drug lord knew the mansion a lot better than he did. Except for his night vision goggles the odds were now stacked against him.

Andy considered his next move. To check the entire mansion he would need the assistance of Corporal Cleaver.

'What's your position Cleaver?' Andy whispered into his mouthpiece as gently as possible.

'Still submerged, I reckon they've given up looking for me though. Hold on a second.'

Cleaver popped his head above the rim of the fountain and spoke again.

'Be careful I think the two goons have just gone back into

the chateau.'

The advice was sound but it was dispensed a fraction too late. The two men had already made their way up the staircase and overheard Andy requesting back-up. Immediately, they launched themselves into the master bedroom, one of the men bashing into Andy and knocking both men to the ground. Andy's gun flew across the floor sliding under the bed. Worse still, he was now pinned to the floor. Although the lights were cut and the room was in virtual darkness, his wrists were held firmly against the cold floorboards as the man's knees rested on his aching thighs. Andy wrestled with the man, his martial arts training had prepared him for this day. However, he was dealing with no amateur. Each move he made was instantly counteracted by another motion. He even resorted to trying to head butt his assailant, which was certainly not taught during the training he'd received. Andy was starting to panic. It wasn't helped by the fact that his night vision goggles had come loose as he attempted the head butt. He squinted his eyes as best he could and concentrated hard on seeing something, anything. As Andy's breathing became heavier and heavier the second man pulled a gun from his holster. Andy could just about make out the gun as some moonlight peered in through the window and reflected off the deadly silver weapon. This was it. Thirty seven years had come to an end for Andy.

During moments like these it's often said people's lives flash before their eyes. It was no different for Andy. The whole world slowed down, the man seemed to take an eternity to pull out the gun and pull the trigger. Now before his eyes lay Anne-Marie and Jack, his parent's image came after that, Andy wondered would it be Amy Fisher or his wife Victoria that he would see next. Instead he saw something very different.

His assassin ran to the window and opened it.

'On y va' he roared in a thick southern French accent.

Into the room flew the drug lord and, just as quickly, he exited it out the gaping hole and slid down the down pipe to his freedom. The two men quickly followed leaping to the ground. Almost as instantaneously Corporal Cleaver entered the room. When he had got no reply from Corporal Pickering he knew he was in trouble. He bounded out of the fountain and sprinted across the forecourt like a man possessed. Corporal Cleaver was now freezing cold and dripping wet, but he wasn't going to let a colleague be killed on his watch. Upon entering the chateau he could just about make out Carlisle who was waiting on the landing for his protectors to finish their dirty work. As Corporal Cleaver galloped up the stairs, two steps at a time, he let off a series of shots at the target. At speed and in darkness it was difficult to keep a steady shot. Corporal Cleaver was disappointed with his shooting, but inadvertently he had saved Andy's life. On seeing the danger to their employer the two men immediately switched their attention to getting him out of the house alive. There might even be a bonus coming up for them for their efforts. With that, the three men had absconded through the window and it was left to Corporal Cleaver to punch Andy to snap him out of his trance.

'Pull your shit together Corporal' Cleaver roared at Andy

'If we fuck up this job we might as well be dead. Get your ass down stairs and I'll follow them out the window.'

Andy hesitated for a moment, clearly shaken by the events. He had never experienced his life flash before his eyes. For the past seven months his confidence had been continually boosted and boosted, but this moment had taken the wind out of his sails. He was now but a man again, a Directacom Area Manager. What the hell was he doing out in France trying to secretly kill a gangland boss.

'Move for fuck sake' Corporal Cleaver bellowed at Andy.

Dazed and confused, Andy picked himself up and brushed

himself off. As he looked up he could see Corporal Cleaver jumping out of the bedroom window. He wanted to follow him out the window or at the very least follow his instructions to go downstairs, but he couldn't. He just wasn't functioning. He made his way into the en-suite and repeatedly splashed water on his pale white face. Each splash hit Andy with the tremendous force of a tidal wave. Ten seconds later he could look at himself in the mirror again. Andy was once again an assassin, a member of Unit Firestorm and a force to be reckoned with. He never again wanted to experience that kind of crippling fear. The last time he had felt that way was in the white room all those months ago. It had changed his life for the better; he hoped this experience would do the same.

The sound of screeching tyres ended the staring match Andy was having with himself in the bathroom mirror. The men had made it to their car and were going to make a ditch for the gate down the long drive. If they made it out the mission was over. The Corporals expected to complete their mission in an efficient manner. The victim was to be asleep and the job quick and clean. As a result a *Ford Transit* is all that lay outside the chateau walls. While fantastic for carrying around equipment, it would prove futile chasing anyone in the large van.

There was no time to make it down the stairs. Andy sprinted to the bedroom window and jumped out. He had not even checked where he would land but as everyone else seemed to land safely he assumed he would too. He landed on the wet lawn and immediately looked at the driveway. The car was half way down and gaining speed rapidly. There was no way he could catch the car on foot. The instruction of the mission was to kill the drug lord, and him alone. Andy knew if he shot the fuel tank that the explosion would surely kill Carlisle, but it would also kill the other two men in the car. He wasn't sure what to do, so more in desperation than hope he sprinted after the car. Then he heard

'Hit the deck Pickering, now.'

Andy rolled onto the grass. As he did so he heard a loud explosion. Andy lifted his head expecting to find an exploded car. Instead he found a crashed one. Corporal Cleaver had rolled a grenade under the very fountain where he had spent much of the night. The hand carved granite fountain centrepiece of the majestic gardens lay in pieces across the drive, and Carlisle's car lay in ruins in front of it.

'Come on Pickering, you haven't had the kill yet' Corporal Cleaver said as he gestured at Andy to investigate the wreck. Both men approached the car with caution. As they peered through the window it could be seen that both front seat air bags had inflated. Unfortunately for the drug lord he started in the back seat but now his blood covered bald scalp had made its way through the front windscreen. None of the men were wearing a seatbelt and the scene was difficult to stomach. Bits of flesh were stuck on the handbrake, on the dash and most of all on pieces of broken glass that lay strewn just about everywhere. Remembering his training Andy checked all three men's pulses.

'Well Corporal?' Cleaver asked.

'The two minders have a faint pulse and need medical attention ASAP. The drug lord is dead.'

Andy wasn't sure how to feel about the whole situation. The mission was complete, it was a relative success, but Andy hadn't got to complete his first kill. He felt his own personal mission was a failure.

The next task was to make the whole ordeal look like an accident. Many people could shoot a man dead in his bed, there was countless numbers of people who wanted Carlisle dead. However, a grenade-exploding fountain would raise suspicion. Corporal Cleaver got the blowtorch from the van and began to use it on the granite stump that remained of the fountain. Five minutes later both men had left the scene. An anonymous call was made to the police describing a loud bang heard at the chateau. The police would come to find that the terrible night had produced a lightning strike on the fountain centrepiece. Two of the three men would survive the night in hospital, the third would be pronounced dead at the scene.

It is said that in difficult times we learn the most about ourselves, and others. Andy had been disappointed in himself tonight, but he had learnt a lot more than in his three previous missions. He learnt how competent Corporal Cleaver was; he saw the level he had to reach to become the cream of Unit Firestorm, the level he had to reach to even remain alive. He had also realised he now had a friendship in which each man was willing to die for the other. Peter's prophecy was coming true, everything he had said in his presentation in the white room was fulfilling itself. Earlier that night Andy questioned himself, he wondered what a Directacom Area Manager was doing in a drug lord's chateau in the south of France. He had his answer, the Directacom Area Manager was here because he was born to do this work. The thought of life without Unit Firestorm now frightened Andy more than a loaded pistol in his face. Now it was time to go back to London, it was time to be back in No. 41 Thompson Avenue, for there was something almost as important going on there.

35

Two table spoons of golden syrup. This was the magic ingredient Victoria had previously omitted. This year things were going to be different; things were going to be perfect. Jack loved nutty chocolate cookies and not just any type, they had to be homemade. As Victoria put the greased baking sheets into the oven she recalled Jack's disappointment this day last year when the cookies just weren't the same. Kids can be cranky at the best of times but Jack was extra cranky at last year's birthday party when his favourite cookies just didn't taste quite right. Victoria had already put in a big morning's work. A sweet smelling and tempting looking chequerboard cake lay cooling on the table. Victoria opened the packet and placed six candles on the cake. Jack could have no complaints today, at least not about the food.

Life had changed more in the past eight months for Victoria than in the previous eight years. As she started washing the baking tin she pondered on whether the changes had been for better or worse. When she first met John Black she fell into a whirlwind romance. The excitement of a new lover, a caring lover, a spontaneous lover drew her in. John was a powerful man and power oozed from his very being. He was suave, wealthy and good in bed. It was exciting times and in a paradox the wrongness of it all seemed to make it right. Even without meeting John, the very act of sneaking around was exciting. It had a snowball effect. She felt good, so she felt more inclined to dress up and look good, and because she looked good she felt even better. Could it last was the question. Yes was the answer, but yes was the answer only to the question of Victoria and John still meeting up. Now the excitement was gone and Victoria was starting to realise some home truths.

Victoria now understood that she was only a mistress to

John. He had not introduced her to his children, or anybody else of note. In fact the only person John had actually introduced her to was Pavel, the gardener. John said it was because she was married. If they came clean her family would be destroyed and his public reputation would be in ruins. He described the headlines. *The Sun* - 'Minister for Adultery', *The Mirror* - 'Black Breaks Family' and *The Times* 'Government in Tatters as Black Resigns'. Victoria understood this too, John was right, but it didn't make things any easier.

Lately she questioned if it was time to end the affair. While she still felt something for John, she knew there was no future there. Andy was now starting to creep into her mind again, and this time in some sexual fantasies. It had been years since Victoria had dirty thoughts about Andy, but now she had a changed husband. John had told her not to ask Andy any probing questions about what he was up to. He said it would be dangerous for her, in fact she could put her life in danger by doing so. Victoria found this very hard to believe, but John was a powerful man and up to now she had trusted him completely. Victoria thought it strange that Andy would not be suspicious that she was not suspicious. He never let on anything even though he often arrived home late at night or with bruises on his body. She thought it ironic how she always knew her husband to be a good, decent, honest man, but now she didn't know her husband at all, and suddenly she was finding herself attracted to him again. It was this that she beat herself up about most. What is wrong with me? she thought to herself. But Andy was now very attractive to her. Physically he was in fantastic shape. He was focused, dynamic and had a swagger in his step. Even the fact that he now didn't grovel for sex made him more attractive to her. Maybe I always want what I can't have she mused to herself. She wouldn't be the first person in the world that felt this way. What she would do about it was the question.

The cake tin was now cleaned ten times over. Victoria put the tin on the draining board as she snapped out of her daydream. She now could smell something unusual. She looked at the cooker in horror. She may have added the two table spoons of golden syrup but leaving the cookies in the oven too long would make it immaterial. Pulling the door open she afforded herself a smile. The biscuits were a light golden brown colour. Jack would be happy after all.

The gathering involved just a few close friends. The Sullivans were coming, no doubt laden down with sweets and chocolate, Chris was coming, as was Victoria's mother. Victoria's father had died some time back and Andy's parents were now living up the country. There was one notable exception to last year's party. This year, Jennifer would not be there. She and Victoria never really recovered from their bust up on the sweltering day outside the Ritz hotel. It wasn't the revelation that Victoria was cheating on Andy that broke their friendship, it was the fact Victoria had now chosen this man over her in all aspects of life. The nights at the Westend had been ditched for her new lover, phone calls were not returned and Jennifer now didn't trust the words emitted from her best friend's lips. The lack of truth was the straw that broke the camel's back for Jennifer. The last thing Jennifer said to Victoria was call me when you sort yourself out, call me when you are the Victoria I met in that Starbucks in Edison. Victoria never called her. Deep down she knew she'd changed and maybe her new life just did not have space for Jennifer. Although she didn't like to admit it to herself, she missed Jennifer. Victoria made up some convoluted story to Andy why they had fallen out. She couldn't even remember what she had told her husband, she doubted he could remember either. He was somewhere else most of the time when it came to Victoria. She so wanted to know where that place was but so far she had to bite her lip. Although she had been warned of tragic consequences, she wondered how much longer she could keep that lip bit.

The table was now fully set, cakes, cookies and crackers covered the mahogany surface.

'Mummy I'm home' Jack proclaimed as he rushed in the door.

It was perfect timing. Victoria was feeling the heat in the kitchen so she had asked the Sullivans to collect Jack from school. She was really glad to have the Sullivans, but surely they must have been suspicious of her. Luckily they adored both Jack and Anne-Marie and never minded taking care of them if Victoria needed some free time. With that, Anne-Marie ran into the kitchen arms stretched out and hands open. Mr Sullivan knew the drill and heaped some jelly babies into the outstretched palms. The party was beginning already. Victoria just hoped Andy would be back in time from his 'Directacom team building convention' to see his son blow out his six special candles.

36

As he stood on the porch he stared at the small silver numbers for a moment. No. 41. It was good to see that number. Andy wasn't sure if he would ever get to see No. 41 Thompson Avenue again. It sure was a good feeling to be home. The events taking place inside mattered as much to Andy as the assassination of some drug lord. He had managed to get an earlier flight from his 'conference' and was looking forward to the shocked expression from Jack when he arrived in the door. Andy turned the latch and he was not disappointed. Jack ran to his dad and Andy lifted him high in the air. Jack always loved this but today was slightly different, it was even better. One, Two, Three, Four, Five, Six. Jack loved his father's birthday bumps and Andy was delighted to be there to give them.

'Mummy, can I blow out the candles now that Dad is here.'

'Go for it Jack, remember to make a wish.'

Jack closed his eyes and squeezed his eyebrows. Then, as if summoning all his energy he caught the table, took a deep breath and blew out the candles. Victoria and Andy watched on, both proud parents, both with broad smiles across their faces. Victoria looked over at Andy and mused to herself what she would wish for if she had the chance. Little did she know Andy was thinking the exact same thought. Andy looked over to Victoria and their eyes met for a brief moment before they both quickly looked back at their darling son. Andy believed that the marriage was now unfortunately defunct. It hurt Andy to accept this but the daily evidence was too great to deny it. Maybe he should be open to taking things further with Amy, maybe it was time to move on.

'Alright mate, long time no see.'

Andy turned around to see Chris' outstretched arm holding

a can of beer in his direction. Andy had only been in the door a short time and thus far all his attention was on Jack. Andy had hardly noticed Chris, but as always it was great to see his face. Chris was one of those guys that instantly put you in good form and today was no different. Andy gladly accepted the golden brew and they retired to the sitting room to have a bit of grown men conversation.

'You should have seen the talent in the pub last night, a hen party from the countryside, outstanding!'

Chris hadn't changed much, and in a whirlwind past seven months Andy was glad that at least some things remained constant.

'Did you do any damage fella?'

'Afraid not, I reckon I could have got the sister of the bride, except with my parents behind the bar I had to cut back a little on the tall tales.'

'I like the way you manage to combine socialising, pulling women, business and family all at the same time!' Andy joked. It was actually true; spending much of his time in his parent's pub meant he could combine all these activities in one location.

Chris then turned to Andy and motioned to speak. His expression had changed. Chris was now actually looking serious for one of the first times in his life.

'You know I never see you anymore, you don't go to the pub after the 5-a-side and you don't even come over for any of the big matches. You might be fooling everyone around you that Andy Pickering hasn't changed, but you can't fool your no. 1 drinking buddy. What the hell is going on with you? Are you in financial trouble or are you having difficulties with Vic?'

Andy, fazed for a moment responded 'I'm flat out at work, that's all. Yes, things could be better between me and Vic, but you know that anyway, nothing new there.'

Chris looked sceptically at Andy, he wasn't going to give up easily and started to continue the questioning. Luckily at that moment Anne-Marie came in the door and ordered the two men out to the kitchen as there were presents to be opened.

Andy avoided any situation where he would find himself alone with Chris for the rest of the night. Chris left the house that night frustrated. Little did he realise he would not have to wait long until everything would be divulged to him. Little did he realise that soon he would be putting his own life on the line in the search for answers.

Victoria and Andy now lay in bed. Andy faced the built-in wardrobe, Victoria faced the bay window, and their backs faced each other. Both pretended to be asleep but in truth, both had things on their mind. Andy wondered how long he could continue in Unit Firestorm, the unit that was revitalising him, before he would lose everyone that mattered to him. The barrage of thoughts going through his mind was deafening. Then a noise came even louder than his thoughts, his mobile phone was ringing. Five minutes later he was in the family car, speeding through the sleepy neighbourhoods of west London. It was too late for an underground, and the Marshal said that this simply couldn't wait. He didn't know what lay ahead of him when he arrived at the Firestorm facility, soon he would wish he never found out.

37

Marshal Pearson strode up and down his office. The office could only have been about fifteen feet wide and the Marshal had marched up and down it more than fifty times. The Prime Minister had given him the instruction and the orders had to be carried out, however difficult they would be. It was the sickest part of the job for the Marshal. Recon had given their encoded investigation report to the Prime Minister. It was up to him from there. These were the only circumstances in which the Chief of the Army and the Chancellor didn't have a veto. It was black and white and it was left to the Prime Minister to decide what was best for the good of the nation.

The Marshal lifted the handset and rang the assigned assassins. He may not have had the frightening growl of The General, but he wasn't the Huggy Bear some of his colleagues described him as either. His eyes welled up as he dialled Andy's number. Andy was to report to The General's office to discuss tactics for his next assignment. The dice had been rolled, the Marshal could do nothing now.

38

Andy ran from his car to the security interlock. Once inside he ran all the way to The General's office. If there was one man in the world he did not want to get on the wrong side of, it was The General.

'Good morning Corporal, apologies for bringing you in at this hour but as you can imagine this mission is critical to the security of the nation. Take a seat while the remaining two members of the team arrive for the briefing.'

This was the best Andy had gotten on with The General in quite some time and he hadn't even said anything to the man. Andy took a seat and waited, he was still drawing his breath form the earlier exertions. Last time he was in The General's office was way back on his second day. He had never discussed that day since but he knew something smelt rotten about Corporal Jack Ryan and the activities of that night. The General too knew that Andy was uncomfortable about the activities, but he was confident that those concerns would never be aired to anybody. The General was right, he never told anybody about that night, not Peter, not Cleaver, not even Amy. Andy took another look around the office. He could still remember the day he met The General, and he could still quote The General's words 'Take a good look around Private, this is my office, I doubt you will ever be in it again'.

As he reminisced, the door opened. It was Corporal Eric Bhana. Corporal Bhana and Andy always got on well but purely at a professional level. He was of average height, had black hair and was of Indian origin. His most peculiar feature was his moustache. He never could quite decide if he liked it and as a result he would grow it for a few weeks, then shave it, then grow it again. Peter even took secret bets on which day he would come in shaved. His facial hair may have been inconsistent but everybody knew where they stood with Bhana, he was strict but fair.

A moment later the door reopened. Clearly nobody wanted to be late for The General. This time it was Corporal Amy Fisher that walked in. Andy was instantly thrown. It was fine to be flirting in the facility when there were plenty more people around, but a mission with Amy might just loosen the lock that secured his fidelity. Amy sat down next to him. He could feel the sexual chemistry as she crossed her legs. It was as if she carried around an aura of sexual energy with her, and right now he was in the mist of its penetrating glow. As he dared to turn his head to look at her, he noticed that she had also turned to look at him. It was like déjà vu. Earlier that day his wife had made eye contact with him in a similar manner, but this time there was no looking away. Andy and Amy stared into each other's eyes for a couple of seconds. He knew tonight could change the course of his life.

'Look alive men, I know it's 2.50am but we have a job to do and we're not going to get it done half asleep.'

Everybody immediately sat to attention as The General continued,

'Tonight is a sad night for Unit Firestorm, we lost a valuable member of our unit earlier tonight. He will be sadly missed. Your job right now is to completely disassociate yourselves from the activities you are about to carry out. When you joined Unit Firestorm you were fully advised of what it entailed, including the dangers, and your loss of right to your emotions. Tonight will test all of you, but the Marshal and I have every faith in each and every one of you.

Unfortunately one of our former colleagues has defected from us. Recon has found that he has disclosed details of the unit to a member of the police force. Recon were unable to ascertain why he divulged the details, but phone tapings were made and emails intercepted which proved the events.'

All three Corporals waited for the words they knew they would surely hear, and The General didn't disappoint.

'Both the informant and the member of the force are to be eliminated tonight.'

It was the moment Andy had dreaded for some time. But Andy knew the rules, he hadn't broken them, and he understood that nobody else could either, otherwise the whole unit, the whole nation was under threat. As with all missions he knew what was coming next. 'Duties' is where The General assigns duties to all members of the team. Partaking in the mission would be difficult but Andy felt that as long as he didn't have to physically pull the trigger on these men that he could carry out any other tasks. At this point the same question was on everybody's lips; which colleague of theirs would they have to assassinate. Nobody dared ask.

Before they could speculate any more The General proceeded.

'The policeman will be dealt with first. Although of sound mind he has previously been for counselling for depression. He will be administered an overdose of sleeping pills. He should be found lying in bed, a photo album will be left beside him on the bed and it will be open on a page of his last girlfriend.'

The General proceeded to hand out a photo of the man's last girlfriend.

'You will find further photos inside the case file. Finally the empty pill containers should be left on the bedside cabinet.'

'Does everybody understand? Remember we require a picture of the scene for our records.'

The General was greeted with silence.

'Do you fucking understand?' The General barked.

'Yes Sir' the trio replied in unison.

'Now for the second part of your mission, the defector is to be killed via smoke inhalation. A sleeping tablet is to be administered before sleep. Then a fire is to be started through an electrical fault. One member of the team needs to wear an oxygen tank and wait in the room checking the pulse of the defector until such time as he is dead. At that point, the team leave and give an anonymous phone call to the fire brigade. Remember we don't want to burn the whole bloody street down. Does everybody understand?'

'Yes Sir'

'All the relevant information of addresses, access points, house layouts etc are as per usual in the file. Normally I give specific tasks but tonight is a team effort, there is no trigger to be pulled. Now I'm sure every one of you want to know who the defector is. Unfortunately he was a good man and a good member of the unit. Of course he is known to all of you, but he is known better to one of you in particular.'

The General was finally about to reveal who would lose their life tonight. Andy and his colleagues were on the edge of their seats.

'The defector is Peter Johnson'

Andy's heart sunk as he grasped his head in his hands.

39

As he left the park bench Peter was confident he was making progress. Eve was a wonderful girl and his brother's pride and joy. He could still see her gleaming white teeth as she smiled at Peter when he last left his brothers house. That was a week ago to the day. How so much had changed in the past seven days. Peter, with five more of Eve's closest friends and family, had carried her remains to the local cemetery. Eve was now six feet under. It had been a bad week in the UK for deaths due to drugs. Four teenagers in the prime of their lives were struck down three days previously. Eve's death was just another statistic. Too high to realise her limitations, she tragically overdosed. It was the death of his niece that had started the ball rolling and Peter was not going to stop until he got some justice.

Tony Cohen was a good friend of Peter's. They grew up in the same area and Tony knew of Eve, even if he didn't know her personally. It was as Peter shouldered the coffin through the cemetery that his eyes caught Tony's. As a policeman, Peter knew Tony was the man for the job. Peter tried to be clever, having seen one of his colleagues previously assassinated he knew he had to be careful. Very careful. Peter bought a new mobile phone, made up a new e-mail address and bought an old car to drive around in so his car wouldn't be tracked. Tony was blown away by the revelations Peter told him. It was mind boggling at first, but Peter had the evidence to back it up. Peter snuck out files from the Unit Firestorm facility, Tony had no choice but to believe him.

Tonight they met in Hyde Park. Peter felt that here there would be plenty of people around so as to not look suspicious with the dark of the night keeping their identities hidden. The discussions had gone very well. As Peter walked through the gravel path out of the park he knew he had chosen the right man for the job. In three days Tony had compiled a near complete case and he told Peter he would give the file to the head detective tomorrow. If all went according to plan arrests would be made within forty eight hours.

Peter's head hit the pillow. It had been a crazy week, he lost his beloved niece and had just put his and Tony's life in danger. Peter tossed and turned at first but he was reassured that he didn't make the stupid mistakes his former colleague had made. He was smart, and there was no reason for Firestorm to suspect him. Unfortunately he was not smart enough.

40

The black *Lexus* was now at high speed in a bee-line for the policeman's house. Time was of the essence. It was now 3.30am and both operations had to be complete by 5.30am, the time that Peter got up as he prepared for a day at Firestorm. There had been silence in the car from the moment all three had entered it. Nobody liked what was going on, least of all Andy. But the choice was kill or be killed. Although Amy was in the passenger seat as Andy steered the car, no sexual aura could be felt anymore. Earlier Andy had known that tonight could change the course of his life. He was correct, but it wouldn't be due to Amy Fisher.

The car was now parked outside the apartment block. Inside the three Corporals sat huddled around the case file. The plan was discussed and final preparations were made. The team entered the building, took the lift, got to apartment 603 and picked the door lock. A gentle purring sound was heard on entry, the noise was coming from Tony Cohen as he lay sleeping in his bed. Next Corporal Bhana wet a rag with chloroform and held it up to the policeman's mouth. Tony woke for a moment but before he had a chance to struggle the chloroform had taken effect. Bhana held the man upright while Andy forced the sleeping pills down his throat. Bhana repeatedly used his thumb and index finger to squeeze the policeman's oesophagus to aid the unconscious man to swallow. Meanwhile Amy found a photo album and identified Tony's ex-girlfriend. The man was put back into a sleeping position, the empty tablet containers were left on the cabinet and the photo album lay by his side.

Within fifteen minutes the team were back in the Lexus. Unlike the messy operation in France twenty-four hours earlier the first half of this mission was a resounding success. However, it didn't feel like that as Andy sped off from the scene. Andy wanted to turn on the radio to quench the deafening sound of silence. Yet he didn't touch the dial as it surely would have been disrespectful to tonight's two victims. It was now 4.30am, within the hour the final part of the operation had to be complete or Peter would be awake. Andy had just killed a man for the first time in his life. It was done cold and calculated and worse still, the man's family would think he committed suicide. Andy didn't even know why he killed him, he just did it because he was told to.

'Check your right hand coat pocket in the morning, it will explain everything' Andy recalled the words that had changed his life. Up to this point they had explained everything, but not anymore. He was a member of Unit Firestorm, he was committed to its endeavours, but he was not brainwashed. He knew what was happening was wrong. Peter was a good colleague at Directacom and at Firestorm, but more than that, he was a good friend. He knew Peter was a hard man, but he was a good man. But he had broke the code, he kept trying to remind himself of this. It was Peter himself who had warned him so much about the cruel reality of violating the code of silence.

There was another option. He knew he would put everybody's lives in danger but at least his conscience would be clean. He was in charge of getting to the target in time. A wrong turn here, a missed exit there and they would be too late to carry out the orders. It was a huge risk. He would put the three members of his team in danger if the Marshal felt that they had intentionally sabotaged the mission. The same fate as Peter could be placed on them. Finally regardless of his actions, Peter would be assassinated the next day by another team. Andy deliberated on Peter's life. He never felt this kind of power before, he also never felt as sick as he did right now. Anxiety overtook his stomach and he felt his whole body cramp. It was decision time.

Kill, kill, kill. It was a horrible answer, but it was the only answer that wouldn't put everybody in jeopardy. Andy knew these roads well. He was back in West Hampstead. If only his family, a mere mile down the road knew what he was about to do. Andy wondered what he had become. A monster was his only answer.

As he gently opened the bedroom door Andy could now see the small but stocky frame of Peter in a slumber beneath his sheets. Andy wanted to catch his shoulders, shake them and tell him to go into hiding. Maybe he could get a flight out of the country tonight, maybe he could make a new life for himself in the Caribbean, lazing under palm trees, leaving all this madness behind. Unfortunately Andy knew the merciless reality, Recon would investigate in the morning. If no remains were found then the shit would really hit the fan. It had to be done, and Bhana was the man for the job. He had always been a Corporal that was harsh but fair, he knew the rules and he expected everybody to abide by them unsympathetically. Robotically Bhana again wet a rag with chloroform and held it up to Peter's mouth.

'I'll keep watch, you start the fire Fisher' At least Andy would not be the one to 'pull the trigger'. Andy took one last look at Peter's face, it was the last time anyone would see skin on it again.

'Move out and have the car ready, I'll give the signal to call the fire brigade' Corporal Bhana ordered to his team. The smoke was now getting quite heavy and without the correct breathing apparatus it would be dangerous.

Corporals Pickering and Fisher waited in the car with faces forlorn and consciences heavy. The last fighting pulse made its way around Peter Johnson's body and the signal was given by Corporal Bhana. Corporal Fisher rang the emergency services and Andy waited with his foot hanging heavy over the accelerator. A minute later Bhana entered the car and Andy's foot fell hard, the Lexus was on its way back to Firestorm. Mission complete. Bhana's signal confirmed it, Andy was now that monster. He drove home wondering how he could have ended up in a situation in which he killed a good friend and work colleague, with the help of a women he was about to cheat with, on the love of his life and mother of his beautiful children.

What have I become?

41

'Thanks for coming Sarah, it means a lot.'

Andy thanked co-worker Sarah Cripwell for her presence. It actually did mean a lot. Andy couldn't believe the size of the crowd in the church, every single available space was taken, with many more mourners defying the bitterly cold weather outside in the church yard. Practically everybody who worked on the 7th floor with Peter was there. Everybody liked 'Fracture'. The reason was simple, almost everybody in Directacom felt the same as Andy. In an office of pen pushers, suits and ties, Peter told it as it was and was a breath of fresh air.

A Tottenham Hotspur flag was draped over the coffin.

'His love of Spurs was widely known and the banter he aroused from this love brightened everybody's day.'

The Pastor continued 'In fact anybody that came into contact with Peter at any stage of his life knew how he could turn a frown into a smile, a sigh into a laugh and a leg into a cast, isn't that right Jeff.'

For a brief moment the congregation shared a smile as those that knew Jeff turned to look at him.

'He was a tough man, many of you may have known Peter as 'Fracture', but certainly was a good man. His loss is tragic and couldn't have come at a tougher time for his family following the untimely death of his niece Eve last week. It is a time to rally round the Johnsons, they need your help, they need your support and they need you to put the smile back on to their faces, the smile Peter would surely have given them.'

Andy listened and tried to hold the tears back, as did much of the congregation. Unfortunately it was all too much for Peter's brother who had opened the gates of the dams that were his eyes. He had just lost a daughter and now a brother. The dealer that is life had dealt him the worst hand in the pack, two weeks running. As the service ended Andy could see George Brownlow approaching with his hand outstretched.

'I know you and Peter were quite close. I just want to say we are here for his family and we are here for you too. Don't hesitate to talk to me about anything if you need to.'

While Andy appreciated the sentiment, he knew he wouldn't be sitting down with his boss to discuss how he was going to get over the fact that he had slain his friend in cold blood. To make it worse, Peter had recently updated his will and Andy was selected as one of the six members to hold the coffin. Andy wished he could be anywhere else but masquerading as a shocked griever.

It sickened Andy that not one member of Unit Firestorm had turned up to the funeral. Apparently all these people were willing to die for Corporal Peter Johnson, instead they had killed him. Andy understood the rational. These people were not supposed to know Peter in everyday life, as a result it would be suspicious if they were attending the funeral of somebody they were not even acquainted with. This rational didn't impress Andy, he felt that surely Cleaver and Fisher could have come, it would be the least Peter deserved.

The walk into the cemetery was horrendous for Andy. Thoughts of suicide crossed his mind. Never in his life before had he let his brain cells contemplate such a fate. Andy felt everybody's eyes piercing him as he made his way to the grave. Paranoia was setting in, he couldn't lift up his head, his weary eyes were fixed on the pavement.

Everybody knows, they all know.

Andy's rational was being undermined by the situation he now found himself in.

He looked at the hole in the ground that lay in front of him. That's the only place I'm fit for he thought to himself. As the men lowered down the coffin his eye caught Jack and Anne-Marie as they played hide and seek behind the tombstone of the grave next to Peter's. Just see it through for them, but you must make this right somehow. He had made a promise to himself.

42

It was only his third night but Chris was ready to give up already. Unfortunately for him he paid for a month's personal training and it would be a shame just to throw the money away. The treadmill was finished with for the night, next up was what Chris most dreaded, the rowing machine. Over the past two nights the rowing machine had turned into Chris' arch nemesis. Kelly was his personal instructor and just because she could row at 15 kph she seemed to expect Chris, a man, to at least achieve parity with her. The difference was while she had spent the last ten years in the gym, Chris had spent it in the pub. Chris pumped pints while Kelly pumped iron. Still, as he moved up and down on the rowing machine he was starting to feel a little bit of pride about himself. It was Chris' mother who told him he was now thirty six and if he ever wanted a wife, he would have to lose that gut. He didn't necessarily want a wife, but a little bit of female attention would be most welcome.

Kelly was trying her best to motivate her client, but Chris wasn't going to take the bait. He was happy to see the sights as he rowed gingerly down the Thames that was in his mind. There was something else on Chris' mind as well, Andy's behaviour. Over time Chris had less and less contact with Andy. Andy's arse had not made contact with Chris's couch for the past three months. At one time, the black leather recliner had a grove that was shaped from Andy's buttocks, sadly this grove was long gone.

Arsenal v Man United had played two weeks ago. It was a crunch game. The papers hyped it so that it was a title decider, but at this early stage of the season only a tabloid could justify a headline like that. Chris rang Andy, he had struck it lucky, Coca-Cola the company he advertised for, had given him first choice on two lower tier east stand tickets for the Emirates Stadium. Chris found it difficult to hide the excitement in his voice as he told Andy. It was tradition, Chris and Andy had only missed one Man United v Arsenal game since Chris had moved into his apartment six years ago. At the time, Andy was disappointed he couldn't watch the game with Chris, but Victoria giving birth to his second child had to come first. Chris was gutted when Andy told him he wouldn't be able to make it. The match was on a Saturday, yet Andy said he had work commitments. Chris didn't even think Directacom was open on Saturdays. Andy could hear the dejection in Chris' voice.

'Pick one of the lads from work or take your Dad he'd love it. Come on Chris, you have to go.'

But Chris declined, he said it was tradition that they watch the matches together and you can't break tradition, unless you're having a baby. To appease the situation Andy promised Chris he would call round to the apartment, that he would be able to make the second half. Andy never showed and one more excuse was added to an ever increasing list. This was the final nail in the coffin. Arsenal won but Chris had lost. Andy had been the best mate a guy could have but Chris now knew he had lost him forever.

'There's a class for twelve year old girls on Saturdays, maybe that would suit you better O'Neill.'

Maybe it would, thought Chris to himself, but he dared not give 'Miss Motivator' any back chat fearing he would get another 'river' to row.

'That's enough, hit the showers and I'll see you Tuesday night.'

Kelly was calling time ten minutes early. Chris was never a man of much faith but at this moment he decided that there was a God after all. Maybe all this time he should have listened a bit more to his devout Catholic mother.

A refreshed Chris left the changing room, the warm shower had done wonders and he was now delighted that he had gone to his third session. As he strode down the corridor towards the exit Kelly chased after him.

'Not so fast Chris, we have compiled your diet plan for the programme. Can you step into the office a moment while we go through it?'

Chris now knew why he hadn't listened more to his mother; finishing early was too good to be true. Breakfast, lunch and dinner were laid out on a sheet of paper. While there were many options available, none looked very tempting. What shocked Chris most was the restriction to eight units of alcohol a week. Hearing this Chris almost had to be picked up off the floor. But Chris had a new found determination after his shower and he promised Kelly he would stick rigidly to the programme.

As Chris drove home he felt revitalised. He may not have looked in shape but mentally he felt in shape for the first time in a long time. He recalled the events that took place at Jack's birthday. Andy was definitely not himself. Something was going on, something was not right. Chris had made one promise already tonight. Now he decided to make a second. Chris was going to find out what was happening to the man he used to call his best buddy.

43

Andy wiped his hand over his rough unshaven face. A musty odour surrounded his body. The underground was full, yet an empty seat lay at each side of him. At each and every stop people were initially delighted when they entered the carriage. They made a bee-line for the unusually free seats until their eyes met with the destitute individual that occupied the seat next to them. In the blink of an eye, their course altered, most tried not to make it too obvious, as if turning nonchalantly would offend the man less than turning in disgust. The last few days had turned Andy into that delinquent. Yesterday was spent in bed, Andy asked for the day off from both his employers. This was the first time he left his bed since the funeral. Thirty two hours straight he lay there. No food, just a little water. The only time he moved was to go to the toilet. Without proper food and drink this excursion was quite rare. Andy didn't know if he got any sleep in all those hours. He certainly felt shattered. It was as if Andy had drank a half dozen energy drinks and couldn't close his eyes. As he lay in bed, no matter how hard he tried, his eyelids just refused to fall. Now he could almost memorise every spot of dirt, every tiny spider's web, and every minute crack in the bedroom ceiling. All three had been sacrificed this morning. Andy just didn't feel like his shit, shower and shave. He was on his way to work. He would have asked for another day to wallow but today was Tuesday, and that meant the mandatory Tactical Tuesday meeting.

When Andy arrived at the facility everyone was shocked at his condition. When Corporal Fisher saw him she caught his arm and dragged him into the store room.

'Andy, you can't let this happen to you, you're a good man, if we didn't do it somebody else would have.'

He remained silent, he was in a different place right now. Habit had got Andy as far as the facility, but in truth, his brain had switched off the ignition and pulled out the key. Amy waved her hands in front of Andy's face. There was no reaction. She could see that while he looked a mess and had physically weakened, worse still he had mentally capitulated.

'Snap out of it Pickering, we can get through this together. Remember, I also knew Peter well but this is the game we're in. We all know what can happen, we could have chosen to laboriously drift through our lives or we could make a real difference to our country. We are heroes, it's just nobody knows it.'

Amy waited for a reaction, then with apathy Andy murmured something.

'I didn't get that' whispered Amy.

'I said…. bullshit' he reiterated, this time with more conviction in his voice.

'We are not heroes, we are a governmental underbelly who doesn't have to get involved with the trivialities of the law, with the trivialities of a moral conscience. So I said bullshit, fucking bullshit.'

'Stop it Andy, this has got to stop right now. If you carry on with this you know you'll end up getting yourself killed.' Amy lowered her voice 'You know how things work around here.'

'Maybe I'm better off'

'Listen to yourself Andy, you can't continue this activity. Peter is dead, he isn't coming back. You are the one with blood running through your veins and with air in your lungs. You can make a difference in this world, this world needs you.'

Corporal Cleaver opened the store room door.

'I could hear mumblings, if you too are getting jiggy then I suggest somewhere a little more discreet.'

'Fuck off Cleaver, it's not like that at all and you know it, we were discussing our last mission, you know it was a difficult one' Amy responded.

Cleaver paused as if recognising he had stepped over the mark.

'Apologies but the meeting is just about to start.'

Andy left the meeting disillusioned. The French mission was discussed first. Andy's flaws were highlighted. The Marshal said he had to get more ruthless, thus his selection for Peter's assassination. Then a minutes silence was observed for everybody's former colleague. From that point on Peter was discussed as if he had never been in this room, as if he had never known the Marshal and The General, as if he had never been willing to spill blood for these men. Peter was a target, Tony Cohen was a target and it had been a stunningly successful mission. Corporals Pickering, Fisher and Bhana were even congratulated at the efficiency at which they carried out the assignment. Andy had grown to enjoy Tactical Tuesday meetings. He had learnt a lot and had moved on a long way from the first day he set foot in the auditorium and didn't even know how to sign in. Andy now often added to the meeting with his views. No longer was he too shy to press the projector button on his screen and contribute with tactical manoeuvres that were shown on the theatre's main projector. In fact, Andy's reputation had grown so much that he was often asked to express his views on different missions. He made no contribution today. The General knew that at present Andy was a shell of a man and refrained from inviting his opinion.

As Andy reminisced on the day, his mind was still in freefall. However, one line that Amy had said stuck in his mind.

'You can make a difference in this world, this world needs you'.

That line gave him hope, a hope he desperately needed. Andy knew he would have to focus on any positive he could find from this unholy mess if he was to pull himself out of the sinking hole his life was becoming.

But what difference?

Then Andy knew.

You must make this right somehow.

He had thought this at the funeral, he didn't know the who, what, where, when or how, but he knew this was his only hope of salvation. He could indeed make a difference to the world.

44

'The FTSE 100 closed down 70 today to close at 5,242, the DAX closed up 14 to 5,170 and the Dow Jones fell 145 with the index closing at 9,560.' The woman proclaimed with efficiency. All around her were moving lines, charts and graphs. In fact there was just about enough room on the television screen for her head. Victoria watched on, bemused that people could actually find all this interesting. *Bloomberg* was the name of the channel in the left hand corner of the screen and it was John Black's favourite.

John and Victoria lay in bed in the 'bedroom under the stars'. John was propped up by a pillow behind his back. His reading glasses were perched on the end of his nose. In his left hand he held *The Times*, it was folded over twice so that it could now be written on by the silver pen he held in his other hand. John peered over his glasses and squinted his eyes as he tapped the silver pen on his extended bottom lip. Then as if hit by a bolt of lightning he briskly put pen to paper. When John studied the markets, which was often, he usually got it right.

John was nineteen when he had his first big win in the stock market. John's father was a carpenter and ran his own furniture business. His mother was a primary school teacher. His parents were loving and hard working and, like most middle class families, they started a fund for their children. Each of John's two sisters and two brothers had their money invested in different shares. John was still a teenager when he struck it lucky. His parents had saved with a mutual savings company, they were floated onto the stock exchange and John had been issued his first shares for nothing. John bought a car, lived the high life and still had money left over for future investments. His life had transformed and he was now a somebody. He liked his new found wealth, it brought opportunities, it brought respect, and it brought an interest from the most beautiful women in the locality. 'Free money' is how John labelled the windfall, John still labelled this type of money as 'free money' and he always made sure he was in on the action.

He quickly lost his remaining monies in investments, within a year the good times were over, the bank balance was nearly empty and his car was repossessed. It was a sharp learning curve, but John would never again forget that share prices can go down as well as up. He now had to work to support himself through his business degree in university. He became a general operative for a local building contractor. His day varied from jack-hammering, to shovelling concrete to cleaning toilets. The toilets were an experience he would never forget. There was a urinal and three cubicles in the makeshift converted container. Everyday he would find something new that disgusted him, be it sick in the sink, pee all over the floor or some gratuitous graffiti on the cubicles walls. When he reminisced on his labouring experience, one day in particular always stood out.

It was the first day in which the engineer paid a site visit. Although everybody treated the man as if they were delighted to see him, in reality his arrival was met with a cascade of dropping jaws. This development changed everything. Twenty men woke from their slumber and ran to check everything was in order before the concrete pour. After some last minute adjustments the engineer was satisfied. The first truck pulled up and the concrete gushed from the pump hose. It was thick and tough and it was almost unworkable, but the engineer insisted it was correct and no water was to be added to it. Everybody knew the engineer was being too strict, but the contractor wouldn't dare argue with him. Instead it was left to John and his fellow labours to feel the burn on their muscles as they shovelled the concrete broth around the first floor. It was gruelling work. With no movement in the concrete each shovel felt as if it was a tonne weight. Shovel after shovel had to be moved, with each scoop John's biceps burnt a little more. Five hours later the torture was over. The floor was almost fully screeded and John's boss showed the labourers a sliver of sympathy by allowing them a break.

John savoured his cup of tea, he had earned this beverage more than he ever earned a drink in his life. It was no more than ten degrees outside but John was covered in sweat. This was toil, this was real life. There was only one topic of conversation during lunch break; the engineer. It was unanimously decided that he was a 'bollocks'. Anybody that even tried to defend his actions was struck down immediately by a torrent of abuse. The engineer was a bollocks and that would be the party line. Break ended soon after, the sausage rolls were devoured, the ham sandwiches demolished and it was time to return to the coal face. For John this meant it was time for the highlight of his day; toilet duty. As he walked toward the ailing cabin he had no idea that what lay ahead of him would ensure his destiny changed forever. Cubicle No.1 contained an excretion that was just too big to make it down the toilet. This was nothing new for John to see. Out with the brush and with a little encouragement it was mission accomplished. Cubicle No. 2 had water all over the floor. John couldn't believe what he was thinking, but he was actually disappointed that it was water and not urine. If it was urine he would just have to mop it up. Water meant a leak. He went for his tool box. Some twenty minutes later he rose from the floor, the problem was fixed but he was covered in toilet water. This day couldn't get any worse he thought to himself, how wrong he was. He now cautiously opened the door to cubicle No. 3 and a used condom which someone had attempted to flush down the toilet greeted him. Now it lay bobbing up and down staring out at John. It was a relatively small site of some forty workers. Of that only one woman worked here and see was just recently married. This meant that either George Michael had secretly organised an onsite party or two of John's work mates had taken the teamwork ethic a little too far. One of the men had literally taken one for the team. John cleaned up, still reeling from this revelation. He threw away his gloves, it was time for a new pair. It was also time for a new life.

His part-time job taught John a valuable lesson. He would never lose money again. A life arduously labouring was definitely not the life for him. He studied business and he took his studies seriously. He loved researching and finding out more and more about how big business operated. He stumbled across many anomalies during the course of his university work. He knew these glitches had the potential to be exploited. Up to this point morality had held him back from utilising these loop holes. Today had changed everything. Earlier he had witnessed the engineer take the action he needed to do. He didn't let the hardship he brought to John and the other labourers get in the way of the end result, a floor poured as per specification. John knew he wanted to be the engineer of the financial world. Morality no longer came into any decisions he would make. When he finished his degree John would not be spending his life at the bottom working behind the desk of some bank. He would be the man making money from young men and women working behind bank desks everywhere. John put on his new set of gloves. Physically, he was shattered, but mentally, he was never more alert.

From that day forth John had a swagger, he finished his degree that summer and quickly became a highly regarded banker. Within a whirlwind year John had found himself in investments. This was exactly where a shrewd John wanted to be. Soon a charismatic John Black was the name on people's lips. Everybody wanted to be associated with him and this is exactly how he wanted it. It was all about image and John had a certain *je ne sais quoi* about him. Everybody thought he knew what he was doing, John hadn't a clue, but he did know who he needed to know, lots of contacts who trusted him. As a nineteen year old he won big on the markets. He was a very lucky boy. As an adult he started to win dramatically on the markets again. This time there was no luck involved, he had managed to perfect insider trading and his empire began to grow. John was where he wanted to be, the engineer of the financial world. Hard cash poured instead of hard concrete. He had the aura that the engineer had on that infamous day, now he felt nobody was every going to question John Black.

John turned and moved his pillow further up on the headrest. He gave it a few pats and then leaned back down again. As he did so he twisted, turned and swivelled his hips as if trying to shape the contours of the pillow to match the shape of his back. Eventually he was satisfied and he peered over the top of his reading glasses. It had been a good day on the markets, but he wasn't a man to rest on his laurels. Something caught his eye and John again put the pen to the newspaper.

Victoria raised her head slightly to look over at John. His head was now stuck in the newspaper and he failed to notice her glancing at him. She stayed looking at him for quite some time. He was an astute business man and she understood his current activities were necessary if he wanted to remain living the life of luxury he was accustomed to. However, she didn't appreciate the timing of his market analysis. The couple had just had sex. Due to the John's adventurous and persuasive nature, Victoria had performed certain acts in certain positions which she wasn't very familiar with. It wasn't as if she didn't enjoy her new more varied sex life, but at the least, she felt she deserved some time to soak it all up, where they would cuddle and chat and laugh. Instead within five minutes of climax John had switched on Bloomberg.

It was bad enough that he had turned on the television to begin with, but to turn on *that channel* of all the channels was a little unpalatable.

Victoria was crying out for a hug. Her lover didn't seem to love her that much after all. Victoria knew she loved John's lifestyle, but at that very moment she was unsure if she loved the man himself or not. She lowered her head onto her pillow and closed her eyes. There wasn't much point staying awake. Her lover was in his own world and all that remained was to muse at the lady on the television surrounded by numbers, charts and graphs.

The Times was laid on the chic oak table. On top of the paper John placed his reading glasses and silver pen. He had managed to avoid attending parliament today as there were few issues of serious note on the table. Besides, when he asked his junior minister to fill in, he was only too happy to oblige. John was glad to get to spend the day with Victoria. It had been a wonderfully exciting and rewarding eight months for him and he knew her presence in his life was the difference. He reached around his hand, pulled out his pillow from behind his back and placed it back on the mattress. As John snuggled up to his lover he placed a gentle kiss on her neck. Close enough to hear her breathing; he could tell she was asleep. He only turned on the television for ten minutes, it was also the middle of the day, and yet Victoria had now gone to sleep. Lately John was more concerned about his relationship with Victoria. His very presence had always caused an involuntary sparkle in her eyes. In recent times he had to look a lot harder for this sparkle. John never worried, he was a practical man and always had the charm and the wit to work his way out of any situation. As he looked at Victoria he felt a twinge of worry for one of the first times in his life. This situation was starting to become out of his control, he was beginning to lose that power he had over Victoria. He wondered if there was another man on the scene who she was saving her sparkle for. It crossed John's mind that her new athletic husband might be tempting his wife, but after all he had heard about how her marriage was dead, he dismissed the thought from his mind. He turned to Victoria again, gave her a kiss on the cheek and decided to get up. There wasn't much point sleeping through a perfectly good day.

John, now dressed, sat perusing the Murray and Associate Developments file. This was one job that wouldn't seem to go away. It had been quite some time since Terry had called to his house to hand him the file. In the interim, nothing seemed to have gone right. If it were any other developer, John would have let it go, as it wasn't worth risking his position in parliament. However, Mr Murray had promised a package too good to turn down. John sighed, it wasn't getting any easier, but he was still determined. If he could put all his weight behind it, maybe he could pull the required levers, and with it, twenty-five million pounds would be his. It was time to ruffle a few feathers. John put on his trench-coat and wrote Victoria a note for when she woke up. He grabbed his umbrella and set off.

45

Salt and Vinegar. There was no doubt in his mind that they were the original and the best. Chris had been very well behaved today, he had eaten only what was on his dietary programme, no more no less. It was his first day and it was a success, in Chris' mind it was time for a celebration, it was time for a reward. Yesterday the bag would have been empty within a minute, this time each and every crunchy sunflower oil covered potato crisp was relished and savoured. He had plenty of time to enjoy it. He had been sitting under a tree for seven hours now and all he could see was a wooded area to his left and a grain feed warehouse facility to his right. By his feet lay two broadsheets and a tabloid newspaper, all three had been read more than Chris cared to peruse them.

When Chris got up this morning he had envisaged a day of excitement, a day of surprises. In a long life it was the earliest Chris had ever gotten up, and he didn't even mind. In fact at 4am Chris jumped from his slumber. He showered, dressed, ate and was out the door and on the road within twenty minutes. By 5.30am he was camped outside the Pickering's. His car was parked a little down the road not to cause suspicion, but unknowingly, Chris was now spying on his best friend only a hundred yards away from where Jennifer also had spied on her best friend.

Within half an hour Chris was on foot and in toe of Andy. As he followed the homeless looking man down the street, he was amazed at the condition of Andy. They both got on the underground and when Andy got off Chris did likewise. Chris followed Andy from the station until he disappeared into the warehouse facility. Chris tried to enter but security looked for his ID badge. Not having any he had to leave, but he decided to stick it out until Andy came out. Whatever Andy was up to he didn't think he would be long in a grain feed store. How wrong he was.

Chris checked his watch. Seven hours had passed. He was thankful he prepared a packed lunch this morning. Without his ham salad sandwiches he would now be a shell of a man. It was a Tuesday and he had made a promise to himself and to his mother that he would make his date with the dreaded gym. He would be leaving without answers. As Chris stood to depart, he saw Andy and many other people emerge from the security turnstile.

Does Andy now work in a grain store?

It appeared so, as Andy along with his colleagues left their shift. It all started to make sense to Chris now. Andy looked forlorn because he had lost his job at *Directacom*, but he was too proud to tell anyone about it, even his best friend. All he could get for employment was to work in a grain store with shift hours. Most likely Andy had to work long hours to be able to afford the mortgage and all the trappings of a dependant wife and two children. He now believed Andy was an unsung hero. It was time to talk to Andy and tell him what he saw today, he would be there for his mate and would help him out financially if necessary. Chris decided he would confront Andy tomorrow night. Andy might be too proud to talk about his new job but he wasn't going to let his best friend degrade any further. But first he had to tackle Kelly and her rowing machine.

46

Victoria awoke to darkness. Through the blackness of the night she could barely make out the time on her watch. She raised her arm above her head and squinted at her wrist. It was now 9pm. Victoria was surprised she had slept for so long. John had obviously decided to let her enjoy her slumber and had left. What surprised her more was the fading memories of the dream that she had just unexpectedly experienced. She was now covered in a slender sticky film of sweat as beads of water ran down from her saturated brow.

She felt all tingly. It wasn't the first time she had woken up to find herself like this, but it had become more common of late. She tried with difficulty to memorise her erotic dream. It was as if it were on a sheet of paper left outside on a window sill with the condensation on the window blurring the view. She tried hard to take a mental picture of the sheet as before long the wind would catch it and soon it would be out of sight and the dream lost forever. Just before the wind took it away, she could make out the man who had caused the unconscious palpitation in her heart. This was her husband, the fit, mysterious, and highly charming Andy Pickering.

She knew some soul searching had to be done. She was at a crossroads and she would have to choose a direction. There was going to be a crash if she stayed at the stop sign too long trying to make up her mind. But that was for later, now it was time to scamper home. Andy was due to return from work some time ago. There was enough reasons for the man to be suspicious of his wife besides adding another one to the list. Moreover, Victoria wanted to be at home this evening when her husband got in, she knew right now he needed support. It had been a rough few days on Andy with the untimely death of his friend and he was going to need a shoulder to cry on. She was starting to feel Andy, the father of her children and the man in her dreams, was the road she needed to travel. She almost wouldn't blame Andy if he cried on someone else's shoulder as lately she had been a terrible wife and terrible companion to him. She hurriedly dressed. For a change she didn't delay to look in the mirror to groom herself. She just grabbed her coat and jumped into the Pickering family car. It was time to make the Pickerings a family again.

On the vanity dresser an unread yellow note lay stuck to the mirror.

'I can make time, see you in the coffee shop tomorrow at 2pm.'

47

'I need you tonight Andy, I have a bit of a problem and I need to discuss it with somebody.'

'I'm feeling sick Chris, can't you just talk to me over the phone?'

'It's too serious for a fucking phone conversation, I need to talk face to face.'

'Seriously Chris, I'm in bits with the flu, can't you talk to somebody else?'

Andy had done his shit, shower and shave this morning. It wasn't easy to drag himself out of his stupor but he had promised himself he would make this right somehow. Although he didn't have the flu, Andy now needed to think. He didn't need to go on the beer with Chris, he didn't deserve to go on the beer with Chris.

'You're my best friend Andy, this is a time I need you, come on don't let me down mate.'

'Okay, but we're not getting drunk tonight, you hear?' insisted Andy

'Absolutely not' Chris replied sternly but both Andy and he knew there was an element of tongue and cheek to his answer.

'Meet me at nine in the pub.'

'Alright Chris, see you then.'

It was just before nine when Andy arrived. Unusually Chris was on time.

'Two pints of lager and a packet of crisps mother.'

Mrs O' Neill duly obliged as Andy and Chris both took their places on the high stools at the bar.

'Well Andy how are ya? I haven't seen you round here in a long time. I hope you're keeping alright?' a genuine Mrs O'Neill asked as she placed the two pints on the bar counter.

'I'm fine Mrs O thanks for asking, bit of a flu at the moment but otherwise all's well.'

'And your lovely wife, she's keeping well I hope?' Mrs O'Neill may have moved countries many moons ago but she never lost the Irish lust for gossip.

'She's fine thanks Mrs O, and your husband, he's healthy and well?' Andy felt he had to get in the next question before she had a chance to prod any further

'Oh his great, gone playing cards tonight, he loves them cards.'

It was at that moment Andy saw his saviour out of the corner of his eye. He was a man with his arm outstretched and a twenty pound note in his hand.

'I think you have another customer there Mrs O.'

Andy said as he pointed in the direction of the man.

'Blast it, I do, I'll be back to ye shortly.'

As Mrs O'Neill pumped the alcohol from the keg below, Chris told Andy that they better take a seat in the nook, they needed privacy for what they were about to discuss.

Now in confidence Andy asked 'So out with it Chris, what's the problem that dragged me out of my sick bed?'

Chris' face turned stern, he began to speak slowly pronouncing each word individually as if they were not in a sentence 'The problem mate is that you're not sick.'

'What do you mean by that?' Andy responded defensively.

'I mean exactly as I said. I didn't bring you here tonight to help me, I brought you here to help you.'

Andy looked on with confusion and in trepidation.

'I know what's going on Andy, I know why you're often home late at night and why you're depressed at the moment.'

Andy moved in closer to Chris and whispered 'What do you mean?'

'I know where you work Andy.'

It was as if a plug hole on Andy's big toe had been released. In an instant, all the blood was lost from his face and a ghost now stared back at Chris.

'Jesus Andy, it's not that bad.'

Andy caught Chris by the lapel of his shirt and dragged him in even closer. Andy's teeth were clenched shut as he passionately told Chris

'It fucking is that bad, this is serious shit, the bastards killed Peter, we could be next'.

Andy's eyes darted around looking at everybody in the bar to see if they might be Recon.

'Why did you bring me to such an easy place to hide a member of Recon? They caught Peter and he went to a secluded park bench to have this discussion, are you fucking crazy?'

Chris thought it was a funny question for Andy to ask him and he knew exactly what to say next.

'Andy look at yourself, are *you* crazy?'

'I'm not messing these people are serious' he replied.

'What people? Who killed Peter? Is this still something to do with the grain store?'

'Of course it's all to do with it' Andy paused and took out a pen from his coat pocket. He grabbed a beer mat wrote on it and handed it to Chris.

Unit Firestorm, never ever say this name out loud. From now on we call it 'cigarettes'.

Chris realised he was wrong about his earlier assumptions. Andy wasn't labouring in a food grain store, something much more sinister was going on.

Chris never let on that he thought Andy was just working in a grain store. Andy also knew that Chris didn't know as much as he had earlier thought. But Andy needed to talk to somebody and the opportunity had come and he grasped it, for better or for worse. Andy began to explain the inconceivable events of the past seven months. Chris' eyes were wide and his ears pinned back as his brain struggled to grasp the enormity of everything he was hearing. Best of all Chris' best friend was a member of this Unit Firestorm. After hearing how Peter Johnson died, Chris understood Andy's dilemma and immediately told him he had no option but to co-operate in his assassination. He didn't want Andy to stay in a dishevelled state and he knew he needed reassurance that he had no choice in his actions. Chris and Andy talked and talked, the questions didn't stop coming and the answers were even more crazy than the questions.

'Cigarettes are very dangerous alright, did you only find this out yesterday?'

'Mum, for God's sake, don't be sneaking up on us like that.'

'I'm not sneaking up on ye at all, it's closing time and I've got a bed to go to.'

'Sorry Mrs O.'

Andy said as he finished his pint. Amazingly, Chris had only ordered one more pint all night. Chris was proud of his activities at the gym and his lack of activities at meal time and at the bar, but this was no time to boast about it. That conversation would be reserved for another night.

'Thanks again mum.'

'Thanks Mrs O, I hope it won't be as long till I see you again.'

A revitalised Andy left O'Neills. The spring was back in his step and the strut in his walk. Chris too was invigorated. This was by far the most interesting night of his life. He was now a target. Andy attempted to teach him how to recognise members of Recon but, in truth, Andy had never even met one, so this was only anecdotal advice at best.

Chris kept his promise, he found out what was happening to the man he used to call his best buddy. Andy too was determined to keep his promise to make everything right somehow, and with the help of Chris he believed it could happen.

'Are we a team?' Andy asked Chris.

'Damn right' Chris responded.

'Do you understand your life is now in danger and you can never tell a soul what you know?'

'Yes I do.'

'Now, let's not get ourselves killed.'

'Jesus, I don't plan on it Andy but I'm happy to do whatever needs doing.'

The two buddies spat on their hands and shook them.

'Catch' Andy said as he threw a mobile phone towards Chris.

'Here's your new mobile, I'll be in contact' Andy said before he walked down the road into the shadows of the night.

48

'Hello' a groggy Chris said as he answered the phone.

'Meet me outside your apartment in ten minutes, I'll be in the parked blue mini.'

'What, you don't own a mini?'

'I do now.'

Chris looked at his alarm clock, it was 5.40am. Chris previously told Andy he always wanted to be either a professional footballer or a private detective. It appeared he was getting his wish, maybe an appearance in the Premiership wouldn't be beyond the bounds of possibility after all!

The door slammed shut.

'Did you get this in the *Antiques Roadshow*?' Chris asked as he quickly opened the glove box, looked into it, and shut it again.

'It's not that easy to get a car in the dead of night. It's not my car, it's not your car and it works, that's all that matters.'

Andy let down the handbrake and slammed his foot down.

Chris continued 'Why couldn't you wait until morning to buy a car, like a normal person. I think that would be less suspicious somehow.'

'Because time is something we don't have, Peter was taken down within 3 days of his first contact with Officer Cohen. The clock started last night in O'Neills, we have 3 days, if we're lucky, before they find out about us and we end up joining Peter pushing up daisies in West Hampstead cemetery.'

'That's a good enough reason for me, excellent car choice Andy!'

'Thank you, glad we're on the same wavelength.'

'Speaking of the same wavelength, where the hell are we going?'

'We're going to find out why Peter risked his life to speak with Officer Cohen, we're going to Peter Johnson's house. Anyway why are you in such good form. Are you not afraid?'

'I know I should be, but I'm just so damn excited.'

'Well I'm not too sure how long that feeling will last but to be honest I'm glad you're on board. As they say, it's good to talk!'

'It sure is.'

Andy parked up close to Peter's house. The last time he parked here it was with the intention to kill him, now he had to put all that emotion to the back of his mind. Andy popped the boot and pulled out a sports bag. He unzipped the bag and handed Chris a long black coat similar to the one he was wearing himself.

'Put that on, now follow me and act natural.'

Andy gently closed the boot shut and pulled up the collar of his trench coat, it was a cold morning but the lapel also hid his face from view. Chris followed like a dog. It was like a scene from a blockbuster movie, Chris watched in awe as with a flick of his wrist Andy opened the back door.

'That was easy' Chris said to Andy as the pair entered the house.

'Easy when you know how.'

Then he turned to Chris and roared 'stop!'

Chris' middle finger was outstretched and only a couple of inches from hitting the light switch.

'So we don't turn on the lights then?' Chris responded.

'I don't think they'll work anyway but no we don't turn on the lights. I reckon Mrs Howell next door may get a bit suspicious if her deceased neighbour is still getting up for work in the morning. Come on, we're looking for a clue, probably a file, get busy, the sun is up, you don't need any more light.'

Both men began searching the kitchen, under cupboards,

over cupboards, in drawers, in breadbins, even under the carpet. Nothing was found except the stench of heavy mouldy smoke which was starting to disorientate them.

'I need some fresh air Andy I can't stick it in here anymore.'

'I know it's sick, I'm coming with you.'

It was nauseating and it felt like it had penetrated every orifice and pore in their bodies. Andy and Chris now stood outside the back door with their hands on their hips. Both took long deep breaths of fresh air.

'Sorry gentlemen, and who might you be?'

Chris' face was startled as he looked around to see an elderly lady with her shopping bag resting on the garden wall. She waited for an answer, it was time for Andy to step in.

'You're up early this morning. My parents always said it was the best part of the day.'

'And they were right' the woman responded, her concerned manner immediately easing.

'So what are you two young men up to this morning' this time the question was asked with a smile. Andy bought himself enough time to gather his wits.

'I assume you heard of the untimely death of Peter Johnson' Andy queried.

'I did indeed, God rest his soul. The whole street did with the fire brigade and ambulances and the commotion.'

'Well we're from Joyce's undertakers and we're just leaving some flowers that were given to the Johnson family at his house as requested by the family.'

'Oh, that's interesting.'

'I know, we don't ask the who or why, we just carry out the wishes.'

'And you're doing a fine job too, I'm only keeping you from your work now. I'll be on my way, have a good day.'

'And you too.'

'Now that was impressive, that was way more convincing than last night when you told me you had the flu!' Chris said as he gave Andy a congratulating slap on the back.

'Come on, remember the clock is on. I sincerely doubt it but that old lady could have been Recon. The longer we investigate, the greater the probability we'll end up dead.'

Chris didn't need to be told twice, they had only checked the kitchen, there were plenty more rooms to go.

'You take the sitting room, I'll go up stairs' Andy ordered almost feeling as if he was on duty again.

The firemen had done a very good job. The smoke was bellowing and the flames were gushing out of Peter's bedroom when Andy had left the scene. Yet the stairs to the first floor were still fully intact. The stench was even worse on the first floor. The air was heavy and the walls were covered in black soot. Andy felt as if his lungs were acting like a catalytic converter. They had a lot of work on their hands just to get some fresh air to his blood cells.

'Nothing here mate' Chris shouted back at Andy.

'Nothing here either.'

Andy knew the best chance of finding the file would be in Peter's bedroom, however, as he peered in the door, all that he could see was a black shell of a room. It appeared the only object to survive the blaze was the metal bed that still lay intact in the middle of the room.

'You okay?'

Chris came into the room and put his sympathetic hand on Andy's shoulder.

'I'm fine, I'm just trying to think what we do now. We need that file, we need a lead.'

Andy knew he had started the clock, it was now a countdown and there was no time to waste.

'Do you think the information was burned?' Chris asked.

'I hoped not, but now my gut instinct is that it is. There is one other possibility, maybe Peter had given all the information to this Officer Cohen. His house hasn't been burnt, so if the file was hidden there it's still hidden there. I think we know our next port of call.'

Andy turned to walk out the door of Peter's bedroom. Suddenly he was struck with a moment of clear déjà vu.

Andy excitedly turned to Chris, that's it, that's the clue. Oh how stupid I've been when it had been staring at me in the face all along. Chris hurriedly stood beside Andy and looked in the direction Andy was staring. In front of them was the door opening to the corridor outside. The door was now off the hinges and what remained of it was up against the bedroom wall.

Chris sighed 'There's nothing there'.

'Oh but there was' Andy enthusiastically replied.

49

The mini was once again on a mission.

'Where are we going now?'

'Just down the road, I need to give a call into an old acquaintance.'

'Come on, stop being so mysterious. What's the plan, what used to be on that door?' Chris asked impatiently.

'I saw something very peculiar on that door the night Peter was assassinated. Obviously for my sanity I've tried to forget the whole event ever took place. That's the reason why I didn't think of this earlier. That night while I kept watch I noticed the dartboard on the bedroom door had a picture stuck to it. Three darts were going through the picture. Three darts were embedded in the face of The General.'

Andy was momentarily surprised that Chris didn't find this absolutely amazing. Chris squinted over at Andy, his expression remained puzzled. Andy then realised that he still had so much to tell his best mate.

'Let's grab a cup of tea and a sandwich, you've a lot to catch up on.'

Chris was glad of the hot tea between his hands. It was another cold morning and it was just hitting the spot. He listened with intrigue, as Andy described the character called 'The General'. He sounded like a caricature, but Andy assured him it was real life and he was a man not to be messed with. Andy continued to explain everything in detail especially the unusual goings on of his first few Firestorm days.

'Sorry, I got a little lost there' Chris said

'Who owned the navy BMW again?'

'Now your catching on' replied Andy

'That's the very reason we're going to the police station'

Andy explained that he knew Sergeant Green, West Hampstead's local sergeant. He was a man that had come to mind when he held the red button in the white room. The sergeant may not have enough power to evacuate the underground network, but he could certainly do Andy a favour and check out the registration of the navy BMW.

'This is where you have to step up to the plate Chris. Peter already got caught for trying to talk to police. That means I certainly cannot walk into that police station without the possibility of attracting Recon attention. That means you will be walking into that station.'

It was music to his ears, Chris was ready, willing and able.

'Hello sergeant, how are you?' Chris waited impatiently as Andy sweet talked on the phone. They discussed the weather, Victoria and the Directacom five-a-side. Finally Andy found his opening and asked for the favour. As Andy expected, he said he couldn't divulge any information over the phone, but that he could come to his office where he could discuss any issues he may have. This is where Andy's ability to produce the white lie once again came to the forefront. This time he had been in a minor accident and the driver of the other car had driven off. Luckily he managed to get the car's registration before it made its getaway. He now had to take the car to the garage but he had a friend in West Hampstead that could call in. Chris was his name and he would be in shortly.

'No problem at all Andy, hope there's not too much damage to your car' said the sergeant.

'I'm sure I'll find out soon enough, anyway thanks again for that' Andy replied and he lowered the mobile from his ear. Andy pulled a pocket notebook from his trench coat, flicked through a few pages, turned to Chris and said

'This is the registration number, act natural, it's all very simple. All you need to know is I was in an accident and need the reg of a car. Basically you're just doing me a favour.'

Chris grabbed the notebook, took three deep breaths and opened the car door. The police station was just around the corner. Chris threw his empty plastic teacup into a street bin as he passed and marched up the steps to West Hampstead Police Station.

Minutes later the door of the mini opened and Chris got back in. It was only 10am, it had been a very productive morning so far and his latest task had proved effortless.

'Well have you got a name for me?' queried Andy.

'I do indeed, his name is Terry White, address 24 Hammer Drive, Greenwich.'

Andy's eyes opened wide, his mouth now ajar. Andy had certainly not expected to know of the driver. Although he had only met Terry on a couple of occasions he was well aware that he was a dark character that led a very secretive life. This information put a new spin on everything. Andy now knew he had a secret weapon that could lead him to the information he desperately needed. Andy wondered if there was a connection between Peter, The General and Terry White. His secret weapon could give him the answers. It was exceedingly dangerous but Andy decided that it was time to add a new member to the team. He pulled out his mobile and began dialling.

'Hey ya, Andy here. I know we haven't talked in a while but I need to meet with you. Are you available at lunch?'

Andy paused 'Perfect, Luigi's around the corner from the library at 12.30. See you then.'

It was time to head to the heart of London town. He debated whether to take the underground or take his poor mini into the gridlock traffic.

'We're taking the mini' Chris said reading Andy's mind.

'Starsky and Hutch had their *Ford Torino* the Dukes of Hazard had their *Dodge Charger* we have Daisy the Mini!'

Andy couldn't help but laugh. At that moment it did seem like they were a crime fighting duo and what duo would be complete without their trusty automobile.

Andy put his hand on the gear stick, pulled it back into first, hit the accelerator and commanded 'Let's go Daisy'.

50

'Thank you Gordon, Thank you so much for everything' said the elderly lady as she left the government office.

Gordon Fletcher had just dealt with another satisfied voter. Her carer's allowance would be backdated and a lump sum would arrive in her account in the morning. Gordon's suit wasn't flashy, his hair was parted at the side and combed through and his cheeks gave off a country red glow. Gordon was always a man of the people. He knocked on people's doors and found out what affected them and always tried to get business into the Gloucestershire area. Gordon was even head of the Gloucester branch of the *Saint Vincent de Paul*. Most analysts claimed Gordon's devotion to his electorate had actually held him back in politics. It was probably a fair analysis, Gordon always saw himself at making a difference in the micro level, not the macro level. Gordon was usually too close to the canvas to see the big picture.

The Prime Minister understood the amount of time and dedication Gordon put into his job. If only every other MP put that amount of energy into their post then none of them would lose their seat in the next election and that government would remain in power. The Prime Minister decided that this kind of dedication had to be rewarded. Others in the party would see that it's not just talking on television and showing up to big sporting events that get you a seat in cabinet; hard work on the ground would be rewarded too. Gordon would probably not accept a full ministerial job. He wouldn't have the manner to deal with the media nor the time for local level issues. Therefore the Prime Minister decided to give Gordon a junior post, he would be the Chief Secretary to the Treasury.

It had been five months since the cabinet reshuffle and

already life had changed immeasurably for Gordon Fletcher. Gordon and his wife were delighted with his promotion. He had recognition for his earnest endeavours and he had a pay rise to match. As Gordon attacked his new role he found that subtlety was in fact more critical than drive to get things done. When asked questions by the media, no definitive action was to be announced on any issue. All answers were to be positive but with no clarity of how goals would be achieved. Even in meetings, much time was spent discussing ideas, little, if no time, was spent putting these ideas into force. The cabinet meetings frustrated Gordon, he wouldn't mind having less time with his electorate if his time was still being used to good effect. Time spent in these gatherings was time Gordon would never get back again.

As a cabinet, decisions had to be made. The country wouldn't run itself. Gordon learnt that decisions were not made in cabinet meetings, they were made in offices, corridors and pubs. It's not that his colleagues were bad people, it's just the way things had been done for years, and the way they would continue to be done. Judgements were generally made for the good of the people and the nation, but there was usually a slight personal angle on all these decisions. Gordon could attempt to sail against the currents and fight the way things worked in the higher offices of power, or he could sail with his fellow ministers and make things better for the people of Gloucestershire and Britain from inside the cabinet. It is here that he would have the power to really make some changes. For the party, for the salary and for the people, he decided to remain a junior minister and make the right decisions in the offices, corridors and pubs around Westminster.

Gordon was used to dealing with the common man. He grew up on a dairy farm and he was one of those people. He was in touch with his public, enjoyed their humour, understood their problems and felt he was there to serve them. These were not the people he met in the corridors of power. Big businesses seemed to make all the decisions around here. John Black was Gordon's front bench minister. John was excellent at dealing with the macro level issues. He had a suave demeanour that endeared him to everybody. Business men found him very approachable and always remarked about the fine job he did. Gordon didn't really know John Black, but from afar he admired his style. While Gordon huffed and puffed to get small matters sorted, John just flicked his pen and made massive decisions without sweat, toil or fuss.

One of the junior minister's assignments was to oversee finances for the 2012 London Olympics. The Prime Minister told Gordon that government finances were getting tight and he had to stick rigidly to the Olympic budget and ensure the taxes that accrued from the construction found their way back to the government coffers. It was on one of these projects that Gordon had most association with his superior. John Black had knocked on Gordon's office door late one evening.

'Come in.'

'Hello Gordon. How are you? I hear congratulations are in order. Well done, I wish you and Mrs Fletcher the very best of luck, especially with the late nights and early mornings!' John said as he reached his hand over the desk and firmly shook hands with Gordon.

'I'm hanging in there John. Thanks very much, I didn't think anybody here knew Claire was pregnant.'

'Ah you have to keep up to date on the lives of your friends. Can I sit down a moment?'

'Of course, what can I do for you?'

'Nothing really, I'm just here to have a chat about some upcoming meetings. As you know the attendance records for government meetings are now available to public access under the recent amendment to the *Freedom of Information Act*. As your aware I deal with most issues from my office, I've always felt most of those meetings are a bit of a waste of time.'

'I'd have to agree there!' Gordon interjected.

'Good, so you understand where I'm coming from. The problem is that it reflects poorly on the finance minister of a country when he doesn't go to any meetings. My political advisors have requested me to attend a number of meetings a week so that the opposition can't use the attendance statistics against me. As you haven't seen me at many meetings I thought it appropriate to let you know why you will now be seeing me more often.'

'No problem at all, will be glad to have your experience in the room' Gordon replied.

'Now, for my own health and sanity, I'm not planning on attending every meeting on every topic available so I've had a look through the upcoming schedule and I've decided that I'll take an active interest in the Olympic village project. It's a big project and my knowledge might come in handy. How does that sound to have an extra pair of eyes and ears on that project?'

'Sounds like an excellent idea John, I'll look forward to your assistance.'

'Good to hear. Now, you should really have an early night and surprise that wife of yours. After all she is pregnant with your child.'

'Do you know, I think I will.'

'Good man' John said as he got up. Again he produced his hand for another handshake, again, it was firm and meaningful.

'See you tomorrow.'

'Feel free to call in at any time' Gordon said as he watched John walk out the door. Gordon went home happy that night. He was glad to have John Black as his chief, and he was pleased that they had a good working relationship. However, the next few weeks would prove interesting at first, then rewarding, but they would end with him fearing for his life and the lives of his wife and unborn baby.

51

'If you're not using the computers for library purposes then please finish up now as there is a large queue of people waiting.'

Jennifer didn't want to drag anybody off their computer, but fair is fair and when there was a queue she always gave people a gentle reminder. It was now a welcome oddity when somebody approached her information desk and asked her a question about a book. Usually the questions would range from

'How long does it take to get on a computer', or 'where are the toilets?', to 'where is the closest McDonald's from here?'.

Still, it was a job she enjoyed and it gave her plenty of time to read all the books that surrounded her.

It was time for lunch. Jennifer took off her reading glasses and put them in their case. Then she put up her *closed for lunch* sign on the desk and went around the corner to the café.

'Hello Andy, long time no see, good to see you again' she said as she hugged Andy.

'And how are you Chris?'

Chris and Jennifer never really saw eye to eye before. It wasn't that they shared any bad blood. It wasn't that they openly discussed how they felt about each other either, it was just both knew they didn't see eye to eye and both didn't push the issue any further. It was just two polar opposites brought together by the union of their best friend's marriage. Chris enjoyed his pint while Jennifer enjoyed her wine. Chris read *The Sun*, Jennifer read Joyce. Chris loved football, Jennifer loved the opera. Chris was proud of the amount of women he had slept with, Jennifer was proud of the amount of books she had read. However, at this time differences, or indifferences, had to be put aside.

'I'm fine thanks Jennifer' Chris answered.

Andy and Jennifer chatted about the past few months and

how sad Andy was that Victoria and Jennifer had fallen out.

'Best friends are best friends, you two should really draw a line in the sand and meet up for a coffee. I know, it's none of my business, that's just my thinking' Andy said.

If only he knew the reason Jennifer thought to herself.

Jennifer had grown to like Andy over the years. As she sat across the table from him she wondered should she continue to stay out of the Pickering's life or should she divulge the truth and show Victoria for what she really is. She didn't have long to debate what she should do as Andy came straight in with a question that utterly threw her.

'Okay Jennifer, I obviously wanted to meet up with you for a reason, that reason is very serious. I can't force you to do anything you don't want to do but let me say your help would be infinitely appreciated. Your help will save lives and bring people to justice. But if you help you will no doubt put your life in danger. I'm really sorry that I can't explain too much more. If I do then your life will already be in danger whether you like it or not. Can you help us, can you help to save lives?'

Jennifer had been stuck in the latest *Harry Potter* book for most of the morning. Although she usually didn't succumb to popular culture there was something about J.K. Rowling's creations that endeared Jennifer to them. There was a large gap in the degree of importance between reading *Harry* behind the information desk and hearing Andy's plea for help. Her brain was still trying to catch up. Finally she spoke.

'What, what and more what? What on earth are you talking about? You work at Directacom as some kind of pen pushing manager. You're not a member of the KGB.'

Andy half expected this response. He wanted to explain everything to make her decision to come on board easier. However, if he told her everything then it would be too late to turn back. It was a case of the chicken and the egg and Andy didn't know which came first. Andy rubbed his chin and sighed

'It's not easy Jennifer. As I say, I'd love to explain everything but if I do, you will be in great danger, even if you don't choose to help us.'

'You're going to have to do better than this' she said shrugging her shoulders.

'Are either of you in trouble with the law?' she demanded.

'Absolutely not, we're not actually in any trouble, we're just trying to do the right thing. Okay, let me put it to you like this. Can you imagine it's 1942, you're living in the Shetland Islands and you had never heard that your country was fighting in a world war. If you knew, it would be difficult, but you would have to join the army and do the right thing. If you didn't know you could continue farming your sheep but fellow countrymen would die because you are not there to help. Which option would you prefer?'

Jennifer weighed up Andy's quirky question. There was a part of her that just refused to believe the situation was as serious to her life as he had suggested.

'Okay, Okay, tell me what it is you have to tell me and I will do my very best to help if I can.'

It was the answer Andy was hoping to here.

'We'd better order some food because this is going to take some time' Andy said. All three looked at Luigi's menu. It was about to be the most interesting meal of Jennifer's life. The questions kept coming with the answers even crazier than the questions. It was a repeat performance of the previous night. In the space of fifteen hours Andy had managed to put three lives at risk.

Jennifer interrupted him, 'Okay this *cigarettes* thing is all a bit 'Tom Clancy' but where do I come in.'

'Well we just found out the owner of the BMW this morning, it belongs to a man you know very well, Terry White.'

Jennifer was truly taken aback. This revelation had shocked her more than all the crazy Unit Firestorm stories Andy had just told. Jennifer had never uttered Terry's name nor did she hear anybody else discuss him since that fateful day almost two years ago.

52

'Excuse me, what do I do now, my mouse has died' Terry asked as he oscillated his hand round and round on the mouse pad.

'You'll have to bury him I suppose' Jennifer replied.

It wasn't the funniest joke Terry had ever heard, but the reply was worth a smile, especially when he saw who he was smiling at.

'I'll fix it for you' she said as she leaned over Terry and pressed 'Ctrl', 'Alt' and 'Delete' on the keyboard.

Terry could smell her hair as she passed him. Every strand combined to smell like a bunch of dark red roses on a fine September morning. As she bent forwards Terry knew he should move his swivel chair back a little to give her some room, but the sweet smelling rose had drawn him in. A lock of her long brown hair now sat on Terry's shoulder. He wished it would never leave. Jennifer could tell Terry had stayed a little too close for comfort, yet she was surprised to find that she still felt at ease. Terry's rugged good looks were a clear draw for her, but even in ten minutes she had found Terry exuded an aura, an energy, that suggested there was substance to this man. Substance was something that was lacking from every man she had ever dated. Once the skin was peeled off, no layers were found.

'No need to get out the shovel, I've given him CPR and your mouse is going again' Jennifer said as she sat down on her seat again.

From that moment on, learning new computer skills didn't seem so important anymore, there was a much more important reason why neither Terry nor Jennifer would miss their weekly computer class.

It had been the best year of Jennifer's life. Terry enjoyed literature, he even had his own private library. He enjoyed the arts and actually listened with interest when she spoke. He also didn't see five pints in the local pub as an ideal night out. He was like *the* perfect man. Fate had intervened to stall Terry's computer and the magic flowed from there.

Insurance. Jennifer had always wondered how a man as talented as this could end up in insurance. It was an anomaly that Jennifer had chosen to ignore. Deep down Jennifer knew there was more to Terry's day than giving quotes and filing claims. Every time she asked about his work the topic of conversation was briskly changed. It disturbed her that she lay in bed with a man whom she didn't really know, yet simultaneously it also excited her. It also helped that life between the sheets was incredible. There was a chemistry between the pair that was explosive. If each were an element on the periodic table then they would be on the opposite sides, ready to react with each other at any given moment. Terry had brutish raw passion and force, and when combined with his gentle artistic side it made for a varied and exciting love life. It was a love life she felt she could never tire of, Terry was a man she would never tire of.

The birds chirped and sang their way to the arrival of a new day. The date was June 21st, the longest day of the year. A sliver of light came through Terry's curtains, it was just enough to illustrate the beauty of the day outside. Terry's arm was outstretched and it wrapped around Jennifer like a glove. The pair enjoyed their one year anniversary dinner the previous night. Three hundred and sixty five days had flown by. Jennifer snuggled into Terry's chest a little more. Last night had been perfect and she knew right now was a moment to savour. She recognised there would be some times in her life to come when it would be challenging, when she would wonder what happiness was. This was happiness Jennifer thought to herself as she took a mental picture of the moment and filed it away in her memory bank. Then it happened.

Terry jumped up and was now sitting upright on the mattress alert for any activity. Terry thought he heard something, and he was right. Five seconds later he heard another creek of a floorboard. It was time to take action. Terry turned to his puzzled girlfriend.

'Be very quiet, get into the wardrobe now and close the door. Stay there until I say otherwise.'

Jennifer didn't know what was going on, but Terry was not a man to argue with and this definitely wasn't the time to start. As she gradually lifted the bed sheets to leave the bed Terry pushed her hard in the back.

'Move' he said in a harsh tone.

It was the first time Terry had done anything physically untoward towards Jennifer. The perfect moment had definitely passed.

The hinge of the wardrobe door was slightly askew. Jennifer tried in vain to pull the door shut. Then came the gunfire. Her heart nearly stopped beating. Not one word was said yet two shots were fired. She peered out from behind the door. Her field of vision was very narrow and all she could see was the end of the bed, nothing appeared to be moving in the room. She craved to see what lay outside the door. Was the love of her life lying in a pool of blood gasping for breath as she stayed hiding only yards away in the wardrobe? It was a horrible image but at this moment it was a distinct possibility. Jennifer weighed up her options.

Stay or Go, Stay or Go.

She then decided, Terry had told her to stay in the wardrobe and that is where she was going to stay.

Fifteen minutes later she remained surrounded by suits,

shirts and trousers. It had only been a quarter of an hour but it felt like a lifetime. She looked at her silver watch and decided to give it one more minute. She picked up an old broom that was lying against the back of the wardrobe and grasped it with both hands. When she dashed out the door she would be ready for whatever greeted her, but before Jennifer had the chance to defend herself she finally heard Terry's voice.

'Are you okay Jenny?'

'I'm, I'm fine' Jennifer stammered in reply.

'Well done, I must just warn you about a few things before you step out of the wardrobe, is that okay?'

Terry was speaking as if he was a negotiator in a hostage situation. Jennifer just wanted to get out of the wardrobe and back to real life.

'Yes fine, what the hell just happened?' Jennifer asked, this time her voice was clear and her tone authoritative.

Terry began 'First of all I'm fine. I waited a while before I spoke with you in case there were men waiting outside that might come in. No matter what happened I didn't want you harmed.'

'Come on, what the hell is going on, can I get out of here now' a clearly agitated Jennifer shouted back at Terry.

'Okay, okay. When you come out there will be two dead men lying on the floor. I know it is shocking, but remember it's them that are dead otherwise it would be us.'

Jennifer was speechless. She cautiously opened the door. Two men lay surrounded by blood on the fluffy sky blue carpet. She looked up, Terry was now wearing gloves and had started to cut the carpet with a utility knife. He pulled up the blood stained carpet and cut it into three sections. Then he grabbed the body of one of the men and dragged it along the ground as if it were a bag of refuse for bin collection. He placed the body on one of the carpet sections and began to roll it.

'I'm so sorry you're here to see this, but I really must be quick and deal with these bodies.'

Jennifer sat on the edge of the bed, her whole body was shaking.

Within a couple of minutes Terry had wrapped both bodies in carpet and tied with string.

'I've got to get rid of these straight away' Terry said.

'You should leave now as well. I'm so sorry you were put through this. I've got to move now. I'll ring you later on and explain everything. The most important thing is we are both alright.'

He threw one of the bodies over his shoulder and motioned to Jennifer to leave the room. Jennifer, still dressed in only a silk nightdress, hurriedly put on some clothes and left.

'I love you. I'll call you tonight' Terry said as she walked out the back door. She didn't reply. Terry loaded the bodies into his car and set out to take care of the situation.

Jennifer's phone rang that night but she didn't answer it. It rang twenty-two times from 4pm to midnight. Each time it rang she stared at it. She wanted to answer the phone, believe any magical fable Terry would tell her and carry on with the wonderful life she was leading. Unfortunately, life isn't that simple. She considered the evidence. Terry held a gun close to his bed and with just two bullets Terry had managed to instantaneously kill two men. He then knew exactly how to dispose of them. She preferred the insurance story. Jennifer didn't answer the phone that heartbreaking night, and Terry had never rung again.

53

'Here, have a drink of water' Andy said as he grabbed the jug and filled Jennifer's glass. She was now pale. A sluice gate had opened that had been firmly shut for a long time and now the memories started to flood out. With the floods of memories came the floods of tears. Andy and Chris looked at each other, both equally unknowing as to what to do now. Chris pulled out a few napkins from the holder and handed them to her. He felt awkward in this situation but at least he had done something. She accepted the tissues gratefully and began to dry her sodden cheeks. Andy was amazed by the outburst of tears. He had never known Jennifer to be a 'drama queen'.

Andy had no idea why Terry and Jennifer's relationship had ended so abruptly. All he knew was that his wife had asked him not to bring it up whenever he met Jennifer. Dutifully he followed her instructions. Whatever happened, from the mountain of crumpled up napkins on the table, it appeared it was something serious. Andy just hoped all the emotion wouldn't be too much for Jennifer and that she could still be their secret weapon.

'Alright Jennifer are you okay? Are you ready to hear how I need you to help me?'

A sniffling Jennifer shook her head, took a deep breath and responded

'I'm sorry you had to see that guys, as you probably understand, the breakup with Terry was a very emotional time for me.'

Jennifer took a final deep breath

'Yes, I'm ready.'

'Terry White has something to do with *cigarettes*. His presence in Canary Wharf and outside the facility is simply not coincidental. We need to find the missing link between Peter, Terry and The General. We need you to see Terry again and get reacquainted so that you can search his house for that missing link. That way we can finish the work Peter was doing and bring the truth to the nation. Can we count on you?'

It was a horrible proposition Andy had given Jennifer. There were so many reasons why she didn't want to go along with the plan. Firstly, she didn't want to open that old wound up again, secondly, turning up to his door would surely appear extremely suspicious, and finally she had seen Terry gun down two men with the ease of a navy seal. Unfortunately for Jennifer, her options were limited. Andy assured her that a countdown had been started last night and all three would be dead in a matter of days if they couldn't expose the truth. She wished she could finish her meal, go back to the library and finish off *Harry Potter* this afternoon. But *Harry* and the Hogwarts crew would have to wait.

'I see my choices are limited Andy, I'll help, but I want one of you guys on call at all times if I'm with Terry. She pulled out her phone, give me both your numbers now.'

Andy reached into his coat pocket and pulled out another mobile phone.

'From now on this is your phone for all contact to us. There are already two numbers in the phone book, Chris' and mine.'

She was taken aback by Andy's preparation but gladly accepted the phone.

'Have you got your car in town?'

'No, I came in on the tube' she replied.

'Okay, you're coming with us then. The plan is that we are going to stake out Terry's house and when he leaves we'll follow him. Then, whenever he stops, be it just for petrol or if he is going to the opera, we will plant you in a situation to accidentally bump into him. Sound okay?'

She submissively replied 'I suppose so.'

Andy continued 'okay that's the bad news, here's the good news. Do you have any other clothes with you at the library?'

'No, why?'

'Because we need to have you ready for any situation; out for a run, going to the shops, or going to the opera. If Terry's still in insurance he won't be home for another few hours. In the mean time we're going on a rapid one hour shopping spree before we stakeout his house.'

Andy put his credit card on the table and looked at Jennifer 'Are you ready to shop?'

54

'Gordon, there is a man here to see you. He doesn't have an appointment but he says he's here to help raise money for the Saint Vincent de Paul.'

Gordon's head lifted from the mountain of paperwork that lay in front of him. His interest had certainly been piqued. Gordon volunteered at his local branch for many years. He loved to see the progress in those that required the assistance but just as importantly he recognised the immense good that volunteering did for the soul. It was a two way relationship and all parties benefited. Gordon laid his pen on the desk, removed his glasses and asked that the unexpected guest be allowed in.

The man was well attired wearing a golf blazer with big golden buttons and a polo neck top. He was mature in age and shuffled into the room using his walking stick for support.

'Damn hip is troubling me again.'

Gordon thought it an unusual opening line from a gentleman without an appointment and for a moment became worried he may be another complainer about the National Health Service. However, the simile which accompanied the comment showed Gordon that no protestations were about to take place.

'Have a seat Mr King, am I correct that this is your name?'

'It is indeed Gordon, you don't mind if I call you Gordon do you?'

The man was warm and kind, and Gordon was intrigued as to why he was sitting in front of him.

'My first name is Robert, I'd prefer if you called me that. It's a pleasure to meet you Gordon.'

He maintained eye contact as he shook Gordon's hand over the pile of paperwork.

'See that red tape. What good does that do for the man on the street? I prefer action to paper, I prefer sharing to gaining, I prefer to sleep soundly at night knowing I've done all I can. Do you understand what I mean Gordon?'

Gordon was amazed at what he was hearing and he did understand.

Robert continued 'I know you understand; I've heard about your good works, especially with the Saint Vincent de Paul. You and me think the same. For me it's the work of Oxfam. My wife lives for the charity and the only thing I live for more than the charity is my beautiful wife. I glow in the knowledge that I have helped hundreds of people make a life for themselves. The reason I'm here is that I have thought of a way to save thousands of lives in Africa, but I need your help to make it happen. For your assistance, I will give a million pounds to your local branch of the Saint Vincent de Paul.'

Gordon stared back at his visitor amazed and excited but a little doubtful about the reality of the proposal. He was impressed at his pitch and Robert had certainly caught his attention.

The men only spoke for another minute before Robert had to leave. Gordon was intrigued by the discussion. Robert arranged to meet him that evening in the Pig and Whistle pub. Gordon felt that maybe this was the good work he could do in the offices, corridors and pubs around Westminster.

Gordon checked Roberts past. It was one of countless donations to charity. He knew he was dealing with a good man that he could rely on.

When the pair met for a drink, Gordon was prepared to do whatever it took to make these works of good happen. Although he had never been involved in unscrupulous activities before, he felt he could sleep with an easy conscience on this matter. He agreed to give Robert King the location for the Olympic Village as soon as it was decided. Robert's development company would buy the site and when the decision was announced it would quadruple in value. Robert would give the profits, minus SVP's one million pounds, to Oxfam. As Robert said, if the charities don't get the money it will end up in some other developer's back pocket.

55

'That's it, that's the navy BMW' exclaimed Andy as 'Daisy the mini' passed by No. 24 Hammer Drive. Andy was lucky to catch a glimpse of the car. It was now evening time and Terry had just arrived home from 'work' and the garage door was closing as he walked away from his car. Andy went to the top of the road and turned the car around, he then drove down close to the house and parked the car. The surveillance began.

'It could be a long night, Chris. I hope we've enough refreshments.' Andy said as he looked at the bag of food they bought in preparation.

Chris pulled out his mobile 'don't worry I've got Domino's on speed dial!'

Everyone shared a laugh. Andy looked around the car; with three people's lives in acute danger, it was amazing to see a chorus of smiles.

'Pull out the sandwiches and we'll have ourselves a stakeout picnic.' Andy's suggestion was met with resounding approval and the happy family began to munch into their meal.

Andy threw his sandwich on the dash and turned on the ignition. The navy BMW was on the move once more. Terry turned left out of the drive and accelerated down the road.

'Step on it Pickering' Chris demanded as they followed the tail-lights of their target. The BMW was making swift progress and Daisy was flat out to keep up with her. Terry was a born driver and he never switched off, especially if he was behind the wheel of a BMW *5-Series* with an impressive 306 brake horse-power.

'Keep going, keep going' was the call from Chris as Andy approached a set of lights on the cusp of turning red.

Andy did as directed, it was the only way to keep with

Terry. Chris was in his element with the excitement of the chase. Jennifer felt in stark contrast to Chris and her two hands grabbed the sides of the seat. To Jennifer's relief Terry pulled in and stopped his car. He got out, walked across the street and entered a computer store.

'Okay, this is our chance. Let's go through a few things first.'

Andy raised his right hand and started to count out each item with his fingers.

'Number one. Your clothes. I think your work outfit is perfect, so no need to change. Number two. Your story. You must be looking for something specific. Something general can be suspicious. Do you have broadband at home?'

'Yes' Jennifer responded

'Excellent, look for a DSL Filter for your telephone line. It's a blocker you need for broadband. Finally, number three. Why are you in Camberwell in a computer store? You are visiting a friend out here after work and thought you'd pop in for the Filter on the way. Any questions?'

The question that was on Jennifer's mind most was how Andy could have turned into this dynamo in such a short space of time. But it was no time to discuss such matters, it was a time for action.

'I'm ready, I have my mobile in my pocket and your number is on the screen Andy. If I feel the need, I will hit the green button while my hand is still in my pocket. When the phone rings, don't pick it up. Just go straight into the store, Chris can be my husband and can whisk me away from the situation.'

'Okay, if you really feel you have to, then press the button, but if Chris drags you away as your husband, we'll never get the information from Terry. Just bear that in mind as we're all in some danger without it.'

'I understand the circumstances perfectly Andy' Jennifer replied, slightly annoyed that he felt he had to explain the situation to her again.

'Best of luck Jennifer' Chris added as he pulled the car seat back. Jennifer hunched her back and squirmed her way out of the mini.

Chris and Andy sat silently, they both looked at the computer store even though they couldn't see inside. Andy pulled out his phone and checked it wasn't on silent. He then put it on the dash. Chris started to bite his fingernails. He had to do something and they were getting a bit long anyway. With the silence in the car, the only noise Andy could now hear was the munching of Chris' fingernails. The noise started to pierce through Andy and he heard each bite as if it were as loud as a kick drum. When Chris put down his hand Andy breathed a sigh of relief. He didn't want to see red just because of a simple thing like biting ones nails. But Chris hadn't finished yet and when he raised his other hand Andy caught a large packet of crisps from the food bag and shoved them in Chris' face.

'Are you hungry, then here munch on a few of these.'

Chris enjoyed a few crisps, but this was the first moment he had seen the pressure get to Andy. Chris knew he had just put all their lives in danger and he had done well to remain calm for so long. Then the silence was broken by the ringtone of Andy's phone.

56

Andy grabbed the phone from the dash and looked at the screen. It was dead, but the phone appeared to be still ringing. Then he realised it was his regular phone that was making the noise. He reached into his pocket and pulled it out. 'Vic' was the name on the screen.

'Don't take your eyes off that shop Andy said to Chris. I've gotta take this.'

'Hello Vic, how are you?'

'I'm fine. I'm sorry I wasn't home last night until nine, I lost track of time at one of the girls houses. I saw your note that you were meeting with Chris for a drink, did he manage to cheer you up?'

'He did indeed, he did a great job.'

'Excellent, you were gone very early this morning, will you be home soon? I'll cook us up something nice' Victoria asked.

'Afraid I can't say, new order in this week and flat out at work.'

Chris hit Andy hard on the shoulder and pointed at the computer store. Terry and Jennifer were walking out together. They crossed the road and both got into the BMW.

'Sorry Vic, gotta go now, chat later.'

Andy ended the call, turned the key and hit the accelerator. Terry arrived back at his house after his errand. He couldn't believe his luck, maybe there was such a thing as fate after all. He needed a new modem for his computer. While surveying his options in the computer store a woman came up behind him and asked him if his 'mouse' was dead. It had been two long years since he had last heard this voice. He immediately turned and smiled, it was Jennifer, the love of his life.

Terry had never got a chance to explain what happened on

that cruel summer's morning. Maybe his time had come. Terry went out on a limb and invited Jennifer out to dinner. To his pleasant surprise she accepted, with one condition. Terry had to cook for her at his house. She had always loved Terry's cooking and Terry felt that he had a chance to impress his shining star once more.

'Daisy' pulled up outside 24 Hammer Drive. Andy was delighted with the way things were progressing. Within twenty minutes of meeting Terry, Jennifer had made her way into his home.

'It definitely could be a long night now' Andy remarked to Chris.

'Can you pass me the bag mate.'

Chris handed Andy the crisps. Chris was due at the gym tonight but Kelly would have to wait. There would not be much point in getting in shape if you found yourself dead two days later.

'It's been a long day Chris, I think we should take it in turns to sleep. I know I'm wrecked. Will you keep watch for the first two hours and we will swap it back and forth? Wake me if you see anything suspicious, anything at all.'

'No problem Andy' Chris was only too happy to be the private eye once again.

57

'I feel we must have that talk Jennifer. I know it's disturbing but otherwise it will always hang over the two of us' Terry said as he put down the tin of almond paste next to the cooker and turned to face Jennifer.

'I don't think so Terry. I spent two years deleting that day from my mind. I really don't want to drag it all back again. It's over, it never happened to me. Make it so that it never happened to you.'

'Okay, but can you do one thing for me?'

'What's that?' Jennifer asked anxiously.

'Can you stir the sauce while I go set the table?'

'That I can do' she said with a smile.

Terry was disappointed that he couldn't tell her what had happened that morning. He was confident that if she heard him out then she could find a way to understand. Hopefully she could find a way to love him again. Terry was elated to have Jennifer back in his kitchen, but without confronting that day, it could never really work.

Jennifer stirred the sauce. When she woke up this morning this is the last place she expected to have dinner. Yet she was strangely looking forward to her dining experience tonight. The meal was guaranteed to be divine, the company intellectual and if anything went wrong help was but a touch of a button away. Even though she couldn't trust Terry for a moment, she noticed something unusual; her stomach was in knots since she first talked to him in the computer store. At first she thought it must have been nerves, but deep down she knew that feeling, she still felt something for Terry White.

'A toast to good books, good films and good times.'

'Here here' reiterated Jennifer as she raised her wine glass in the air. Her fork then pierced the chicken breast and the juices flowed out. She dipped the piece of chicken into the accompanying sauce and put the fork to her lips. The meat almost melted in her mouth. Once again Terry had come up trumps at the dinner table. The taste of tender Indian butter chicken mixed with cashew nuts was heavenly and her overjoyed taste buds brought memories flooding back of the last time they felt this good. Maybe it was a strategy by Terry, Jennifer couldn't be sure, but it certainly had worked a treat. The last time Terry cooked this meal for her was the night they first made love. It was a magical summer's evening in which Terry cooked the food, put it in Tupperware in a basket and took the food and a blindfolded Jennifer out to his Porsche 911. He then drove for ten minutes and lead Jennifer down a path for short walk. Finally he told her to remove her blindfold. Jennifer was standing in a park surrounded by ancient chestnut trees. Terry held out his hand and asked Jennifer to sit. She was dining inside Greenwich Park bandstand, lit only by a glorious full moon and a solitary candle that helped illuminate the dining table. Terry took the food from his basket and arranged it neatly on the table. He then sat down and clapped his hands. Jennifer looked a little perplexed as she turned to see what Terry was looking at. From behind the large chestnut trees came four men dressed in black trousers, white shirts and black bow-ties. Each had a classical instrument and they began to play. As the string quartet took their place inside the gazebo Jennifer's heart began to melt. The very nature of the occasion was immense but the choice of tune had made it all the more special. 'Air on the G String' by Bach; it was the tune Jennifer's mother would play on her violin when she tried to get her daughter to sleep. Jennifer couldn't even remember when or if she had told Terry about this, but he always just seemed to know how to touch Jennifer the way no other man ever could.

Terry removed the ware from the table and walked towards the kitchen. Jennifer sat staring into the flame of the lone candle on the table. The meal was the most enjoyable she had had for some time. It wasn't just the quality of the food, it was the quality of the company too. At this moment in time it almost felt as if she actually had deleted the unspoken memory. A small gust of wind came from the slightly open window and blew out the candle. This shook Jennifer out of her trance, she was here for a reason and it wasn't to fall in love again.

Terry came back in to the dining area and sat next to Jennifer.

'I've had a wonderful night tonight Jennifer, it's been simply amazing to see you again.'

'Thank you Terry, it has been amazing to see you too. Thank you for the dinner as well, it was as good as always.'

'Okay, I know we could stay talking for the next few hours and that would be amazing, and then maybe more might happen and I'm sure that would be incredible too. But we have something special, you and me, so I don't think we should rush anything. We have come this far in one evening and that will keep me happy for now. What do you think?'

She wasn't sure what to think. If Terry was any other man he would have pounced on the situation and she would be staying the night. The problem for her was that Terry *was* the perfect gentleman. Regrettably for Jennifer she wasn't looking for a gentleman right now, she had a job to do and she couldn't do it without Terry. Jennifer was about to ask Terry if she could stay the night but as she moved her lips she decided against it. If she requested sex with Terry, after just meeting him again, after all they had been through, it definitely would look suspicious.

'I think that's a sensible idea Terry, I really have enjoyed tonight.'

'Excellent, will I drop you back to your friend in

Camberwell or drop you home, you still live in the same apartment?'

Jennifer wanted to be dropped in Camberwell but Terry being the perfect gentleman would wait until she was inside the door of her 'friend's' house. With no friend to go to Jennifer was left with little choice.

'It's a tad late now to call to my friend. But I do still live in the same apartment and I would be grateful if you could drop me back there.'

'Pleasure' Terry said as he took their coats off the wooden coat rack.

'Daisy' followed the pair all the way to Jennifer's apartment. Andy and Chris watched on as Terry kissed her goodnight. Andy didn't want to ask it of Jennifer, but secretly he was hoping she would stay the night. This would give her a much greater chance of finding something to link Peter, Terry and The General. However, circumstances had seriously changed. As Andy pursued the couple he now felt very pleased with the night's progress. The missing link had been found.

Jennifer waited inside her apartment for five minutes before remerging and walking around the corner to meet Andy and Chris. Chris was outside the car and once again pulled up his seat to let Jennifer into the back.

'I'm really sorry guys but I got nothing. We're still on good terms though, so I can meet him tomorrow night again and really start searching' said a disappointed Jennifer.

'Quick question Jennifer, why did Terry not drop you home in the BMW?'

'Oh, it had a flat, he said he would drive me home in his other car and fix the puncture when he got back.'

Andy turned around and gave Jennifer a noisy and dramatic kiss on the lips.

'You're a legend, I now know what is going on. That red

Alfa Romeo is the car that was parked suspiciously outside the *cigarettes* facility on my second night in the unit.'

It had dawned on Andy that Corporal Jack Ryan was Terry White and The General was up to something very sinister.

58

After dropping off Chris, Andy arrived back to No. 41. It had been a long, but productive day. Chris and Andy arranged to meet at 7am tomorrow morning to continue their investigations. Andy felt time was of the essence and every minute wasted was a minute closer to death, but he had no choice except to wait until morning. Andy hung up on Victoria tonight as she offered to make him dinner. It was rude and inexcusable behaviour but at the time he had no choice. Now he regretted not ringing her back to apologise but with all the excitement of the night's proceedings he had completely forgot about the earlier phone call. It had been two days since he last talked to his wife. Last night he only popped into bed for a mere two hours. It was now 11.30pm; he knew if he got up in the middle of the night again his marriage might as well be over. As it was, his wife had been more than understanding about his busy 'work' schedule. He knew when to draw the line, the last thing he wanted to do was get his wife, the mother to his beautiful children, in danger by having to inform her of Unit Firestorm.

He slipped under the covers. Victoria was already in bed, no doubt worried and somewhat confused by her husband's recent behaviour. He knew he would have to wake her, otherwise she wouldn't even know he came home tonight. He cuddled up to his wife's back and wrapped his arms around. He then gently stroked Victoria's hair to remove it from around her neck and softly began to kiss her tender flesh. It had been sometime since he had any physical relationship of note with Victoria. Even though at this moment she lay asleep and unaware of Andy's advances, it still felt really *really* nice. He continued to kiss her neck and squeezed her hard as he embraced her. Victoria murmured some approving noises but she never awoke from her slumber. He decided to let it be. Falling asleep with Victoria in his arms would do for now. Surely she would wake at some stage, feel his touch and realise her husband still cared.

The most annoying sound in the world woke Andy. He had always promised himself to change his alarm clock but since joining Firestorm he had been rejuvenated and the daylight now called Andy. It was the first time he had not woken before the alarm clock for as long as he could remember. He needed that sleep. Last night he was running on empty and it was critical to refill his tank before he broke down. Victoria too woke with the sound of the alarm clock. Momentarily she felt his warm touch before he jumped out of bed to go to 'work'.

'I won't even ask what had you so busy last night, but can we make some time for the two of us tonight? I'll cook, you relax!'

Andy really wanted to make time for his wife, especially now she seemed so interested in making an effort to have some quality time together. But her advances had come at the wrong time. He needed to keep everyone alive and saving his marriage was no excuse for letting innocent people, innocent friends, die.

'I'd love to Vic, I really would. I am just up the proverbial walls at work. It's gone crazy in there, it really has.'

Victoria looked at him, it was different from any other time he had made up an excuse, she was now looking deep into the openings to his soul. What she saw upset her. Her husband still lied to her even though see was making every effort to engage with him again. Maybe it was over. It's not like it wasn't her own fault, but she still felt terrible. A single drop hit the sheet Victoria had wrapped around her body. A second followed soon after. She tried her best to hold her emotions until he left, but the well was full and it needed to overflow. A guilt ridden Andy couldn't bear to watch his wife cry because of his uncaring and unjust actions.

'Victoria, you have to believe me, I'm flat out at work. I would kill to have dinner with you tonight, I really'

Andy was interrupted mid flow.

'No you wouldn't, let's face it, our marriage is over. Do you have any interest in me Andy, do you?'

'So much you wouldn't believe. Our marriage is not over. Give me two days, our deadline is midnight Saturday night. You will wake up Sunday morning to poached eggs on a puffy croissant, freshly squeezed orange juice and a vase with a red rose for my beautiful wife. After that I am yours to do as you will for the whole day. How does that sound?'

'I don't know how it sounds, but I know how it smells. It smells of bullshit. Fuck you Andy, Fuck you.'

'I'm serious Vic, just give me until Sunday.'

'Whatever, just go, just get out of here.'

Andy turned and looked at his wife one last time before he walked out of the bedroom. He knew it might be the last time he would ever see her, as his wife, again. Two days was two days too many for Victoria. Andy didn't blame her for being angry, he understood the situation. In fact he was often surprised how she hadn't asked more questions of him before. But two days and it would all be over, either the truth would be revealed or he would be dead. If only she could just wait two days. Deep down he knew the last straw had been pulled, he just prayed their solicitors would be busy until Monday in the hope he wouldn't arrive home to a horrible set of divorce papers.

59

'I have it, I bloody well have it' said an overjoyed Andy as he punched the air.

Chris, Jennifer and Andy had spent the morning in Chris' apartment with a black marker and a whiteboard. Names, events, cars, and anything else the trio could think of were written on the board. A series of lines then connected each item to another and they hoped by squeezing their brains hard enough an answer would simply have to fall out. And it did.

'It was so obvious' exclaimed Andy as he got up from the couch and grabbed the marker from Chris. Andy excitedly began his lecture.

'Okay guys, an arrow points from Peter's niece, Eve, to Peter, then to Officer Tony Cohen. Another arrow points from Terry to The General because The General set him up as Corporal Jack Ryan to gain access to Unit Firestorm. A final arrow joins Peter to The General. The only reason we know of so far is that for some reason Peter threw darts at The General. So there needs to be something to connect all the dots and reveal the picture.'

'Good man Andy, we already know all this, out with it' Chris said impatiently

'Blow, Snow, Charlie, Icing, Cocaine whatever you want to call it, that's how this whole mess got started. The night I let Corporal Jack Ryan into the facility something very valuable was being stored in there. Forty million pounds worth of cocaine. It was due to be destroyed the next day but The General must have gotten Terry to pinch several kilos of it before the rest went up in flames. Peter told me that The General had taken a special interest in this case. He was more focused than he had seen him before.

He really wanted this mission to go perfectly, he wanted to nail these bastards.

Peter knew The General was crooked, he just didn't know what he was crooked in. Somehow, Peter found out about The General's dirty tricks. Only two weeks ago a thirty million haul of cut cocaine was stored in the contraband room. The cocaine had been tested and was only 40% pure. It had been cut with phenacetin, a pharmaceutical drug banned some years ago in Britain for causing kidney failure, and with prolonged use cancer. The kidneys are the part of the body that filters out impurities so if you're using cocaine, impaired kidney function is particularly serious. As is the *cigarettes* policy this cocaine stash was again due to be destroyed.'

Andy again pointed with his black marker at the whiteboard, becoming more animated with his revelation.

'A week later Peter's niece Eve died due to the dreaded white powder. Peter must have done his own investigation and traced the drugs backs to The General. The General had got greedy and was even selling dangerous cut drugs to his dealers. The General's actions killed Peter's niece, and *cigarettes* had made it all possible. It was time to bring down The General. It followed that the only way to catch him was to bring down the unit as well.'

'Top marks Andy. So what's the plan?' Chris asked.

'Proof, we need proof immediately, there's no point in going to Scotland Yard empty handed. We need to have a file that Scotland Yard can act on. Remember, we're already a day and a half behind where Peter was before he started to gather information and he still ended up dead. The clock is definitely against us but we have the numbers. We're going to have to split up.'

Andy was pacing about the room as he spoke, he was talking faster than he normally spoke as he felt each second wasted talking could cost them dearly.

'Okay, let's make a list of what we need and who is to act on it, grab that marker and start writing. We are all going to meet back here in three hours time, that's twelve midday' Andy said pointing to an eager Chris.

'Number 1 – Proof Eve died due to The General's drugs. We need that autopsy report. Chris you find out which pathologist carried out the post mortem, I want a copy of the findings.

Number 2 – We need proof of who Terry gave the cocaine to. Terry must have information somewhere in his home. You've seen the house Jennifer, is there any way we could break in there?'

Jennifer painfully recounted that fateful day again. But she had to be strong, everything was now on the line.

'Terry has been broken into before, but it's not an easy job. There are alarms, sensors and CCTV cameras outside. Whatever the latest technology in security measures, Terry has installed them. Trust me, he is a dangerous man, no matter what you do, don't get caught trying to break into his home.'

Andy was disappointed, but he trusted Jennifer's judgement. This was going to get more difficult now.

'I'm afraid we have no choice but to get that information. I understand it's suspicious, but can you try and get into Terry's house today? Maybe you can call by his office and collect the keys because you left something behind last night?'

'It's going to be difficult Andy but I'll try.'

Jennifer knew in her own heart and soul she wouldn't find Terry working behind some office desk in an insurance brokers. But she would have to try and find him where ever he was and get that key.

'Right Number 3 – We need proof The General set this robbery up. The only way I think Terry White aka Corporal Jack

Ryan could have accessed the cocaine was via the door to the contraband room. This means that Terry must have had a swipe card to access the room. My money would be that card belonged to The General. If I can get a swipe card log for that night then we have our proof.'

'Is everybody clear on what has to be done?' Andy asked as he looked at Jennifer and Chris. He was pleased to see the same conviction in their eyes as existed in his own.

'Absolutely Sir' Chris said as he light-heartedly raised his rigid right hand to his head and gave him a military salute.

'Thanks Chris' replied Andy with a smile.

'Okay, 3 hours people, everybody put their hands in, on three, *cigarettes* are going down.'

The trio chanted in unison.

'Let's go' Andy said as he grabbed his coat from under the mess of clothes on Chris' couch.

As Andy pulled on the warm coat he realised the phone in his pocket was ringing. He instantaneously pulled it out and looked at Chris and Jennifer. Both were staring right back at him.

'Who the hell has this number?' Andy said looking to his motley crew for answers but knowing there was none to be found.

'Should I answer it?'

'No, just let it ring out, it must be a wrong number' Chris said looking much more composed than Andy.

Three minutes later Chris didn't look one bit composed. The phone was now sitting on the dining table staring up at Chris, Jennifer and Andy as they sat huddled around it. The room had been quiet except for the piercing tone of the *Nokia* tune for what seemed like an eternity. A restless Jennifer eventually broke the silence.

'Just answer the damn thing Andy, you might find out what

our hopeless fate is instead of staring at the bloody phone all day.'

Andy had never heard Jennifer curse before. If ever a curse carried weight to an argument it was right now. He knew he had to answer the dreaded phone.

'Unit Firestorm is NOT going down' said the lady at the other end of the line.

60

'The location for the site is in Stratford John, I'll email you the details. Things are developing well and the subcommittee have agreed most of the details.'

Since getting the post Gordon was required to keep John updated regularly on the details of the Olympic Village. John was delighted with the developments and reassured Gordon that he was doing an impeccable job.

John put his finger on the telephone hook and dialled another number. It was another extremely short but extremely successfully phone call. The location was divulged and according to Mr Murray, by noon tomorrow John would have his money. It was more that John could ever spend on his own, without Victoria it would all be for nothing. From now on she would come first. Bloomberg wouldn't feature in the 'bedroom under the stars', Victoria would get the attention someone so beautiful deserved.

John was very concerned about Victoria. He knew he hadn't treated her very well, but then he had never treated any woman very well in his life. *It's what makes them like me.* But maybe she had put up with enough. All the signs were pointing at something and he was now obsessed that she was in love with another man. He was sure that man was her husband, but he needed proof.

John was both surprised and disappointed when Victoria failed to show for lunch yesterday. There could only be one reason in his mind, big athletic Andy had wrenched her away from him. John rang her but the call rang out. He wanted to ring again and again until he got her back under his wing but he knew that it was his suave manner that had won her over in the first place. If he lost his cool it would surely be all over.

It was time to find out where Victoria's allegiances really lay. John got his P.A. to act as Andy's secretary.

'Hi Victoria, this is Sarah, Andy's secretary. He's busy in meetings at the moment so he asked me to ring you. He'd be delighted if you'd join him for dinner tonight at La Talpa. The reservation has been made for 7.30pm. Thank you, goodbye.'

Now for one more phone call.

John rang Victoria's voicemail again. This time it was John who left the message.

'Hi Vic, John here. I'm sorry I left for the office the other day, I just saw you sleeping and didn't have the heart to wake you. Things have changed Victoria, I have closed a deal that will make us very wealthy. Bloomberg will never be switched on in the bedroom again, I can guarantee you that! It calls for a celebration. I have reserved a table in The Ritz Restaurant for 7.30pm. I look forward to your company as always.'

61

Her voice was husky and hoarse. From his training, Andy was confident the person at the other end of the line was using a voice changer to hide her identity. Andy put the phone on loudspeaker and placed it back in the centre of the table. Again everybody huddled around the table.

'Can you repeat what you just said please?' Andy requested

Again the lady responded 'Unit Firestorm is NOT going down'

Andy looked at the distressed faces around him. He had caused this mess. He had killed Peter and in trying to 'make it right' had as good as killed Chris and Jennifer too. The game was up, Recon had found them. Andy put his index finger to his mouth and made the sign to be quiet. He then moved to the window to check for any suspicious vans parked outside. He used his fingers to slightly open the blind so that he could peak through. For all he knew, Unit Firestorm members could be on their way up to the apartment right now. Andy's 'friends' were about to kill him, Chris and Jennifer. He saw nothing suspicious outside the window but it was hard to tell with so many vehicles parked by the road. He started to perspire, it had been a long time since he hadn't felt in control of a situation. The last time was as he held a glass of brandy by the fire fearing he had lost control of his own destiny. Firestorm had showed Andy how to gain control of his life. Now they had just taken it away again.

The raspy voice spoke once more.

'Are you not interested in what I have to say? Can one of you please respond to me?'

This comment threw Andy.

'Why would you think there are more people here than just me?'

'I don't know, why would you think there is anything interesting outside the window?'

An air of disbelief descended the room.

Andy reached down and put the phone on hold.

'Follow me.' He said as he beckoned the pair to follow him into Chris' bedroom.

'She can see us somehow. They must have a camera in the living room somewhere. They know exactly where we are. It's not looking good, but we are not going to go down without a fight. I've only got two semi automatics on me. That's one for you' Andy handed the gun to Chris.

'And one for you' he placed the second Beretta $M9$ in Jennifer's palm.

'Watch closely.'

Andy showed the two how to operate the safety, how to aim and how to shoot.

'Don't ever be afraid to use these, it's us or them, but remember that when you shoot, everybody then knows where you are.'

Chris and Jennifer listened carefully to the words of their leader, their Marshal. Everything had suddenly spiralled out of control but Andy had to do the best he could in the situation. He was grateful that Jennifer and Chris were willing to follow his command. He went into the kitchen and grabbed the biggest knife he could find.

'Okay hide your weapons, we are going back into the living room to try and talk our way out of this. If that doesn't work then you know what plan B is. Any questions?'

Both shook their heads, apparently they had no questions. The reality was they had so many questions that they just didn't know where to start.

The team marched defiantly back into the living room. Andy reached for the phone and took it off hold. The lady was still on the line.

'All our operators are busy at the moment. Please hold and you will be forwarded to the next available operator. Remember we value your call. I didn't think I was ringing to pay my gas bill when I picked up the phone to ring you Andy. Now first and foremost, let's get things straight. No more fancy tricks like going into Chris' room and getting weapons. If I ever get put on hold again, you will regret it. From now on you will listen to me and follow my orders. You may not know me, you may not trust me, but right now I am your best chance to stay alive. You need to leave the apartment within the next five minutes. It's nine o' clock now; I will talk to you again at Baker's street station, one hour. Believe me, I am with you, without me Unit Firestorm is not going down. With me you've got a chance. Talk to you in an hour. Now move.'

The line went dead.

'Is it a trap Andy? What do we do now?' Chris asked his marshal.

This time his marshal didn't have the answers, a decision would have to be made in the next four minutes. Andy could hear the clock on the mantle piece ticking, with each tick he felt the four walls of the room close in on him.

Should I stay or should I go? Andy thought to himself.

'The Clash' never gave an answer in their well-known song. Andy didn't have an answer either.

62

A twenty-four carat diamond ring sat proudly, bulging from the middle finger of a tanned but wrinkly left hand. The obscenely large piece of jewellery dwarfed her finger to such a degree that it appeared as if it acted as a counterbalance, if taken off, the lady would immediately fall over. Mrs Rosaline Georgina King would not fall over because the ring was not coming off; she was devoted to her husband, even now.

Two hundred or so guests sat at their tables before Mrs King, listening to her every word. A dropped fork could be heard reverberate off the floor with everybody remaining utterly silent as they looked up at the vibrant woman. She may have been elderly but she certainly had lost none of her ability or indeed her feistiness. Most people were undoubtedly focusing in on her distinctive oversized glasses and full brown curly hair that added an extra three inches to her height. She had a beautiful way with words which were not lost on her audience. A glare from her deep blue eyes could pierce though a man and look into his soul. She implored the crowd below. She commanded the podium with her determined stance and unwavering voice. The elite of society sat eating over priced food below her. She knew she had to push the buttons to their conscience to open the wallets below.

'It's up to you, it's up to us. They don't have the chances we do, and we have the chance to make a difference. It's easy to make a buck, it's a lot more difficult to make a difference. Make that difference, stop stepping on the people of the third world, and let them put their arm around your neck so you can help lift them up, lift them to new heights. If you step on people in this world be careful as you might come back as a cockroach in the next. Nobody here wants to come back as a bug to be trod on.

There's one sure way to avoid that scenario. So, I ask you, put your hand in your pocket, pull out your cheque book and feel good about yourself as you lay your head on the pillow tonight.'

A quarter of the gathering reached deep into their suit pockets and clasped their cheque books. Silly figures could be written on most of these. Mrs King looked down with contempt and raised her finger in the air. Then she proceeded to point at individual people below.

'Do you want to come back as a cockroach, do you want to come back as a cockroach, because that's what's going to happen.'

She pointed down menacingly at another man who was keeping his head down during all this ridicule.

'Sir, yes, you the man who is intent on examining his own shoes.'

The man gingerly raised his eyebrows in hope more than expectation that the woman wouldn't be staring down at him. It was no surprise that when he looked up, her eyes once again bore into his soul.

'You're going to be stepped on too sir.' She insisted

He was in a corner now, surrounded by his peers he was left with no option. The man pulled his cheque book from his coat pocket and waved it defiantly in the air.

'Oh no I'm not Mrs King.'

'That's the spirit. Now I know none of you want to come back as cockroaches, and you all want to make a real difference in this world, so let's see everybody raise their cheque books in the air and shout 'We're gonna make a difference'.

A sea of cheque books were raised like a Mexican wave rolling from the right side of the dining hall to the left.

We're gonna make a difference' the audience joined in on the show.

'Again' Mrs King proclaimed her arms outstretched.

'*We're gonna make a difference*' the crowd replied with passion.

'Now don't be shy with the ink. Thank you for coming here today to the Annual Oxfam black-tie dinner. You're presence and contributions are much appreciated by me, but far more appreciated by the smiling children of the drought and war torn countries of Africa. Thank you and good evening.'

Fait accompli Mrs King thought to herself as she stepped down from the podium and joined her fellow organisers at the top table.

It was a slow walk, although the operation was a success, her recent hip replacement made travel on foot a tough process. Everybody congratulated Mrs King. It appeared today was going to provide a windfall for Oxfam.

'Outstanding Mrs King; that was one hell of a speech you gave up there' a sharp Dutch accent pronounced.

She was sitting next to Gretta Von Humber. Gretta was the head of Oxfam in England and had all the hallmarks of a do-gooder. She would go out of her way to help people, found it hard to see the bad in anyone, and she could never keep her mouth shut when it most needed to be.

'It's the least I can do, all these good people are only too happy to give to good causes, they just need a little encouragement.'

'Well you certainly know how to encourage them Mrs King.'

Gretta then whispered into the ear of the woman on the other side of her. She nodded at Gretta knowing there was no real option.

'Thank you, I knew it was a good idea' Gretta said to the overwhelmed lady as she turned and grasped her champagne flute.

'Everybody raise your glasses to Mrs King, the hero of the hour.'

With no option everybody did as the do-gooder said.

'To Mrs King, the hero of the hour' but the response was subdued and there was no joy in anybody's voice.

It wasn't that the others gathered there that evening didn't like Mrs King, it was that they felt the whole toast was a little inappropriate.

It had been less than a week since her husband died. She sat at the top table dressed from head to toe in black and Gretta Von Humber had still thought it a good idea to have a joyous toast in her honour. Mrs King was always interested in charity and it was this mutual love that brought Mr & Mrs King together thirty eight years ago. The couple met in Sudan on a building programme. Robert King was a developer and had many building contacts through his work. He decided to set up a fund, The King Fund, to help bring basic infrastructure and housing to the poorest people in Africa. At the time he was working on sinking a well when a young female volunteer was assigned to help him. Romance flowed from that well and with it came a strong and beautiful marriage. Mrs King wanted for little as her husband was a successful property developer, but neither she nor her husband ever lost sight of the unjust suffering in the world. All and sundry in Mrs King's social circle dressed to impress, be it the latest Gucci bag or the latest Tiffany earrings. Mrs King couldn't bring herself to spend so frivolously on herself when she knew the cost of a bag could give a lifetime's education and a chance at life to an African child. Today she was once again dressed elegantly but modestly in her all black outfit. Yet she did allow herself one luxury. Her wedding ring was a grotesquely large and expensive chunk of jewellery. But this meant more than the price tag it carried, it was a symbol of her love and loyalty to her husband. She lowered her champagne flute and looked at the ring. As she twisted it she could see an image of her husband in bed covered in pool of blood. 12

bullets had passed through his defenceless body. Whoever wanted him dead was taking no chances. She was taking no chances either. Her ring was not going to come off until the perpetrator was brought to justice. She now believed that the very perpetrator was sitting in the same room as her, wining and dining as if nothing had happened. Her elbows were now on the table and her hands raised in the air as she continued to play with her wedding ring. She then glanced down at the man she suspected of murdering her husband. She hoped his stomach turned when his eyes caught her ring. The man was the brains behind the second biggest developers in London. William H. Murray glanced back, raised his glass and nodded in Mrs King's direction. He then turned and continued his conversation.

63

'I hope the tomatoes are in there' the woman said as she pointed at her boyfriend's ruck sack.

'They were out of tomatoes' her boyfriend sheepishly responded.

'What do you mean they were out? It's a fruit and veg shop, all they sell are bloody tomatoes.'

The overweight couple stood on the landing of the narrow stairwell. She was loaded down with two big brown bags in her arms while he rummaged through his pockets for the keys to open the apartment door. The woman wasn't best pleased with him and he knew he was in trouble. He was only asked to get one thing this morning when he left for work and he had come home empty handed. On the other hand, his girlfriend had been flat out baking this evening to try and make the night special. She organised a gathering for tonight and wanted everything to be perfect. All he had remembered to buy was a few bottles of beer, now stored safely in his rucksack.

'Move it, move it, out the way.'

The shouts came from up the stair well. Then there was the thud of people running down the stairs. Andy looked over the banister, he could see the couple arguing below. The stairwell was exceptionally tight and their bulky mass completely obstructed the way down. Andy knew there just wasn't room for everybody.

'Get out of the way' Andy roared down.

The man fumbled through his pockets and eventually found the key. He aimed at the keyhole but the pressure of three people shouting at him made his hands quiver, his fingers were too fat and chunky to control the key and he let it slip from his grasp.

The man stooped to the floor to rescue the key. He looked up to see a group of people who had the fear of God in their faces hurdling his torso. His girlfriend was now also on the floor and jars of bolognaise, apples, and chocolate muffins were rolling down the stairs chasing after the trio.

Andy slowed when he got to the bottom flight of stairs. He raised his hand showing Chris and Jennifer the stop signal. He peered around the corner into the lobby. It looked clear but it was impossible to see everywhere. They didn't come down the lift in case Firestorm were in the lobby, then they would be sitting ducks when the elevator door *binged*. A bloodbath confined to the elevator would be an easy clean up exercise. Andy wouldn't give them this opportunity, instead they'd have to work to assassinate the defectors.

Andy pointed and whispered 'We should use the side doors to get out of here'.

Chris cut in 'they're nearly always locked, don't do it it's too risky.'

'Okay, guys, on three' Andy whispered as he pointed at the revolving door.

It was the only guaranteed open entrance and exit point to the apartment block. The countdown was given and the group sprinted across the marble tiles.

Jennifer was now in a very compromising position. Her head lay firmly on Andy's groin with her bum resting on Chris' lap. Jennifer grasped Andy's gear stick and moved it where he wanted it. It wasn't lady like and it wasn't very gratifying but it had to be done. There was no time to pull up the passenger seat so Jennifer could edge into the back seat. Firestorm could have been anywhere and 'Daisy' needed to get moving. Now the mini had three in the front, one to drive, one to change gears and one to read the map. If the police stopped the car Jennifer would have a red face to challenge any farmer's weather beaten cheeks.

She tried to keep her mind off her compromising position stretched across the front seats as she listened for Andy's next order.

'Fourth.'

Jennifer lifted her abdomen and slotted the gear stick into place. They were now making serious progress as they ripped through the side streets of greater London.

'Daisy' and her crew were destined for Baker Street in the centre of London. Andy had equated the situation. The woman on the phone had placed cameras in Chris' apartment and knew of their every move. If she wanted them dead, then they would be dead. Blind faith is the only choice they had left. Andy made the call. He would try and keep his wits about him, but he had to follow the woman's advice, she was in control now. Andy was a puppet on her string and if he cut the cord he would fall to his demise.

64

Mrs King examined the animal's leg. She was clearly in pain. With nothing obvious jumping out at her, she decided to call the vet. It looked like it was going to be a disappointing few months for *Mercury King*. The filly had gotten sick before her last race six weeks ago and hadn't run yet this season. Last year was a tremendous year for Mercury King. She won four of the six hurdles she ran and Mrs King was planning on entering her into Cheltenham this year. Unfortunately, at this moment in time, that looked more and more doubtful.

Mrs King didn't have any children of her own and she always considered her horses as her adopted children. With the loss of her husband her 'children' were all she had. The stable was in Kent, a little over an hour outside London. Every single day she would train her horses. Every single night she would go home to her loving husband. Anytime in between was spent doing charity work. It was a simple life, but it was the life she loved. That life had been ripped away from her. Mercury King now played a big role in her life. Her success brought her momentary happiness. More importantly the horse led her to a new hope, a hope that justice would be served.

Robert King had often told his wife not to do any business with Jeff Redford.

'He is as bent as a ten bob note' he would often say.

Being embedded in the horse industry she too had heard rumblings about this character. Yet just over a year ago she purchased a one year old from the man and it had proved to be the best purchase of her career. Although wary of the dealer she loved the look and pedigree of the horse. Sentimentally she also recognised that it would be nice to have success with a horse with King in its name. The name Mercury King became quite famous that year and she kept in contact with the dealer on the progress of his horse. She may not have liked the rumours about Jeff Redford but she felt she had no choice but to seek his assistance. Jeff Redford, aka The General laid out his price; for £500,000 he would find the killer and produce the evidence. It was an obscene amount of money but she felt it was her only option. So far he hadn't let her down, he had already done more to investigate her husband's death than the police had managed.

The General asked Mrs King to try and recall any strange activity her husband may have been involved in before his murder. She told him that everything seemed normal but that he had told her that they could be making a few thousand people in Africa very happy this year. Mrs King had asked her husband to elaborate, but he said things were only at the early stages and he couldn't divulge anything yet. The conversation intrigued her, but she knew that almost everything Robert did was for starving children. Hearing a comment like this wasn't as daft as it would appear to be.

The General told her to go through all her husbands' appointments for the past six months. Any curious entries should be investigated. Mrs King did as she was told. Soon she had a lead. His name was Gordon Fletcher, the Chief Secretary to the Treasury. His post was the second most senior position in HM Treasury. Regular meetings were held with Gordon. For the two weeks prior to his death, Robert had met with Gordon Fletcher almost every working day. This was the suspicious information The General was looking for. The General would find answers; he would prove who murdered Mrs King's husband.

A green Land Rover came up the driveway and pulled into the yard. A man dressed in blue overalls got out and greeted Mrs King.

'Where is she?' the vet asked

'Follow me' Mrs King replied as the two set out to the stables. Unfortunately the vet was about to uncover a serious problem with Mercury King. Meanwhile The General was uncovering a serious problem with very big brown envelopes.

65

It was like a fortress, but Gordon felt it was a necessary measure to ensure the safety of his family. Each room now had a sensor, every window and door was connected to the alarm and new eight foot cast iron gates were installed at the entrance. Gordon was a man of the people and never wanted to disconnect himself like this, but he now felt he had little choice. Robert King, an associate of his had been murdered in cold blood. Gordon was rattled, but today's measures were due to a recent visit from a gruff and dangerous man who called himself Jeff Redford. As Gordon fiddled with his new house alarm he recalled the day that brought fear to the Fletcher home.

Gordon's secretary lifted the handset and pushed a button on her phone.

'Gordon there is a man here to see you. He doesn't have an appointment but he says he has some important information to discuss with you.'

'What is his name Marie?'

'Jeff Redford sir.'

'Thank you Marie, send him in.'

Gordon didn't know a Jeff Redford but if he had something important to say Gordon would rather hear it than not.

'How do you do sir?' asked the short, heavily overweight man.

'I'm fine thank you, now what can I do for you.'

Redford, aka The General, turned and walked back to the door. He then rotated the key and locked the door.

'You can do a lot for me Gordon, nobody is leaving this room until I get all the answers I need' The General said in a determined tone.

'What do you think you are doing? Hang on a minute' Gordon said as he reached for the phone to get some help.

The General calmly walked across the room, caught the telephone cable and yanked it out of the wall socket.

'I am perfectly calm. Now do you know a Mr Robert King?'

'I know *of* him yes.'

'You know *of* him?' The General repeated sarcastically.

'Have you not been meeting the man almost every day for the last couple of weeks.'

This was the moment Gordon really started to worry. His meetings with Robert King took place in various pubs around the city. Nobody knew they were meeting. Things had just gotten very serious for Gordon Fletcher.

'Why do you think that?' Gordon asked

'Don't play me for a fool. Speak the truth or you won't speak again' he said as he pulled back his shirt to reveal a pistol tucked inside his trousers.

Gordon swallowed. He had no choice but to tell the truth and hopefully that would be enough to save his life.

'Okay, okay, okay, I'll tell you everything you need to know.'

The General let his shirt cover over his pistol again. He sat down across the table and told Gordon to tell him everything from the moment he first had contact with Robert King.

Gordon told him the pair met regularly discussing proposals until the cabinet subcommittee finally made the decision on the Olympic Village. Robert was informed immediately, within twenty-four hours he had placed a bid on the large site, within forty eight hours he was lying in a pool of his own blood gasping his last breath of air.

'Now you're playing ball, so where is the Village to be located?' The General growled.

'Seriously I can't leak that, it has caused enough trouble already.'

'Do I have to show you my gun again? Tell me the fucking location' said The General as he banged his fist of the table.

'Okay, take it easy, I can tell you it's located somewhere in Stratford, I can't tell you the exact location, it's too dangerous for both of us.'

'That will do fine' said The General as he pulled out his phone and his chunky fingers hit the number keys.

'Hello Jack, tell me can you do me a quick favour? Look up the purchase of a large site at Stratford, North London.'

The General nodded his head.

'That's a Murray & Associate Developments, is that correct? Thank you.'

The General hung up and dialled again.

'Hello, I have some information for you. Do you know a Murray & Associate Developments?'

The General paused as the lady on the other end of the line spoke for a moment.

'I can't really talk, I'm at the annual Oxfam black-tie dinner and I'm due to speak in a moment. But I do know them, William H. Murray, their owner, is here at the dinner. Why?'

'Because that's the man that killed your husband' exclaimed The General. 'We have no proof, but to me it's too suspicious to be coincidence.'

'I told you before that I need proof.'

'I'll get you that proof' The General said and he put the phone back in his pocket.

'You've done well Gordon. I'm not a member of the police so make sure you don't inform anybody of my visit. If you do, I may have to do more than just *show* you my silver piece. Do you understand?'

'Absolutely Mr Redford.'

Gordon pushed the button to activate the alarm. This was a dangerous man and Gordon had his family to protect. He wished he had never become a junior minister. He wished his biggest worries were if Mrs Nolan would be able to get her benefits backdated.

66

Andy looked at his watch, they had made it with five minutes to spare. They had ditched the mini and after a short walk they now stood outside an entrance to Baker Street underground station. Chris was leaning against the black railing. Beside him stood a large bronze statue of a great British icon. He towered over the street puffing on the tobacco in his wooden pipe. Andy looked up at the famous statue of Sherlock Holmes. How he could do with his help right now. Andy had no pipe to muse over, all he could do was scratch his furrowed brow.

Baker's street station is one of the busiest stations in London and it has more platforms than any other station on the London underground network. Andy had no idea what was about to happen but he knew that standing around the memorial of the fictional detective definitely would not help their cause. They had taken a minute to pause for breath and that minute was up.

'Everybody okay?' Andy asked.

There was no response, just a jerk of the shoulders. It didn't matter what Chris and Jennifer felt now, they were under the command of Andy and they were not going to stand in his way.

'Good enough, Lets go.'

Andy led the pair down the steps and into the main ticketing area. He told Chris to get three single tickets so they could quickly get out of here if necessary. There were ten platforms in the station, which meant there were ten different directions in which they could escape. Andy checked the large schedule poster fixed to the tiled wall. He then pulled a pen and paper from his pocket and began writing.

He turned to look at the large digital clock hanging from the ceiling in the centre of the ticketing area. It read 11:58:20. The countdown was on, in one hundred seconds the puppet master would pull the strings once more. Right now he was willing to dance as long as he could stay alive.

'Here you go' Chris arrived back from the booth and handed out the tickets. Andy then pulled out a sheet from his notepad and handed it to him, he pulled out a second sheet and handed it to Jennifer.

'The plan is we stay here until I give the signal. The signal is me dropping my notepad. If you see this you go to the destination shown on the piece of paper. A different direction is shown for every two minutes. If I give the signal straight away you go to the platform that's written at the top of the page, at 12:02:00 you go to the platform that's written second on the page and so on. We follow what is on the paper and everybody will end up on a different line, leaving straight away if the trains are on time. Everybody sync your watches to the main digital clock. It's coming up to 11:59:00.... Now. Do you both understand the plan?'

Jennifer looked at the sheet of paper she held in her hand and started to speak.

'Sorry, but what happens if you drop the pad after 12:10:00, there's nothing written after that time.'

'I don't think we have to worry about that, if I haven't dropped my pad by then we don't have to worry about escaping, we'll already be dead' Andy stated.

'Okay spread out in the station but stay in this area. Remember to look natural and relaxed and don't forget to keep an eye on me.'

Chris joined the queue for a cup of coffee. Jennifer walked to the ticket booth grabbed a tube pocket map and began examining it. Meanwhile, Andy stayed with the masses next to the popular schedule poster. Everybody was peering over the next person's shoulder to get the information they needed, Andy was peering over his own shoulder; would 'the voice' give him the information he needed. He counted down the digital clock, each of the orange figures seemed to take an age to change. The slow motion of these ten seconds would no doubt be offset by the ten seconds of panic that was sure to follow.

Five, Four, Three, Two, One.

67

Andy surveyed the vicinity. Everybody looked normal, yet everybody looked suspicious. One woman had her hoodie jumper covering her head. She walked staring at Andy, but only because he was staring at her. His eyes followed her bright pink clothes as she made her way in the direction of the Bakerloo line. Once she was out of sight he chose the next available person to suspect. It was a woman who appeared to be kneeling down tying her shoe lace for an age. His eyes were glued to the woman, Chris and Jennifer's eye's were glued to Andy's notepad. Something had to give, and it did. The crowd swelled in the station and a person accidentally bumped into Andy. He looked to where the woman had been kneeling, but she had left and was in amongst the crowd. Then his mobile phone rang. This was it, this was the call he had been waiting for.

To Andy's dismay the caller ID displayed *'Chris'*.

'What?' Andy growled in a disgruntled tone.

'There's a big sheet of paper sticking out of your pocket, you better look at it.'

Andy reached down and grabbed the paper.

'Read it out, read it out' Chris demanded.

'12.07 Hammersmith and city line, towards Hammersmith, fifth carriage, the back seat.'

'It's 12.02 now' Chris said

'I know. You guys go somewhere secure. I'm doing this one on my own, stay safe.'

As he finished the last few words Andy began to run. Once the phone was safely back in his pocket he started to sprint. He assessed the turnstiles queues as he sprinted, and got through without delay, next it was the escalators.

Stairs are for walking, escalators are for standing.

It seemed to Andy that there was always one asshole that could never wait the fifteen seconds to ride an escalator peacefully. It would usually be a business man in an Armani suit, Blackberry in hand, and he would shout to some unfortunate eighty year old grandmother to get out of the way. Today Andy was that obnoxious escalator pest, but drastic times cause for drastic measures.

'Keep right, keep right' Andy demanded as he ran taking two steps at a time.

Buskers to his right, commuters to his left, Andy slid through the crowd like a hot knife through butter. The train was already at the platform when he arrived. It was difficult to tell which was the top carriage but he had no time to check. He jumped into the carriage as the door slid closed. He looked at the back of the carriage. There were empty seats there. He sat down at the back of the carriage and crossed his fingers he was on the fifth one. Beside him sat a young woman with a beanie on her head and a scarf covering her face. It was particularly cold but he was in suspicious mode. The woman stared out the carriage window.

'Stay looking straight ahead.'

He turned to the woman as it appeared she was talking to him.

'I said stay looking straight ahead.'

He did as he was told.

'I told you I was here to help and I am. We will no longer stand in the shadows. We will turn on the lights and illuminate the murky dealings of Unit Firestorm.'

Andy couldn't believe she had risked saying the hallowed words. He knew this woman was serious, whatever she was about to do.

'I will help turn on that light, obviously I cannot tell you may name, but you can know me as *The Light*.'

'Okay, so what is The Light going to do to help me? I already have a plan and as far as I can see you are only delaying me.'

'Check under your seat.'

Andy nonchalantly reached down and grasped the file that awaited him.

'This is Peter Johnson's file, this is the reason you were sent to kill him. It contains all the information you planned on gathering this morning, autopsy reports, swipe card reports and names of dealers. It's a good report, but it is not good enough to take down The General. He is a man of many contacts and is very strong willed. If you want him, you need definite proof. You have the ability to get that proof.'

As she spoke she remained looking out the window and Andy remained looking straight ahead. He needed some answers.

'Okay, so you say you can't tell me your name, but can you tell me who you work for?'

'You know who I work for Andy.'

'Recon?'

'Of course.'

'And why are you doing this?'

'Because I knew Peter Johnson very well and yet it was me who reported him defecting. I killed Peter Johnson as much as you killed him. Peter wasn't even exposing the whole of Firestorm, he was exposing The General, but still, they decided to kill him and Tony Cohen. I started with Recon because I wanted to do good. My work was for the good of the nation, I don't believe that to be true anymore. It's only with my help that you can achieve your goal and bring down Unit Firestorm. Are you willing to trust me?'

'Do I have any choice?'

'Well you can trust me, or I can report you which I should

have done already.'

'Okay, you have my trust, what do I do?'

'It's not what *you* do, it's what Jennifer can do. Terry White links everything. If we can get a testimony of the truth from him then we have all the information we need. Terry's testimony will bring down The General, the decision to kill Peter and Tony to hide the truth will bring down Firestorm. Terry is the lock, and Jennifer is the key. I need you to use that key. Can you make it happen?'

'I can try. How long do we have?'

'You have tonight, they're already on my tail. Don't worry about saying the name Firestorm. It's pointless at this stage, you are going to be found out. I may have to give them some information about you to keep them off my back. You must understand anything I do is not to get any of you caught, it's to make sure Recon don't get too suspicious. Don't try and follow me, I'll be in touch.'

'Paddington Station, please mind the gap.'

Andy her through the window as the tube made its way towards Hammersmith. He pulled out his phone.

'Chris, get the mini, meet me at Hammersmith Station as soon as you can.'

68

The General sat in his office, his chunky fingers pressing on the numbers on his phone. There were a few important calls to be made this morning.

'Fletcher' The General barked down the phone.

'I hope you've been behaving yourself, I just want to check how your wife is doing.'

'She's doing fine, why?' Gordon Fletcher responded.

'Oh, no reason, just wanted to see how she was doing. Keep behaving, I'll be in touch.'

The General had nothing to gain from Gordon Fletcher at the moment, but he made sure to keep the fear of God in him to ensure he would not disclose their earlier meeting.

The next phone call would be a first for The General, but he needed help if he was to prove who killed Robert King. The evidence would give him his biggest ever pay day. He lifted the receiver again.

It was the first time The General had used his contact in Recon to investigate a case. Only he and the Marshal knew the Head of Recon. It was a separate organisation run out of a separate facility. Both were a product of Unit Firestorm, but like the police and the judicial system, they were kept very much apart. The Head of Recon was the person who gave the encoded missions to the Prime Minister, Finance Minister and British Army chief. He knew more information about the nation than any other single member of society in Britain. The General and Marshal were only told about missions when they were given the green light. The Head of Recon knew every dirty secret in the United Kingdom, and beyond.

The General asked him to investigate William H. Murray as the murderer of Robert King. From what The General told him, it was a fair investigation. As the police came up with nothing, the Head of Recon saw no issue with Recon stepping in. It probably wasn't a case that put national security at risk, but as a colleague of The General's, he accepted to put some member's of Recon on the case. Recon were about to discover something that would set in motion events that would change the face of Britain forever.

69

'Well done Jennifer' Andy said as he munched his way through the fresh chicken Caesar salad.

'This is going to be a nightmare Andy.'

'You'll be fine, we'll be right outside if anything happens.'

The trio decided their stomachs could take no more neglect. It was time for dinner and a de-briefing of the day's events. Chris and Jennifer were amazed by Andy's revelations. The fact that he was alive was incredible. To top it off, Andy now had more information at his fingertips than they could ever have gathered today. If what The Light said was true, and they had no alternative but to believe her, then a frank discussion with Terry is all that stood in their way of achieving their goal.

'So what do I have to do exactly?' asked Jennifer.

'First of all, you need to wear a wire. Don't worry, it's not a big microphone strapped to you with duct tape like you see in the movies. I'll give you a small recording device that you can put in your pocket or handbag. All you have to do is try and have a clear passage from the recording point, that just means have your handbag open. Then tell Terry you need to have a serious discussion. Tell him a man who called himself The General rang you and told you to stay away from Terry. He said Terry worked for him and that you would only be a distraction to his work. Tell Terry that The General warned you not to say anything about him ringing, but you felt you had to explain why you have to leave him for your own safety. If he feels as strongly about you as you say he does, then he will divulge everything to try and keep you. With the recording, we can go to Scotland Yard and all this will be over. How does that sound?'

Jennifer hadn't touched her meal yet. Her stomach grumbled and the smell of the sautéed walnut and almond from her chicken teriyaki was almost celestial, but right now she couldn't bring herself to swallow either her food or the nonsense that she was hearing.

'Sounds a bit simplified to me' she retorted. 'Surely that sounds suspicious, why would The General possibly ring me? Did he ring all Terry's other girlfriends and ask them to stay away from him? I don't like it Andy, I don't like it one bit. I was Terry's girlfriend for a full year and I didn't ask a peep about his extracurricular activities. I bump into him yesterday and I go and confront him with this. Then to top it off I have a recorder on me. This man is dangerous Andy, trust me. I will be lucky if I come out of there alive.'

'I don't mind what way you get the information, but without touching a nerve and provoking some emotion there's no way Terry will tell you what we need to hear. I know it sounds dodgy but I know The General, he's a crazy eccentric man and he's not a man you can predict. Anything is possible with him believe me. Can I count on you?'

'So my choices are face assassination tomorrow or risk being killed tonight to avoid tomorrow's fate. I suppose I don't have much option.'

Andy was relieved to hear her agree. He could see Chris mimicking wiping his brow. Without her it would all be over. The date had been arranged, tonight it was Jennifer's turn to cook.

'Well I'm getting desert anyway' Chris said to try and lighten up the atmosphere a little. He and Andy were finished their meals but Jennifer still couldn't swallow her first bite. Her stomach was in knots, and it wasn't going to get any easier.

70

Victoria was dressed in a shapely little black number. It was a night for high heels, heavenly fragrances and Tiffany jewellery. She couldn't believe it when she listened to her voicemail, it was the last thing she had expected to hear. It was a special night and she wasn't going to have to put up with the chewing gum stained seats and stench of B.O. of the underground. The taxi rolled up outside the restaurant and the porter opened the door for her. She gracefully stepped from the taxi. She could sense the eyes of every man and woman gazing at her. Since hearing the message Victoria set off and had her hair done, her nails manicured and received a cleansing facial. She looked like a celebrity, but more importantly she felt like a celebrity. Tonight could be the start of something amazing.

The waiter showed her to her seat. He pulled her chair back to allow her to sit. Tonight was her night and she would milk all the attention she could get. In her eagerness to please, she arrived ten minutes early. As yet there was no sign of her date so she ordered a glass of Shiraz and sat listening to the music made by the talented fingertips of an old woman. The woman had long grey hair and creases on her face, she looked like she had experienced many worries felt from being on this earth so long. But as she sat behind the beautifully crafted piano, she found the ability to bring an inanimate object to life. She was lost in her own world where worries mattered little. It was magical to watch the wonder of such a musician; her frailty disregarded by the power of her stirring composition. Victoria felt privileged to be in her presence, the whole restaurant was within her enchanted bubble.

'Young lady you look so beautiful tonight, would you like to request something special, something to perhaps bring back a beautiful memory?'

Victoria was flattered that the lady chose her for a request, but as her table was located next to the grand piano it seemed a likely option. Maybe her date arranged for their table to be located here, after all, Victoria always loved classical music.

'I would love a request. Beethoven's Moonlight Sonata would be just lovely.'

She closed her eyes as she listened to the transcending range of soul touching notes that emanated from the grand old instrument. The moonlight sonata was the perfect choice. The moonlight on their first meeting illuminated the gently rippling sea. The passion of that first encounter was spellbinding. Tonight brought it all back.

71

'Would you like another drink sir?'

'No I'm fine thanks.' responded the man. But he wasn't fine. The waiter knew the man's fate, even if he didn't want to believe it himself. The headwaiter had worked here almost all of his life. He had seen people come and go, the rich, the richer and the richest. He was still learning how to deduce how wealthy people were, but one thing he could always identify was when somebody was stood up. He had waited upon many gloomy individuals who found out that their night would involve a lonely meal. It always amazed him that people could stay and eat a meal at a table set for two. The majority decided to do so, maybe out of spite or maybe out of egotism. His patron had waited long enough. As he left the restaurant the waiter was surprised to see little in the way of a gloomy hollow man. Instead, determination was etched all over his face.

John Black was confident he now knew what the problem was. The next step would be proof. La Talpa was just five minutes' walk away. As he walked down the road the blood started to boil in his veins. Blood vessels in his temple were throbbing. He offered Victoria everything she could ever want. Money beyond her wildest dreams, the highest class parties in the world and a man that would now give her his attention.

How could anybody throw all that back in my face?

He rounded the corner and looked through the glazed front of the restaurant. Victoria was looking more beautiful than ever. He could see she was making every effort to impress her husband. She had a simple choice and she chose the middle class Directacom employee over him. It seemed absurd to him, but the evidence was right in front of his eyes. He was gutted, but he always got what he wanted and in love it would prove no different.

He pulled out his phone.

'Hello. Sorry for calling you out of hours so to speak. I have a proposal for you worth an awful lot of money. However, it does involve more of you than I have ever asked before. I have a situation that needs resolving and unfortunately the only way to do it is to see a certain individual eliminated out of the picture. I trust I can count on your help in this matter for the appropriate rewards.'

John paused and listened. He was very surprised at the response he was hearing. His contractor had never shied away from any jobs in the past. Maybe he was all about reputation and this repute meant he never had to do any of the dirty jobs.

'Yes, and you trust this man?' John asked

The instant he asked this question he knew he shouldn't have. Judging a man's character wasn't part of his work and it never would be.

'Okay, Okay, you cannot trust such a man but you say he is German and typically efficient. I have a pen, what's his name again. Deisler; and his number?'

John had the name and number of a complete stranger on the back of one of his business cards. He would prefer if someone he knew could do the job but it wasn't to be. Deisler would push Victoria back into his life. John made one more phone call. It was a quick exercise, Deisler sounded very efficient indeed. By this time tomorrow night it would all be over.

Mr Murray's money will be transferred into my new account, Victoria will be on her way back into my open arms and the cool, calm John Black will be back.

'Good evening Mr Black. I'm afraid we've reset your table. We inexcusably thought that you had left for the evening. Once again our sincerest apologies.'

The headwaiter barked at his staff to reset a table for their prestigious guest. A young waiter quickly set about his task. A small table was cleaned, new covers were draped over the mature oak surface, and the places were reset.

John looked over disapprovingly at his table.

'You can tell that eager apprentice of yours that he can blow out that candle and take back one set of cutlery. I have had a phone call to inform me of an unfortunate event that has taken my date from me tonight. However, I have decided to dine, I need to eat anyway.'

The headwaiter did exactly as requested. It was unusual behaviour. However, his job was not to ask questions but to see to the smooth and efficient running of the restaurant. Throughout the night John appeared to be acting very strangely. He bought the most expensive bottle of red wine in the house, enjoyed six courses and acted as if to do so on one's own was perfectly normal. During the course of the evening the maître d' took note of this behaviour as he oversaw the running of the room. There was something unusual about John Black. He had often dined here before, but tonight he showed a change in temperament. Something had fazed him and he was starting to act somewhat irrationally.

Only a few remained sipping from their glasses as the clock struck the wee hours of the night. My job is not to query but to serve; the headwaiter reflected as he helped a visibly inebriated John Black from the establishment.

72

The kitchen door slammed behind her. Jennifer covered her mouth with her hand as she made her way through the wafts of smoke. She loved cooking but the knots in her stomach made her nervous. Even the most basic tasks became complicated. She pulled open the oven door and took a few steps back to leave the smoke waft out. She hoped it wouldn't be a salvage mission. Eager to find out the extent of the damage, she waved the smoke clouds apart with her hands and poked her head into the oven. A relived cook stepped back from the roast beef satisfied that all was not lost. A fork made its way through the floury centre of a large potato. A quick mash and it was almost perfect and the coup de grace was the Yorkshire pudding that was just about ready in the top oven.

Terry White had all the sophistication of a Londoner but he originated from the north of England. It was a special night and she knew his favourite dish; roast beef with Yorkshire pudding. Terry always said that no Sunday roast was complete without Yorkshire's finest. She hoped he would say a lot more than that tonight. There was a knock on the door. She took off her apron, ran to the mirror over her fireplace and put the finishing touches to her mascara. What stared back at her looked fazed and edgy. Her long deep breaths were interrupted by further knocking on the door.

He can wait.

She had to relax. Tonight was the most important of her life so far, but that burden couldn't be shown on her face. Once more, she looked into the mirror. Happy with her reflection she went to the door, turned the key and pulled down on the latch.

'Jennifer, you were supposed to make contact with us at least every half an hour. We need to know if you're okay. If you can't make contact with us please give us a signal. One flick of the lights signals all okay, two flicks means we come in and take action. Please contact us soon, if we get nothing in the next ten minutes we will have to go in.' Andy pressed send.

Chris and Andy were waiting impatiently in the mini. Jennifer agreed to send a text every so often to let them know she was all right. Andy received two texts already tonight. Both were blank. Just hitting the 'send' button was clearly the easiest way of sending a message without Terry knowing about it. The last text they received was over an hour ago and both were starting to worry. She had never poked and probed before and Terry was an intelligent man. This combination could spell disastrous results.

'What do you think Andy?' Chris asked

'I don't know, just sit it out another few minutes.'

Andy was here for Jennifer and if she needed help he would be right behind her. But he knew if he busted into the apartment and everything was fine, then the case was blown for no reason.

Sit it out Andy. Sit it out.

Jennifer once again enjoyed her evening immensely. The only thing Andy's recorder had taped so far was the sound of a happy couple. Although the roast beef was a tad crispy Terry truly enjoyed his traditional meal. It set the tempo for an evening of nostalgia. A lot of happy memories were reminisced. Like a wily freshwater crocodile Jennifer had moved slowly toward her prey, when the perfect moment arrived she would pounce. For a very random reason Terry mentioned something about football jerseys in passing. This was her link, this was her moment. She leapt from the safety of her imaginary billabong to try and catch her prey.

'Speaking of football jerseys...'

As if by divine intervention Terry's mobile began to ring.

'Hello, yes, one moment.' he covered the mouthpiece and apologised.

'Can you bear with me a moment while I take this call?'

Terry walked back into the kitchen to gain some privacy.

She was deflated. It would be difficult to muster the same courage when he returned, but no choice was available. She checked her phone. She knew it had been some time since she pressed the send button, but when she read Andy's message she realised just how long it had been. The night had gone so well, she didn't notice the time fly by. She texted Andy back, this was no time for any macho heroics, this one she had to handle herself.

She had never done it before, but tonight was always going to be a night of firsts. She decided to stand at the door and eavesdrop on Terry's conversation. If she was going to probe into his criminal activity, she might as well start now.

'I don't do that kind of work John. No, not even for you. I'm about collection and delivery, I'm a middle man, not a hit man.'

She was amazed. Nevertheless, she was delighted to hear Terry wasn't a hit man. Since that infamous summer's morning this was the very profession she feared he practiced.

'Okay, okay, I can give you the number of a guy that can help you. He's nothing to do with me and you didn't get the number from me.'

Terry called out the digits. This signalled it was time for Jennifer to sit down again. As she sat twiddling her thumbs he returned to the table.

'I'm so sorry about that, some people have no respect for private time. Anyway, where were we?' he asked with a gentle smile. 'Ah, I remember, I'll always know that expression on your face, you were about to ask me a question.'

'Was I?' she hesitated.

'Yes you were, don't be shy.'

He reached across the table and placed her hand in his. It

was firm yet gentle, she couldn't quite explain it, but it was the most genuine act she had ever felt.

'You know you can ask me anything' he invited her as he looked meaningfully into her eyes. He could see her pupils dilating, she definitely wanted to say something but she was nervous. Terry kept her hand in his and gave it a gentle squeeze.

'Alright' said Jennifer plucking her hand from his grasp. 'Let's talk, let's really talk.'

Passion was in her voice and this fervour conveniently masked the anxious twitch of her vocal cords.

'I loved you, I really did. I could imagine nobody else in the world that was more suited to me. When we first met at the computer course I thought I had struck gold. But, I always knew something about you didn't fit. Selling house and car insurance, it seemed so out of character. If you were going to make something up then you could have surely picked a different cover story. But in a crazy paradox how unbelievable it sounded actually started to make me believe it. I decided that no matter what you did; I loved *you*, not what you did for a living. I made a conscious decision not to ask you any work related questions. That way I could love you unconditionally and I could trust that you would have never lied to me. I always said to every girlfriend I ever had, relationships are based on trust. This was my way of getting around that stumbling block. Porsche *911*'s, designer clothes and best of all a wonderfully educated mind. All three are not normally associated with an insurance sales agent. Something funny was going on, but I hid it all somewhere in the back of my mind, in a place I would never look. Then one day, everything changed. I came out of the wardrobe in your room and all the stuff I had hidden away for so long came rushing out of the closet. I couldn't hide these worries any longer. With two bullets you killed two men. You didn't even blink. I squirm when I see someone get an injection. Without any panic or

263

anguish you dealt with the bodies as if you were cleaning some spilt red wine on the carpet. Now, it's true we are having a beautiful evening tonight, but I've managed to bundle all those insane memories and push them kicking and screaming back into the closet. Right now they are bursting to get out. The hinges of the door are getting weaker and it won't take much for a screw to come loose and, once again, we're back to where we started. So tell me everything. I may pick up your stuff and throw you out, I may even call the police, or I may somehow understand and we can move on from here. This better be the truth, there are no second chances.'

Terry sat patiently listening to her as she lunged head first into her rant. This had already impressed her. With every other man that had been in her life the couple would now be involved in a pointless bickering argument. Terry was cool, he was always cool. Antarctica is cool too, and beautiful, but it can kill, and that was the problem.

Terry began calmly.

'My name is Terry White and I come from Halifax. I have never told you a lie and never wish to do so. I do work in insurance, but not the kind you would be led to think. I insure my client's endeavours run smoothly. I am a glorified postman. The only differences are I don't have to wear the uniform and each stamp costs a minimum of £5,000. This is the truth. My clients are unknown to me. They are generally in high-class society. As with many people who reach this privileged position, they didn't achieve this success by helping old ladies cross the road, they reached it through corrupt behaviour. I am simply the middleman in their games. I'm like a referee in a football match. Both teams want to play but sometimes they fight and disagree. I am the man in the middle who maintains order. But what you need to know is what happened on that notorious summer's morning, right?'

Jennifer readied herself for the earthquake she knew she was about to experience. Her only question was how high the reverberations would reach on the Richter scale. She sat, arms folded across the table. She tightened the grip on her biceps and hunched her shoulders upwards. She was now braced for impact.

'Car park space No. 627. I will never forget how that car park space changed our lives.'

Terry recounted the night he would never fail to remember. It was the night he lost his treasured Porsche *911*, and within twelve hours he had lost the love of his life too.

'When you came out of the wardrobe did you notice anything unusual about the two men?'

Jennifer squirmed as she attempted to recount the taboo events. Her eyes were squeezed firmly shut and her cheeks were elevated to new heights. Her open hand now covered her face. Terry wasn't sure if it was to hide her horror at the thought of the proceedings, or if it in some way helped her to concentrate. He faintly hoped it was the latter.

'There was one very strange thing.' she began

'Yes, go on.'

'They were both wearing white football jerseys.'

'Exactly, they were Tottenham Hotspur football jerseys. They had infiltrated a plan, but whatever listening device they used they obviously didn't hear the name of the football club that they were supposed to follow. The moment I saw they didn't have Chelsea jerseys on I left parking space No. 627 faster than I had left school when I heard the bell ring. I lost my car to their bullets, but worse still, they somehow tracked me down and I lost you as a result. Yes, I am proficient in the use of firearms. But if a postman delivered *my* mail, he would carry a handgun too. Yes, I wrapped them up in the carpet like they were sandwiches in cling film. But these men were scum, and I wasn't going to prison for the sake of these criminals. The street would be safer without them. I'm sorry for the pain I've put you through. Believe me, I'm not a bad man, but I am a thorough professional. My work has made me the man I am today; it has paid for my education, made me stay in shape and gave me the affable life I live today. Without it, I wouldn't know that you love 'Air on the G String' by Bach, I wouldn't have been able to cook you the Indian butter chicken you enjoyed so much last night. I wouldn't have been able to love you, and I do love you.'

The tears came to Jennifer's eyes. They had become glassy and it was difficult for her to make out Terry. She didn't want it to look like she understood him. A few nicely put words wouldn't make it all all right. But inside, she still felt something for him and this explanation didn't shake the foundations of her being as she had envisaged. In fact, it was pretty low on the Richter scale. The only vibrations she now felt were those from her phone that was on silent.

'One moment' she said wiping the water from her eyes. She opened the message.

Have you got the information on The General? What is the status? You have been in there almost three hours now.

I am about to be assassinated in the next twenty-four hours and here I am worried about my love live, she thought.

Immediately she asserted herself. If she was alive tomorrow she promised that she would allow herself to think again about her love life. For now it was about survival. Everything Terry told her tied up all the loose ends in her mind. She was satisfied that he wasn't a bad man and he wasn't going to kill her if she asked for some more information. That was exactly what she would have to do. She glanced at her handbag; the recorder's head was peering over the top of the bag at her. It was time to record something useful. She looked into Terry's eyes and began

'The General rang me.'

73

The witching hour had arrived. The air was crisp and white sparkles of frozen crystals covered the roads and pavement. The clear night sky housed an extra large full moon. An owl that perched on the branch of an ancient oak tree, hissed and screeched at his eternal foe. The owl only dined under the cloak of darkness. Tonight the owl would go hungry and it wasn't happy. The incessant screeching woke Andy from his soothing slumber. Chris was on watch. Andy turned to see him munching on salt and vinegar crisps.

The driver's seat of the car had been let down so that it was almost horizontal. It was perfect for a snooze, but it wasn't perfect anymore. Andy pulled the lever and sat upright. With the vertical position he felt his mind aligned to the gravity of the situation again.

'Chris what's the status?'

'Terry has been in the house three hours, twenty-two minutes. Jennifer has texted us six times. All texts bar one have been blank. The last text was blank and we received it fifty-two minutes ago. The kitchen and living room lights are the only lights that are on. No other lights in the house have been switched on except for the bathroom light twice, both for brief periods of no more than five minutes. The last time somebody entered or exited the apartment block was approximately one hour ago. And my shift is due to end in five minutes!'

Andy felt Chris had grasped the nettle that was this investigation harder than him. He believed, in fact he knew, if he grasped hard enough he would not get stung. Andy realised that a packet of crisps in Chris' right hand may be a constant but the man could certainly adapt to a situation. He was a valuable ally.

'Okay mate, you seem to be on top of this private detective

stuff. What are we missing? Can we do something while we are in this car? Can we push our heads together until an idea falls out?'

'Well you just threw that file from The Light into the back. Have you even read it?' Chris responded.

'Fuck it I haven't.'

'You donkey!'

'Maybe it's all the late nights and lack of sleep that's got me a little off form. Anyway, I just want to say fair play Chris, it's good to have you here.'

This was as close to an emotional bonding hug as the two buddies were ever going to get. Chris knew it too and appreciated Andy's simple words.

Andy browsed through the report. Everything appeared to be in order and exactly as The Light had described. Swipe card reports pinned The General. A list showed dealers and their drugs transactions. An autopsy report showed kidney failure, due to the use of cut cocaine, was the cause of Peter's niece's death. A lab report showed that this was almost certainly the same cocaine to that confiscated by Firestorm. However, this is not what caught his eye. Instead, a different detailed report had engaged him.

'So what have you got fella?' Chris asked sneaking a peek at the sheets he was holding.

'Something every British person should know. In my hand I hold how Unit Firestorm began.'

Andy was about to begin reading when Chris interjected.

'Look, there's somebody coming out the revolving door.'

'That looks like Terry to me, what do you think Chris?'

'Definitely Terry. Do we follow him?'

Andy plucked the phone from his coat and raised it to his ear.

'I'll ring to see if Jennifer is alright and check what the

status is.'

'I've got everything we need from Terry. I need you, and only you, in my apartment now. Don't ask questions just come' said the voice at the other end of the line.

'But what about.'

'I said no questions, see you in two minutes.'

A slightly fazed Andy pulled the door handle.

'I gotta go, stay here.'

He left 'Daisy' and Chris behind and made his way to the apartment.

It was very tempting. It lay next to Chris on the driver's seat calling out for someone to pick it up. The moonlight caught half the top page. The other half fell into darkness. It reflected the fact that Andy had seen the outline of the document, and as yet Chris was in the dark. It wouldn't remain this way for long. It was time to read exactly what every man, woman and child in Britain should know.

74

Jennifer and Andy exited the apartment. Chris lifted his head out of the file to see the revolving door spinning in their wake. Both marched over to the mini. The determination on their faces was evident. He lowered the passenger window.

'What's wrong?' he asked.

'Nothing, just get out of the car now' Andy responded pulling open Chris' passenger door.

'What, what's wrong?' he said staying put, waiting for a reasonable answer.

'Get out of the fucking car Chris.'

This time there was a tone of anger in Andy's voice that concerned him.

'Alright, Alright, calm down.'

The moment he left the seat Andy slammed the door shut. He raced around the car and jumped into the driver's seat. In a matter of seconds the door had been closed, ignition turned on and the accelerator had felt the weight of his heavy foot.

Chris blinked. When he opened his eyes Andy was turning around the street corner and suddenly 'Daisy' was out of sight.

'What the hell just happened there?' Chris demanded to know.

'You'll find out soon enough but I'm afraid I can't tell you right now.'

'What, why am I left out of the loop?'

'Trust me, it's better to be out of the loop than in it. Now move it, it's getting late and there's a big day ahead of all of us tomorrow. We need every bit of sleep and recuperation we can get and until I drop you home I won't get that sleep.'

'My jacket is still in the mini, is Andy not coming back?' Chris remonstrated.

'Not a chance. You can survive one night without your jacket. Now follow me, it's time to call it a night.'

Chris put out his arm to stop Jennifer.

'Hold up, first I've got some serious news, this is amazing stuff.'

'I don't care what it is, now follow me or you're on the street for the night.'

It was Chris' first time in a Toyota *Yaris*. He noticed the speed dial read like a Formula 1 car. He felt the huge digital numbers changing every split second would almost encourage the driver to go faster and faster. The only reason he took any notice of the feature was that although the heating had raised the temperature in the car, he could still feel the frosty reception coming from the driver. He decided to risk her wrath and break the ice.

'Can I ask, did we get everything on tape?'

'Yes, everything, but I don't want to talk about it. We're not going to talk about it, okay Chris?'

'That's okay.'

It always struck Chris as an oddity. Something so simple and so natural could cause such unease. People could be faced with the wrinkly saggy flesh of a topless eighty-year-old woman on a Mediterranean beach and feel more comfortable with the situation than with this. Chris never much believed in the term 'comfortable silence'. A silence by its nature was always uncomfortable.

He stared straight ahead and focused on the white dotted centre lines as they came and went. The awkwardness would surely be magnified if their eyes, even momentarily, accidentally met. He reached for the radio, if he was too chicken to end the impasse then getting the help of some DJ seemed like the next best alternative. He fiddled with the knobs, and pushed every button. The wireless remained soundless.

'The radio broke last week. Don't know what's wrong with it, but it just won't come on.'

Finally Jennifer said something, but they were words that he just didn't want to hear. He sat back in his seat and began staring at the white dots again.

What he didn't realise is that an awkward silence is uncomfortable for both parties. She was feeling the force too. Soon she too couldn't take it anymore.

'So what is this serious news you have for me?' she finally asked.

The standoff was over. Chris took his eyes off the mesmerising white dots. He relaxed a little and looked at Jennifer.

'This could take a while but it's good stuff.'

'Okay all this information is coming out of the file The Light gave to Andy. I can't verify it, but everything else in the file was spot on so I assume this is too.'

'Is that the file there?'

'It sure is, I'll try and give a synopsis as best I can. First of all Unit Firestorm is not a new phenomenon, it has been in Britain for a long time. It's the brainchild of a Kenneth McKenzie, later to be given the title Sir Kenneth McKenzie. His Scottish family had a long tradition of military service. It seems the genes ran true in Kenneth. He served with the British Royal Artillery during World War I as a Lieutenant. Following the outbreak of World War II McKenzie quickly distinguished himself in the handling of the British forces in the...'

'Come on Chris, get to the good bits' Jennifer said. She didn't really care about a man she had never heard of before, and his achievements in the world wars. She wanted to know how a unit could be set up so that she, a trouble-free librarian, could have her life put in danger.

'Okay, okay, bear with me. May 1941 saw the worst of the

London bombings. The air raid sirens rang across the city and the sky oozed German bombers. Invading London was a big coup for the Luftwaffe. Even the Houses of Parliament were hit. Thousands died.

McKenzie was convinced spies were amidst the ranks of the British Forces. The nights of the raids were particularly vulnerable for London as the Royal Air Force had a large maintenance schedule planned for that weekend and much of the force was grounded. This information had been leaked and he felt the nation had to get a handle on any spies. He was a close ally of Winston Churchill; he conveyed his opinions and suggested starting Unit Firestorm. They were radical plans; too radical for Churchill. Britain was still a democracy that fought for justice and defended the right for a fair trial to all. Churchill didn't want to change what people had fought for, for centuries. However, the war gained incredible momentum.

Anyway, in December the Japs launched a surprise attack on the U.S. fleet at Pearl Harbour. In the next week the shape of world political affairs completely altered. Japan declared war on the Philippines and some other countries. Germany and Italy declared war on the U.S. India and Hungary declared war on somebody too. Basically it all kicked off in a big way. We had a few big battleships sunk by the Japanese; Churchill was feeling the squeeze. World order was lost, he realised that there were no rules to be broken anymore. Drastic measures were called for. He needed his right hand man to be a man of action. He needed McKenzie and he was appointed Chief of the Imperial General Staff or CIGS. That basically means he was in charge of the British Army. It's ironic that we randomly chose our code name *cigarettes* as it was CIGS that actually began the unit. So what do you think so far?' Chris asked Jennifer.

'It's actually very interesting, I've read about most of those events at work. The only thing is, I'm not studying for a history

273

exam and, we've only got about five minutes till we get to your place so you better speed the rest of it up!'

'Don't you worry, I'll be done when we arrive. I've just set the background, the best is yet to come.'

75

'Daisy' screeched to a halt. Andy got out of the car and slammed the door shut. He didn't care what time it was or how many people were woken or saw him. The blood coursed through his veins, his heart raced and his hands began to shake.

Control yourself, control yourself he reiterated to himself.

It was a testing situation but after all the good work of the previous few days it would be a shame to see it all ruined by some ill-advised action tonight.

He opened the door and marched into the kitchen, he marched to the sitting room, then upstairs. The light was on in their bedroom. He opened the door and was surprised by what he saw.

'What are you doing Victoria?'

'Are you blind, I'm packing my things and getting the hell out of here.'

'Calm down, I know I've been busy these past few days but this all looks a little dramatic. Is this to do with the fact I couldn't make dinner tonight?'

'Of course it's to do with the fact you didn't make dinner tonight' she said despairingly.

'I sat there for a full hour, and waited for you, my solitary candle and me. I spent the whole day making myself look special for you. Every inch was waxed and plucked, I would take any pain for you. I dressed in that short black dress you complain you don't see me in anymore. I made every effort I possibly could. And then you don't turn up. What do you expect me to do? Lie down and accept this as a marriage. I don't think so.'

She turned back to pack her clothes, more to hide her damp eyes than to get out of the house any sooner.

'This is bullshit, I'm sorry that you went to all that trouble, but how can you be so disappointed? Did you really expect me for dinner?' Andy hissed, his voice raised and agitated.

'Yes, I expected you for dinner, why would you arrange dinner if you weren't planning on showing up?'

'What?' he retorted with his hands wide open in an appeal for sanity.

'I told you this morning that I wouldn't be able to make dinner. I apologised and asked that you give me two days and you would have your husband back again. I understand you're upset that I can't seem to make time for you at the moment, but it looks like you've added another nasty trait to your box of tricks. Are you now clinically insane as well as an abysmal shameless cheat?'

76

'So when the Second World War finished didn't they close down Unit Firestorm?' It was an apt question but Chris was ready with all the answers.

'I'm glad you asked me that!' he embraced the discussion and was acting more like a college professor all the time.

'Calm down Chris, just tell me what you read in the report.'

'Well, you're right. After the war a new Prime Minister was elected. Labour leader Clement R. Attlee took up residence in No. 10 Dowling Street. Unit Firestorm was disbanded and Attlee was never made aware of its existence.'

'So how are we in this mess today then?' Jennifer asked her 'professor'.

'Because Winston was only on sabbatical. In 1951 Churchill came roaring back to power and after discussing matters with his new CIGS, they decided to reinstate Unit Firestorm for use in 'exceptional circumstances of compromised national security'. At this point a new member was added to the team. During the war, costs had spiralled out of control. Post-war money was tight with rations the order of the day. Any money used for the unit would have to be well hidden; the Chancellor of the Exchequer was the man for this job. And so over fifty years on, the unit is still here, unknown to almost everyone in Britain.'

'That's great, now is it a left or a right from here?'

'It's right, then second left and keep going, I'll give you a shout when we're there.'

It was a quick response, Chris was on a role and he didn't want to stop now.

'Attached with the document is a list of all the missions the unit carried out. Have a listen, I think you'll find this interesting. There are two pages of missions coving operations from inception until early 2009. Each page contains about one hundred missions. The first sheet covers years 1945 until 2004, the second contains 2004 to 2008.'

'So?' Jennifer said, wishing he would just spell out exactly what he was getting at.

'So that equates to an average of three assassinations a year from 1945 to 2003, and from 2004 on, the average is twenty-two kills a year. Basically, the average jumps like a heartbeat on a hospital EKG monitor. Something happened to Unit Firestorm around March 2004 and it brought the unit to life. As far as I can see, Britain's biggest serial killer is the Prime Minister!'

Suddenly he raised his voice 'Hold on, hold on, hold on.'

He grabbed the dash in front of him as Jennifer slammed on the brakes.

'I said second left.'

'I know, sorry. I think your story finally got interesting and I got distracted.'

She completed a neat three-point turn and got back on track.

'Nice driving Jen, anyway I think The Light gave us this information for a reason.'

'And that reason is?'

'That's for tomorrow's lecture' he said with a smile. They had arrived at his apartment. He stepped onto the pavement and stuck his head back into the car.

'6am my place sound okay? It's gonna be a big day tomorrow.'

'Sounds good, do I get course notes to study tonight?' She joked.

'No exams if you cook breakfast for me tomorrow!' he winked at her and closed the car door.

Jennifer executed another neat three-point turn and made her way back home. Chris had certainly helped her to relax. His bubbly personality had often grinded against her, but tonight the pair finally seemed to be getting on. Regardless, anything was better than an awkward silence.

77

The birds chirped. The wind brought the trees to life. The sun peered over the horizon and combined with the cloudless sky it cast a red hue over the homes, cranes and offices of London. On this winter's morning, trepidation had now been replaced with disillusion. This was the last place Andy wanted to be right now, but he had no choice. The Light had contacted him earlier that morning. She ordered him to ring his boss and inform him he was sick again. He had not gone back to Directacom since the funeral and The Light didn't want Brownlow, or anybody else having a cause for suspicion. Then she ordered him to make an appearance at Firestorm or risk exposure. Recon's systems had highlighted Corporal Pickering was absent for three days running. Now it was all about not getting caught. Andy was still on a tight rein, and like a good dog, he did what he was told.

'Hey hey stranger, I see you found the razor blade!'

Andy sat in the canteen eating some slightly burnt toast with marmalade. He turned to see Corporal Cleaver whose head was inside the door although his body had remained outside. It always seemed odd to Andy that a person could wish to talk with someone but felt they were in such a rush that they couldn't afford the time it would take for that one extra stride inside the door.

'Earth to Planet Pickering. I said I see you found the razor blade!' Cleaver reiterated.

Andy lifted his head from the plate and looked at him with a hollow stare. A few seconds later he eventually asked.

'For What?'

'To cut your beard.'

Andy's hollow stare remained.

To cut my beard.

The last time Andy saw Corporal Cleaver he left the facility a defeated man. Hearing about his 'good' work in assassinating Tony Cohen and Peter Johnson was harrowing. Cleaver had just picked up on how Andy was looking much better than earlier in the week. However, it was also clear he certainly wasn't feeling any better.

'Yes, I found it alright' Andy said as he turned back down to his burnt toast and contemplated whether to eat the burnt crusts.

Cleaver's head joined his feet in the corridor and he left Corporal Pickering to play with his breakfast.

'Pickering, my office now.'

Andy knew this voice, it was unmistakable in authority. This time both head and feet entered the canteen. Andy doubted if The General could boast the agility to have it any other way. He jumped to his feet. Maybe the big man and his moustache was exactly the tonic he required.

'Yes Sir.'

He followed The General down the corridor and into his office. Inside sat Corporal's Bhana and Fisher. Something very fishy was going on and Andy didn't like the stench.

'First of all, let me congratulate each and every one of you. Last week's mission was a great success, but that mission is now over and it's time to move on. The three of you obviously have a great bond as a team. We need to harness that. A mission has come up. The Marshal and I have discussed it and we have decided you three's talents are what we require.'

'When's the mission?' Andy blurted. The moment he said it he knew it was a mistake. The General got up from behind his desk and walked around until he stood in front of Andy.

'Because?'

'Because I think that's pretty important' Andy said with a

cocky tone. He had decided to fight fire with fire, and he was right.

'Tonight Corporal. Now, no more questions until I have finished.'

Andy was glad he hadn't felt the wrath of The General, but a mission would take up all his time. The clock was ticking. Recon would give the information on him anytime soon.

Maybe Fisher and Bhana are going to assassinate me.

It was the most plausible thought Andy had had for some time. It made perfect sense.

What better way to kill someone than to invite them along to their own murder scene?

The General began his tactical briefing. All Andy could hear were muttering murmurs. The General's voice was one of conviction, but right now, it exerted as much influence over Andy as *Mystic Meg's* daily horoscopes. Andy's mind was elsewhere. It was in paranoia mode. He looked from the corner of his eye. Maybe he could reason with Bhana and Fisher. At least Amy would listen to him. He almost sacrificed his marriage for this woman, surely she wouldn't kill him in cold blood. Or would she? He started to seriously contemplate killing both Bhana and Fisher.

Maybe it's the only way.

78

Chris fell in a heap on the floor. His abdomen cramped as he clutched it. He had one minute to gather his composure. He dragged himself to his feet and propped himself off the wall. The short snappy breaths he was taking were giving insufficient air to his lungs. He felt very weak. He concentrated and attempted to regulate his breathing. The minute was almost up. He pushed himself off the wall and gingerly walked over to his ab rocker. It was time for another twenty-five sit-ups. Chris was determined to do a quick workout, despite the clearly extenuating circumstances. It helped to clear the mind.

The sight that greeted Jennifer wasn't very appealing. It was only 6am and this view would shake anybody's head and knock the remaining nuggets of unwanted sleep from their eyes. It was a smelly, sweaty Chris that opened the door. Complete with wet white vest top and short tight shorts, it was a difficult sight for people with the toughest of constitutions. Jennifer waited in the corridor.

'Won't you come in?' he asked guiding her with his hand to show her inside.

'Won't you disinfect yourself first?' she retorted.

He leaned back, unsure if he could have heard her right.

'Yes, I said won't you disinfect yourself first?'

'Well I'm not sure I've enough *Dettol* to fill the bath.'

'Chris, I don't even want to know what you've been up to. Just please, have some dignity and some respect for everyone else and go straighten yourself up.'

Her head was lowered and her hand placed over her anguished brow to hide the horror ahead of her. Now she quickly took a peak between her fingers and was pleased to see he had taken her advice. Whatever brief bonding had taken place in the car last night had been quickly dissipated. Order had been restored.

Chris enjoyed his shower. Whatever the snotty nosed, arty farty Jennifer thought was immaterial. He was developing a new found respect for himself and it was all due to sweaty vests. The exercise cleared his brain too. He now reasoned with clarity. Random pieces of a jigsaw could be seen for the full picture they represented. They would need this clarity today more than ever. He made sure that if today were his last day to walk on this earth, then he would have given survival his best possible shot.

'Yes, yes, you can remove your hand from your horrified face. I am dressed in suitable attire for the lady!' He sarcastically stated as he re-entered the living room.

'Why thank you Chris, you really know how to treat a lady' she responded.

Bloody idiot is what she really thought but other things were on her mind right now.

'I've tried ringing Andy three times since I got here and it keeps going straight to voicemail' Jennifer said.

'Well you should know more about it than me, what the hell did you show him in your apartment? He was demented when he left last night.'

'I can't tell you Chris. It's not like I'm trying to be a bitch, it's just he made me promise not to tell anybody and I must respect that.'

'Trust me, you don't have to *try* to be a bitch.'

Before she had time to respond, her hand started to vibrate. Wrapped inside her fingers, her phone had begun to ring. She looked at the screen and raised her eyes to Chris.

'Is it Andy?' he asked wondering if the *bitch* would even tell him.

True to form she said nothing. Instead she placed the phone on the table and put it on loudspeaker, just as Andy did the previous day.

'Good morning to you both. Good to see you up so early, and hats off to Chris for his exercise routine, very impressive!'

With all the happenings of the previous day, it had slipped his mind that his apartment had been bugged. 'Straight to business. Recon has stepped up surveillance on Corporal Andy Pickering to Level 4. He was away from the unit for three days straight. This triggered the alarm. Combined with recent circumstances it was decided that he is now a high level risk. I was previously the woman assigned to monitor him. Unfortunately, Level 4 means a more senior member of staff is assigned to the case. By tracking movements, I estimate we have approximately ten or so hours until all three of you are caught. It may take a further two hours for approval of the assassination plan. The clock has officially begun. It's now 6.30am. At 18.30 you *will* become a target of assassination. Have no doubts about that. Due to the nature of the case, i.e. exposing Unit Firestorm, you are a Code Red Alert. This means you will be assassinated within the hour. I hope your wills are in order.'

The past three days had been fraught with disbelief, danger, delusion and deception. Yet somehow, it hadn't struck home how real this whole pursuit had been. It now hit Chris very hard indeed. He loved skydiving. Whenever he was on holiday it was always the first activity on his itinerary. Now, it felt as if he had pulled the string and his first parachute had just failed. The whole experience of the chase had been a mind blowing, adrenaline pumping experience. With skydiving, the worry comes before you jump out of the plane. The pursuit of the truth had been the same. The moment Andy told him about Unit Firestorm he jumped out of the plane. There was no going back and no time to worry. But the flawed cord was now pulled and the exhilaration had been replaced by the devastating reality that if he didn't release his parachute in the next ten hours, he would end up lying dead on the ground after staring his own death in the face. He wanted to skydive again, but literally, and on a well-deserved holiday.

'Alright Ms Light, I know what you gave us in that file is a clue, but we need direction from you' he appealed

'And that I can give you. First of all, let me tell you where we stand. Andy has passed on the recording from Terry White's house. It's definitely enough to take down The General. Peter Johnson's work is now complete and we could arrest The General right now. However, something rotten is going on in Firestorm and it's more than just some on-the-side drug dealing. If you read the report, I'm sure you have seen the sudden increase in assassinations in recent years. If we expose Firestorm now, it will be quietly disbanded and nobody will be brought to justice.'

'Fuck Firestorm' Jennifer interrupted. 'I'm not dying for this, hand in the file, arrest The General and get me into police protection.'

Chris was taken aback by her outburst, but he could defiantly see her point.

'Ya, I'm all for heroics but not going to the police now is suicide. Let's get The General and let Firestorm sort themselves out.'

'Suicide' crackled through the phone. 'Not seeing this through is suicide. Do you want to live your life looking over your shoulder? Because whoever this is, they are going to get you. Maybe not when you are in police custody, but someday they will come looking. There is only one winner, and it won't be you. I'd seriously advise not doing that. You must trust me. We need to find the ringleader.'

The conversation turned to silence as Chris and Jennifer looked at each other weighing up their options. Finally Chris spoke.

'But don't you think the ringleader is The General?' Chris asked.

'It could be, he certainly has a motive for his drugs trade, but we need proof, not coincidence. So where should we begin to look?'

'Around March 2004?' Chris suggested

'Bingo' said the crackly voice, her voice changer still in use.

'I really have no more information. I haven't been investigating this myself. I was horrified at Peter Johnson's assassination, that's how I got my hands on the file. The information is as new to me as it is to you. Anyway I must go now. I've got to go try and delay Mr Andrews. He's Recon's best field officer and the man looking into this case. Best of luck.'

'Hold on' Jennifer shouted with an air of desperation in her voice.

'Do you know where Andy is? Is he okay?'

'He's okay for now, he's in Firestorm, they were getting suspicious by his absence. Look, forget about Andy he can look after himself. It's up to you two now. I mean it, best of luck, we're all counting on you.'

The line went dead.

Chris walked determined into his bedroom. A moment later he arrived back at the table with an A4 pad and a pen in hand. He opened the pad and began writing. Jennifer peered over his shoulder. All she could see was one to ten written down the side of the page and inscribed at the top was written *Events March 2004*. It was time for some serious investigating and he was ready for it. He was embracing his free fall again. If he stayed cool he could solve the crisis and release the 'problematic parachute'.

79

Chris paused a while. The pen felt heavy in his hand. It was surprisingly difficult to think of major events that took place in March 2004. He could only think of one significant moment. It was an event that was close to his heart. The date was the 18th of March and he collected a cool £1000 from his best mate William Hill. *Best Mate* was the name of the horse and William Hill was the name of the bookmaker. It was an incredible triumph and the whole nation stopped still for a day to honour their champion. It was the gelding's third consecutive Cheltenham Gold Cup victory. He equalled the achievements of the legend Arkle.

To hell with it he thought and Chris wrote down event No. 1.

'What is Best Mate?' Jennifer asked confused.

'The Beethoven of horse racing.'

It was an explanation she could immediately identify with, but she still wasn't impressed.

'Come on Chris, can't you take anything seriously? Grab my laptop, we're not going to solve this by memory.'

Jennifer typed an encyclopaedic website into the address bar and hit return. Although not fully reliable, it was a brilliant place to get loads of information at the touch of a button. Chris was impressed. In two seconds there was enough information on March 2004 to write a book. Immediately, almost like an impetuous schoolboy, he checked March 18th. To his utter disappointment, the inclusion of Best Mate's historic win wasn't seen as necessary.

'So, of the thousand events shown, your horse didn't feature, what a pity!' she said, taunting him.

'Well it's staying number one on my list anyway!' he said putting his hand over the A4 pad as if to protect it.

'Come on, enough bickering. We're dead in ten hours. We need to focus. Let's go through these and write down anything that jumps out at us' Jennifer said as the pair began to study every major occurrence during the month in question.

Finally they agreed on their shortlist. In brackets they put down their own thoughts.

No. 1, 3G to be rolled out in Britain. Government award 3G license after sealed bid auction. The European Union Council recommended that the 3G operators should cover 80% of the European national populations by the end of 2005. (Not sure but biggest UK business deal to go down in the month)

No 2, HMIF oil industries hostile takeover of Rostech fails. An eighteen billion dollar takeover bid failed when HMIF industries were refused credit to finance the deal. (Big money, no other reason to be suspicious)

No. 3, Three tons of cocaine with an estimated street value of thirty million pounds was intercepted off the coast of Cornwall near the coastal town of Porthleven. (Cocaine = The General Connection?)

An hour had passed, but the list was complete. Chris looked at his watch, nine hours to go till they were caught.

'Nine hours for three investigations. I don't think it's going to work. What do you think we should do?' he asked.

The odd-couple had actually worked quite well for the past hour and Chris now valued her opinion.

'We've got to go with our gut. I think we only have time to check out one idea.'

Chris nodded.

'I agree entirely. So what's it to be?'

'Surely it's got to be the cocaine?'

'Good plan, now, let's say a little prayer!' Chris said sarcastically. The sarcasm was a front. His Irish upbringing was lurking in all but a few corners of his consciousness. He closed his eyes and said a prayer to Saint Anthony to help him find the answers he was looking for.

It was decided. There was no need for bickering this time. Both Jennifer and Chris had similar thoughts. The connection with coke ran deep in all the discoveries made so far. It looked the safest bet.

'So where do we begin to investigate this?'

'I know exactly where to start.' he confidently answered.

'Follow me' he said as he grabbed his coat from the chair and made a beeline towards the door.

80

The digital display not only looked like a F1 car, it now read like an F1 car. Jennifer knew how to drive her baby when it mattered, and it mattered at this instant. Upon reaching their destination the car grinded to a halt. Chris was impressed. Last night she completed some very nifty three point turns. Now her ability to parallel park was tested by a space fit only for a car the size of little 'Daisy'. Once again she passed with flying colours as she gave Chris a wry wink.

'Hop to it. You've brought us all the way out here so you better get some answers.'

'No pressure!'

Chris knew he had just made a big call. Either he was a good judge of character and all the required information would be his, or he had over stepped the mark and lost the best part of two hours crossing the city for absolutely nothing.

'See you soon darling' he playfully said before he scampered across the street and up the oversized limestone steps.

'Hello Chris, step into my office. You know the way, I'll be with you in a moment.'

Chris did as he was told and sat waiting in the office. The office clearly wasn't designed for the waiting person in mind. There were no trashy magazines or newspapers to keep Chris occupied. He always found it difficult to do nothing. Reading was a way to avoid such an unpleasant state. He often read the Sunday newspapers while on the toilet attending to nature's business. If using a friends facilities and no reading material was to be found then the back of the closest product within arm's reach would be carefully scrutinised. As party tricks go, knowing the ingredients of toilet cleaner or an expensive shampoo isn't a very good one. However, if requested by friends on a drunken night out, he was always available to oblige. The only reading material available in this room was on the walls. Wedged between a variety of soccer photographs was Sergeant Green's police certificate. This too was difficult to read as most of the text was in Latin. Having nothing to read often made Chris fidgety but thankfully he would avoid that fate today. No sooner had he visually dissected the walls than the Sergeant walked in the door.

'Now son, has Andy got you here on another errand?'

Jennifer had been a busy lady while she waited in the car. This was no time for her to twiddle her thumbs. She studied arts in University College London. She spent fond times in Travistock Square where she lived for most of her third level education. She only sporadically kept in contact with her former university friends. However, a minimal amount of contact was enough of a link and she hoped that one of them could help get her out of the hole she had suddenly found herself in. She had made no progress after three phone calls. She wasn't giving up yet.

'Hello Ann, how are you? It's Jenny here.'

'Sorry who did you say?'

'Jenny, Jenny Penny.'

Jennifer hated her university nickname. She couldn't even remember where it came from, but it seemed everybody else just loved the name.

'Penny baby, how the devil are you?'

'I'm good thanks, you know trying to keep the best side out.'

'My main problem is all sides are coming out! Think I need a man to help me burn of some of my love handles. So how's your love life hun?'

Jennifer was in no mood for pillow talk, it was time to get

down to business.

'Quiet. The reason I'm ringing is I am hoping you might be able to help me with something. As a business journalist, would you be able to recall HMIF oil industries hostile takeover of Rostech back in 2004?'

'I remember it vividly. I broke the story for the paper. It was the news of the business world that year but the bid failed. So are you still working in the library or are you planning a takeover bid yourself?'

'Definitely just a librarian, but I do have a particular interest in this case. Can you tell me, was there anything unusual about the attempted takeover? Something out of place or suspicious?'

'There most definitely was, it was something very unusual.'

'Go on' Jennifer said as she listened with interest.

81

She looked so beautiful. Her little tartan hat kept the cold out, hiding her flowing strawberry blonde locks. It was only three weeks ago the picture had been taken. After a sprinkling of snow Jack and Ann Marie enjoyed some good-natured snowball fights in the back garden. Jack didn't feature in the picture, instead Ann Marie's new friend joined in the fun. 'Frosty' was complete with scarf, hat and an old smoking pipe and the snowman looked quite handsome next to his maker. Andy sat staring at the photograph from his wallet. He was transfixed on the image before him and tears began to well in his eyes. It was almost four years since Andy first held her in his arms. It was a wonderful moment in the hospital but a moment that also sparked fear into him. Without ever having sisters and without any young female relatives, he felt nervous about what lay ahead. It would sicken him if he couldn't be a good father to her. Four wonderful, educational and emotional years later he was the good father he had longed to be. As he looked at her snow-covered face he couldn't bear the thought of not seeing his angel again. She needed him and he needed her. He rubbed his eyes. He may have been alone in the canteen but he definitely couldn't afford anybody to see his raw emotion. The picture was slipped back into where it came from. He put the wallet back in his pocket and in the one movement of his right hand he pulled the gun from the holster around his waist. Lifting the gun into the air he checked its moving parts and made sure the weapon was clean. If he was going to kill two more of his colleagues, he would have to be convinced it was for the right reason. The only right reason was his beautiful pride and joy.

'Have you got everything ready Andy?' Amy Fisher said as she popped her head in the door.

'No, nothing ready as of yet, just having a quick cup of tea first' he responded.

'Come on Andy, knock it back. We've got a mission to get ready for and by all accounts it's not going to be easy.'

'Okay, okay. Give me two seconds' he said as he let the now cold tea flow back into his throat. After a quick rinse, he left the cup on the washboard and walked down the corridor with Corporal Fisher by his side. It struck him as quite unusual that she had just called him by his first name. If any feelings of guilt were to come over her she would surely have addressed him by his Firestorm title. Maybe, she just didn't care about him anymore, or maybe she wasn't actually about to assassinate him after all. Paranoia had left him believing he detonated a bomb on the London underground system, when in fact he had merely called for assistance. He almost wished he was bound to that white room chair right now. At least then he couldn't do any more harm. The possible paranoia was highly dangerous and he knew it. He set himself a new rule; he would have to be shot at before he would shoot his colleagues, his friends.

'What are you thinking about in that serious head of yours?'

He turned to see what looked like a genuinely concerned Amy. He looked searchingly into her eyes but failed to find the answer he was looking for. He turned away in silence only to feel a warm touch on his right shoulder. Amy put her arm around him and continued with her line of questioning.

'Come on Andy, you can tell me, what are you thinking about in that head of yours?'

He wanted to tell her exactly what was occupying his mind. He wanted to pretend that telling her would make everything bad just go away. She was the embodiment of physical perfection in his lusting eyes. She also appeared to have a keen attraction to him and only one week ago it looked as if she might make a move on him. Right now she was comforting him from a mental turmoil that involved matters of life and death. All this on the back of a night in which he just discovered that his beloved wife had been cheating on him for almost an entire year. He could have easily fallen into Amy's gapping arms. It was a quick fix solution, but it could also have far reaching and fatal consequences. He knew better. He picked up his pace and walked out of her embrace. It was no time to get sentimental.

'I need to go to the toilet Corporal Fisher, I will see you in the weapons room.'

He detoured left and pushed the door open to the male toilets. As soon as he was inside he stood with his back to the door, closed his eyes, and tried to think logically. Nobody was going to brainwash him today. Nobody could be trusted.

He walked to the wash hand basin and turned on the tap. As he doused water on his face he caught his eyes in the mirror. They were scattered and weary. He needed something to help him focus. He didn't have to wait long. As he turned off the tap his mobile phone rang.

'You are caught Pickering.'

Good news was hard to come by for Andy and The Light wasn't going to change that trend.

'I'm afraid my supervisor Mr Andrews has obtained information that puts you and Chris in severe danger. Already a plan is being formulated to eliminate you both. After some thought I have come up with a solution. You will have to attempt to do something which sounds horrendous, but it is the only way.'

Unfortunately, alternatives had become limited. Andy listened as The Light explained his next move.

'So just remember, don't miss his chest and everything will be fine.'

'So you're telling me this is my only option?' a flabbergasted Andy exclaimed down the phone.

82

So, have I been of any assistance to you Penny?'

'I hope so' Jennifer answered, frantically jotting down the last few details from her former classmate.

'Thanks so much Ann, we've really got to catch up again soon. See you'

Jennifer ended the phone call without giving Ann a chance to respond.

The car door opened and in stepped a panting Chris. She had seen him run down the steps from the police station. For a man with a few too many pounds, in a few too many places, he could still move when he wanted to.

'I've got the information' he exclaimed. Then he paused for a moment to catch his breath.

'But it's not what we were looking for'

'What do you mean?' she demanded, squinting her eyes as she tried to comprehend her confusing collaborator.

'Sergeant Green was so helpful it was almost unnerving. Anyway to cut a long story short, normally the drugs are transported to the nearest main police station for analysis and then destroyed. However, Porthleven is a long way from the nearest main station. It was decided not to risk moving such a large quantity of drugs. Instead it was analysed on site and destroyed that night at an army sealed site near the find. As Sergeant Green put it; In Cornwall they do things that bit differently!'

'So what does this tell us?' she asked, her right hand holding the key in the ignition ready to turn it and set off on a new assignment at any moment.

'It tells us that there wasn't enough time for The General to interfere with the drugs. Basically, we can obtain no proof whatsoever from the event. It means we've got to go back to the drawing board, unless you found out anything in the mean time?

'Well as it happen I..' Jennifer was interrupted by Chris' ringing phone.

'You and Andy have been discovered conversing on Firestorm by Mr Andrews. They plan to terminate both of you immediately.'

83

A candle was placed on the stereo, a candle was placed on the table, and a series of candles were placed on the mantel piece over the fire. In fact, the room was enveloped in a sea of dimly lit candles. Next he moved to the table, out of the corner of his eye he spotted a mark on a spoon. He immediately plucked it from the table and whipping his handkerchief from his breast pocket, he rubbed away the unwanted stain. Taking a step back, John Black examined the room. It now looked perfect. In his eyes everything *was* perfect.

He had been off form all morning. His eyes narrowed as he thought back to the embarrassing events of the previous night at The Ritz Hotel. He was making sure this would never happen again. Earlier today he received a phone call. It was the answer to his prayers. Tonight John would finally have everything. He walked back to the stereo. The hue from the candles illuminated his music collection arranged in alphabetical order on a CD rack. He flicked through the collection, pausing sporadically to examine one CD or another a little closer. He perused the Beach Boys, Michael Jackson and Depeche Mode. None made the grade. Finally the choice was made. The luscious lilting tones filled the room. Only one man's voice could touch a woman like this. Tonight Black and White would combine as the sound of 'Can't Get Enough Of Your Love Babe' drifted through the dining room.

Foam exploded everywhere. It sprayed on the table, on his hand and on the carpet. He didn't care where it spilt. There would be plenty more where that came from. Manners would suggest he wait until his guest arrived before he opened the vintage bottle of champagne, but he just couldn't help himself. There was a personal triumph to be celebrated first. How life had changed from the days of working on construction sites. He recalled that unforgettable day in which he had to clean the cabin toilets. Staring back at him was the horrific sight of that used condom bobbing up and down. The moment had changed his life. He knew this was his lowest ebb. He knew he would have to turn his life around. Now, staring back at him was twenty-five million pounds, which only two hours previously, was transferred into his laundering account by William H. Murray. Champagne could now be for breakfast lunch and dinner and in his eyes, he had deserved every single penny of it. It's not easy to build a life of deceit, corruption and immorality without either some busybody or your own conscious getting in the way. He had managed to avoid those two dreaded traps and came out the other side an incredibly wealthy man. He filled another glass as he looked at an old black and white picture of himself on the mantel piece. He was fifteen in the photo and wearing his older brothers hand-me-down clothes. How far he had come.

'To me' he said as he raised his glass to the photo. In one swallow he consumed the entire contents of the flute.

No sooner had he put the glass on the mantel piece than the doorbell sounded. He rubbed his hands together and walked to the front door. Opening it, he saw the most wonderful sight before him. Victoria was looking ravishing. Her blue dress was simple. There were no frills, no fancy cuts, but it hugged her body like a roll of coloured cling film. Her presence gave an aura like no other woman he had known. Quite simply, she was stunning. Unfortunately, her expression was cold and listless, but after the news she told him on the phone today, he could well understand why. Hopefully a glass of champagne and the promise of a life without financial limits might bring some rosiness back to her cheeks again.

He gave her a gentle kiss on the cheek.

'Come in, come in. Care for a glass of champagne?' he said as he produced a flute glass from behind his back.

'I don't know John' said a hesitant Victoria.

'I'm celebrating, I'll tell you all about it later. You'll have to have a drink tonight.'

With that Victoria hesitantly outstretched her hand and John filled her glass to the brim.

'To the good life' he said toasting his glass in the air.

The moment was interrupted by the sound of a phone ringing.

'I'm sorry, terrible timing' he said apologetically as he wrenched his phone from his pocket.

'Unfortunately I have to take this one, why don't you move into the living room and make yourself comfortable by the fire.'

Victoria did as suggested and John answered the phone. A man in a German accent began to speak.

'I am in position. You were correct with your information. The target has just left the grain store. I am now in pursuit. Am I still to carry out orders as discussed?'

'Absolutely, I don't want any more phone calls until you confirm he is dead.'

John didn't wait for any more chitchat. He put the phone down, shook his head, regained his composure and headed straight for the living room. He knew he had been losing control of Victoria. He had been neglecting her in recent times but he definitely didn't want to lose her. Now it was time to work his magic. She rang him earlier in the day and said it had been a crazy night and she needed to see him. He was ready to comfort her, but he would be comforting her about something a lot more serious soon. First though, it was time to break the good news.

'Victoria, my darling, I have something I want to tell you, but first we should fill our glasses again.'

John raised his glass for the third time tonight.

'Victoria, the past ten months have been incredible. From the moment I saw you outside the Theatre, to that wonderful day at the Ritz, to every other moment we've been together it's been amazing. Now let's take it to the next step. Let's enjoy a future without boundaries. I have just become a millionaire, twenty-five times over and I'm so happy that I have you to enjoy it with.'

She looked at him in disbelief. Twenty-five million was a hell of a lot of money. John leaned into Victoria and embraced her with a kiss.

84

Chris didn't know why, but he was now speeding towards Scotland Yard. He wished it was for a reason. He wished he had all the information he needed to end Firestorm and guarantee his safety. Instead he was making his way empty-handed. He didn't even know what he would do when he entered the foyer. Who would he talk to? What would he say? It was all a mystery, but he had no choice but to place his faith in The Light's hands.

Her familiar distorted voice had instructed Chris to immediately make his way to Scotland Yard. It didn't matter that they hadn't found the evidence they so desperately needed. He had to leave and arrive there within the hour.

'You and Andy have been discovered conversing on Firestorm by Mr Andrews. They plan to terminate both of you immediately. You need to get to Scotland Yard within the next hour, Jennifer is to remain to carry on the investigation. I must go, make sure you are there within the hour.'

Nothing made sense anymore. Yesterday, Chris felt their destiny was in their own hands. Now they had nothing. Andy went to Firestorm for the day to make an appearance but had been caught by Mr Andrews. He had walked into the lion's den and if he had survived thus far, he was now a dead man walking. All the while Chris was bound for a destination but he didn't know why. He didn't even know who the woman was that was dragging him there. All he knew was that the skilled Mr Andrews had caught both he and Andy and that he had just a few hours to live, at the very most.

The iconic structure stood tall and proud looking over its people as it had done so for almost one hundred and fifty years. It was dusk on the cold December evening as the large hand made its way to a vertical position. Big Ben now confirmed it was four o'clock. Chris glanced at Westminster and the clock as he whizzed by. Two minutes later and he would arrive at his destination. From here he could see the famous rotating triangular sign. New Scotland Yard. He pulled up on the curb. Tentatively, he opened the door and stepped nervously onto the pavement. This made no sense but he would have to do it anyway. He made every effort not to look suspicious, but without a reason for being there it was hard to look focused. To relax, he pretended in his mind that he himself was a police detective. 'Good day ma'am' he said to the first passerby he noticed. He walked assuredly up the street and started to approach the entrance of the grounds, this new confidence would only last so long. What would happen once he entered the building? What would he do? What would he say? He didn't need to worry.

'Do not turn around. Continue walking, go past the entrance and walk down the first alley to your right.'

On hearing the voice Chris' natural instinct was to swivel his head to see who was speaking to him.

'I said don't fucking turn around unless you want a hole in your head' said the voice.

This response immediately over ruled his natural instinct and he kept his head firmly facing forward. They turned down the alley and he felt something against his back. He tried to spin to see what happened when he once again was told in no uncertain terms not to turn around.

'Stop there Chris. Listen very carefully to me, we do not have much time.'

Chris now knew who his assailant was. Facing down the alley with The Light behind him Chris listened in anticipation and apprehension.

Deisler lifted the device from the passenger seat and began

to check it over and over. The timer was working and all the connections were made. This was his speciality. He never liked using guns. Guns were too precise; it took a sharp eye to hit a man from two hundred yards. He much preferred to just press a button. 'Boom' and it was all over. Deisler was almost caught by the police on one unlucky evening four years ago. Since that night he never used a gun in anger again. It was much preferable to be in a remote location when assassinating someone, rather than the immediate vicinity of the crime. Tonight would be no different, he had a job to do and a cheque to collect.

Deisler loved a good explosion, but the more people who witness an event, the more it seemed police felt the need to investigate. His employer hadn't told him the target would be driving with two other people. He preferred to minimise unwanted casualties, but a job was a job and killing people is what he did. He lost his morality many years ago. It was a bit late to get worried about two more people's lives. These would be just a blip in the enormous list of lives he had already cut short.

Deisler smirked as he considered his current location. He looked at the device in his hands, then he looked out the window at the rotating sign for New Scotland Yard. The irony was not lost on him as he tried to hide his smile and refocus.

Andy's finger quivered. His granduncle had experienced the degenerative effects of Parkinson's disease towards the latter end of his life. Andy saw how it had changed him, how it robbed him of so much. It had taken years for the onset of the disease; it now appeared to have come upon Andy within a matter of minutes. He was in the perfect position, the shot was open, the orders given and yet his index finger remained quivering over the trigger.

'What the fuck is wrong with you Pickering? Do it already' said an impatient Corporal Bhana. From a tactical view point

Bhana was spot on. Delaying the kill meant narrowing their window of escape. Chris' chest was in Andy's scope. This is what all the hours spent in the range were for. Andy murmured under his breath 'Please God, keep my shot true'. He pulled the trigger. It was a perfect shot, the target was down.

Deisler looked on in disbelief. If he knew he was dealing with a skilled marks man and possible psychopath he would have insisted on a much bigger fee for the kill. It was clear this guy was not to be messed with.

'We have got to go' said Bhana as he pulled Andy's sniper rifle in the window.

'Time is ticking, let's go, go, go' repeated Bhana as he became more agitated. Of all places to hang around after killing someone, Scotland Yard was not one of them. Corporal Fisher sprinted across the street and jumped into the car. Andy turned the key and drove away from the scene, his mind troubled by the events that had unfolded. It was an unexpected detour and one Andy felt he may never forget.

The team was already on the road to complete the assigned mission when the following message came in on the Firestorm in-car display.

Emergency unscheduled mission to be carried out immediately. Location, Broadway, Westminster, SW1H, London. Man will be walking holding green file bound for entrance of Scotland Yard. Assassinate on sight. Does not need to look like accident as time is of the essence. File to be obtained and destroyed. Upon completion continue with assigned mission.

Andy tried to concentrate on their getaway but it was difficult to black out the fact that he had just shot his best friend.

The Light better have had everything organised.

85

New message from The General read the display. Bhana opened it.

'What does it say?' asked Corporal Fisher as she leaned out between the two front seats

'He is just asking if we completed our added detour, and if all went according to plan.' Bhana replied.

Fisher queried The General's motives 'It's strange he's taking such a special interest in this evenings activities. He has never interfered on a mission before. Do you think something else is going down tonight?'

'I'm sure of it' replied Bhana.

All the time his colleagues were discussing the night's events, Andy couldn't help but wonder what The General was playing at.

Why would he send this message knowing full well I would read it? Why would he order me to make the kill at Scotland Yard knowing full well that I would then know we were caught? Why am I still alive? Is it just for his amusement? Will my next mission be to kill Jennifer? Or is the next mission to kill me?

The questions were endless, the answers were few.

Andy decided it best to drive as fast as possible.

If they kill me now, they kill all of us!

Deisler followed, waiting for his moment. He looked at his speedometer. They were still in the streets of London but the dial read 64mph and was rising. This guy was not holding back. Deisler kept following but at this speed it all looked a little suspicious. As a result, he kept his distance as much as he possibly could. So far, he was confident he hadn't been detected.

It was approaching Christmas and streets were busy with shoppers. One little girl had lost her mother in the festive crowds. She was the only motionless person in a sea of people trying to get places. She kept getting bumped and shoved, more often than not it was accidental, but now the little girl had got frightened. Finally their eyes met. Across the street she could see the smile of a loving and relieved mother. Immediately she ran across the road to find her warm embrace. It was at this point Andy spotted her. He swerved as best he could. The car pulled one way then another. There was a collective gasp as the street stopped their busy lives for just a brief moment to witness the outcome. The little girl froze as her mother screamed. The screams could be heard ringing through the entire street. The screams were overpowered by the clanging noise of metal upon metal. Andy had just hit a lamppost. It sounded worse than the damage it caused as it scraped along the side of the Lexis. Once the car was back on the road and under control all three Firestorm assassins turned around to see the little girl still frozen in the same position as her mother ran across the road to embrace her little miracle. The occupants of the car breathed a collective sigh before Fisher shouted to Andy what the hell was he doing driving so fast.

'I'm just trying to carry out the orders Fisher. Look, nobody is hurt. We need to keep moving.'

He kept his foot on the pedal and he kept his heart in his mouth. He would never forgive himself if he had killed that little girl, then again, he wasn't sure if he could ever forgive himself for all he had done.

By the time Deisler passed the mother embracing her little girl, the busy street was no longer paused. The moment was over and the thousands of shoppers, workers and local residents continued about their business as if nothing had happened. Deisler continued the pursuit but was now becoming mindful that police might get involved. He didn't understand why his target was driving at such excessive speeds, but if he continued to do so it wouldn't be long before a waiting copper would turn on his siren and begin his pursuit. In fact, Deisler was already concerned that this may have begun. Occasionally he caught a glimpse of a car in his rear view mirror. Every so often he could see the car and, although it was not a marked police vehicle, Deisler was suspicious. It seemed unusual that a police car wasn't already in toe. Deisler assumed they were undercover and were looking to catch the suspects in a criminal act, whatever that act might be. He put them out of his mind. He had never been caught before and he wasn't going to buck that trend tonight.

86

Jennifer sat in the library. It was now closed to the public. She had locked all the doors to barricade herself inside. She was armed with a kitchen knife and a plank of timber she found in the storeroom. She also had an aerosol can of women's deodorant and a lighter. It wasn't much of a defence but it was better than nothing. On her desk lay all the information they had gathered to date. She looked at Peter Johnson's information, the top events of March 2004 and Andy's notes he had given her the previous day. It was as if she was looking at a thousand-piece jigsaw puzzle but she didn't have the cover of the box from which to work to. The sweat dripped from her brow and crashed like a gushing waterfall onto the page. The library was so quiet that it appeared to make a splashing sound as it hit the stack of papers. Then the large antique clock made a single bong as the pendulum swung and the hands moved into position. It was now five o'clock.

Tick tock, tick tock. Jennifer could think of nothing else.

If The Light's calculations were correct she had but ninety minutes to save everyone.

Victoria couldn't believe the news. Twenty-five million pounds was a lot of money. It was mind blowing. Her children would never need to worry about the drudgery of life. They could now just enjoy every day; they could make decisions about their lives instead of life making decisions for them. Money wasn't happiness, but it certainly didn't do any harm. She stood by the fire as it crackled sending warmth throughout the room. As she looked into John's eyes he moved towards her and kissed her lips.

It was a wonderful taste. Not alone did Victoria wear a

delicious apricot flavoured lip-gloss. John could also taste victory as he kissed her sensual lips. He knew from her limp kiss that she wasn't fully committed to him just yet. Deisler would see to that. Soon she would throw her arms around him looking for support. She would cry on his shoulder and he, and his money, would be there for her in her hour of need. John Black always got what he wanted and in love it would prove no different.

The General knocked on the Marshal's door.

'Come in' said the Marshal as he lifted his head out of a stack of paperwork. As soon as The General sat down he started to speak.

'Tonight is the most critical night this unit has faced since I took over. If it goes wrong in the next hour we're all seriously exposed. The media will be over this story like flies on a shit. Strange information is coming from Recon. Who was this guy we just killed at Scotland Yard and what was in those files? As head of the unit I need to know. Do you know General? Are you keeping anything from me?'

The General stared back at his Marshal. He too had realised it was the biggest night the unit faced since he had become General. Yet the Marshal was starting to ask a lot of questions. He had never done this before, why would he start now? The General didn't like being asked into the Marshal's office, and he didn't like his tone.

Corporal Amy Fisher glanced at the rear view mirror. In it she could see a determined Andy Pickering. He was still driving at excessive speed despite both she and Bhana telling him to slow down. Even the earlier near miss hadn't deterred him. Something was wrong. From the moment she had placed her arm on his shoulder as they headed for the weapons room she knew Andy was a distracted man. It was obvious to her that he didn't need to go to the bathroom, it was clear that he was just trying to escape her presence. At that moment Amy got a text message. She looked at it and saw it was from The General. All correspondence in relation to missions had to be sent through the Firestorm database computer. It was one of Firestorm's basic rules to ensure all action carried out had been fully authorised, so the sight of this communication surprised Fisher. Apprehensively she opened the message.

He was nearly there. Andy checked his rear view mirror. He could see Amy Fisher looking at her phone. Suddenly she looked up at the rear view mirror and caught his eye. As if embarrassed she instantly looked down at her phone again. Andy had no idea what was going on, he was tired of trying to read into things, paranoia had almost driven him crazy already. All he knew was logic meant his team were going to assassinate him.

Deisler again glanced at his rear view mirror. This time he was shocked by what he saw. If the car following him was an undercover cop he was doing a very inept job. Instead of lurking in the back ground, the pursuing car was now right behind Deisler and looking as if it were about to hit him from behind. Deisler braced himself for impact but it never came. Instead the car veered to the right and overtook the hired gun. Deisler knew he was now caught up in the middle of something big. He glanced to see if he recognised the man driving the car. He was of average height and stocky, nothing really stood out about the man. Deisler did not know him. All he knew is that he sure could drive a Toyota *Yaris* to its limit.

87

Chris read the speedometer. The big blue digits read 102mph. He had just broken the ton and the car had nothing more to give. By now they were out of the busy streets and a straight road opened up in front of them. A new moon meant it was pitch black outside and the lights of the city were starting to fade away. In the distance he could just about make out the taillights of Andy's car. He rang Andy's mobile phone for what seemed like the tenth time, again; he got no answer. It was going to be a battle to catch him, but he simply had to.

Moments before Chris was shot, he saw a man place an object under Andy's car. He had now managed to overtake the man but he needed to go faster. He needed to tell Andy. If only he had started going to the gym a month earlier and lost a few more pounds, the extra weight he was carrying didn't help the *Yaris*'s cause. Thinking about the extra weight he was carrying, he looked back at the bulky object lying on the back seat. He reached back, caught the item and pulled it out to the passenger seat. He kissed it, then he opened the passenger door, still at top speed, and pushed it out. Looking in his rear view mirror he could see the car he just passed swerve to avoid a crash. He hoped he could lose him. The blue numbers now read 106mph. It seemed to him that The Light's bulletproof vest must have weighed at least a stone in weight.

Chris rocked back and forth in his seat. Ahead of him, Andy's taillights were now getting closer and closer. Behind him, a now furious assassin began to draw nearer. The futile rocking awoke the nerve endings in his abdomen. He lifted his hoodie to see a massive contusion on his stomach. He afforded himself a brief smile. He thought maybe it wasn't such a bad thing to have an extra few pounds of fat there to protect him.

He moved his right hand onto his stomach to comfort the pain he felt. Adrenaline had taken him back to the car and got him this far; reality now kicked in. The incessant aching caused him to squint as he attempted to grin and bear the anguish. Through his squinted eyes he looked at the dash, he had dropped to 90mph. The pain had distracted him. He looked in his rear view mirror. The assassin was only twenty yards behind him. He pushed his foot to the floor once again.

Andy glanced at the GPS on the dash and swung a right through a grand entrance. He was a hundred yards from the mission location. He felt relatively safe while driving the car at top speed, but soon Bhana and Fisher would have no reason not to kill him. He turned to look in their eyes. Both kept their heads down. As he searched for their tell tale signs he found something else. It was Jennifer's car in his rear view mirror.

How on earth? But he didn't have time to decipher the possibilities.

The driver of the car was holding a newspaper to the front window, with black markings on it. Andy squinted to read it; the writing was done with a shaky hand. Finally the *Yaris* was close enough to read the sign.

Jump out of the car now: Chris

There was no time for questions. Andy pushed open his door and roared in his authoritative voice 'Out of the car now'.

Deisler whizzed past the entrance. He was happy his work was done. The detonator was pressed and the magic would happen in five short seconds. He hit the green button on his phone. It was time to collect his well-deserved pay cheque.

88

John lifted the telephone handset. No sooner had he answered the phone than a thundering noise reverberated throughout the house. The walls even shook for a moment. He dropped the phone; he didn't motion to pick it up. There was the sound of hundreds of panes of glass, breaking and shattering everywhere. The majestic conservatory featuring John's beloved 'bedroom under the stars' just came shattering to the ground. A panicked John cowered under the food-laden table.

Andy lay on the ground, sore but alive. In front of him a pile of burning metal lit up the night sky. The *Lexis* was destroyed and whatever was in Chris' green file had been destroyed with it. Still rooted to the ground he craned his neck to see who else survived. Behind the burning inferno lay both Fisher and Bhana. Both were very close to the flames. The heat from the blast would no doubt have begun to burn their flesh irreparably. It was clear to him that they were unconscious. Gingerly he picked himself up and dusted himself off. He noticed blood dripping over his eye. He wiped it away but twice as much came gushing back. He would just have to deal with it later. Regaining his composure he moved towards his colleagues. The heat from the petrol-fuelled explosion was now becoming extremely uncomfortable. He decided to make a dash for it and sprinted as best he could into the blaze. He returned from the flames dragging a person in each hand. Away from the flames he laid them in the recovery position and checked their pulse and airways. Both were breathing and it appeared the burns were not life threatening. Andy knew what he had to do next. He reached inside Amy Fisher's trousers pocket and pulled out her mobile phone. He opened the last message received. It was indeed from

The General.

Although it was as he had suspected, it was still both unbelievable and unnerving to read the message.

'Unit member uncovered speaking of Firestorm and attempting to bring down the unit. Mission does not need to look like accident. Assassinate Corporal Andy Pickering.'

Andy shook his head in disbelief. It was that easy to take his life. Just a simple text message and the deed would be done. An instant later he felt a blow to the back of his head. He was knocked to the ground. Above him stood a determined Corporal Bhana. Bhana moved towards the shell shocked Andy and kicked him into the stomach. Andy was winded, and he was disappointed. He knew he should have handcuffed both of them while he had the chance. Bhana kicked Andy again, this time in the head. The cut over his eye exploded with blood. It now gushed like a leak in a water main. He started to feel faint as he looked up at his attacker. Bhana pulled a gun from his holster and aimed it at his head.

'You know you shouldn't have fucked with the unit Andy.'

A near unconscious Andy greeted his comment with a defiant grin.

The sound of the gunshot brought Chris back to consciousness. The newspaper, he was trying to get Andy to read, obstructed his view. At the time he had no choice but to drive blind. It didn't come as a huge surprise that he crashed Jennifer's beloved *Yaris*. Chris muscled his way through the air bag that had inflated and found his way out of the car and onto the ground. Hunched over on his hands and knees he looked to where the gunfire occurred. These people wanted him dead and he wasn't going to give them the chance. He quietly crawled along the grass towards the main road. Once it was within forty yards, he got up and sprinted. The gym work came in handy after all, even as a dynamic twenty-year-old Chris had never moved as fast as he did right now.

The screaming almost hurt Andy's ears. Bhana lay with his leg cocked in the air. He clutched it in a futile attempt to stem the flow of blood. Andy turned to see Fisher still lying on the ground but with her semi-automatic in hand. An embattled Andy pushed himself to stand up. Every muscle in his body now hurt like hell but he had to keep going.

'Thanks Fisher, but I'm really sorry I have to do this' he said as he pulled the gun from her hand. She was still too weak to get up which made it very easy to disarm her. He proceeded to handcuff both Fisher and Bhana. Ripping some material from his blood stained tee shirt, he tied it around Bhana's leg to help stem the flow of blood. With that job complete he turned to the smashed car to see if Chris was all right. As he turned he saw what looked like an Olympic sprinter leave through the entrance and head back out onto the main road. Although the dynamic action gave no clue as to the identity of the runner, Chris' chubby rear end was all too evident as it raced away from view.

Before Mr Andrews' information had changed the course of the evening, The General had stated that this was the biggest and most important mission that had been undertaken by Firestorm. For the first time since Andy's arrival, the unit had not been given the name of their target. It was considered 'classified' information even for Unit Firestorm members of Corporal rank. Andy was fascinated to see who their secret target was. Despite the trauma of the past hour Andy was still thinking clearly. Whoever was in that house was extremely important and most likely extremely dangerous. He knew there was no point trying to run. If he tried to run with his injuries he would surely be gunned down. He knew what he had to do. First, apprehend the suspect to be assassinated and handcuff him. Second, call Jennifer and ask what the fuck was going on. Clearly there wasn't much point in ringing Chris if he had just run away from him. Hopefully they had the incriminating evidence and Jennifer had taken it to Scotland Yard. If so, Andy could just wait with his three prisoners for the police to arrive and end the madness of Firestorm.

Andy stood next to the front door with his back to the wall. His index finger wrapped around the trigger of his loaded semi-automatic. The cut over his eye had begun to dry up. Andy was not sure if it had begun to heal or if he simply had no more blood in his head to give. He debated whether to pick the lock or simply knock the door in. Normal code of practice states to make as little noise as possible when entering a target's place of residence. He was pretty sure that rule was now null and void. The target had certainly heard the car explode outside his front door. Andy couldn't help but think of the difficult mission he experienced in France a fortnight ago. He almost lost his life that night because Recon didn't do their job properly. He found it ironic that tonight he would lose his life if Recon did do their job properly. As with the French mission, the target was now aware of their presence. He would have to be very careful tonight.

With his sweaty back to the wall Andy gathered himself, still debating how he would attack the entry point. Finally he decided to pick the large brass lock. He removed a small metal object from his right trouser pocket and cautiously motioned it towards the door. Delicately he forced the object into the key slot and began to twist it. He believed he was carrying out the task very quietly. Unfortunately for him, he hadn't been subtle enough. Gunfire rang in his ears as three shots sprayed through the oak door.

Andy, now with his back to the wall again, patted down his body. It felt as if no shot had hit him. To his utter relief he found nothing. With no back up available, a wound would most likely have finished him. He took another deep breath, whoever fired those shots meant business. Being quiet was not an option anymore; it was time to subdue the gun-wielding target. He riddled the lock with a full round of bullets. Discarding the magazine he then reloaded. Staying rooted to his position behind the wall he flicked out his leg and kicked the door. It opened with ease. He had been trained not to wait around; it was always best to confront a situation as soon as possible. Andy counted down.

Three, two, one.

Once again gunfire rang out. Andy sprayed bullets everywhere as he sprinted inside. He now lay behind a dark brown leather couch. It was again time to change magazines. The plan worked and it kept his target at bay. As he reloaded his gun he couldn't help but notice the family pictures that hung on the living room wall. Andy now knew his target.

No wonder it was secret.

Firestorm wanted the Chancellor of the Exchequer assassinated. Andy felt a momentary remorse about shooting an elected MP, but right now he knew he had no choice.

Right now it's either him or me.

89

The previous night

Sarah Cripwell ate her chicken salad sandwich. The elaborate high street store food packaging was added to the growing mountain of wrappers stacked up on her desk. Late nights had become common place for her. Not that her boss Andy Pickering took any notice. He hadn't been at work for the past week since the death of their colleague Peter.

Sarah's eyelids no longer had the strength to hold themselves open, but sleeping was not an option. When Recon wanted an investigation completed they wanted it done fast. Lately, working for Recon seemed to be almost a full time job. She had been told the police may need a helping hand on a difficult case. The latest request was unusual, Recon looked after national security, not individual police cases. However, this was in keeping with the odd direction the organisation appeared to be moving in.

She was at a particular estate agency practice earlier in the day. A little financial lubrication had confirmed that it was William H. Murray who held the current bid on the large site in Stratford. He also confirmed that there was another bidder but due to his untimely death only Mr Murray remained interested. The generous offer was expected to be accepted by the developer who owned the land. Already some interesting developments had taken place. Within the first hour Recon field officers monitoring Mr Murray witnessed a suitcase drop. A man met Mr Murray outside Cafe Rosa near Canary Wharf. The man shook hands with Mr Murray, then got into the passenger seat. Shortly afterward he left the car carrying two large briefcases.

The Recon officers decided to split up and follow one man each.

Recon sent the photos back to Sarah Cripwell. Once she saw them, she knew who she was dealing with. Terry White had come across Sarah's path before. When probing a shady deal a number of years ago Terry had a role to play. It appeared this time would be no different.

A large blob of relish hit the papers that lay on the desk. Her head was now tilted forward and began to bob occasionally. Sarah's mobile phone broke the silence of the eerie office. The shock caused her to drop the sandwich but the call had woke her up. She answered the call.

'Hello, Code in.'

'3478, Suspect seen giving a suitcase of cash to unknown male.'

'Tip off the police. This unknown male is almost certainly Robert King's murderer. The original suspect's name is Terry White, continue to follow him. Thanks for the update. Keep on the suspects tail. Over and out.'

Progress was quick and it was an interesting few hours but unfortunately she currently didn't have the energy to investigate any further.

She pushed the papers to the side and wiped the relish off of the desk. She had no more to give and a power nap was required. As soon as her head hit the desk she entered the land of dreams.

Once more her mobile phone broke the silence. She looked at her watch, two hours had passed. She felt fresher. It helped that the heating was now turned off for the night, and the cold air brought life back to her mind. Sarah answered the phone in the same fashion.

'Hello, Code in.'

'3478, I can hardly believe my eyes. Suspect seen giving the other briefcase to a slightly intoxicated John Black, the

Chancellor of the Exchequer.'

Sarah was flabbergasted. The investigation had thrown up another twist. Normally a reconnaissance mission involved sitting in cars for hours on stakeouts, trawling through paperwork or listening to hours of phone calls. Today, a few hours of work had, in all probability, found Robert King's murderer and had also linked the Chancellor of the Exchequer with the same sordid event.

'Great work. This night just doesn't stop giving. Stick with him, keep me posted.'

'Will do, I'll be stuck to him like glue, over and out.'

The following day 3478 monitored John Black, he watched his movements, tracked his internet use and listened to all his phone calls. He saw him nurse a hangover with paracetamol and fruit juice, put the suitcase he acquired last night in his safe, eat a microwave dinner and discuss the weather with Pavel the gardener. However, it was when he spoke with his lover that the most interesting revelation occurred. She said the words

'I need to see you, Andy has changed since he joined the unit'

This development needed to go straight to the Head of Recon.

90

Andy peered over the back of the couch. He caught sight of John Black who was peeking out from behind an alcove wall.

John stood in the living room recess. Behind him stood his drinks cabinet. He craved for a forty year old scotch. He definitely needed something to calm his nerves. Until this moment he had no idea who was invading his home. Having just seen Andy Pickering's face, he now knew who wanted him dead. It was poignant that the man he introduced to the organisation would now be the man sent to exterminate him. As far as he was aware, Firestorm had a 100% success rate. He didn't fancy his chances. Andy had trained for moments like these for the past eight months; in contrast, it was the first time John had fired his gun at another human being. John knew he needed something to even up his chances. Luckily that something was just an arm's reach away.

Andy couldn't believe his eyes. It had been a crazy night so far and it had just taken one more outrageous turn.

'Drop the gun or she gets a hole in the head.'

Andy looked into Victoria's eyes. They were filled with fear and yet they were filled with love. Victoria had become a human shield and above her head a desperate John Black held a gun pointed directly at her.

Last night had been an emotional rollercoaster. It rolled from Jennifer's bombshell, to seeing his wife packing to leave him, to hearing her admit to the affair. Then came the tears, followed by her plea to rekindle the magic with the father of her children. She explained that the affair should never have happened, but it occurred because Andy appeared to have lost his lust for life. She needed more from life, she needed more from her man. She never said whom she had the affair with, but she did say she wanted it to be over. Victoria noticed the recent changes in her husband and once again felt the love that first attracted her to a dynamic confident Andy Pickering. Hearing of the affair, Andy felt dejected. As he thought about the situation he saw how he had become everything he did not want to be in his life. Sedate, boring, conservative, unspontaneous and comfortable. Firestorm may be a shady organisation, but it helped Andy become the man he always wanted to be. Although it galled him, he could see why she had strayed. An emotional night came to a close with both vowing to go to counselling to help with trust issues and to reignite their marriage. Victoria promised Andy she would meet with the man the following night and explain that the affair was over, she loved her husband and she would never meet this man again.

Andy had inadvertently popped in on the break up and now stood face to face with the man that had been screwing his wife for the past ten months. The twisted bastard was now using her as a human shield. Andy wanted for nothing more than to pump lead into every part of his sick, disgusting body.

'What do you want with her, let her go and we can work this out. She's got nothing to do with this.' he said as he attempted to reason with a frenetic John Black.

Victoria had both fear and love in her eyes. Somehow she had found herself in a situation with the two men in her life and guns pointed in every direction. While she feared for her life she was strangely pleased with herself. Even if her life was immeasurably cut short tonight, she was glad that she had told Andy that she loved him. She truly did. She was glad too that she had told John she didn't want to be with him, or his dirty millions. Her current plight proved she had made the right choice, unfortunately, she had made it at the wrong time. Victoria stared with love into her husband's eyes. Her knight stood tall, blood oozing down his face as he stared down John

Black.

'Just do what you have to Andy.'

Andy viewed the situation. He stood approximately ten yards away from his target. In front of him was his wife. John held her tight. Andy had nothing but a few inches of a forehead to aim at. He was trained for this. He had improved immeasurably from his first day at the firing range. He was now ranked the second best marksman in the unit, for a man of his accomplished ability it was a relatively easy shot. But this was no shooting range. Tonight he was William Tell and if he failed to split the apple his children would lose their mother forever. Andy closed one eye and took aim, Victoria closed both eyes and John tightened his grip on the trigger.

91

'Drop your weapons, everybody drop your weapons right now.' The man's voice amplified by a megaphone.

'You are surrounded, drop your weapons now.'

Andy wasn't sure what was going on but there was no way he was dropping his gun just yet. The only logical possibility was that Chris had come back to save the day. Andy knew there was no way the building was surrounded but if he could get John to drop his weapon he would willingly drop his weapon too.

'Okay John, what are we going to do?'

'Do you take me for an idiot Pickering? I saw what happened outside. There were three of you and you handcuffed the other two. I'm surrounded by two injured and handcuffed people. I won't be dropping my weapon for that. Listen here Pickering, I'm giving you your final chance. I have the upper hand here, you better start realising that. You have ten seconds to drop your weapon, else the blue dress your slut of a wife is wearing will begin to turn red. Time for talking is over.'

John turned to a horrified Victoria and whispered in her ear 'We'll see who loves you now'.

He then turned back to Andy, looked him in the eye and began the countdown.

Time was running out for Andy. Again, he weighted up his options. If he dropped the gun, John would either let them go, or kill them. He looked in his eyes, they were frenzied. His pupils danced around. Andy knew there was only one option available to him. It eased his conscience that Victoria told him to do what he had to do. He again took aim at the few inches of sweaty forehead he could set his sights on. He wiped the blood from his brow and closed his left eye. He was ready.

Victoria screamed as John dropped to the floor in agony.

Immediately she kicked the gun from his grasp and followed it up with another kick into his torso. She felt dirty for ever having slept with the diseased animal that lay at her feet. She ran to her savour and jumped into his waiting arms.

'I love you Andy, I'm so sorry. I love you so much.'

Victoria did not expect the response she was about to receive. Andy caught Victoria and flung her behind the couch.

'Somebody else is here, I didn't take that shot.'

Victoria and Andy lay covered in sweat behind the living room furniture. Their hearts raced, and almost beat as one. There was blood, sweat and tears. There was passion. A moment later the man on the megaphone spoke again.

'This is the police, we are now entering the building. Throw down your weapons and you will be unharmed.'

Somehow, the police made their way to John Black's home. Andy didn't care how or why. He could only presume he had Chris and Jennifer to thank. Victoria already disarmed one man tonight. She now set about disarming another. She took Andy's gun and flung it across the room, she then pulled him close, wrapped her arms around his neck and began to kiss him. He felt the passion behind his wife's embrace. He had won back Victoria, he had won back his marriage.

92

'Legend!'

Andy couldn't help but describe his best mate who was waiting for him outside the house. Chris just saved his life, and the lives of countless victims that would have been killed in future Firestorm assassinations. Not only this, but he now stood in front of Andy holding a six-pack of cold beer. Andy was covered in blood, and was just about able to walk, yet he never felt better in his life. He was surrounded by a long lost lover, and the best friend a man could wish for. He was also surrounded by a police investigation that would change Britain; Andy knew that *he* helped change Britain.

The golden nectar of the effervescent malty beer washed away the pain as it eased its way to the back of Andy's throat. Nothing could ruin this moment now.

'Excuse me sir, but we need to arrest you as part of our investigations' said an almost embarrassed police officer. Chris couldn't believe it but Andy knew the authorities had to do their job. Andy became the third member of the Firestorm team to be handcuffed tonight as he was led to a waiting police car.

'Can I come too? I need to talk with him' Chris pleaded.

'I'm afraid not Sir, it is against police code of practice.'

'Fuck the code of practice, this guy is a national hero and you are treating him like a common criminal!' snapped Chris.

'Okay, calm down, you can go with Mr Pickering to the police station.'

'Thank you' Chris responded sarcastically.

Andy and Victoria shared a final embrace before the police car drove past the carnage and away from the scene.

'I can't believe I'm alive Chris, I can't believe we're all alive. But I can't get my head around what just happened tonight.

Give me the low down blow by blow.'

Chris began the story when The Light rang him that morning. He told him of March 2004, of meeting Sergeant Green and of how Jennifer went up a blind alley in her investigation of HMIF industries. He told him what happened at Scotland Yard and informed him that The Light gave him a dummy green file to hold when he was shot. He then thanked him for his straight shooting. Then came the most interesting revelation of all. Jennifer had faxed information to Scotland Yard. It contained information that John Back was to be assassinated. This was the reason the police came out to the house. Firestorm had been exposed and Jennifer had uncovered its corrupt mass-murdering ringleader. Andy listened with bated breath.

'So who is Edward Simmons again?' Andy asked as he tried to keep up with an excited Chris.

'He's the computer programmer. His company had the rolling contract since 1962. Every year the Firestorm codes were updated to ensure the safety and security of the system. However, one year the Head of Recon managed to attain these codes. Simmons was just a geeky computer programmer, he had no idea what impact giving the codes directly to his client the Head of Recon would have. Later that month the Prime Minister received a message that Firestorm had been disbanded in the interests of the country. The message came from the Head of Recon and was apparently sent to all three. A majority was needed to disband Firestorm. This simply meant that both the Head of the British Army and the Chancellor must have decided to break up the unit. Only those two men had the codes to make this agreement. There was nobody for the Prime Minister to question on this. In his eyes, a chapter had been closed, and he was not disappointed. It must have been a difficult affair when the Prime Minister was sworn into office and informed of Firestorm's existence. Having to make decisions on assassinations for the greater good of the country was something a Prime Minister could do without. So from March 2004 the Prime Minister no longer made these moral decisions. Instead, the Head of Recon made them. He had supreme control, he could now supply missions for approval, and then approve them himself acting as if he was the Prime Minister. The codes gave him absolute power. For the past number of years Britain has had a dictator and not even one citizen knew about it.'

It was mind-blowing news. Andy listened to Chris in awe and amazement. He could just imagine every television and radio programme in the country being interrupted to give the breaking news.

Mass murder funded by the government.

In a sick way, the Head of Recon was a genius. But who was he? Andy needed to know, the pieces of the puzzle were coming together but he still couldn't see the big picture.

'Out with it, who is the Head of Recon?'

Chris paused for a moment just to add to the already considerable tension. Then he revealed the bombshell.

'Brownlow, the head of Directacom'

'What, George Brownlow, my boss?'

'The very man' Chris responded.

Andy had expected everything to become clear, instead he was even more confused. His boss was the biggest British mass murderer of his lifetime.

'I knew that would take you by surprise' Chris remarked as he saw Andy's face turn a little pale.

'His first job was the assassination of the CEO of *In Line*. Two weeks later the government awarded Directacom the 3G licence after a sealed bid auction. In Line was Brownlow's only serious threat to attaining the single licence to be issued in

Britain. With its CEO deceased the company was in disarray for a number of weeks and it pulled out of the bid. As a result, for a much reduced cost, Directacom now owned the rights to 3G. Brownlow was about to become a very rich man. He should have left it at that, but that first murder changed Brownlow. He fell in love with the power. It was so simple it was incredible. When he first joined Recon it was over twenty years ago. It was to bring some life to his mundane existence. Initially the spying and surveillance excited him. He improved his work performance and then decided to start up his own company. *Directacom* was born. It wasn't a pure coincidence that both you and Peter worked for the company. After all, it was the ideal workplace for someone who wouldn't even show up half the time. Brownlow understood the demands of Recon and Unit Firestorm. He allowed time off for individuals. Employees felt he was just a forward thinking boss allowing them to work at home. Instead, as Head of Recon, he knew their every move. His employees were more dynamic than the competitions. They worked hard when they did work, and when they were not working for Directacom, they worked for George Brownlow's new pet project. From now on, he would decide law and order in the country. The power went to Brownlow's head. Occasional murders were for *the good of Directacom*, the rest were a Brownlow justice. It appears he hated drug dealers more than anything else in the world. His father was a drug dealer and he had abandoned him as a child. It seems in his eyes they all had to be exterminated.'

93

The city lights now illuminated inside the police car. They couldn't be far away from the station. Andy could finally see the big picture, but he still had so many questions that needed to be answered before he was taken into custody.

'How on earth did Jennifer figure all this out?'

'It was actually your notes that helped her most' answered Chris.

'But I didn't have anything even remotely connecting Brownlow on my notes?'

'True, but the heading at the top of your notepad read: *Directacom is a telecommunications company specialising in mainstream mobile communications*. Jennifer knew about the 3G deal, she knew both you and Peter worked at Directacom and she knew she had nothing else better to investigate.'

The car was now stationary. Andy knew he would be dragged inside, but he truly wanted to stay. Chris was a fountain of knowledge and he was thirsty for more facts.

'Please Sir, get out of the car, watch you head.'

Andy had no choice but to leave the vehicle. He was surprised by how difficult it was when his hands were cuffed behind his back. With the help of an officer, he managed to step onto the pavement and he was then escorted into the police station.

'If I'm not released by tomorrow come visit me' Andy shouted back to Chris as he stepped into the foyer.

Andy couldn't believe what awaited him in the station cells. There was Corporal Bhana and Fisher, The General, the Marshal, Corporal Cleaver and every other member of Firestorm. A thirty strong crowd shared a cell the size of Andy's office. It was pretty crowded, and pretty loud. Most people couldn't understand why they had just been arrested and detained in a prison cell. Andy knew exactly why. The bunch of keys clanged as one hit off the next. He thought he might be given special treatment, he thought wrong. He was thrown in with the rest of the Firestorm team.

'You alright?' a genuinely concerned Cleaver asked Andy.

'I've been better, but I'll survive. Can you tell me who are all the people in the opposite cell?'

Andy pointed to the cell on the opposite side of the corridor. It was a similar size and contained almost as many people. He scanned across the group to see if he could recognise any faces but it had been an unfruitful search.

'That's Recon' replied Cleaver. 'Apparently the big fellow on the right is the head guy.'

Andy's scanning eyes locked on to the man Cleaver picked out. What he saw confirmed everything Chris had said. George Brownlow sat on the damp cold concrete floor of his prison cell. This would be no overnight stay. Britain's most prolific mass murderer would surely never be a free man again.

'It's opening again' Cleaver said pointing to the door separating the cell corridor from the station.

'It hasn't stopped for the past hour, one person after another, after another.'

Almost everybody in both cells turned to see who was the next detainee to join them.

John Black limped down the corridor. A leg of his trousers had been cut off. The dressed wound where he had earlier been shot was visible for all to see. He appeared to be in much distress. Andy was delighted he hadn't been given an easy time of it and taken to hospital for the night. He would be treated the same as everyone else.

'You fucking bastard Pickering, all this mess is your fault, why couldn't you just die like you were supposed to.'

333

A possessed John Black snarled and scowled at the Firestorm cell.

'What will we do with this one, we can't put him in with these? He'd harm them or maybe himself in the process' noted the officer, all the time trying to keep him restrained.

'There's only a single one man cell left, put him in there, next to Mr Murray's cell.'

'Fine, but help me get the lunatic under control first.'

As the two officers wrestled with Black, Andy recognised a girl in the opposite cell, the Recon cell. He couldn't believe his eyes. It was an exhausted looking Sarah Cripwell.

He stood looking at his secretary trying to figure it all out. All the time she stared down at the damp floor. When John had been escorted away to a separate cell she finally raised her head. As she did so Andy caught her eye. Immediately she smiled. It was a genuine expressive smile; the kind one might get after completing a marathon. Andy politely returned a smile. She appeared to be pointing at something in the ceiling. Andy looked but could see nothing of note. He turned back to Cripwell. She remained adamantly pointing at the ceiling. Finally he understood, the last piece of the jigsaw was put in place and Andy could now see The Light.

94

'Good afternoon Mrs. Howell' Andy said as the old lady, weighted down by her shopping bags, made her way past.

'And a very good afternoon to you Mr Pickering. I wish you and your lovely wife the very best of luck.'

Over the past month Andy had become a minor British celebrity. On the other hand, in his home suburb of West Hampstead Andy was a superstar. Ms. Howell turned as she walked past.

'I see you've given up the undertaking' she said giving Andy a playful wink. They both shared a knowing smile.

It was another smile to add to the lovely growing list. Yesterday was the first of January and it had been a truly fantastic day. Jack scored a goal for West Hampstead Under 10s football team. They lost, but Jack didn't care, he was only six years old and he scored for the Under 10 team. He dreamt of playing for Arsenal, and Andy encouraged him all the way. Anne-Marie was still amazed by Oscar the recent Christmas arrival. The Labrador kept running up and down at the back of the goals and Anne-Marie kept giggling and running up and down after him. She had a new best friend in Oscar, he would not just be for Christmas, he would be her best friend for life. Victoria stood by Andy's side as they watched and encouraged Jack from the sidelines. The counselling had gone well so far, in fact, the marriage had reignited. When Andy looked around at all the other couples he could see they were the only parents still laughing, embracing each other and holding hands. Despite the madness of the previous months Andy felt proud and thankful for everything he had.

'Who was that old lady, I think she has a thing for you?' Victoria joked as they both shared another smile. Today too had been a wonderful day. This morning a delighted Victoria showed Andy a postcard they had just received in the post. Not alone had Anne-Marie a new best friend, but Victoria had regained an old one. The postcard was from Sri Lanka. Jennifer knew the tapes sent to incriminate The General would also implicate Terry. As a result, she rang Terry and asked him if he loved her. Terry's answer ensured his freedom and they fled the country on the night of the arrests. They had now made their way to the east coast beaches of Sri Lanka and the postcard suggested it was a happy escape.

Andy could also afford himself another smile today. The judicial system recommenced this morning after the Christmas break. Brownlow would face the justice he so richly deserved. The General on the other hand had the best lawyer in town. Mrs Rosaline Georgina King backed him to the hilt. Terry White's taped evidence was thrown out. Terry White was a phantom, there was little proof of his existence and now he was nowhere to be found. The General was found innocent of any charges. All the other members of Firestorm and Recon were released without charge with a tribunal put in place to establish the exact extent of the unit and the atrocities untaken. The scandal brought down the government.

Andy spent little time thinking about the scandal. He was too busy living life. Everything was perfect, well almost everything. There was a hole in his life, and it was starting to get bigger. A new CEO was appointed to Directacom and Andy got a promotion. He was now 'Region Manager'. Even the sign on the door had been changed. *Progress* he told himself.

95

The world's most annoying sound woke Andy. Andy couldn't remember the last time he didn't wake up naturally. It was Monday morning and the start of another week. He was a bit more sluggish this morning; the shave had to be cut out of the traditional pre work routine so that he would arrive at work on time. He gave Victoria a gentle meaningful kiss on the forehead and headed out the door. The fresh air from the five-minute walk to the tube definitely helped wake him up.

The sardines went into their can to start the week. It was the Monday after the festive holidays and everybody was back to work. The carriage was jam-packed and everybody remained silent as they endured the journey. The holidays were defiantly over now.

As he entered his office he could see another pile of papers to be signed on his desk, luckily he had ordered replacement ink cartridges for his lucky fountain pen before Christmas. Sarah entered his office.

'I have those cartridges for you' she told her boss as she lay them on his desk.

'Thanks Sarah, I hope you were able to relax over the Christmas after all the excitement.'

'Too much relaxing, I think I put on a half a stone!'

'I think I put on a stone!'

They both shared a smile.

'Thanks again Sarah, for everything, I mean it.'

'My pleasure, I kinda had to save your life, I couldn't bear the thought of getting a new boss, better the devil you know and all that!'

'Seriously, thanks again.'

'Just forget about it, isn't *that* what we are supposed to do.'

It was what they were supposed to do. All members of Firestorm and Recon were attending therapists to help them forget the unit ever existed. The sessions weren't working for Andy and he could see that the same was true for Sarah.

'I know, just forget about it huh.'

Sarah began to feel awkward. She could tell Andy had the same hole in him that she did. There had to be more to life than buying ink cartridges. There *was* more to life, just not anymore.

'See you later, I've some more papers that need reviewing on my desk. I'll pop them into you in a while.'

Andy loaded the cartridge. The pen was ready to start signing but Andy wasn't. The pen hovered over the page as Andy's mind wandered. There was still one thing that he couldn't reconcile. It was in his mind now, it had been in his mind last night, in fact it disturbed his night's sleep ever since it happened. It was time to make his peace with his good friend and time to make peace with himself.

The frozen grass sparkled in the sunshine. Thousands of headstones lay before Andy and Sarah but they were heading towards only one. Andy had earlier attempted to tell his secretary that he had to pop out for the morning to attend a meeting. Sarah detected something was amiss. Before he had time to fabricate a credible story, she had extracted the truth. Years of Recon work made such an assignment a simple task. There was no way he would be allowed to go on his own. She too had to grieve, she also felt responsible.

Peter 'Fracture' Johnson; the family decided to put his nickname on the tombstone. It was a nice thought. It made it all the more real. Their work colleague, their Firestorm colleague, their friend. It was time to speak with his friend and ask for forgiveness.

'I'm so sorry Fracture, I hope I did you proud by bringing

down the unit. The madness had to stop, I'm just sorry you are not here to see Brownlow, the man who ordered your murder, get what he deserves.'

Sarah looked on as an emotional Andy relived the moments before Peter's death. He could see the small but stocky frame of Peter in a slumber beneath his sheets; the rag full of chloroform dangled in front of his eyelids. Amy Fisher was holding the Zippo lighter ready to engulf the house in flames.

'Are you talking to yourself Corporal? Are you daydreaming when you should be making things happen. Pull yourself together Pickering.'

It could only be one man. In unison Sarah and Andy turned around. There, leaning against a tombstone, was The General, his demeanour brazen and unfazed.

'What the fuck are you doing here?' swore Andy.

'Before you use up all your pathetic little curses and get yourself all caught up in a big dirty knot, let me explain why I am here. If you want to rant and rave later, then by all means but not on my time Pickering.'

Andy was taken aback. He wanted to speak but all he could do is swallow and no words came out. The General still had an effect on him and he didn't like it.

'Pickering calm down and listen to me, but before we speak, who is your beautiful friend? Not your cheating wife I see.'

'She is my secretary Sarah Cripwell.'

'Very nice Andy. A pleasure to meet you Sarah. Would you mind giving Andy and I a moment to discuss men's business?'

'Yes I would mind' retorted Sarah. 'I'd be very interested in what you have to say Jeff Redford, very interested indeed.'

The General took a step back. Andy hadn't seen this before and he liked it. In fact, it gave him the confidence to speak up to The General.

'Sarah was with Recon, she probably knows more about you than your mother does.'

'The boy has found his tongue. Well, this is interesting. I think your friend may want to hear what I have to say then. As difficult as it is to believe, I'm not here to cause you any trouble. I also grieve for Peter. I never wanted to give those orders, that was my job. I was the middleman. I liked the work just not the boss. Now let's get this straight. Peter's niece died from a cocaine overdose. I don't know if it was the coke I sold or other coke. Regardless, you take too much, you die, that's what happens. I didn't kill Peter's niece. He was understandably angry but the facts are she took too much of the stuff.'

'Ok, but you made a lot of money from Firestorm' replied Andy.

'So fucking what, it was money that was about to be put in the furnace, better in my pocket. Anyway the reason why I'm here is because I can see it in your face. It's funny, I can see it in your face too Cripwell. It's the eyes we see before we took people to the White Room. It's those dead eyes.'

Andy and Sarah looked at each other. They both wondered the same thing, where was The General going with all of this?

'There, that's it, I guarantee this is the first time your eyes have lit up all day. I already said I liked the work just not the boss. The new Chancellor of the Exchequer is a gentleman by the name of Gordon Fletcher. I've made his acquaintance on a number of occasions. He's a good man, he's a charitable man and he can be trusted. Most importantly, I have him wrapped around my little finger. I've come to an agreement with him. We fight drug dealers, sell the drugs and he will give the money to charity. It's doing bad to do good. It's what we did anyway, but this time we'll do it right. Gordon Fletcher has offered, admittedly under duress, to finance the start up of the unit. I want you. Sarah the offer is now also open to you to be our

340

Recon. We can do it for the right reasons this time.'

The General reached up, grabbed Andy's shoulders and looked into his eyes.

'Well Pickering you know your choices. What's it going to be. You can go back to your 'monkey can do' job and Directacom 5-a-side or you can choose the alternative.

END

ABOUT THE AUTHOR

Willie O'Regan is a Chartered Engineer. He currently lives and works in Cork.

Made in the USA
Charleston, SC
01 December 2014